The Fish Murders

Suzanne Visser

Clear Mind Press

The Fish Murders

Suzanne Visser

Translation from the Dutch by Jonathan Smith 2017;
"De Vismoorden" Uitgeverij Atlas 2000, The Netherlands
ISBN 978-0-6456547-1-4
Clear Mind Press, Australia
Copyright © Suzanne Visser
Legal deposit in the National Library of Australia
Design and layout: Clear Mind Press
Clear Mind Press: www.clearmindpress.com
Typesetting: Clear Mind Press - Baskerville 12
Cover Design: Clear Mind Press

Published in Dutch as *De Vismoorden*, in Spanish as *Sushi*, in German as *Das Japanische Rätsel*, and in French as *Les Meurtres au Poison*.

In memory of

Carrie Sakai and Raul Fogelstrom

who were there then

In August 1997, after eight people, all non-Japanese, have been brutally murdered in Tokyo, the decision is taken to establish an international team to find the perpetrator of the "Fish Murders". From the experiences of the seven investigators and criminologists emerges an account of the relationship between Japanese and foreigners attempting to integrate into Japanese society.

The novel describes a society on the brink. The roaring eighties of the "economic bubble" in Japan has just finished. The banks have just caved in. Mobile communication is not there yet. Recent disasters have not happened yet.

The pre-Fukushima, pre-Covid novel, is an ode to pre-disaster Japan. It feels nostalgic to those who knew Japan in the 1980ies and early 1990ies and informs those who try to imagine that dynamic era when anything seemed possible, and then everything collapsed.

The novel is set in a time before wokeness hit the world. This is reflected in habits and speech.

CHAPTER 1

The drain holes of sinks, baths and washbasins are the size of saucers. Below them hangs a sieve, the size of a small beach pail, to collect tea leaves and other waste matter. A handle enables the sieve to be lifted out of the waste pipe and emptied. Sometimes the drain holes are fitted with rotating knives that shred the waste finely enough for it to pass easily through the drainpipes.

Washing machines, only half the size of European models, are made of smooth plastic, including the screws and nuts, so they can be left outside; they wash with cold water and complete a wash cycle in half an hour. No more than a tablespoon of washing powder is needed for a whole wash, which means that washing powder can be sold in small packets. A Japanese wash cleans just as well as any other in the world.

The cistern of a toilet sits low on top of the WC and has a stoneware cover in the shape of a wash basin. When the WC is flushed, the water to be used for flushing flows from a pipe into the wash basin, and thence from the wash basin into the cistern, so that you can use it to wash your hands before it reaches the cistern.

Mattresses for sleeping – *futon* – are folded up and stored in a built-in cupboard, precisely sized, providing extra space during the day. The empty tatami room, with an alcove for a flower arrangement and a calligraphy display appropriate to the season, primarily provides visual tranquillity.

At locations where people need to fill in forms, such as post offices and banks, plastic spectacles with lenses of all possible strengths hang above the counter.

On telephones there is a 'parrot button'. By pressing on this button you can increase the volume of the sounds made by a heavy breather and make them echo back into his ear.

In cars, an unbearable whistling sound is emitted as soon as the car exceeds the speed limit.

You can buy books in a format half the size of an ordinary European paperback. When these are sold they are not wrapped up, but are covered in plain paper, so that a curious fellow-passenger on a train cannot immediately discern the political or sexual preferences of the reader. Into each book, large or small, is stitched a cotton bookmark.

You can buy winter coats, 'mama coats', designed to fit both a mother and a child attached to the mother's back. Recently, 'papa coats' have also made an appearance in the shops.

You can buy not only fountain pens, but also refillable ink brushes.

Houses are warmed sparingly. During the winter, people wear warm clothes inside the house. In the main room, on a thick rug, stands the *kotatsu*: a low table with an electrical heating bulb attached to the underside. A second thick quilted coverlet is spread over the table, and on top of this is placed a second tabletop. The legs and the second coverlet are heavy, to give stability to the whole. Sitting 'in' the kotatsu, half enclosed in the coverlet, the lower part of your body stays warm while your head is cool: an excellent state for doing homework, writing letters and other things that require concentration. And in the evening, everyone slowly becomes more drowsy under the quilted coverlet, and a pleasant warm heap of legs, socks, cats, slippers, books and saké bowls accumulates under the table.

At the local fast-food restaurants you can order complete meals to be delivered hot to your home. The food prepared is healthy: buckwheat noodles, dishes with rice, soup, vegetables, fish and tofu. They are delivered in chinaware dishes which you can leave empty by your door, where they will be picked up again by the staff of the restaurant, usually on a small motorcycle equipped with a box hanging on springs.

And finally, there is the Japanese word that is used most, the most useful word in the world. It means 'thank you very much,' 'not at all,' 'oh dear,' 'I'm sorry,' 'how are you,' 'good day,' 'bye for now,' 'I don't know,' and hundreds of other things. Literally, it means 'many,' or 'very much.' You can use it in any situation, even if you don't know what you ought to say: *Domo*.

Bertus Hogenelst shuts his book and looks at the ugly cover. Brightly coloured fish and beer cans are floating in the tranquil landscape of a Zen garden. His ears start to hurt because the aeroplane is preparing to land. He tries to make the pressure on his eardrums more bearable by pinching his nose and keeping his mouth wide open while he leans towards the window and looks out; a gap opens in the cloud cover and a carpet of fields becomes visible. The patchwork quilt rises rapidly towards him and more details come into view.

Oh, he thinks, *the roof tiles are blue here.*

CHAPTER 2

Bertus Hogenelst is a member of an international police team that has been convened to solve the cases of the 'Eight Fish Murders' in Tokyo. The murders have been so named because they were committed with a long fish knife, and because the remains of the victims resembled fish that had been sliced open ready to be served: with the two body halves lying like flaps, pressed against the ground on each side of the backbone.

As the victims had all been non-Japanese, these murders have not only captured the attention of the whole of Japan, but in recent months have also made headlines worldwide. Since the first murder in March, the police in Tokyo had made little progress with the investigation, probably because the trails had turned back on themselves into various circles of the foreign community. In the Western media Japan had been the object of finger-pointing, and had even been accused of being autistic. Finally, at an international conference in Honolulu organised by the United States, it has been agreed that seven foreign investigators and criminologists, in cooperation with Chief Inspector Ichiro Mochizuki from Tokyo, will take on the case. The conference coordinator has also added to the team two office managers, an interpreter and a psychologist. The latter will help the team construct profiles of the perpetrator and victims, and will be on hand at times of excessive workload. The United States has insisted on having this kind of stress management expert. The seven team members, the psychologist and the office managers have been put up in the Akasaka Prince Hotel in the centre of Tokyo. Two floors of this enormous building have generously been made available, at the request of Chief Inspector Mochizuki.

The victims of the Fish Murders were:

Hendrik Mechanicus, 36, a Dutchman. He had been murdered on the night of the 12th of February. Mechanicus had worked part-time as an administrative assistant at the Japan-Netherlands House and had been studying Japanese five mornings a week at a well-known language school in Yotsuya. To learn Japanese quickly, he had been lodging with a Japanese family in Chiba. His remains were found on a service road next to a station in Chiba, lying in a hollow on the verge, like tuna ready to be served up on a plate.

Marcus Bopp, 42, a Swiss expert in security systems, was found dead on the 2nd of March in Sendagaya 5-chome, in Shinjuku ward. His remains, filleted like a fish, had been discovered in a quagmire next to a fence of concrete piles on the far side of Shinjuku Park. Enquiries made of neighbours, family members in Switzerland and subordinates in his business – which had suspended trading in the meantime – have so far revealed nothing.

Ian Wackwitz, 32, a German, had been found, slashed open in the same manner, on the 19th of April, by some rubbish disposal workers on their way back to their truck. The body was almost completely filleted, and rubbish sacks had been placed around it in an oval. According to his family in Germany, Wackwitz had been looking for work, and now and then had worked as a substitute teacher of German.

Jacob Parker, 36, an American, was the founder of the Harvard Academy for International Communication in Odawara. The pastel-coloured pamphlets of this institute promised a 'creative approach' to teaching English to Japanese. According to the light yellow application form, the fact that Japanese still do not speak English was attributable to their not having learned to use the left half of their brains properly. Parker's body was found on the 27th of May by seven middle-school girls, on a railway bridge in the Koganei area, over the new Koganei Expressway. The operations of his school have since been suspended.

Irina Skoynich, 33, was a Polish woman who had lived an isolated life as a housewife in an out-of-the-way part of Iitabashi ward with a Japanese man, Morio Abe. She painted in her free time. She was found on the 12th of June, under a dome-shaped climbing frame that was going to be installed in a playground.

Marco Polo, 36, an Italian, died on the night of the 30th of June. His body was found by a boy playing in a ditch next to the embankment of a paddy field, in the suburb of Hachioji. Absolutely nothing was known about Polo.

Larry Maxwell, 34, an Australian, was a video artist who lived in a small apartment in the Yotsuya area. To finance his artistic videos, he gave English lessons and sometimes worked as a model for drawing classes. His remains were found close to his apartment on the 18th of July, in the garden of an empty house. The body had been laid out almost artistically, in a butterfly of flesh and bone, on a rocky outcrop by a small pond.

Hughes De Keuninck, 34, a Belgian, ran QueBook, a small bookshop in Chiba that sold second-hand books in English, German and French. He was murdered on the 15th of August.

On the 17th floor of the Akasaka Prince Hotel, in a dining room that has been converted into a conference room, Chief Inspector Mochizuki is on the point of officially transferring the tasks and responsibilities of the Japanese investigatory team to the international group. Mochizuki cuts an impressive figure immediately. He stands head and shoulders above his subordinates. Alone among the Japanese, he has curly hair; the curls are short and stiff, as though they have been wound too tightly, using rollers that were too small. His hair does not move when he turns his large head. Unlike his subordinates he is not in uniform, but wears an old-fashioned tailored suit. His hands are held flat against the seams of his dark blue trousers.

Over the course of the previous afternoon and evening the members of the new team had flown into Narita Airport from various parts of the world, before being picked up by white-gloved colleagues of Chief Inspector Mochizuki and driven into Tokyo in grey Toyotas.

Mochizuki has only to gesture to his subordinates – there are twenty-two, Bertus counts – to make it clear that they should take their places at a U-shaped table. They sit down immediately, ready and quietly attentive. By contrast, the foreigners who form the international team sit together round a table, disorganised and noisy.

Mochizuki walks up to them, closely followed by his interpreter, requests that they sit in a row on one side of the table so that the two teams face one another, and asks them to put on the headsets lying on the table. He speaks to the group with authority, without looking at anyone. Then, together with his interpreter, he mounts a small podium behind a lectern, where he introduces first himself and then his interpreter, Ichiro Watanabe. The long speech that follows is spoken loudly into a microphone that generates too much feedback. He begins by enumerating the names and ranks of the members of the old team and thanks them for their commitment, after which each person mentioned stands up and gives a slight bow.

He notes that the Japanese and international teams will not actually be working together immediately, but that the Japanese team will be continuing to do a lot of routine work behind the scenes. Then he lists the names and nationalities of the victims and expresses his sorrow to their families for their deaths. He also acknowledges the finders of the bodies, who had included children and a pregnant woman. The woman had lost her child the day after she found Irina's remains. Mochizuki deals with these matters in a neutral voice point by point, as though he is reading from a shopping list. His hands remain together on the surface of the lectern. His fingernails glint as though they have had polish applied to them.

The members of the international team form an untidy row. Some make scribbled notes; others smoke, leaning back a long way. Four of the ten have removed their headsets and are listening to Mochizuki directly, some with their eyes closed.

Mochizuki introduces the new team to the old. Gerardo Silva from Mexico; Lucia Valenti from Italy; Jack Fowell from Australia; Mark Croo from Belgium; Bertus Hogenelst from the Netherlands; Robynne Green from the USA; and Bettina Welt from Germany. Then come the two office managers, Yvonne Lacoste from France and Yukiko Inoue from Japan, and finally the psychologist, Zhiqiang Li from China. All the members of the new team stand up as Mochizuki announces their names. Two of them also bow: the Japanese Yukiko Inoue and the Chinese Zhiqiang Li.

The team will be staying at the hotel for the entire investigation, except for those who live in Tokyo. These are Li, Watanabe and Mochizuki himself, although rooms will be kept available for them in case of extreme pressure of work.

Mochizuki announces that the investigator and criminologist Gerardo Silva will be giving a lecture that evening, and requests that the members of his old team be present.

The members of the Japanese team then stand and bow deeply, all at the same angle, with their hands tight against the sides of their thighs, and in chorus as one, make the request, *"Yoroshiku onegaishimasu."* The members of the international team are not sure how to react to this and stand up somewhat cautiously behind their table. One of them waves slightly, as though he is the Pope, or Michael Jackson. It is Jack Fowell from Australia.

Mochizuki and Watanabe step down from the podium

and Mochizuki opens the door. Both teams leave the room; the Japanese shyly and in a single line, the Westerners chaotically. Robynne Green walks along talking loudly with Bertus Hogenelst. Bertus stumbles and falls against her; Zhiqiang Li holds out an arm for him. Gerardo Silva and Lucia Valenti are laughing loudly about something somewhere, Bettina Welt bends down to pull up one of her socks; Jack Fowell touches her bottom as he walks behind her. Bettina jerks as though she has been stung, and looks back at him angrily. Yvonne Lacoste and Yukiko Inoue are walking around and studying the floor plan of the hotel.

Watanabe waits patiently until the gaggle of foreigners has passed him.

Mochizuki is the last to leave the room. At the hotel entrance he turns his head slowly in all directions, like a warrior in an open field, looking over the heads of his new subordinates and back towards the plastic wallpaper and the lift doors of imitation mahogany.

Bertus rubs his large hands over his fleshy face. His fingertips massage his closed eyelids with their pale eyelashes. He sits on the edge of the bed in the brown and beige hotel room and thinks about the long flight from Amsterdam to Tokyo, and about the two policemen standing waiting for him at the airport, one with a little yellow plastic flag in his hand bearing Bertus's name and the word WELCOME. Hogenelst spelled wrongly: Hogenelsk. Then the drive into Tokyo in the grey Toyota; an hour or two, first on expressways and then through the strange city, a city of grey cardboard. As if it has been cut out. A collection of construction slabs on the obverse sides of cornflake packets: little flat black windows, small neon tubes installed in the cardboard buildings; not beautiful, not charming, not endearing. Strange. Hustle and bustle in the lights behind the tens of thousands of little windows.

The Japanese policemen had said almost nothing during the journey. Their English was nearly incomprehensible, and Bertus had been too tired to make a serious attempt at conversation. He just left it like that, and had felt a little awkward with the two silent men.

And Mochizuki, he had set to work so formally. The endless speech. The bowing. Bertus grinned.

Something in his body seemed to have changed. The proportions and sizes must be different here, he thinks; walls, staircases, steps, pillars, seem different from those at home. I've spent the whole morning swaying as though I was drunk. He takes his clothes off, shakes open the blue and white printed starched cotton *nemaki* lying on his bed and puts it on. Cardboard, he thinks vaguely; and sitting on the edge of the bed, with his head in his hands, elbows on his knees, bare feet apart on the carpet, he looks at the pile of crumpled clothing on the floor.

"Better get to sleep," he says out loud, then stands up stiffly and walks to the bathroom. His ears are still bunged up and his nostrils dried out; under the shower he tries to clear them by rubbing his ears and blowing his nose. Back in his room and in the sleeping robe, with his hair dripping, he inspects the contents of a small fridge. He takes out a can of tomato juice. He doesn't like the taste. He stretches out between the starched sheets under the light duvet. Everything here is made of cardboard, he thinks, I am dead tired but wide awake and cannot sleep, that's it. There's nothing more to think about. I'm bored; my thoughts have not yet arrived, they are still hovering above the ocean. I'm an empty husk, between cardboard sheets in a paper robe.

He walks to the window and works out how to open it. It is tightly sealed in its grooves. There is a metal clip overhead that can be used in conjunction with a lever. He opens the window and damp air strikes his forehead. Close it again.

He lies in bed once more: lucid, empty, the duvet too light, the pillow too hard, his body too big, his feet wet and cold. The knot in the belt that encircles his nemaki irritates him. Get up. He takes the photograph of Martha, his wife, out of his suitcase. "Hello Martha, my darling," he says, and puts the portrait on the night table next to the bed. He leans on his elbow and says to the face in the frame: "I am completely homeless, Twitty. I hope that we can get this bastard quickly, and then I can come home."

He falls asleep around two. At six-thirty, the alarm goes off for the first team meeting.

Bertus observes that he is not the only one who is swaying when he walks. Inspector Fowell, a tall, thin man in a rust-brown off-the-peg suit, is staggering uncertainly, with his hands moving towards the table. In the harsh light falling through the window he looks like a spider creeping sideways. Fowell is also feeling the effects, thinks Bertus; is he jetlagged too? Or is the building being blown back and forth by the wind? He looks at the staff walking past: small Japanese people. They move purposefully; their bodies are as compact and expressionless as eggs. He chooses a place at the table laid for the team opposite a window. The serrated city lies in an ochre fog and stretches right to the horizon. He thinks he can see mountains in the distance.

A good-looking, attractive, middle-aged Asian woman taps her pencil against her coffee cup.

"Good afternoon everybody," she says in English. "My name is Zhiqiang Li, and I am a psychologist, as you learned from Inspector Mochizuki this morning. Mochizuki-san has asked me to open this meeting. We have been brought together here to track down the perpetrator of a gruesome series of murders. It is important that we get to know one another well so that we can work together harmoniously and bring our joint task to a successful conclusion as swiftly as possible.

"I will therefore begin right away with an introduction that consists of a round of questions. The first question is: who are you? I will start with myself. I am Chinese, born in Hong Kong in 1947. I studied clinical psychology in London and obtained my Ph.D. in Berkeley, California, after which I returned to Hong Kong. When I was offered a partnership I moved to Tokyo. I now have a practice here with an American business partner. I specialise in making profiles of perpetrators and victims, and I know a lot about group processes, which is why I have been asked to provide you with guidance. I am not married and never have been. I have no children."

Watanabe, the interpreter, translates this almost simultaneously for Inspector Mochizuki, who is sitting next to Zhiqiang Li. Li smiles coquettishly with her bright red lips and offers the floor to her neighbour with a gesture of her hand.

"My name is Ichiro Mochizuki, and I am in charge of this investigation, as you know," he says, with a drawn-out accent that makes him almost incomprehensible. He pronounces his own name very quickly; the words in English emerge whistling and hissing from his throat. He insists on speaking in English; this is evident from the way he gestures to Watanabe, the interpreter, to remain silent. He is not accustomed to being challenged. He looks round the table with the unimpaired self-confidence of a pampered boy. The foreigners turn their heads in his direction, the better to understand him. It is clear that he has learned this text in English by heart.

"I would like to welcome you all, and I hope that you will all feel at home in Japan, despite the onerous and unpleasant task that lies before us." He seems to be about to say more, but suddenly he remains still, bows stiffly and then looks straight ahead, as though he has not said anything.

The blonde woman next to him takes over.

"My name is Lucia Valenti. I work for the Criminalpol department of the police in Palermo. I'm a sociologist, specialising in sexual offences. I have been asked to participate in this investigation because I speak, read and write Japanese, and am very familiar with Japanese culture. I've been taking Japanese lessons for many years from a Japanese lady living in Palermo and am fascinated by Japan. I collect Japanese pottery. I've lived and worked in Palermo my whole life." She laughs childishly. She is extraordinarily beautiful: her hair is very long, straight and blonde; her eyebrows are thin and black, her brown

24

eyes childish. She is tall; her hips and breasts are full, her clothes a little on the cheap side. Her skin is a transparent white, her hands long and delicate. She seems to alter as she speaks; she becomes more ordinary. Everyone looks at her, and she laughs. It is difficult for her neighbour to take the floor, because everyone keeps looking at Lucia Valenti. The man clears his throat and speaks into the void; he blushes. The group's attention shifts slowly and awkwardly.

"Yeah, it's not easy to sit next to such a beautiful woman," he says haltingly. Almost no one hears this; Lucia Valenti pulls a face, like a girl of ten. He clears his throat once more, blushes again slightly and says, "I am Mark Croo, from Belgium. I come from Ghent and work for the police in Brussels. I worked on the Van Golberdinge affair last year. You may possibly remember that at that time the Netherlands and Belgium had to deal with a spate of murders. From that investigation I know Bertus Hogenelst, as I worked closely with him for six months. I was pleasantly surprised to see his name on the list here, as he is a very competent man." He looks at Bertus and gestures; Bertus says, "thank you."

"I have been in Tokyo since the beginning of this year in connection with the investigation into the Miyazawa affair," continues Croo. "I am researching the relationship between violence in films and violence in everyday life. In 1992, Miyazawa killed seven pre-school children. After his arrest, a large quantity of violent visual material was found at his residence. Copies of all this material have been sent to the university for research purposes. Until recently I had an office and a room on the campus of Todai, Tokyo

University. The research there was concluded two weeks ago, and now, just like all foreign members of this team, I have a room here at the hotel. I became very lonely during my research at Todai. I have made almost no friends here in Tokyo, and scarcely left the campus. I am glad I can work in a team now."

"Did you spend the whole day studying pornography, sitting in that little office at the university?" asks the youthful-looking woman next to him.

"No," answers Croo. "I was mainly comparing large amounts of information. I was studying statistics."

The woman nods, and then says, looking around the group, "I am Robynne Green. I come from Salt Lake City; yes, my parents are Mormons. I'm thirty-five and I like dancing, especially salsa." She wears a brown check jacket over a white silk shirt. Her head is small and masculine; her short hair is sleekly combed back. "I am married to a Japanese man, I have no children, and we live in Palo Alto and both work in San Francisco. I work as an inspector with the police. I don't use my husband's name because no one can pronounce it. It's 'Kuroyanagi'." She looks at her neighbour.

"Gerardo Silva. I am Mexican, and I'm too fat. I am married and have two children, both now at university. We live in Mexico City. I did a lot of rough street work in my earlier years with the police, with gangs among other things. But my eyesight became bad and I started to concentrate more on my other obsession: the scientific side of police work, criminology. People with bad eyesight become fat. And who are you?" He turns to the woman next to him, a small Japanese with a broad face. She laughs shyly, but her voice is determined and clear; her English is almost accentless.

"Yukiko Inoue. My family name is quite common in Japan. I come from Hokkaido, Japan's most northerly island; there are only cows up there. My parents are farmers. I studied in Tokyo and now work for the police as an office manager. Homicide department. I was also working on this project before you all came here, and I was selected for your team because I speak English. I'll do my very best to help you process the information in this investigation."

"Jack Fowell. Australia, inspector, Vice Squad. Unmarried, that is divorced. Thank you." His face is thin; he looks too loose in his skin, as though he had once carried more weight.

"I am Bettina Welt," says the young woman next to Fowell, with an unmistakable German accent. She has a friendly, rather peasant-like appearance: blonde hair in a ponytail, red cheeks, blue eyes, a round face. "I am German, born in Munich, but I have been living in the Netherlands for eight years. I am a criminologist and a sinologist and I work at the Ministry of Justice. Through my marriage I have taken on Dutch nationality. My husband, Matthijs, is Dutch and also a sinologist. We met in Berlin." She turns to the woman sitting next to her and gives her a friendly, curious look.

"My name is Yvonne Lacoste. I work in Paris as an office manager with the police Département Judiciaire Criminelle. I used to live in Tokyo because I used to be married to a Japanese man, and I have a daughter, Lei, from that marriage. Before my marriage, and for the first years afterwards, I lived in Tokyo for seven years. I was divorced when Lei was three and went back to Paris with my daughter. When Lei was six, we married a Frenchman. Lei is now twelve."

"*We* married?" asks Inspector Mochizuki.

"Lei and I," says Yvonne Lacoste with a mischievous laugh. Mochizuki looks at her uncertainly.

"It is only a joke, Mochizuki-san," she says. He glances at her suspiciously.

"I started studying Japanese in Paris," continues Yvonne Lacoste. "I speak the language well now and I still know Tokyo like the back of my hand. I am happy to be back here again. Yukiko Inoue and I will be working closely together. I shall mainly be doing translation. My native language is French, but I speak English, as you can hear, and Spanish, Italian and German as well. That is the reason I have been chosen for this investigation."

"Ichiro Watanabe. I am your interpreter. Welcome to Japan." He is small and weasel-like. His skin is dull and yellowish, his suit a smaller version of Mochizuki's; tailored, with narrow lapels; the legs of the trousers are too short, the sleeves of the jacket too long. Like many Japanese men, he wears shoes with elevated heels in order to appear taller. Everyone looks expectantly in his direction, but he says nothing more.

Bertus begins to speak. "I am Bertus Hogenelst from Amsterdam. I am an inspector and work for Department of Serious Offences at the Chief Bureau of Police. Last year, as Mr Croo has already told you, I collaborated in the Van Golberdinge affair in the Netherlands. That case concerned a serial killer, just as this one does now. As a result of that investigation I was asked to join this team. I do not know how you ladies and gentlemen are faring here, but I feel just like an elephant on this little chair. I am one metre ninety-eight tall. I am fifty-nine and I am married to Martha. We have five children who have all left home. My wife is a pianist and I play the double bass. We both like music very much. You know, I thought the buildings in Tokyo would all be romantic and made of wood."

Zhiqiang Li laughs, her even teeth showing, and thanks everybody for the first round. There is lipstick on her teeth. "From now on I suggest that we call one another by our given names," she says. "What I would like you to do now is give one word describing how you feel; this is what we call 'taking the temperature.' Ichiro, over to you."

"What?" asks Mochizuki.

"How do you feel?"

"I don't understand."

"It's very simple. How do you feel?"

"Fine. Why?"

"No, I should have started with myself. I feel surprised."

"Me too," says Mochizuki politely.

Li shrugs her shoulders. "And you, Lucia?"

"Nervous," says Lucia Valenti.

"Ready to get to work," says Mark Croo.

"That is not a feeling," says Zhiqiang Li.

"Oh, okay, er… stimulated."

"I played this game once before," says Robynne Green. "It is very American. I feel calm."

"Impatient," says Gerardo Silva.

"Insecure, says Yukiko Inoue.

"Give me a break," says Jack Fowell.

Zhiqiang Li looks at him in annoyance.

"Happy," says Yvonne Lacoste.

"Surprised," says Watanabe, and swiftly translates for Mochizuki.

"I'm enjoying it," says Bertus Hogenelst. Everyone looks a little cautiously at Zhiqiang Li.

"This is not an innocent game," she says. "It is important, please work with me. You will see that it is worthwhile." She looks in the direction of Jack Fowell, who returns her look sullenly.

Mochizuki stands up and takes Zhiqiang Li to one side. Then he informs everyone that Li and he have agreed that both office managers can now go to their office. Yvonne and Yukiko leave the room. Yukiko bows slightly, while Yvonne raises her hand in farewell.

Zhiqiang Li continues with the game. "The next round concerns all your names and nicknames. Shall we go round the other way? Once again I will start with myself; Bertus could you go next?" Bertus nods.

" 'Li' is a very common Chinese family name," says Zhiqiang Li. "Literally, the character means 'plum,' as in the fruit. And 'Zhiqiang' is a boy's name, which I was teased about a lot when I was young. The most important meaning of the character for 'zhi' is 'will' or 'ambition'. As a verb it means something like 'to desire, to strive after, to be ambitious.' The character 'qiang' means 'strong' or 'powerful', but also 'to exert oneself', or 'strive after', depending on how it is pronounced. My name is written like this."

Li takes a paper napkin and on it writes three Chinese

characters: 李志强. She holds the side with the writing on up to her audience. "My father tells me that the name can be used just as well for a girl, but I think he really wanted to have a boy. I'm an only child. I was happy to move to London and later to California, even though I studied with some Chinese there who found the name 'Zhiqiang' hilarious. In Tokyo I have had no trouble with it. It occurred to me far too late that I could have changed my name, and now that's no longer necessary." Her red mouth produces an expression that is both prudish and mischievous.

"My name is Albertus Maria Hogenelst," says Bertus. "My parents come from the south of the Netherlands and I grew up there. Later I moved to Amsterdam. The south of the Netherlands is Catholic, hence my name 'Maria'. I had various nicknames when I was young. First, Bertus Higherup because I was so tall. Also Lighthouse, Red, Stoplight and that kind of silly name, because of my hair, which used to be much redder. My brother calls me Koos, I don't know why, and I call him Rinus, although his real name is Jan. My wife sometimes calls me 'crook' because I often call her 'Twitty'. That means something like oh, how can I put it, a 'fluffy'? No, that is too soppy."

"A cunt?" Robynne Green suggests helpfully, at which Croo, on the other side of the table, blushes.

"No," says Bertus Hoganelst, "it is less crude than that."

Robynne Green knits her brows.

"My son calls me Ludwig," continues Bertus, "because he thinks I look like the bust of Beethoven we have on our piano at home."

The foreigners laugh; Watanabe is a little late with the

translation. When he has delivered it, Mochizuki laughs as well.

"I have never had a nickname," says Watanabe, "but Ichiro means 'first son.' My full name is written like this…" He scrawls on a paper napkin with his fountain pen, just as Li had done: 渡辺一郎. "My family name is composed of two characters, one meaning 'cross over' and the other 'a side,' one side of a river, for example. 'Ichiro' is also written with two characters, can you see? I have two younger brothers and one sister. It is a big responsibility to be the oldest son: I have to decide everything if someone in the family gets married, or dies, or if there is any disunity. A lot is expected of me, it always falls on my shoulders." He hesitates to translate this into Japanese for Mochizuki. Zhiqiang Li indicates with a frown that he should do so.

Jack Fowell starts to speak. "When I was small I used to dress up in my younger sister's clothes and sing. So my father called me 'Sweet Jacqueline'. You cannot imagine how I suffered from being called this. Other than that I have no nicknames, fortunately."

"Jam jar," says Silva. "That's what they call me at work behind my back. I pretend not to know that it's because of my spectacle lenses."

"I have a whole load of them," says Robynne Green. "My husband calls me 'Chan', after the suffix 'chan' that follows Japanese names. It is a diminutive: little Robynne. First it was Robynne-chan, and in time that became 'Chan.' My mother always buys dolls with Japanese faces for my nieces, and all the dolls are called Chan. At middle school I was 'Sweetlips,' God knows why, and then there was 'Hobbes', which my father called me, and 'Hobbeles',

32

and 'Canary', and later 'Knee.' Why 'Knee'? I've no idea, it started around the time I was in middle school." She laughs loudly and heartily.

"My nickname was 'Hein,' because I was so thin," says Mark Croo. "In Dutch, and also in Flemish, the language of northern Belgium which is my native tongue, we call the figure of death, the one with the scythe, 'Magere Hein,' 'Skinny Hank.' I blushed a lot, and because of that I was also called 'Lighthouse,' just like Bertus Hogenelst, or 'Peony.' I still blush."

"Mouse," says Lucia Valenti. "My father called me 'Mouse' when I was a small child. Apart from that I've not had any nicknames."

"I've never had a nickname," says Bettina Welt.

"Neither have I," says Mochizuki rather awkwardly, "but my name is written like this…" He sketches out the characters with broad strokes on the cardboard back of his notepad: 望月一郎. "My family name means 'looking at the moon.' The given name is the same as Watanabe-san's. In Japanese families we put 'kun' after a boy's name. So I am 'Ichiro-kun'. He gestures imperiously to the interpreter, as if to say 'translate that, for heaven's sake'.

"I would also like to ask you to call me 'Mochizuki' rather than 'Ichiro,'" he continues. "First because Watanabe-san is also called 'Ichiro', and it could be confusing if we are both called by our given names. Second, we Japanese are not accustomed to the use of given names outside the family circle. It feels too intimate. Would you mind calling me 'Mochizuki'?"

Zhiqiang Li looks round the table. The members of the team shake their heads. No, they would not mind calling

Mochizuki, 'Mochizuki.'

"And how do you feel about this, Ichiro?" Zhiqiang Li asks Watanabe. "How would you like to be called?"

"Watanabe, please," says Watanabe.

"So that's that," says Zhiqiang Li to Mochizuki.

Mochizuki nods and takes the floor. "Thank you very much, Li-san, for this interesting and extremely unusual game." He places a slightly mocking tone on the word 'game', then has Watanabe translate the rest of his speech. "I would now like to distribute reports that you can study in your rooms. They contain details of the investigation by the Tokyo police. A huge pile of paper, but as you will see, the documents are very precisely labelled and numbered and are provided with an index and a list of key words. Dinner will be served at six o'clock in this room. After that you must go to the large conference room. There, Inspector Silva will deliver a lecture. At ten o'clock there is a press conference in the lounge. I would request that you drink no alcohol during the press conference and keep your comments as brief and general as possible." He holds his hand out to Watanabe, who passes him some thick brown A4 envelopes. Mochizuki reads out the names on the envelopes and has each member of the team sign a declaration of confidentiality.

"*Yoroshiku onegaishimasu,*" he says each time, as everyone signs the paper and takes delivery of their envelopes.

"Not at all, thank you," Watanabe translates freely, ten times.

The group disperses itself silently over the thick broadloom carpet of the seventeenth floor of the Akasaka Prince Hotel. There are no staff to be seen in the corridors.

The vending machines for drinks, flowers, condoms, diamonds, snacks and newspapers hum in unison.

Gerardo Silva stands behind a wooden lectern, ready for his lecture. He half closes his eyes and looks at the room. Watanabe sits at the back behind a microphone. The Japanese attendees have headsets and sit still, waiting for the presentation to begin. The members of the international team sit talking noisily to one another. Silva clears his throat and grips the sides of the lectern tightly with both
hands while he looks at the sheaf of papers in front of him.

After a few moments he looks up again at his colleagues in the investigation team. His thick glasses, with their black frames, dominate his whole face.

The gestures diminish, the loud whispers subside. The room becomes very quiet as he begins to speak.

"I have researched the psychology of serial killers," he says, "which is why I have been invited to give this presentation. My book about the subject came out last year. *Cold Blue Fire: The Psychology of a Serial Killer.*" Silva speaks clear, accentless English.

"I'm having a problem with the last two rows of fluorescent lights at the back of the room. Can someone turn them off? They're reflecting in the lenses of my glasses and distracting me."

Nothing happens for a moment, and then a man at the back of the room gets up quickly, puts his notepad on the seat of his chair and clicks the light switch next to the door. Silva waits until the man is back on his chair with his pen at the ready above his notepad.

"That's better, thank you. We have come together here before we get down to work so that we can take our bearings with respect to a very regrettable affair, one that has been generating a stir in the media for some time under the name of the 'Fish Murders'. Journalists are a creative bunch of people, and I shall not attempt to add anything further to this very expressively chosen name.

"What has happened, ladies and gentlemen, is that eight of our compatriots – Marcus Bopp from Switzerland, Ian Wackwitz from Germany, Jacob Parker from America, Irina Skoynich from Poland, Marco Polo from Italy, Larry Maxwell from Australia, Hendrik Mechanicus from the Netherlands and Hughes De Keuninck from Belgium – have been murdered here in Tokyo, and their mutilated corpses have been found by passers-by. All these passers-by described the human remains they found as having been very carefully arranged, as though they had been prepared in order to be served up. The investigations of the Japanese police have revealed that the bodies were carved up with a 'yanagi-ba'.

Silva takes a long narrow knife with a wooden handle from his lectern and holds it in the air. The point is fitted with a plastic cap. The knife is about forty centimetres long; the blade shimmers in the fluorescent light.

"It is certain that the person who caused the injuries used a similar knife and wore black leather gloves. Traces of these gloves have been found on the bodies of the victims. The state in which the remains of the victims were found points to ritual murder, which is a characteristic of the serial killer.

"Another characteristic of the serial killer is that he selects his victims carefully according to particular criteria. And this is the point at which the police find themselves completely in the dark: we do not know what the victims have in common with one another. So on this last point I can tell you nothing, except that the victims were all non-Japanese. But I can comment on what is known about serial killers. I would like to emphasise that in putting forward my argument I do not seek to evoke either compassion or sympathy for the perpetrator. What we are trying to do is get an insight into his behaviour and motives, so that we can find a swift and efficient way of working. It is quite possible that at this very moment the murderer is dreaming about his next victim: choosing him, stalking him, seducing him or killing him. Because these are the phases that a serial killer goes through: those of fantasising, selecting, shadowing, seducing and killing. A terrible obsession forces him into his fantasies, his silent pursuit, his choice, his 'game', if I can put it like that, his act; and finally, into a depression that makes him plunge back into his fantasies.

"I use the word 'he', but it will be apparent to everyone that a serial killer can also be a woman, although history shows that female Jack the Rippers are rare. During the research for my book, I came across three. On was in the Middle Ages, one in the sixteenth century and one in the seventeenth. The first was called Angela Jesus. She murdered farmers' sons by cutting their throats, after which she flayed her victims, then dried the skins so she could make garments from them. She reached the age of sixty and lived at the foot of Mount Vesuvius. Then at the beginning of the sixteenth century there was Erzsébet Báthory in Hungary. To preserve her beauty for eternity, she bathed in the blood of young virgins. The third female killer was called Bata, and lived in Romania. She drank the blood of children in order to attain eternal life. It could be that Bata and Erzsébet Báthory were the same person, and that in the oral recounting of the tale one has split off from the other.

"You might ask yourself: is the serial killer ill? The answer to this question is not simple. It has to do with a combination of genetic, social and psychological factors which are interconnected and reinforce one another. Hence, in the brains of eighty percent of serial killers known to us in the past seventy years, damage to the limbic system has been found. The limbic system is an ancient part of our brains. I will not go into too much detail here, but the limbic system governs the primitive drives. The more savage impulses are normally kept under control by younger parts of the brain, but with the serial killer this appears not to be the case. We are dealing with a kind of human being who is operating like an automaton, who is overcome by forces that he does not control and does not understand; forces of which we can have only a vague conception, because we have never experienced them. We do not know the extent to which damage to the limbic system also occurs in normal people, because no normal person with this kind of damage has ever been examined. Damage like this can, for example, be caused by severe abuse in childhood.

"Imagine that a young boy is caught off-guard by aggressive sexual feelings. He takes the cat into the back garden and torments the animal until it quickly dies of exhaustion. He experiences a strange kind of arousal. Having killed the cat, he hides the body and then comes to his senses. The appalling nature of his deed overwhelms him. If the parents of this boy are observant people, they are likely to notice that the cat has gone missing and that something has changed in the boy. A boy who has committed such a terrible act will not behave as though he's unaffected. The parents will question him, and the truth about what happened to the cat will come to light. If he is fortunate, the boy can now give expression to his shame, his pain and his disgust. And this is what matters. If the boy has a way of giving form to his feelings, by having a good cry, or expressions of regret and promises to improve his life, then the intensity of these feelings will diminish. Only this way will he be less inclined to torment the next cat.

"Now, imagine that the parents of this kind of boy are violent, stupid people. They don't notice what's happened to the cat, or they do notice it and they hit the boy. They shut him up and bully him. Eighty-eight percent of the serial killers researched in the last seventy years suffered repeated severe physical and psychological abuse as children. What kind of consequences does this have on the psyche of a child? It is forced back into a fantasy world. If the child has never experienced friendship and warmth, it will not even know how to fantasise about these. Its fantasies will be bizarre and violent. It is these kinds of fantasies that we are dealing with here. They are partly sexual in nature and release the individual from tension which has built up in its organism as a consequence of not knowing the feeling of being loved. Just as an orgasm releases the sexual tension of a human organism that knows itself to be loved, murder releases, as it were, the tension in an organism that does not feel loved. I will now review the different stages of tension and release that a murderer passes through.

"As soon as the serial killer feels tension grow in himself, the fantasies begin. The situation in which he now finds himself is comparable to that of sexual arousal. He imagines himself committing the act, in all its details.

"The normal requirements of everyday life don't matter any more. They are satisfied automatically, or they are neglected, and are replaced by an intense, all-consuming feeling of lust. Terry Middler, a serial killer condemned to death in 1961, describes the feeling as 'a cold blue fire that there is no way of avoiding'. Mickey Delthy, convicted in 1964, said, 'It seemed as though I was being drawn into a place where other rules applied'.

"This phase can continue for days or weeks. In this period, the killer begins to look around for a victim. The victim must conform to the image the murderer has: one with a particular kind of voice or appearance, or who engages in a particular kind of behaviour. The victims of a serial killer always have something in common. For the victims of Caesar Varano, who was convicted in 1972, it was a particular way of looking at people. In fact, the common characteristic of the victims is the most important trigger for the consequent act of the murderer.

"Once the killer has located his prey, the stalking period

can begin. The murderer tries as far as possible to get to know his future victim. In that way he can feed his fantasy with more and more new details and keep that 'cold blue fire' burning. He will engage in conversations with the victim, or draw him or her into friendship or love. He is convincing and appears to be sincere. People who have escaped a serial killer at this stage describe their stalker as charming, warm, disarming, open-hearted, childishly innocent and attractive. If the murderer has gained the trust of the victim, he then sets up his prey to go to a location that he has sought out well in advance.

"While committing the murder, the murderer experiences a feeling of release, and of what in theology is called 'integration'. He feels omnipotent and in direct contact with the universe. This ecstasy can last for several days, and then descends into its opposite: fear, and finally, lack of sensation. This last feeling, which in my book I refer to as 'un-feeling', is the precursor to the next fantasy, because of all the intense feelings that persist, un-feeling is the worst.

"The un-feeling is the basis of the serial killer's existence, and so he will do anything at all to prevent this numbness occuring. In this way he is the prisoner of a terrible cycle, one which, if it is not broken through by outside intervention, continues until the killer dies. He will not stop murdering until he is safely under lock and key. This bizarre phenomenon is what we are dealing with.

"We have to break the cycle as quickly as possible. I venture to suggest that this is less complicated then it appears at the moment. I am convinced that, deep in his heart, the perpetrator wants nothing more than to be caught. His arrest will at least put an end to the acts that he has to commit over and over again. A life sentence in prison would be far preferable to compulsively submitting to the impulses that enslave him at the moment. Because of this he will become more and more careless. As soon as we work out some leads, he will make our investigation easier. He might even lure us to him. We should always be aware of this possibility. The man or woman we are looking for might even be giving us signals at this very moment."

Several of his audience involuntarily look around.

Zhiqiang Li stands up, comes over to Silva and leans over the microphone. "We, the members of the international team, will be under great pressure during the investigation. We may be confronted with strong and unfamiliar emotions. These could hinder our investigation. I would like to request the members of the international team to keep a diary during the investigation, and if necessary talk to me. Do not hesitate to contact me as soon as you notice that you can no longer think clearly."

An air of muffled amusement runs through the room.

Chief Inspector Mochizuki, followed by Watanabe, comes to the front of the room and requests the new team to devote any free moments to studying the reports from the Japanese police and the layout of Greater Tokyo, and to learning their way around the hotel.

"There will soon be a press conference," he adds. "Tomorrow morning at seven o'clock we have a breakfast conference in the dining room on this floor. You should have received a floor plan. You also have a list of the telephone and room numbers of everyone concerned.

In this hotel there are jet-lag rooms for anyone who feels disoriented after the plane journey. You can go and have a course of artificial sunlight and ozone. Thank you for your attention. Does anyone have any questions?"

Bettina Welt addresses Silva: "Do you have any idea why serial killers are mostly men?

"No. There are certainly theories about this, but in general I do not find them credible or satisfactory, and for that reason I don't want to recapitulate them here. I would like to emphasise once again that the killer could also be a woman. In recent years we have seen criminality among girls and women increasing, even in Japan."

To Silva's surprise, there are no more questions. Not one question came from the Japanese side, he thinks. He goes over to Watanabe, who has stayed behind in the room, and whispers that after that lecture anywhere else in the world he would have been overwhelmed with questions. Watanabe answers that Japanese people are very reticent about putting questions in public. "Asking questions is discouraged from the first class of primary school," he says.

"Aha," says Silva vaguely, pondering this explanation.

Little groups are forming in the room. There are handshakes; name cards are exchanged; and Mochizuki distributes new thick brown envelopes containing reports.

In the large conference room, it is smoky and noisy. Gerardo Silva is giving an abbreviated version of his lecture for the press. The journalists make assiduous notes or hold miniature tape recorders in the air. Mochizuki sits chain-smoking behind a small Japanese flag and a glass of pineapple juice, pulls a sulky face, for reasons that are unclear to Silva, and reacts with irritation when after his lecture Silva demands a translation of every word spoken in Japanese.

The journalists are intrusive and loud, and barely speak English. They address the members of the team in Japanese as if that is the most normal thing in the world. With a discontented expression, Watanabe tries as far as possible to translate simultaneously. Silva asks the press specifically to publish the descriptions and photos of the victims again, and to encourage the reading public to share any information via specially established contact points open twenty-four hours a day. Calls in other languages will be channelled to the 'language bank', which will have forty-two people of various nationalities at its disposal. Silva has to shout to make himself understood. Finally, with a thick felt pen, he writes the telephone numbers of the hotlines onto the tablecloth, then yanks it out from under the cups and glasses and holds it up with both hands so that it can be seen by the press.

Mochizuki walks up to Watanabe with long strides, leans past him and loudly calls 'test, test test' into the microphone. He signals authoritatively to a technician. The journalists have put away their notebooks and tape recorders and launch themselves en masse at the members of the international team. In violation of the rules set out by Mochizuki, Robynne Green has ordered a gin and tonic. The journalists ask what they think about the Japanese weather, eating with chopsticks and the taste of Japanese food.

"Rather trivial questions they're asking," says Bertus, when Yukiko Inoue comes over and stands next to him.

She sighs deeply and rolls her eyes dramatically.

"Typically Japanese," she says.

"How do you mean?" asks Bertus.

"Most Japanese only want to talk about trivial things," she answers. "You sometimes get really fed up with that in this country."

"Oh yes?" says Bertus, surprised.

"The land of small talk." From her expression it is impossible to know whether she means this facetiously.

Bertus turns to Robynne, who has been standing looking at him in silence. "Shall we go to the bar downstairs for some small talk?" he asks, more to Robynne them to Yukiko.

"Sounds good," says Robynne eagerly.

"I'm going to bed," says Yukiko. "Sleep well. I hope you will have got over the jetlag tomorrow."

Robynne and Bertus go to the lifts. They pass Gerardo Silva and Lucia Valenti, who are deep in conversation in Spanish.

"Do you feel a bit wobbly?" Robynne asks Bertus. Her manner of speaking is direct, relaxed, and in a nice way, flirtatious.

Bertus immediately senses he is being flattered. "Yes," he says, "I thought it was me."

"I think it's because of the time difference," says Robynne. "My head feels as though it's in a ball of cotton wool."

Bertus looks at her face. "You look quite awake otherwise."

"Were you able to concentrate properly today?" asks Robynne, pulling herself up onto a bar stool. Gerardo

Silva and Lucio Valenti, still deep in conversation, are coming over to sit at the bar next to them.

"Strangely, well enough," says Bertus, and signals to the barman.

In one corner of the enormous lounge a lady sits behind a grand piano, singing 'Fly me to the moon' at length into a microphone with too much echo. The melody coming from the piano is drowned almost immediately in the thick red carpet.

"Terrible, isn't it," says Bertus.

Robynne grins, her lips greedy. Bertus looks at her mouth, and knows that she knows he is looking at her mouth. For her part she looks at his face, while she says: "Shall we not speak about our work late in the evening? Shall we agree on that?"

"Good," says Bertus, "what would you like to drink?"

"Gin and tonic," says Robynne.

Bertus orders it.

"So you come from the Netherlands," says Robynne.

"Yes, and you're from Salt Lake City. Mormons."

"That's right. My greatest fear is of going back to being a Mormon against my will."

"Against your will?"

"Yes, as if I were standing on top of a mountain and suddenly wanted to jump off. You understand what I mean?"

"No, not really."

"Well, let me explain. All my brothers and sisters are Mormons. I'm the only one who left the religion. My parents have no idea that I drink alcohol, and if they come to visit me I give up coffee. I'm afraid that one day my resistance will give way, out of laziness. It would make things much easier for me just to be an ordinary Mormon."

"An ordinary Mormon," says Bertus; and then, "Do Mormons not drink coffee?"

"No. At least my parents don't, and they don't drink tea either."

Bertus offers her a filtered Caballero cigarette.

"No, thank you."

"Do Mormons not smoke either?"

"No, it's not that. I used to be a heavy smoker. I stopped five years ago. Feel free, it doesn't bother me."

"Thank you," says Bertus, and lights a cigarette.

"And how is it being Dutch? I always hear that it's a very liberal country."

"That's right. For me, the Netherlands is Amsterdam. I hardly ever go anywhere else. I really like Amsterdam, despite everything."

"Despite everything?"

"Yes, it is noisy and has a heap of problems, but it's a wonderful city. Very different from Tokyo, certainly, much smaller, almost a village… I only saw Tokyo from the car yesterday. What an enormous city."

"I like Tokyo," says Robynne. "I heard that you are interested in art. If you like I'll take you to the galleries in Ginza when we have a couple of hours free."

"What is Ginza?"

"That's the area with the expensive department stores. And bars, and hundreds of small galleries. The galleries that show the work of the lesser-known artists are often especially interesting. You can read about them in the Thursday edition of the *Daily Yomiuri*."

"Yeah, that would be great. How nice for you to know all that."

"Which religions are mostly practised in the Netherlands?"

"Protestant and Catholic, mainly. I'm not anything; I don't have a religion. My parents were Catholic. We have a few good writers in the Netherlands who have used religious traumas in their work."

"In that case, maybe I should consider a career as a writer."

"Was it that bad?"

"I don't want to get that close right away," says Robynne, laughing. "Shall we go up? It's a very early day tomorrow."

"Yes. It was very nice to get to know you better."

"For me too," answers Robynne. She slips down from the stool; Bertus looks down from his high position on the bar stool into the neck of her T-shirt; he sees the curve of her small breasts; and then, as she turns away from him, watches her long back in the brown checked men's jacket.

She knows I'm looking at her, thinks Bertus, as he follows her.

They wave to Silva and Lucia Valenti, who are still engaged in heated conversation, and walk to the lifts.

Alone in his room, Bertus sets his alarm clock for six o'clock, before the breakfast meeting. After taking a shower, he wraps the *nemaki* around his body. He has a semi-erection.

"Down, boy," he says. "We have no time for that now, and we're not interested." He gets between the hard sheets, turns the portrait of his wife towards him and purses his lips at it.

"Good night, Martha the Wife," he says.

First of September

This is the first time I have been more or less forced to keep a diary. And for the first time since I have kept a diary, which I have been doing for nineteen years without missing a single day, I have no desire to write. I once promised the old lady who I will one day become that my diaries are for her, so that when she is tired and weak she can analyse her life at her leisure. So I am forcing myself to sit at this dreadful wooden hotel desk and write with an Akasaka Prince pen.

What a day! What a situation! But it's very interesting to be back. The smells! When were Matthijs and I last here? Five years ago, six? I don't know, right off the top of my head, and forgot to ask Matthijs on the telephone just now. The darling did not first enquire after my well-being, but immediately asked whether Narita still smelled of iron filings; and indeed, the first thing I did when I landed on Japanese soil was breathe in deeply. For a sinologist of limited means like me, the business-class flight with Japan Air Lines was certainly a step up. Back then with Matthijs we flew Aeroflot. But I found the elbowing Russian hostesses with the thick red upper arms at least as intriguing as the Japanese hostesses speaking unusually good American, in their kimonos with the giraffe-skin motifs. The mechanical dance that they performed on boarding, dressed in bright orange masks and lifejackets, was so synchronised, and in its own unique way beautifully enacted, that I didn't realise it was a demonstration of what to do in an accident. A man sitting a couple of rows in front of me who spent the whole flight looking at a pile of reading matter turned out to be a fellow team member, Bertus Hogenelst. Strangely enough we were taken in separate cars from the airport to the hotel. There he disappeared immediately into one of the rooms. I've only been able to meet him today.

After a particularly disturbed night because of jet lag, today has been strung together in such a mad rush that I found no time to write it all down coherently. How did all this happen? I have been the victim of an unfortunate statement made earlier this month by a high-ranking bureaucrat in the Japanese Ministry of Justice. This bureaucrat, referred to as 'Adolf' in certain Western publications, was so stupid as to say out loud that the Japanese and the Germans work so well together. Of course the whole world got to hear about this, including all the German candidates for our research team. That is why I was chosen even at such a late stage: as a German living in the Netherlands. I found all this out from Lucia Valenti, who also learned only at the last moment that she had been selected for this team. In her case it was because the Americans had insisted that it should preferably be a woman who was chosen. They pressured Japan to make a male colleague of Lucia Valenti stand aside, a man whose suitcases had been as good as packed. The poor man now has the honour of being ready on-call in Italy as Lucia Valenti's 'assistant.' No-one else has that kind of assistant. Now I sit here, uncertain of my place in this team, ignored by Mochizuki, groped on my bottom by Jack Fowell, an

Australian inspector with the drooping cheeks of the kind of dog that is popular with the English aristocracy.

Zhiqiang Li, the psychologist, has instructed us to keep a diary. It will be interesting to see who does and who doesn't. To judge by the expressions on people's faces, no-one had much stomach for it. So I will go just a little further in this journal, for my old lady. It was silly of me not to have brought along an extra notebook from De Zaaier. I swear by De Zaaier. The covers give me a homely feeling, and I could do with that here in this bare, brown and beige hotel room.

After an insanely formal transfer of power, in which form took precedence over content, Mochizuki immediately provided us with dozens of pieces of paper concerning the findings of the Japanese police; double-labelled with long numerical codes. There are three piles ready on my particularly uninspiring beech veneer desk. Really my style of working! As if there was not enough paperwork in the world already.

In the afternoon, still pretty shattered, I went out onto the street. You always forget the humid heat and the repugnant cold in the buildings. Around the hotel there was nothing visually endearing other than the trees on the square that are wrapped up to protect them against insects. The heavy trunks and branches are wound around with gauze dressings like linen, and the tops are wrapped in dark blue nets. They are just like modern sculptures. Other than that, everything is businesslike and functional.

The introductory game led by Li, who watches everything with her surprised round psychologist's eyes, was only just tolerated by a contemputuous Mochizuki, but it was amusing and perhaps even useful. I found the lecture from Silva about serial killers rather too focussed on the situation in the United States, but he is an impressive speaker.

The press conference was downright messy. Watanabe, our interpreter, became more and more weaselly. Almost broke in half with his bowing. He must be suffering from stress fatigue in his pelvis.

I had some light therapy and took a jar of vitamin D from the jet-lag room. Nevertheless I'm dead tired, but I still can't sleep again. It's half-past three. I have to get up at seven.

After I had called Matthijs, but not for long because there was so much echo on the line that talking was not much fun, I read the newspapers: the *Japan Times*, the *Daily Yomiuri*; listened to the Armed Forces Radio, the Far East Network Tokyo; and watched TV: channels one and two on NHK.

The Great Kanto Earthquake of 1923 was commemorated today. Around 7.7 million people took part in excercises on what to do in an earthquake. Imagine this city being hit! They say it won't be long until the next big one comes. Major earthquakes happen every sixty years on average. Better not think about that. I thought I felt some small ones today, but Bertus Hogenelst said that this building sways back and forth in the wind.

In the corner of this room there's a fridge that wheezes like a sick old man. I call him Herman. The air conditioner thrums, you can't stop the noises, I'd forgotten that about Tokyo as well. If you go into the hallway there are hundreds of humming vending machines selling a huge variety of items. In one of them I quickly had a *meishi* printed, because without a name card, and the accompanying ceremony when people meet one another for the first time, you're nothing here, a nobody. A person without work, and so without a card, has no identity in Japan. I'd forgotten that as well. The machine can even combine Japanese characters with Western script so that my name is printed in *katakana* with a transcription underneath, and my profession in *kanji*. Thus equipped, I shall bravely hurl myself into battle.

CHAPTER 3

Over breakfast on the second day of the investigation, Zhiqiang Li continues the introduction game. Once all the members of the team have shuffled past the row of covered dishes to assemble their breakfasts, the muffled clink of cutlery and dishes has faded away and everyone is sitting at the table, she tries to bring the table to order. To achieve silence she has to tap her spoon hard on a bowl. She sees Robynne incline her head towards Fowell, who simply turns away from her.

"I would like to play a second round today. The intention is to stimulate your imagination and creativity. Does anyone have any objections?"

Watanabe raises a hand tentatively to head height.

"I am Mochizuki-san's assistant, and as such I am not really part of this team. I also feel a little uncomfortable with this game. Could I absent myself from it?" He points steadily at the end of his nose.

"What's he doing pointing to his nose?" whispers Bertus to Robynne Green.

"Japanese people point at their noses when they mean 'I', just as we point at our chests to indicate our hearts."

"Ah."

"It makes no difference what jobs the participants here are doing," says Zhiqiang Li to Watanabe, "but if you don't feel comfortable with the game, then you can go with that. It is played on a voluntary basis."

"It's not so much that I don't feel comfortable with the game, but my participation seems to me inappropriate," answers Watanabe.

"Once again, you are free not to participate," says Zhiqiang Li, a little acerbically. "Would anyone else like to follow Watanabe-san's example?"

There is no reaction.

Mochizuki stands up and says loudly, "Our time is valuable. The game is important in some people's view, but others find it unnecessary. I would like to follow a middle course. I suggest that the central members of the team play the game, while our office managers and my assistant bow out. Watanabe-san here has already indicated that he would prefer it to be that way. How do the ladies, Lacoste and Inoue, feel about having a separate table?" Yvonne and Yukiko are already standing, holding full cups of coffee.

"No, just a moment, we will have a table laid," says Mochizuki. "Watanabe should stay with us at our table, to translate."

Zhiqiang Li looks at Mochizuki angrily. "Everyone can just eat quietly for now," she says. "We'll start again by taking the temperature. Unlike last time, I'll go last. The question is, how are you feeling at this moment? What about you, Mochizuki-san?"

"Particularly irritated," says Mochizuki, in halting, throaty English.

"Particularly irritated," repeats Watanabe, also in English, and then claps his hand over his mouth.

"As if my head's got cotton wool in it," says Lucia

Valenti. "Really jittery."

"Confused," says Jack Fowell, and by way of illustration shakes his head rapidly, like an animal shaking water off its skin.

"Shocked," says Marc Croo.

"Disturbed," says Gerardo Silva.

"Restless," says Bertus Hogenelst.

"Alienated," says Bettina Welt.

"I have jetlag," says Robynne Green.

"Anxious," says Zhiqiang Li. "Help yourselves to some fresh tea or coffee and then we can continue. The second question is: what kind of heating arrangements did you have at home when you were younger? How was your house heated?"

There is a slight buzz of amusement, then Robynne Green begins. "Well, if you really want to know, our house in Salt Lake City had oil-fired central heating. There was a big white boiler in the concrete basement. In the winter my mother used to dry washing there, so it used to smell fresh. The basement makes me think of how tidy my mother is and what a slob I am myself, and my husband as well. We still live like students in our little apartment: sprawling on the sofa, eating hamburgers in front of the television. Sometimes we rent three films in one evening.... But I was talking about my parents' basement. It's a cool white cube, with a steady flame behind a window, in a grey space smelling of soap powder."

"Nice," says Zhiqiang Li. "Just what I wanted. Let your thoughts flow and don't be frightened of free-associating."

"When I was a child I lived in the province of Zuid-Holland," says Bertus Hogenelst. "The winters there are long and cold. We were the first in our neighbourhood to have a central heating system, a primitive one, with radiators that took up a lot of space. It was often stuffy and dry at home. In the winter my father was always busy with wet gloves and humidifier boxes. The boxes were all different, horrid oblong flower boxes that he had bought at the flea market. I remember one was made of knobbly moss-green earthenware. My mother often thought of buying some nice ones made of Bakelite. You could hang them on hooks behind the radiators. My father thought it made no sense to spend money on Bakelite ones, and I don't think we ever bought any."

There is a small round of applause for Bertus. He bows a couple of times, laughing. "Your turn, Silva," he says.

"Our house was built in a U-shape around a courtyard," begins Silva. "At that time it was no longer customary to provide heating with open fires, but I come from a stubborn family and my parents had had the house built according to a traditional Mexican style. They wanted to have open fires in all the rooms. In the end this took a lot out of my mother; I can still hear her grumbling all the time because she had to look after nine open fires. We didn't have to heat the house because of the cold so much as because of the damp. It brought out yellow circles in the plasterwork on the walls and ceilings. The ash from the fireplaces was strewn onto the courtyard, and it must have been a very good fertiliser because we used to have enormous pumpkins growing there. In the kitchen we had no heating, but we did have an ultra-modern electric stove. It was always cold there, and my mother used to complain bitterly. In the winter she had blue hands when she served up the food. She always made too much food, which again used to annoy my father. My parents came from poor families. They always wanted to have the latest things, and plenty of them, but were not really up to dealing with them. So there was always something going slightly wrong, for example with the fireplaces. I remember the fires smouldering when fuel was short, then being blazing and warm. No one felt any connection with the fireplaces, nor with the stove."

There is profuse applause. Silva stands up and bows.

"At home we used to have a Leuven-style stove," says Marc Croo shyly, blushing. Nobody hears him, and he puts his hand up to ask for quiet.

"We had a Leuven-style stove," he repeats. "A Leuven-style stove consists of a heating unit containing a bowl-shaped fuel burner, enamelled in yellow on the outside, with a big cover on top that you can cook on. Underneath the fuel burner, which could burn wood, coal or briquettes, there was an oven with a chrome-plated door. Below that there was a thick bar going round the heating unit for you to put your feet on. The stove was in the middle of the living room. Right under the ceiling the chimney bent towards the wall. So there was also some warmth coming from the pipe. You could sit in a circle around the stove. My father played flamenco guitar, and we often had guitarists and singers round to visit. They sat around with one foot on the bar of the stove and drank lemon gin. There was sometimes even a female dancer, complete with castanets. When I was a child I really liked these kinds of get-together, especially when there were solos being clapped. Then the guitar music fell silent, but the song continued, with long silences built into the rhythm of the clapping." Marc pauses a moment, sighs, and says, "Well, that's pretty much It."

The applause is exuberant.

"Croo, man, you even have a soft 'g' when you speak English," Bertus says in Dutch, laughing.

As the noise dies down, Jack Fellows begins to speak. "I used to live in a large house outside Sydney. It was heated with sun and wind energy from units that my father had built himself: solar panels on the roof, a thirty-metre high windmill on the land. The energy collected was stored in batteries in two sheds that had been built below the windmills. Later my father also built a digester, into which we put cow and pig slurry. These three sources of energy provided the whole house with electricity, light and heat. There were gratings in the floor for warm air to come through. There was also an open fireplace in the living room. It was a huge bugger, so it was really hot round the hearth. I am very interested in what Lucia Valenti has to tell us."

The group claps cheerfully.

"My story is less pleasant," begins Lucia Valenti.

The room immediately falls quiet.

"It is even shocking. But I'll tell you anyway. I grew up in one of the poorest parts of Palermo. My father drank, and squandered money on illegal horse races. We had no heating at home, so I don't have much to divulge. Instead I will tell you a little about the neighbourhood. The area is called Borgo Vecchio. It's in the north-west of Palermo, by the sea. To the south there is the Via Libertà, where the rich people buy their fur coats and patent leather shoes. The affluent neighbourhood starts behind it, and the contrast makes Borgo Vecchio look even more squalid. The most striking building in the surrounding area is the prison. Borgo Vecchio is an old harbour district with narrow dark alleys. In addition to large families the houses often shelter racehorses, and when this happens the lower floor is turned into a stable. It is not uncommon for the children to sleep with the animals, and I used to do that sometimes. It was nice and warm. Sometimes the stables are on the first floor, for example if the grandparents of the family are a bit unsteady on their legs. When this happens the horses have to be brought down the stairs to be taken to the illegal races, and after the races they have to go upstairs again. A horse weighs six hundred to eight hundred kilogrammes. The stairs are rotten. Sometimes a horse plunged through the staircase."

Lucia Valenti falls silent.

The dining room is quiet. Watanabe's and Mochizuki's heads are bent over deeply; they stare at their hands in their laps. Watanabe is muttering a translation.

"How did you escape that kind of past?" asks Marc Croo.

"I was lucky," says Lucia. "I didn't go to school very often. But at the primary school which I attended now and again I had a teacher, a Palermo man from 'behind the Via Libertà' who was very committed, a socialist and an intellectual. He often took care of me. My father inherited a market stall from an uncle. It sold mandarin oranges, but my father immediately ran the business into the ground. This teacher taught me where I could buy mandarin oranges, and once a year, prickly pears. I was eleven when

I went to work at the market stall. My teacher encouraged me to come to school in the afternoon. Later on, he helped me through middle school and into university."

"Thank you for being willing to share that with us," says Zhiqiang Li.

Silva looks thoughtfully at Lucia Valenti.

"Not at all," answers Lucia cheerfully. "Over to you, Mochizuki-san."

Mochizuki clears his throat slowly. "Apart from the *kotatsu*, that wretched thing, we had an air conditioner that could also blow out warm air," he says. He gestures impatiently to Watanabe to translate.

"But you are speaking English," answers Watanabe. Mochizuki scratches himself in surprise on the back of his head. "Was I speaking in English?"

Everyone nods.

"Oh yes." He laughs out loud and continues in Japanese.

"I will not bore you with stories about the *kotatsu*. I don't understand why people have a soft spot for them when they look back. In the winter it always used to be freezing cold at home, and that was not pleasant. Fortunately, when I was about nine we moved to an apartment on the outskirts of Tokyo, and there we finally had air conditioning. It brought an end to a lot of trouble with fans and ventilators and sweat rags, because in Tokyo it is too hot for much longer than it's too cold, so air-conditioning is more important than heating. Our air conditioner blew out warm air in the winter and that solved all our problems. Perfect. Not cosy, but that wasn't what we were after. It did make a terrible noise, though. Our bathwater was heated by solar panels on the roof. Japanese *o-furo* baths are the best in the world; perhaps Li-san will make bathrooms the next part of the game?" Once again he utters the word 'game' slightly disparagingly, so he forfeits his applause.

Bettina Welt looks around attentively before she begins speaking, as if to confirm that there really is going to be no applause for Mochizuki. Some members of the team clap feebly; Mochizuki stares directly ahead, imperturbably.

"Your turn, Bettina," says Zhiqiang Li.

"As a child I moved around quite a lot, so I experienced a whole range of heating systems. I will try to tell you what they were in chronological order. Coal. That was in the city. My parents lived on a small upper floor, and in the winter my mother had to descend three flights every day to bring the coal up. She also did the nappy wash on the stove. After that, we moved to an apartment in a small city. There we used coal as well, but this time in a small level fireplace with porcelain tiles. I had the same sorts of tiles in my box of bricks, so I often used them to build a play stove next to the real one. After that, gas. That was in a detached house in a village. There was a grey wall heater in each room. We had evidently gone up in the world a bit financially. Then central heating, in an apartment in the big city. We missed the cosiness of a stove or hearth. The place we lived had no centre any more, like a village without a church square." She looks around triumphantly as the applause rings out again.

"Good, so there is only my story to go," says Zhiqiang Li, sounding satisfied. "When I was very young we used to have a large stone pot full of white sand in each room. On the sand there was a heap of burning charcoal, and that was the stove. Sometimes there were also sticks of incense burning in the sand. Nowadays, if I burn incense when I go to a temple or shrine, it immediately takes me back to that atmosphere. The same goes for the odour of burning charcoal and open fires in general. At that time there were open flames everywhere, even in the big city. The flames were often associated with something for sale; roasted sweetcorn or chestnuts, or sweet potatoes." She bows.

There is applause from the room. Everyone has had their turn, and the mood has significantly improved. The group is relaxed and people are enjoying themselves; there is laughter and little exchanges of conversation.

"Good," says Zhiqiang Li. "The faces I see are already less anxious. But be careful: the investigation will take its toll. I cannot force anybody, but I would really appreciate it if you would come to ask my advice whenever necessary. After all, it is important for the investigation that you be as lucid as possible. See it as a question of mental hygiene. I'm available in the afternoons and evenings in my room. Do not worry – there is no couch, but there are a couple of easy chairs. You can ring me beforehand. And don't forget the diary. A diary can help order your thoughts and keep your feelings under control."

There are absent-minded nods; the team members are still thinking about the stoves, and about the unexpected insights into the backgrounds of these investigators who have been brought together by chance.

Silva stands up and goes over to sit next to Lucia Valenti. "What a story, Lucia," he says. Lucia smiles at him.

At noon, Bertus Hogenelst stretches. He has been able to bring a clear focus to the material in the envelopes that Mochizuki had given out. It is astonishingly well organised. The Japanese police are clearly very keen on procedures and numbers with compendious codes. He now understands Mochizuki's and Watanabe's formality rather better. Nothing in the police reports that he has just thoroughly read through is expressed with even a hint of informality.

Bertus is not a man for procedures. He looks carefully at the photos of the victims. Full of impatience, he wants to mount them on the wall as quickly as possible, but the walls are too hard for the drawing pins he has brought with him. He calls room service and asks for a roll of adhesive tape. The voice at the other end of the line asks him to wait a moment, and Bertus listens, bored, to an electronic version of *Home on the Range*. They don't have any adhesive tape, the voice tells him, but they can send someone to the shop. Bertus answers that he'll do it himself. It is a good opportunity for him to stretch his legs. He goes to the four lift doors, one of which emits a polite ding-dong, and descends soundlessly to the lobby, where tourists of the well-heeled variety are standing next to their soft leather suitcases. He walks past them and goes outside, through glass doors which open automatically and close tightly, and crosses the vast empty square in front of the hotel. The clammy heat enfolds him.

On one side of the pavement around the square a huge tide of people is moving. Bertus merges with the crowd. There are no shops to be seen near the hotel. He looks up along the giant glass facade of the building, which is constructed in a jagged V shape. The edge of the roof looks like a flight of birds in the air. He has been outside for only a minute, but senses the drops of sweat forming in his armpits and running down his sides to his waist. The waistband of his trousers immediately feels soaked, lukewarm and cloying. He tightens his belt and shivers, despite the heat. He crosses over two large sets of crossroads, walks past thick concrete pillars under an expressway and sees an orange sign for Kentucky Fried Chicken on the corner of a narrow street. He has to pass under an archway bearing large Japanese characters to reach it. The spacious, quiet world of the hotel and the square around it might never have existed. Suddenly he finds himself in a teeming crowd, between little stalls and close-packed hanging signs. Music merges with electronic noises. Hawkers cry out. On the pavement, a row of shoe-cleaners sits on grubby blankets. Bertus smells eel, fruit and freshly roasted chestnuts. There are schoolchildren in uniforms wandering around in groups, businessmen in three-piece Burberry suits walking along smoking and laughing, middle-aged women hobbling past in kimonos, girls in heavy make-up with hips swaying, and old women lugging large boxes tied to their backs. Bertus walks on uncertainly. Cautiously but hastily he scurries past fast-food restaurants, fashion stores, shoe shops and windows displaying expensive cakes and fancy tins of biscuits. A side street catches his eye. The alleyway is full of steam and air-conditioners working at full capacity, generating yet another noise. He strides quickly past filthy windows, and then comes straight out onto a spotless street that could have been in a suburb, being used over its entire width by cyclists and pedestrians. Open shops have set out some of their merchandise on the street. It is barely conceivable that the shopkeepers can bring the goods back in in the evening, into shops where goods are already piled to the ceiling. Finally, Bertus sees a shop offering notebooks and exercise books, wrapping paper and bows. Above it is a sign bearing the words, 'Animal Backstyle'. He looks down at the heavy plastic racks. On each piece of merchandise there is a picture of a small line of red pigs' backs. The pigs are wearing coloured dungarees, with curly tails poking out. Droves of schoolgirls are milling around the goods on display, giggling and talking, alternating strange high screeches with low humming sounds. Bertus finds a small roll of adhesive tape in a holder of thin plastic with small pigs on it. Even on the adhesive tape itself there is an endless row of pictures showing little pigs' backs. He takes two packets in his large hands and walks over to the cash desk. The cashier asks him something in Japanese, and Bertus shrugs his shoulders helplessly.

"No Japanese," he says. The girl begins to wrap the goods carefully in crackling silver wrapping paper. Bertus gestures that this is unnecessary. She looks at him uncomprehendingly and quietly continues her work. The wrapped goods are placed into two large plastic Animal Backstyle bags and handed to him.

Back in his hotel room, he attaches the photos to the wall above his desk with strips of Animal Backstyle adhesive tape. First, the wide-angle shots of the areas where the remains of the victims had been found, then the 50-millimetre pictures of how they were arranged, and the detailed pictures of the injuries and incisions. By

66

the time he has finished, the wall is covered in gruesome pictures right up to the ceiling. He then sticks the pictures of the victims to the wall above his bed. These are enlargements of their passport photographs; they are in colour, apart from the black-and-white photo of the Dutchman, Hendrik Mechanicus. The pictures are arranged according to the dates of the murders: Hendrik Mechanicus on the 12th of February; Marcus Bopp, the 2nd of March; Ian Wackwitz, the 19th of April; Jacob Parker, the 27th of May; Irina Skoynich, the 12th of June; Marco Polo, the 30th of June; Larry Maxwell, the 18th of July; Hughes de Keuninck, the 15th of August.

Bertus scrutinizes first one face and then another, feels around for his office chair using his bottom, and reaches out for one of the reports by the Japanese police. He underlines 'Common Characteristics of the Victims' a couple of times with his Akasaka Prince pen. Then he circles various points:

1. They were murdered in Tokyo.

2. They were non-Japanese.

3. Seven were aged between 30 and 36. One was older: Marcus Bopp, 42.

4. There were seven men and one woman.

5. They were white.

6. Six of them were unmarried. One was living with somebody: Irina Skoynich. In the case of one, we don't know: Marco Polo.

Bertus stares again at the row of photos and then writes hesitantly in the margin:

7. Although the mouths of the victims are very different from one another, their expressions share one thing: the

person felt slightly wronged in some way. This is true even of Hughes de Keuninck, although he was laughing when his picture was taken.

Bertus taps his pen on the desktop. Are there similarities that he is overlooking? He examines the photos from close up, paying attention to the details of the clothing: Irina's brown-orange-yellow flecked shawl, Ian Wackwitz's frayed collar, Hendrick Mechanicus's corduroy shirt; and he shakes his head. What was it that had attracted the serial killer to these foreigners? Was the perpetrator Japanese, and had the motive been racial hatred? He rummages impatiently through the heaps of paper on his desk, grabs a sheet from the pile of plain paper and rapidly scribbles:

To: Yukiko Inoue
From: Bertus Hogenelst
2nd September, 17.05
Did the victims speak Japanese?

He dials Yukiko's number into the fax machine and watches the sheet of paper as it is drawn through the device in fits and starts. Five minutes later the fax machine starts to beep, and a rustling piece of paper bearing the reply slides towards Bertus. He reads the text as it appears, line by line, emerging upside-down through the plastic slit.

To Bertus
From Yukiko
2 September, 17.10
See sheet number 221 from report number A1.23 CX.255 – 455Bis from the Japanese police. (Copy follows, in case you don't have this yet, in Japanese syllabic order).

Hughes de Keuninck: spoke Japanese well, but could not read or write it.

Irina Skoynich: spoke reasonable Japanese, could not read or write it.

Jacob Parker: spoke reasonable Japanese, could not read or write it.

Marcus Bopp: spoke Japanese well, could read and write it fairly well.

Marco Polo: Not known.

Larry Maxwell: spoke reasonable Japanese, could not read or write it.

Hendrik Mechanicus: spoke reasonable Japanese, could also read and write it.

Ian Wackwitz: spoke Japanese well, could read it a little but not write it.

Bertus writes under the list:

8. Seven of the eight are known to have spoken Japanese. We do not know about Marco Polo.

This increases the possibility that the murderer was Japanese: serial killers want to make contact with their victims.

"How is it that the fax machine in my room is so slow?" Bertus asks Yvonne Lacoste, on the way to the dining room.

"Tomorrow you can come and see whether there's a better one for you upstairs in our office; we have plenty of them there. The colour copier is so good that you could forge banknotes with it. The rest of the equipment is years behind, as usual in Japan."

"How do you mean? I thought Japan was a Mecca for modern equipment."

"Not as far as word processors are concerned. The script is too complicated for that. Ten years ago, the ward offices in Tokyo still used huge typewriters. The keyboard was as large as a tablecloth and contained around four thousand characters," says Yvonne.

"Gosh," says Bertus. "Did you work with one of those here?"

"Yes," says Yvonne, "they might still be in use somewhere. Ask Mochizuki whether the police still use them. It wouldn't surprise me. You find modern computers in companies, but in government offices a lot is still done by hand or on an old *wapuro*."

"What is a *wapuro*?"

"The Japanese word for word processor. They are big plastic boxes without any internal memory that you can only use in Japanese."

Like Bertus Hogenelst, Jack Fowell spends the afternoon going through Mochizuki's reports. He has set out the photos along the skirting board of his room. The previous night he slept badly, which has left him irritable. He considers what he scornfully thinks of as "the blunders of the Japanese police". First, immediately after being formed, the international team had requested Mochizuki and his team to open a telephone hotline. The Japanese had never really seen a reason to canvass the public for help in this way. They saw it as a loss of face. Fowell's mouth forms a cynical line under his large, hairy nostrils. Now the photos of the victims will be published again in all the newspapers, accompanied by an appeal to readers to phone the hotlines that have been set up. The obscure posters which had been put up near police stations will be replaced by clear pamphlets in bright colours.

Fowell becomes angry again as he thinks of the behaviour of the Japanese when they selected the members of the international team. How an official had explained on television that "the German mentality and discipline at work are the closest to those of the Japanese." Also, for reasons that were completely unclear, the Japanese had opposed the nomination of the Polish expert in connection with the Polish victim, Irina Skoynich – so much so that eventually this expert had taken umbrage and pulled out.

And then the reports by the Japanese police! He had become irritated at their endless concern with minutiae. The impression was really that no single author wanted to be responsible for what was written. Every report had referenced other reports to an absurd extent, as if the authors were all hiding behind one another.

Fowell reflects on his reputation as a super-tough policeman; on the seriousness with which his subordinates at the police station in Sydney took complete responsibility; on his nickname – 'Robocop' – which he had kept to himself during Li's game; and on his dedication to his work, which had cost him his marriage and alienated him from his son. He stretches and goes over to sit on the edge of his bed. He rubs the shiny material of the brown off-the-peg suit jacket that sits on his aching back, stands up, hawks, staggers to the bathroom while he pulls up his trousers, spits into the wash basin, and looks in the mirror. As if his own reflection gives him energy, he rubs his hands with glee. "We're going to ginger this place up a bit," he says out loud.

Before dinner, the group goes through the newspapers. The press has done what Silva requested: the photos of the victims appear in all the papers, mostly in colour on the front page, and appeals have been made to the public to call the hotlines, which will be open in a few hours. The teams of telephonists who are to staff the lines are introduced to the group. The twelve Japanese form a line against the wall and recite their names, followed by the useful phrase *yoroshiku onegaishimasu* and a bow. The forty-two foreigners who will be working at the language call centre go along the table and shake the hand of each group member. The entire call-centre team then leaves the room to set up work rosters, view the facilities and then take their places at the telephones. In the dining room, the following day's tasks are to be allocated. Mochizuki takes the floor. He has another pile of envelopes lying in front of him.

"Valenti-san will handle the Marco Polo case; Fowell-san, Larry Maxwell; Croo-san, Hughes de Keuninck; Hogenelst-san, Hendrik Mechanicus; Green-san, Jacob Parker; Silva-san, Irina Skoynich; Welt-san and I the cases of Ian Wackwitz and Marcus Bopp. I will give you the instructions and information you will need for your investigation very shortly. You can now go and eat. I hope the dinner is to your liking. You can choose between Japanese and Western menus."

After dinner, Bertus studies the map of the underground railway. He has an appointment with Adinda Buisman of the Japan-Netherlands House in Aoyama. On the Ginza line it is three stops away: Aoyama-itchome, Gaienmae, Omotesando. Quite some names, thinks Bertus. He turns the hand-drawn map of the Omotesando area that he has received by fax from Adinda Buisman round and round in his hands.

At the top of the staircase at the underground station he studies the map once more, then walks over a crossroads and down one of the narrower streets. There is a Swedish bakery with orange windows on the corner, just as the map shows. The street is quiet and trendy. The shop windows display designer brand names: Yoji Yamamoto, Kenzo, Y's, Issey Miyake. Even at this late hour, the shops are still open. Bertus walks slightly awkwardly into a cool, almost empty shop with a wooden floor. He looks at the price of a large, loosely woven shawl. More than fifteen hundred guilders, he calculates. "Sorry, Martha my darling, can't run to that." He walks out of the shop as he turns his map so that the Japan-Netherlands House is ahead of him. The smooth paper has become damp in his hands. Left at a green garage door, straight on past three trees as far as the greengrocer's, right then along past a shrine, right again by the tofu shop. What a heavy-handed description, he thinks.

"I felt just like a hunter chasing wild game with that little map of yours," he says to Adinda Buisman, an energetic woman of around thirty-five. She pours a cup of coffee for him in a dingy kitchenette.

"That's the way it is here. Everyone draws maps, because in Tokyo the streets have no names."

"There's Tamachi-dori in Akasaka-Mitsuke. I thought that was the name of a street."

"You're right," she says. "The larger streets have names. But the smaller ones don't." She passes in front of him and moves into her small, neatly furnished office. A glass wall offers a view onto innumerable lights shining in the high-rise building that makes up the block.

"What can you tell me about Hendrick Mechanicus?" asks Bertus once he is sitting opposite her at her desk, the plastic cup with steaming coffee in front of him.

"Just say what you want and I'll do the same, if that's okay. What you want to know?"

"Everything. What kind of a person was he? Did he have friends? Did he mention contacts outside the Japan-Netherlands House?"

Adinda Buisman thinks for a moment. "He was my assistant. He worked here part-time. He was pleasant, a bit aloof, a hard worker. He never objected to doing simple chores like stuffing envelopes or making copies. In that way he took a whole lot of boring work off my hands. He never used to complain about it. I used to tell him sometimes that I was sorry I didn't have any more interesting work for him to do, but he said I shouldn't worry about that because he enjoyed doing simple work, as it allowed him to think. He was a slightly dreamy, quiet type, with a charming way about him. In the mornings he went to school to study Japanese. He sometimes mentioned another student, someone called Tim; a young American who could speak a bit of Dutch. They sometimes went walking in the mountains. Tim was a gardener by profession, if my memory is correct. He had once been a trainee at a nursery in the Netherlands."

Bertus made a note. "Do you know his surname?"

"Tim's? No".

"Have you told the Japanese police about Tim? I haven't come across his name in their reports."

Adinda Buisman thinks for a moment. "No. The interview with the Japanese police was chaotic. At that time I didn't think about him at all. And oh, did you know that Hendrik was living with a host family, a business acquaintance of his father's?"

"Yes, that family has already been interviewed by the Japanese police. And Hendrik's father arrived in Japan yesterday."

"God, how terrible for the poor man. Has he come to Japan especially because of the investigation?"

"He is also here on business." Bertus massages his eyes. "What else can you tell me?"

"Let me think for a moment. I had lunch with him at the restaurant on the corner a few times, and he did tell me a bit about the school at that time. How difficult it was for the Westerners there, because they were put into the same classes as Chinese people who knew even more characters than the Japanese did. He had to practise ten new characters per day, and write each one thirty times with an ink brush, and remember the direction of each stroke and the stroke order. He told me they sometimes gave him nightmares. In his dreams the characters grew above his head and ran after him on stilts. He was annoyed about the Chinese in his class because they had been brought up to be so studious, and were as proud as peacocks if they got better marks in their exams than the Westerners. The Japanese annoyed him too; the way they always used to ask him the same questions and stare at him. Oh, we talked about silly little things. And he never stopped dreaming about Japanese women. That was sometimes embarrassing. He used to wolf-whistle if he saw a beautiful woman. He spoke very frankly – no, too frankly – about the desires that Japanese women evoked in him. He was completely oblivious to the fact that I found it embarrassing when he got onto this hobby-horse of his, but I just let it go, I had no interest in talking about the subject." Adinda Buisman falls silent.

"Anything about the host family?" asks Bertus.

"Yes, he was crazy about the mother. She treated him like a prince. She cooked special Western food for him, did his washing, ironed his shirts. They sometimes took him into the city at the weekends, and once to Kyoto for a couple of days. They stayed at an expensive ryokan there. He said that he didn't know 'how he could reciprocate.' He gave Dutch cigars to the father, and Delft blue tiles to the mother, and clogs and chocolates to the children. They were thrilled with them, we often sat and smiled about that, but whenever he gave out presents he always found that a couple of days later he got one back, usually something that showed superb taste, such as a varnished wooden soap dish with a lid, or a set of hand-made writing paper with his initials on it.

"Oh, there is really nothing special I can tell you about him. It is inexplicable that he's dead. It's terrible." Adinda hid her face in her hands. "Everyone here at the House is really shocked. And the poor parents. Do you have any leads yet?"

"No, our team has only been engaged in the investigation for three days."

"I'm really sorry that I have so little to tell you."

"No, no, this chat has been very helpful. I have to get a mental picture of the victim. If you had to describe him in one word, what would you say?"

Adinda thinks for a moment. "Lonely," she says.

Bertus walks back across the dark square to the hotel. He has one more appointment, with Hendrik's father. Back in his room he puts on a clean shirt and drinks a whole bottle of mineral water. In the corridor he encounters Yvonne Lacoste.

"Mechanicus's father is sitting waiting for you in the small meeting room."

"Thank you. Yvonne, could you find out something for me?"

"Yes, of course."

"There was a young American in the same class as Hendrick Mechanicus. Someone called Tim. We don't know his surname yet. Could you call the Japanese language school for me and ask them to set up a meeting with Tim? I've written the name of the school here." He gives her a yellow sticker.

"Certainly."

"Thank you. And oh, Yvonne, could you also find out

whether this Tim is mentioned anywhere in the reports from the Japanese police? And if so, could you send me the numbers of the relevant reports?"

Yvonne wastes no time in setting off to the office. Bertus walks quickly to the small conference room, where he finds Hendrik's father, Reinier Mechanicus, sitting and looking straight ahead, with a scowl on his face. As Bertus comes in, he closes the door softly behind him; Mechanicus's wrinkled face turns towards him. He remains sitting and nods abstractedly. Bertus walks resolutely towards him and shakes his hand. Mechanicus rises from his seat, then sinks back into it as soon as Bertus has shaken his hand. Bertus remains standing next to him.

"Mr. Mechanicus, it's really good of you to have come."

"Have you found anything out yet?" asks Mechanicus abruptly.

Bertus shakes his head. "We've only been on the case for three days."

Mechanicus sniffs contemptuously. Bertus put his hand soothingly on his scrawny shoulder. Mechanicus rises quickly and brushes his shoulder as if an unpleasant insect has landed on it.

"I've been hearing '*I am sorry*' for six months now. I've received very long letters, in terrible English; 'letters of apology'. Strange, copied documents with red stamps at the bottom. And the same letter three times, one after another."

"From whom did you receive these?" asks Bertus, taken aback.

"From the Japanese police."

"Oh."

"Yes, I bet that's shut you up, eh?"

"Mr. Mechanicus…"

"Be quiet, man! We have been treated appallingly. Appal-ling-ly. My wife has been absolutely devastated by this, do you understand that?"

"Mr. Mechanicus…" Bertus shrugs his shoulders helplessly.

"Didn't they tell you that? You should see how it feels some time, when someone phones you up to tell you in the most dreadful English that your son has been murdered."

Bertus has come round the table and now sits opposite Mechanicus. "Is that what happened? How awful."

"Yes." The voice softens a little. "We want to bury my son. He's here somewhere, lying in a freezer."

"Yes, that is awful."

Mechanicus nods silently.

"I had hoped that I might be able to ask you some questions about Hendrik. What kind of young man was he?"

"What's that got to do with anything? The Japanese police didn't ask us anything at the time. And when you were in Amsterdam I didn't see you either."

"At the time your son was murdered I had no idea that I would be working on this case. That was decided much later."

"Be that as it may, I am over on a business trip, and I've only come here to say how scandalously we have been treated."

"We are investigating what the victims had in common with one another. From that we may be able to form an image of the perpetrator."

Mechanicus looks silently at his shoes.

"Did Hendrik sometimes write home?"asks Bertus.

"Yes, he did. About one letter a month." Once again, his voice is a little less acerbic.

"Do you still have the letters?"

Mechanicus nods. "At home."

"Could you possibly have them faxed over to me?"

"Yes, okay."

Bertus slides his name card with his fax number over the table. He tries again.

"Could you just tell me something about the contents of the letters?"

"His Japanese host family, his work, his school, a friend, Japanese women…" Mechanicus recites the list grudgingly.

"Was the friend called Tim?"

Mechanicus starts in surprise. "Yes, Tim Smith."

Bertus makes a quick note. "Did Hendrik have girlfriends?"

Mechanicus gives a brief laugh. "No".

"Why you laughing?"

"They were so unattainable for him, Japanese women."

"Why was that, do you think?"

Mechanicus smiles again. "He found them so beautiful. He was intimidated by their beauty."

"Did that affect him really badly?"

"I don't really know. My son was not extreme in any way. He was a bit solitary."

"Could you tell me a bit more about him, so that I can get a picture of what he was like?"

Mechanicus shakes his head slowly. "I can't tell you any more."

He reaches slowly round to his back pocket, pulls a photo out of his wallet and gives it to Bertus. "That's him."

Bertus looks intently at Hendrik's childish face. The mouth is laughing, but the eyes are sad.

"You read the letters, then you will get a sense of what Hendrik was like. I haven't come here talk about him. I wanted to say to you personally that you must get your hands on whoever did it. *Must*, do you hear?"

Bertus picks up on the fact that Mechanicus has stopped using the informal Dutch 'you' and shifted to the formal version. "I can see that you are upset. I will read the letters. If I have anything else to ask you after that, then I'll be in touch with you. It's a pity that you can't tell me anything more about your son. You are here now; it's a unique opportunity to talk."

"For you, not for me." He stands up laboriously and shakes Bertus's hand. His hand feels damp and cold.

"I won't detain you any longer, Inspector. I have to call my wife right away. You can expect the letters this evening."

He walks away abruptly. "Goodbye, Mr. Hogenelst."

Bertus keeps right behind him in the corridor, but he lets the lift doors close right in front of Bertus's nose.

Bertus sighs.

Gerardo Silva walks, panting, over a derelict patch of land. In his hand he holds a crumpled piece of paper giving directions. He is wearing a T-shirt with an enormous stain on the chest from a patch of sweat. His jeans are new, and of an expensive brand. He has knock knees. A leather belt cuts into his fleshy stomach and hips. He has just paid a visit to the scene of Irina Skoynich's murder. It is covered in plastic sheeting; there was nothing to see other than dry mud and pebbles. He walks over to a recently installed playground on the edge of the patch of land.

Then he goes to sit on a bench in the shadow of the nearest block of flats and looks around him. The tubes of the climbing frames and roundabouts are still new, sprayed yellow, red and blue. Perfectly dressed toddlers are playing there. On the benches all around sit their mothers, carefully made up and just as perfectly dressed, talking quietly, occasionally taking morsels of food from plastic lunchboxes with their chopsticks. They hide their mouths behind their hands when they are chewing or laughing. They all wear nylon stockings. In this heat, thinks Silva. He allows his eyes to roam back and forth over the playground, then turns round and looks up at the twelve-floor concrete facade of an apartment building with tiny windows.

He stands up and walks towards the still-unpaved path that leads to the new housing estate. He feels the eyes of the young mothers on his back. Their conversation has ceased. As Silva disappears around the corner of the first apartment block, an excited discussion breaks out in the playground behind him. He takes a second piece of paper from his pocket and peers at the number written on it: 12 C. Apartment 401.

The flats stand in rows of four: A, B, C and D. Apartment 401, where Morio Abe, the boyfriend of the late Irina, is still living, is four floors up. Silva looks for a lift but cannot find one. Puffing, he climbs the external staircase to number 401 and rings. It is it is a long time before signs of life are audible behind the iron door. The door finally opens, and a narrow head wearing large black spectacles peers out.

"*Konnichiwa*. Are you Morio Abe?"

The head nods.

"My name is Gerardo Silva. I am investigating the murder of your girlfriend, Irina Skoynich."

The door swings open to reveal a spindly figure in crumpled but clean clothes. The two men, each in heavy black spectacles, stand opposite one another in the narrow corridor; one fat and panting, the other thin and motionless. An arm gestures that Silva can approach further.

"My English is poor," says Abe, once they are sitting uneasily next to one another, on a salmon-pink stuffed sofa in the living room.

"That doesn't matter, we will work things out. I don't speak any Japanese. Sorry. I will speak slowly. My condolences, Mr Abe. I am really sorry about what happened to your girlfriend," says Silva, leaning over. "We are doing everything we can to track down the person who did it."

Abe nods briefly, his face betraying no emotion. His eyes are even and slanted behind the lenses of his spectacles. He sits straight up, his posture symmetrical and giving away as little as his face. Silva estimates that he is in his early thirties, though he finds it hard to tell the ages of Japanese people. "Would you find it difficult to talk about her?"

Abe shrugs. "I can if you want."

"Can you tell me something about the period before Irina's death?"

"I've already been interrogated by the Japanese police."

"I know that," says Silva. "I've read the reports. I would like to ask you a couple of 'open questions', as we call them. Questions that you can't answer directly with 'yes' or 'no'. I hope you don't have any objection to that?"

Abe looks at him uncomprehendingly.

"A closed question is, for example, 'was your girlfriend at home the day before she was murdered?'"

"Yes," says Abe, "I've already told the police that."

"That was an example," says Silva. "An example of an open question is, 'Can you tell me how you were feeling around the time of the murder?'"

"I was sleeping on a futon under my desk at my office."

Silva's eyes dart uncertainly back and forth. Is this man not very bright, or is it a language problem?

"I would like to ask you rather more personal questions; open questions. Do you have any objection to that?"

Abe shakes his head. "Irina was a Westerner. I am used to having to talk about personal things," he says, and starts doing so right away, his speech sporadic. "We had difficulties. A lot of arguments towards the end. She was Polish, I am Japanese. I am so busy. I didn't know how I could help her. I could not go to Poland. My business. The money is good in Japan. She was depressed. So was I. We used to have arguments about small things. It was not good. She had too few friends here. A couple of Poles, a couple of Americans. Not really good friends. She used to paint. She used to paint a lot. Every day. I rented a studio for her."

"I understand from the reports that the studio is still there?"

"Yes."

"Where is it?"

"Five minutes' walk from here. It has already been examined by the police."

"I know that. Even so, could I have a look at it?"

"Yes." Abe stands up and walks to the door. Silva follows. Outside they walk together in silence. Abe indicates an ochre-yellow two-storey rectangular building with a corrugated roof. Off a short walkway on the second floor, there are four doors. "A cheap apartment," he says over his shoulder, while he climbs a rusty staircase to the walkway. He takes a key from his pocket and opens one of the doors. The two men stand in a square *genkan*, and Abe indicates that Silva should take off his shoes. The space further inside consists of two tatami rooms divided by sliding paper doors. Silva steps onto the smooth, slightly springy mats in his soggy socks and looks at the damp footprints he leaves behind, embarrassed. Abe appears not to notice.

Taking small steps, Silva walks around the low-ceilinged space. In the furthest room there is a wooden easel on which sits an unfinished painting. Dozens of canvases are neatly stowed on wooden racks. Behind the easel there is a small table with clean paint brushes and ink brushes in tins, a row of palette knives and some tubes of paint. Under the table is a wooden chest full of tubes, and a row of bottles and tins. The air smells pleasantly of turpentine and linseed oil. Frosted glass windows filter the light from outside.

"May I have a look at the paintings?"

Abe nods.

Silva takes a couple of canvases from the rack and turns the picture side of one towards him. It is a colourful, dynamic work, composed using thick strokes of oil paint. He takes a step back to look at it better. Abe sets a pair of canvases against the wall. The same dark red, dark green, deep blue… they make Silva think of jungles.

"Flowers," says Abe, "recently she only painted flowers." He takes some canvases from a rack on the opposite wall. "These are from a couple of years ago."

The subjects are rather more intellectual: nudes, still lifes, portraits of Abe. All painted with the same robust strokes.

"Not bad," says Abe. "She could have become good."

Silva nods. He looks around the room. It breathes a sense of order. In the corner by the exit stands a radio-cassette recorder. Silva presses the play button; sentimental music comes out.

"Polish pop," says Abe.

Silva presses the stop button. "Did she ever have visitors here?"

"I don't know. Her teacher, yes, he came now and then, but apart from that, no one as far as I know. She was studying *sumie*, watercolours of flowers." He opens a cardboard folder and shows Silva some watercolours on thin paper. On some of the pictures of branches, leaves and blossoms, gold flakes have been strewn onto the paint.

"Yes, the teacher has already been interviewed by the

Japanese police. I have read the report."

Abe closes the folder. "It is hot," he says.

Silva nods. "Is there anything else you would like to tell me? I fully understand that this is difficult for you, but even so…."

"No, don't worry about that. I don't know anything else. It is just as I said. She was homesick. But she didn't want to go back to Poland by herself. Much too difficult. No work. She was not happy, but she did her best. She was lovely. And beautiful. I could do so little."

"Did your girlfriend have a good friend, perhaps even another lover? Did she sometimes go away at night? Did she ever talk about a close friend? Someone she shared her problems with?" Silva fires his questions quickly, one after another.

Abe's thin shoulders rise helplessly, a long way. His hands turn outwards, with the palms up. "Maybe yes, maybe no. I was often away overnight. Sometimes I used to sleep in my office."

"Your girlfriend was murdered by a serial killer. I think that person must have got close to her. It is very probable that they sat together in the playground down there."

Abe shakes his head. "She wrote letters," he says. "A lot of letters. To Poland."

"To whom?"

"To her mother, to a girlfriend, maybe to others. I don't know her Polish friends. The police have taken away her address book."

"Yes, I saw that," says Silva. He looks alternately at Abe's face and at his own wet socks on the tatami. Then his huge upper body suddenly lunges forward, and he brings his head closer to Abe's. The two pairs of spectacles are very close to one another.

"Mr Abe, do you ever speak with a Japanese person as we are doing now? Would that be possible?"

"No, that is absolutely out of the question," Abe answers quietly.

"How is that so? Can you explain that to me?"

"A membrane. I have a membrane in my head," says Abe, without hesitation. "It divides my brain, my heart, my being into two. Whenever I speak with a Western person, I pass through the membrane into my other personality. Western thinking, Western feeling, the Western sense of being are completely different from Japanese thinking, feeling and the sense of being. There are people who claim that Japanese people and non-Japanese people function in the same way, but I am not a supporter of this idea. It makes things blurred. If I speak with a Japanese person again in the near future, I will first go back through the membrane in order to communicate with him in a Japanese way."

"Does that also mean that you communicate with the Japanese police in the Japanese way?"

"Yes, of course," Abe answers.

Silva stares again at the tatami mats, and then says decisively, "Thank you Mr Abe. I shall not trouble you any longer. If anything important comes to mind, please phone me about it immediately." Abe nods, takes the proffered name card respectfully and bows.

"I'll make my own way out," says Silva. At the door he sees a coloured silk shawl hanging on a hook. He brings his head up close to it; it gives off a vague scent of perfume.

Silva shivers. "Poor girl," he says softly. Then he speaks in the direction of the studio. "You really don't know the name of Irina's girlfriend in Poland?"

There is a moment of silence, and then Abe comes through the sliding doors and towards the genkan. Silva sees his shape indistinctly against the yellow light from the studio. Abe stands motionless in thought.

"Katharina."

"Did your girlfriend have a telephone here?"

Abe shakes his head.

'I have a membrane in my head', Silva repeats mentally, as he walks back to the underground train. I must tell the others that. 'More open and more personal than with the Japanese police'. Perhaps the Japanese police didn't go into personal details. Didn't Hogenelst's case have something to do with a Japanese host family? Maybe he should go along and see them again, even if the members of the family had already been questioned by the Japanese team. Who knows what that might throw up. Maybe Mechanicus had been depressed and lonely, just like Irina, and they were both looking for someone to trust. That was very plausible.

Mochizuki has brought along Bettina Welt and Watanabe, his interpreter, to visit the residence of Frau Fischer, a German woman who lives in a small flat in the Sendagaya 5-chome district. He has instructed Bettina to restrict herself to being an observer at this first enquiry. She can take over the investigation later, he argues. His rationale for this strange decision is that while Bettina Welt has had experience at the Ministry of Justice with theoretical criminological investigations, she has never done any work at street level. Bettina Welt is determined to put up with this humiliating start to the proceedings, and to comply with Mochizuki's order not to interfere in the conversation with the interviewee. She walks behind the Japanese pair and watches their preoccupied, blue-clad backs, half-amused by the absurd situation.

Mochizuki is miffed. He has learned via a tip from the hotline that Marcus Bopp had visited Frau Fischer the evening before he was murdered. He is very tired, and the prospect of having to interview another foreigner, with all the language problems and other misunderstandings that implies, makes him bad-tempered. Watanabe skulks along next to him, bowing apologetically, as they walk through the narrow streets, where air conditioners are endlessly and noisily recycling hot air.

"You must translate clearly, I mean precisely. I never know what foreigners are talking about." Bettina, who understands Japanese well, hears Mochizuki complaining to Watanabe.

"I will try to do that, Mochizuki-san,"

"Hmm."

"Yes, Mochizuki-san."

"What did you say?"

"Yes, Mochizuki-san."

"What did you say?"

Watanabe bows in desperation.

"They all speak different kinds of English," says Mochizuki loudly. Watanabe is silent.

Frau Fischer's bell seems to be out of order. Mochizuki

knocks, much too hard, on the door.

"Keisatsu," he bellows.

"Police," translates Watanabe.

"Louder," says Mochizuki angrily.

"Police," bellows Watanabe. Bettina Welt waits below by the outside staircase.

Frau Fischer opens the imitation wooden door. Behind her, an enormous fan revolves on a stand. She gestures to the men to come in. Bettina climbs the staircase and shakes Frau Fischer by the hand while she introduces herself. She briefly explains the situation in German. Mochizuki looks at her impatiently. Bettina speaks slowly for a couple of minutes more, and then, at the invitation of Frau Fischer, goes to sit on the floor on a *zabuton* cushion. She falls silent and looks around her.

The fan takes up a lot of space in the small apartment. There is also a drawing board and a low table with a sewing machine. On the tatami floor are pincushions, crayons, bobbins with yarn, scissors and boxes of buttons. A pile of thin patterned paper flaps and rustles in the wind from the ventilator. Frau Fischer throws a magazine onto it. A small corner of paper continues rustling.

"Please don't look at the mess, I'm working. Please sit down. Would you like some tea?"

Watanabe nods and says, "Oh, yes, please."

"Nan deshitaka?"

"Would we like some tea."

"O-cha arimasu desyoka?"

"Do you have green tea?"

"Yes, of course. Would you like some green tea?"

"Yes, please."

91

"Nan deshitaka?"snaps Mochizuki.

"I said, 'do you have green tea?' Then she said, 'yes of course, would you like some green tea?' And then I said, 'yes please'."

"Oh," says Mochizuki.

"Hajimemasyoka,", says Mochizuki, into space.

"Let's start," translates Watanabe, hesitantly and in a low voice.

Frau Fischer sets water to boil in the kitchen. Over her shoulder, she asks Bettina Welt in German what she would like to drink.

"O-cha kudasai," says Bettina, in order not to confuse Mochizuki further.

Once they are all sitting on the floor around the low table, with steaming cups of tea in front of them, Frau Fischer says, "Marcus Bopp."

"Yes. Why did you not contact the police earlier?" asks Mochizuki. Watanabe translates.

"I've only just heard about the case. I don't read any newspapers, I don't watch TV. I've only known about it since the telephone call from your secretary, the day before yesterday. It is terrible."

"I'm really sorry, Miss," says Mochizuki, in his slow, heavy English.

"Thank you."

"Nan deshitaka?"

"She said, 'thank you'," says Watanabe.

"Ja, gaikokujin no eigo wakaranaiyo," says Mochizuki.

"What did he say?" asks Frau Fischer.

"He said that he doesn't understand the English that a lot of foreigners speak."

"Nan deshitaka?" says Mochizuki.

"I said that you don't understand the English that a lot of foreigners speak," says Watanabe.

"Idiot, you don't need to translate that."

"Oh, I'm sorry."

"What are you talking about?" asks Frau Fischer.

"Oh, let it go, it doesn't matter."

"You were a friend of Marcus Bopp's?" Mochizuki asks Frau Fischer via Watanabe.

"Yes, we knew each other superficially. We sometimes used to go out to Ni-chome."

"To Ni-chome? The homo area? Was Bopp homosexual?"

"The gay area, you mean? Yes. No, Marcus was not gay."

"Are you?"

"No, it is actually possible to go to the gay area without being gay!"

"I don't know. So neither of you was gay?"

"No, are you?" Frau Fischer towards Bettina as she says this. The latter looks dispassionately from one speaker to the other, as though she is learning an enormous amount from this interrogation.

"I?"

"Yes, you."

"I don't have to answer that question," says Mochizuki.

"Oh, so you don't, but I do. That's how it is, is it?" says Frau Fischer, in a low voice.

"Are you opposed to the police? Opposed to this investigation?"

"Oh no, but I don't see what your questions have to do

93

with the fact that poor Marcus has been murdered."

"I'll be the judge of that."

"I'll be the judge of that," translates Watanabe.

"Oh, yes, right," says Frau Fischer, quietly.

""What did you do in Ni-chome?"

"Oh, talking, dancing, drinking."

"Drugs?"

"I'm going to hand you that one on a plate, of course. What do you get at the moment for a couple of grammes of hash? Five years?"

"So, drugs, then."

"Oh, God."

"What happened the night before Marcus was murdered?"

"We went to Ni-chome, just as normal. We set off around midnight and went to three bars; first to Tonoyama, then to the SixtyNine, and around three o'clock, to Zazai. There we parted. At one point Marcus wanted to leave. I stayed at Zazai because I was dancing and I didn't want to go home yet."

"How can you remember that so well? It was six months ago, and you have only just found out that Marcus is dead."

"It was my birthday. The first of March. Marcus had come looking for me on my birthday. He gave me a lizard."

"A lizard?"

"Yes, he'd caught it on the way. We called it Liz, after Liz Taylor, you know? Unfortunately Liz died a couple of days later."

"And after that you went to the bar?"

"After we had set Liz up in a terrarium, yes."

"Have you never asked yourself what happened to

Marcus? I mean, you didn't hear from him for a long time."

"Oh, you know how it is in Tokyo. Everyone is so busy. Friends come and go. In that sense it is a terrible city. There is no time for friends. This is a place where you have to work, Mr. Mochizuki." She bangs a roll of fabric. "In order to pay the rent, Mr. Mochizuki." She bangs the flat of her hand on the tatami mats. "And that was true of Marcus as well. I thought, he'll turn up again. I did phone him, but got no answer. I thought he must be on holiday in Thailand. He did that quite a lot."

"Thailand?"

"Yes."

Mochizuki raises an authoritative hand to interrupt the conversation and says to Watanabe, "Write that down." Watanabe takes a notebook from his thin briefcase and waits with his pencil paused above the paper.

"Ni-chome," dictates Mochizuki. And to Frau Fischer, "those bars, what did you say they were called?"

"Tonoyama, SixtyNine and Zazai."

Watanabe writes.

"A lizard," says Mochizuki. "Write that down. A lizard. And Thailand."

Mochizuki turns to Frau Fischer again.

"Did Bopp have friends at these bars?"

"Friends? I wouldn't call them friends. You always come across the same people, people you only meet there."

"Can you remember who Bopp talked to that evening?"

"Oh yes, let me think, it's a long time ago… yes, there was a Japanese man at SixtyNine. He was called Tomo, an entertaining young guy. And in Zazai we met Johnny,

95

a dancer from Ireland, and then there was Raul, a young guy from South America, I don't know exactly where. Marcus spent a while talking to him."

"What did they talk about? Can you still remember that?"

"I've no idea. I was dancing. I just saw them talking together."

"Do you think those people still go to those bars?"

"Oh, probably. I haven't been to them for a long time."

"Can you tell us anything more about Bopp? What kind of a man was he?"

"He was handsome. He had a very striking face."

"Yes, we know what he looked like. We have photos of him."

"Now you mention it, I have some photos of him as well. We took them with a self-timer." She stands up, rummages in the chest and comes back with an album. "Here, you can see them."

In the photos, Marcus Bopp stands with his arm round Frau Fischer. They are both pulling silly faces.

"When were these taken?"

"About January."

"Do you have any other photographs of Bopp?"

Frau Fischer furrows her brow and scrabbles around in a shoebox. "Yes, there is one here that was taken at the beach."

Mochizuki leans over the photo. It shows Bopp standing laughing, his upper body bare and tanned. He is wearing wide, colourful Bermuda shorts. His hair is much longer than in the other photos and has bleached highlights from the sun.

"Who took this one?" asks Mochizuki.

"I don't know. Marcus gave it to me. He had a whole set of them, I think."

"May we take these photos away with us?"

"Yes, certainly," says Fischer.

"Please tell us more."

"Oh he was friendly, not hard to be with. A bit lonely, just like everyone who lives and works here, the foreigners I mean. He sometimes said he felt depressed. Then he used to go to Thailand. To recharge his batteries. When he came back he was cheerful and he could face life here again, he used to say. He earned a fortune. He dealt in security systems. But he spent money like water. He always paid when we went out to Ni-chome."

"What did you talk about mostly when you went out to Ni-chome?"

"Oh, nothing special. We laughed and joked a bit. We ate and drank. Sometimes we talked about literature and the theatre."

"Write that down," Mochizuki gestures to Watanabe, who is already diligently making notes. Watanabe shrinks into himself and writes faster.

"Do you expect the man to translate and write at the same time?" Frau Fischer looks directly at Mochizuki.

"What did she say?"

Watanabe is silent.

"What. Did. She. Say?" repeats Mochizuki.

"Oh, er, nothing."

"I want to know what she said."

"She said, 'Do you expect the man to translate and write at the same time?'"

Mochizuki shrugs his shoulders. "He is my assistant," he says.

"I am his assistant," Watanabe translates.

"I can see that," says Frau Fischer. "What a job!"

Watanabe is silent, and Mochizuki does not ask him to translate the last remark. A smile plays on the lips of Bettina, who is still looking interestedly from one to the other, as if she is calmly watching a tennis match.

"Can you tell us the locations of the bars you went to with Markus Bopp?" asks Mochizuki.

"Yes, of course. I'll just draw a map for you. They are only a couple of minutes' walk from one another. Shall I use your notebook?"

"Thank you," says Watanabe politely, and passes over his notebook and pencil.

"Tsk, tsk, tsk," Mochizuki hisses through his teeth when they are back on the street, and with an angry gesture throws down the handkerchief he is holding. The carefully folded object drifts onto the dirty asphalt. Bettina steps over it. "Now we have to go to Ni-chome as well. We still have that job to do."

Watanabe is silent.

"If you like, I can visit the gay bars," says Bettina in Japanese, to the back of Mochizuki's suit.

"We'll talk about that shortly, at the hotel," says Mochizuki, as he politely turns right round to face her.

"Did you see the poster on the wall at Frau Fischer's, the one that looked like a seventeenth-century painting of a couple with white dogs at their feet?"

"I didn't notice it," says Mochizuki, though Watanabe nods.

"Under the picture was written 'Báthory and Nádasdy'. Báthory, wasn't she one of the mediaeval murderesses Silva described in his book?"

"No idea," grunts Mochizuki; but Watanabe says, "early 1600s."

"What?"

"Erzsébet Báthory, Hungary, early seventeenth century," says Watanabe.

"A book about Erzsébet Báthory has just come out," says Bettina. "Isn't that curious?"

Jack Fowell sits at his desk in his hotel room, writing the words 'Larry Maxwell'. He underlines the name a couple of times, and continues: 'was a video artist and lived in a small apartment in the Yotsuya district of central Tokyo. He gave lessons in English, had occasional small jobs as a model for painters and photographers, and used these to finance his experimental videos. Used to hang around in artists' cafés with other artists. All the regular customers of these cafés have been interviewed'.

'Maxwell's body had been found by two housewives at twenty to ten in the morning, very near his apartment, in the garden of an empty house. The two halves of the body had been laid out almost artistically, on a large rock next to a small pond. The entrails lay next to them, in a hollow'.

"What a joker," says Fowell aloud to himself, and continues writing.

'Maxwell's family lives in Sydney. He had had little

contact with them. His parents run a small supermarket'.

"Oh yes, a supermarket," says Fowell cynically. He thinks back to his visit to the anxious couple who lived on the outskirts of Sydney, at their little shop smelling of shoe polish, just before he left for Tokyo. It rather looked as though the old couple did not know what their son got up to in Tokyo.

Someone knocks on the door.

It is one of the hotel's *shiatsu* masseuses. He signals that she should come in. She bows to him and says something. Then she gestures that he should take off his shirt and trousers and lie on the bed.

She sits on the small of his back, as if she is riding a horse, and puts her thumbs on the sides of his scalp. Fowells' shoulders and neck are unusually painful and stiff from all the reading he has been doing. He has been altering the settings of the knobs on the climate control mechanism according to a careful system over the entire day, but the wretched thing has stubbornly kept the room either too warm and too humid, or too cold and too dry. He is still irritated by the Japanese police reports, and the Japanese names confuse him. Hundreds of people have been involved, and many square kilometres of terrain mapped out. Diagrams have being made of how the teams were organised, and of which person within each group was responsible for what part of the investigation. Mostly, different people were responsible for a small part. So a small group of three people, all called Yamada, had been responsible for cleaning the scrapers used to rake the terrain. And then to think that that during these intensive searches for clues, nothing had been found other than a couple of flecks of black deerskin that had come from a glove, and some blonde hairs. The gloves were of the CiCi brand, sold under that name in their thousands in department stores. The hairs, which had been found in various locations, appeared from DNA tests to be from one and the same person. That is something, but not much.

The DNA from the hairs will be useful once we have found the perpetrator, thinks Fowell, as the masseuse pulls his earlobes downwards. He also thinks about the incisions visible on the photos of the victims. Earlier in the day he had subjected the photos to a careful examination and concluded that these incisions had been performed with great professionalism. There is almost nowhere where they are uneven. They are the cleanest incisions he has ever seen. They remind him of Christmas festivities at home, when he is slicing the joint, or the bird, on a large board with a deep gutter for the blood. Fowell himself is a proficient hunter and butcher. In the past, together with friends, he used to shoot kangaroos from a pickup truck. They had deboned the animals themselves and barbecued them over a camp fire.

He smiles at the memory while the masseuse puts her thumbs into the backs of his knees. Suddenly she sits on his shoulder blades with her bare knees, and simultaneously uses her knees and hands to massage the uppermost part of his back. Fowell is surprised at the strength she can bring to bear on his body, slender as she is. He feels a slight nausea dissipating as she pulls up the loose skin at the nape of his neck, away from his vertebrae, as though she is picking up a cat. It is painful, but pleasant at the same time. Now he is free to lie here and think about

Lucia Valenti. The masseuse works slowly downwards on her knees, along his spine, still pulling up the skin with her hands. Her knees make circular movements, like an orbital sander. Fowell feels relaxed and sensual, like a lion in the sun inside its ample skin. He stretches and yawns four times in succession.

"Good, good!" says the masseuse, laughing.

"You can stop now," says Fowell after a little while. She pummels her way down his back a little more with the sides of her hands as far as the crack of his buttocks, as though she is playing the head of a drum, then gently caresses the length of his backbone in a zigzag movement. Fowell shivers and gets goose-pimples. The masseuse shakes her hands in the air, as if they have water on them. Then she stands to attention by the door and bows, while he gets back on his feet and has a stretch next to the bed. His boxer shorts hang low on his bony hips. He pulls them up.

The small woman in the impeccable white cotton jumpsuit crosses her hands over her chest. She smiles warmly and politely, bows again and walks backwards out of the room. "Thank you," Fowell calls after her; the door is already closed, and she is halfway down the corridor, walking soundlessly in her white trainers with short, compact steps.

"Wow," he says aloud to himself, while he shakes his head roughly and reaches for his trousers. "What a lady."

The 'lady' is currently in the lift, zooming down towards the lobby at thirty kilometers an hour to collect her pay. She concludes that Fowell resembles an old Irish setter. The same leanness, the same loose skin, a similar bump at the back of his balding head, even his red-brown colouring. She giggles softly into her cupped lustrous hand and brings it to her mouth. Her thin pink shell-shaped nails glisten in the yellow light.

Still enjoying the sensation, Fowell strolls to the lift. On the hot square in front of the hotel he looks around for a while and decides to go towards Tamachi-dori, under the expressway, past the thick concrete pillars. Then he sees the orange sign of a Kentucky Fried Chicken on the corner. There is a coloured, larger-than-life polyester statue of Colonel Sanders on the pavement. Fowell looks at it from close up, amused. The thick artificial head wears a real pair of spectacles. The temples of the spectacles are too short to bridge the distance to the ears, and disappear into holes bored in the sides of the Colonel's head to accommodate them. Fowell gives the hollow statue a gentle punch on its dark brown necktie; then, observed by a small, curious group of uniformed schoolchildren, he walks under the ornamental gate that marks the entrance to the vibrant Tamachi-dori.

Three kilogrammes of beefsteak, a turkey, a large piece of tuna and a knife; a yanagi-ba, thinks Fowell while he looks around. Where would I find all those? He walks along to the end of the street and discovers the entrance to a station. He sees people with plastic shopping bags coming out of it. I'll take the train, he thinks, this neighbourhood is not right. He walks down the staircase to the underground station, energetically taking two steps at a time, and then sees to his surprise that the people with the plastic shopping bags are emerging from a set of a glass doors in the station concourse. He slips adroitly between the doors, worms himself through a crowded section to a less crowded one, and looks around. He finds himself in the shoe department of a department store, where it smells of food. Following the aroma, he takes an escalator down into an enormous supermarket. Bingo, he thinks, when he is halfway down with a good view and immediately spots a meat counter.

The beefsteak laid out in front of him is the best Fowell has ever seen. It is also sold in Australia, for shabu-shabu, which has become very popular. Fowell knows that the cows that produce the meat are raised on beer and massaged daily. This results in the red meat being marbled with white fat. It melts in the mouth. He has eaten it at a hotel in Honolulu, during the negotiations about bringing the international team together. His mouth waters as he thinks of the tender meat with the mild sesame sauce. Fowell gestures to the serving assistant that he would like to have the whole piece of beefsteak. At the next counter he finds a turkey, and further along a huge cut of tuna. Without blinking an eye, within a few minutes he spends more than thirty-four thousand yen on foodstuffs. He strolls contentedly over the marble floor of the luxury supermarket. It is pleasantly cool, with a smell of fresh fish and fruit. He leans over a wooden box containing two melons. They are an almost fluorescent green, and are covered with a regular pattern of white veins. He looks at the price. Thirty thousand yen. "Holy shit," he says aloud. On impulse he buys a small packet of nettle-like sheets wrapped in cellophane, because he doesn't know what they are, and a persimmon. Then he hurries back up the escalator, and from his elevated perspective looks at the goods offered on each floor. It strikes him that the checkouts are placed very unstrategically and that everywhere there are goods lying around for the taking. Then he remembers having heard that there is almost no shoplifting in Japan.

His curiosity is aroused by a department that has silk kimonos hanging on poles, like colourful tropical birds with broad wings spread out wide. Once he has reached the household goods department, he steps off the escalator. He finds a wall full of Japanese knives and takes a piece of paper out of his trouser pocket. Looking at the paper and comparing it with the goods in front of him, he selects a knife. It is the longest yanagi-ba available.

'Holy shit', he thinks again when he looks at the price; but nevertheless, he takes the knife to the nearest checkout. Startled, the cashier takes the razor-sharp object from him carefully and says something to her assistant at the wrapping counter. The assistant disappears with the knife and comes back with a long wooden box. She opens the box and holds it out to Fowell. The yanagi-ba glitters against the purple velvet. There are characters engraved deeply on the blade. The handle is made of wood, and is attached to the blade by an elegant, glossy black band.

"Black belt. Kendo. Fourth Dan," Fowell jokes to the girl in English. He performs sword-fighting moves in front of her. She looks at him a little fearfully, closes the box and starts to wrap it in nautically themed paper with pictures of white clouds on it. Fowell gestures that this is not necessary. She looks at his motioning hands, smiles politely and continues imperturbably with her artistic wrapping of the knife. Once he has given up his attempts to stop her, Fowell watches her in fascination. When the wrapping has been completed and the package is equipped with a fan-shaped decoration of bamboo sticks and a red ribbon, the box goes into a coarse grey paper bag fitted with string handles. Bowing deeply, the girl hands the bag to Fowell.

Back in his hotel room, he rings room service and asks for a plastic tablecloth and a large cutting board. These arrive immediately, brought by a young man who behaves as though he is unaware of the meat and poultry lying on the plastic bag on the bed. Fowell covers his desk with the plastic tablecloth, places the cutting board on top and sets to work on the meat with the knife. From time to time he looks at the photos of the mutilated victims lying along the floor against the skirting board. Very thoroughly, he goes to work; first with the point of the knife, then with the blade, flat against the flesh. His hand slips a number of times, making the cut frayed or jagged. He undertakes the same experiment with the poultry and the fish. Once all the meat has been sliced into small pieces and is lying on the desktop, he calls Mochizuki and asks for a photographer. After the pieces have been photographed, Fowell calls room service again and orders the stoic young man to take the pieces away. Once again, the man behaves as if this is something he is called upon to do every day. While he wipes the plastic tablecloth with an absorbent cloth that slowly becomes dark red, Fowell sits at the seat by the window, looking again at the photos from time to time, and removes from its thin film packaging one of the nettle-like leaves that he bought in the supermarket. He crushes the leaf between his fingers and smells it. It gives off a surprisingly fresh odour which is completely new to Fowell. He turns towards the man, holds up the package containing the leaves and asks, "What is this?"

"*Shiso*," says the man amiably, "Japanese herb. Very good."

Fowell nods. He points to the persimmon on the nightstand. "And what is that?"

"*Kaki*," says the man. "Japanese fruit."

"Kaki," repeats Fowell, and then, "Shiso."

"Very good Japanese," says the man, as if he were dealing with a child.

"Yes, yes, you can go now" says Fowell, and gestures impatiently at the mess. The man shovels thirty-four thousand yen's worth of meat and fish into a rubbish bag.

"Take it home with you," suggests Fowell. The man shakes his head.

"*Saishokushugisha*," he says

"Pardon?" The man thinks for a moment. Then: "Eat no meat," he says.

"Oh, vegetarian," says Fowler.

The man nods. "*Sai-shoku-shugi-sha*" he says again, slowly.

"Forget it," says Farrell, "I can't pronounce that." Then he stands up and stretches.

"Don't throw it away," he says. "Put it somewhere cool, so I can use it later this evening."

The Japanese have some very particular skills, thinks Fowell. They build the best bathrooms in the world, they are good masseurs, and good carvers. Fowell remembers a documentary about decorative cutting. The Chinese are good at Baroque: whole tree-trunks with birds of prey from one root, lotus flowers from radishes. The Japanese can fillet enormously skilfully and finely. Fowell thinks of

107

the *Fugu*, the pufferfish with the poisonous gall-bladder which he had eaten in the company of a number of colleagues during the conference in Honolulu. This is the Japanese version of Russian roulette: if there is a nick in the gallbladder, the poison is rapidly diffused throughout the flesh. The poison has no taste. A diner can fall dead at his seat if he eats a morsel of fugu that has been incorrectly prepared. The chef must have a special licence to cut the gall-bladder out of the flesh. At the restaurant where Fowell dined with his colleagues, the certificate was hanging up on the wall. Nevertheless, eating the fish still generated a certain suspense. The glassy flesh had been cut very thinly. It had been prepared in the form of a bird, a crane, on a decorated plate. The designs on the plate were visible through the flesh: bright red and veiny blue.

The way in which the victims had been arranged by the murderer reminds Fowell of the shape of the crane.

Second of September

I feel that normal life does not penetrate into this hotel. I am longing to see a child. I haven't seen any children for days, neither on the street nor at the hotel. I feel shut up in this air-conditioned box, I look at intestines, smeared plastic, moist earth, faces sliced through the middle.

It is unbearable to know that Irina's melancholy face was cut up with a knife. I find Irina's case the worst, it affects me the most, perhaps because she was the only female victim.

I've been here for three days now, and it feels like three

weeks! That's because I can't sleep. I've just been down to the bar, but there was a conversation going on between Jack Fowell and Gerardo Silva, and it was so boring that I've fled back to my room. It was about Japanese women. Bertus Hogenelst was sitting telling Robynne Green about the visit by the father of Hendrik Mechanicus, one of the victims. It seems that Mechanicus was obsessed with Japanese women. Fowell claims to be as well, and he was talking philosophy with Silva. Silva went out today and had obviously had time to look at women. Fowell had ordered a masseuse in his room. Basically, both of them wanted to 'try something out' with a Japanese woman. Robynne became angry and asked Fowell if he sometimes imagined that Japanese women had horizontal pussies. At that point, Hogenelst had to laugh uncontrollably. Fowell pointed out again that Japanese women haven't yet been messed up by feminism. Yeah, yeah.

My handwriting is terrible. I have to catch up with my thoughts by writing very quickly. Mochizuki let it be known today that he thinks it is a good idea for me to be on the sidelines. I find him obnoxious. He sits with his groin pushed forward. His wide stripey tie hangs absurdly between his legs. It's much too long, that tie.

Watanabe is also worth observing. He's all straight and stiff. His body can only move backwards and forwards from the waist up. During lunch he drinks a cup of tonyu, soy milk, that he's brought himself, through a straw, though there is already an enormous buffet available at the hotel. Mochizuki always brings his own lunchbox as well. Watanabe ate kaki today. An unappetising, gory fruit. We have already had enough of looking at blood and entrails.

He fussily puts the pieces into his mouth, after he has sat peeling the thing and dividing it into pieces, so carefully, as if it is if it were a bundle of heroin worth millions. He stacks the peelings up precisely in the middle of a plate, and pops the stones out with the top of a chopstick, then places them in a little pile next to the peelings. After eating each piece, he wipes his mouth with a tissue from a little case. The tissues are laid in a tidy pile next to the plate. Watanabe is completely wrapped up in himself while he eats.

Mochizuki eats out of a box packed in a furoshiki, a cloth bag tied at the top with a knot. His lunch is probably prepared by his wife.

Sometimes I wonder what their wives are like.

Bertus Hogenelst has been to the Japan-Netherlands House. Gerardo Silva has visited the friend of Irina Skoynich. This afternoon I went with Mochizuki to the home of a certain Frau Fischer. My job was to observe.

This evening, after dinner, we were unexpectedly rounded up for a demonstration of butchery by Jack Fowell. The only one who could not be there was Bertus Hogenelst; he had an appointment to talk with the father of Hendrick Mechanius. Fowell wanted to demonstrate that the murderer must be a person who routinely handles knives. He was very convincing! He is good at his job, that's obvious. It is always fascinating to watch and listen to experts. He explained how to fillet fish and how proficient the Japanese are at it, and pointed out that the perpetrator could certainly therefore be Japanese. God forbid, because there are only fourteen million in this city.

So even an evening spent with Jack Fowell was very

tolerable, until he started talking about Japanese women, of course.

In the afternoon I went out to buy a pen. I came back with a handful of Animal Backstyle ones. I promised Matthijs I would buy twenty of them. Once again the line was too bad to talk to him easily on the phone. I miss Matthijs, my love. I would so much like to lie next to his nice red cheeks.

It's two forty-five and sleep will not come. The newspaper says an agreement has been reached about sharing out fishing grounds between China and Japan, the Far East Network reported on the falling yen, and on TV I saw something about the mistreatment of rabbits and guinea-pigs at primary school. As far as I understand it, regional contact points have been set up for them, sort of child clinics. I also ran through some Japanese soaps; these are often about young mothers with cancer. Impossible love relations and consequent double suicides are also a favourite topic. I couldn't understand everything because the dialogue was too quick.

CHAPTER 4

"Good morning," says Zhiqiang Li, opening the breakfast meeting. "Today we will once again start by taking the temperature."

"I feel trapped," says Robynne Green.

"Excited," says Silva.

"Irritated," says Mochizuki.

"Irritated," says Watanabe.

"I also feel irritated," says Zhiqiang Li.

"Tense," says Lucia Valenti.

"Confused," says Bettina Welt.

"Finally managed to sleep a bit, so quite fresh," says Jack Fowell.

"Insecure," says Mark Croo.

"Impatient," says Bertus Hogenelst.

"Thank you," says Zhiqiang Li. "Today's question is a little more personal than yesterday's, and you can choose not to answer it. I would like to follow the order that we're sitting in, anticlockwise, beginning with Robynne. The task is to describe one of the most magical moments of your life."

This evokes laughter and chatter.

"What do you mean by 'magical'"? asks Mochizuki.

"I mean a very special moment that you will always remember; a moment that was enchanted," answers Zhiqiang Li.

Mochizuki exchanges whispers with Watanabe for a moment. "I think I understand," he says, and gives a slight but genuine smile.

"Maybe you could start, Mochizuki-san, as you look so cheerful?" says Robynne Green.

Mochizuki nods. "All right. I am thinking of one morning a long time ago. I was still a child. My brother and I had run away from home; I no longer remember why. We had gone into the mountains, and there we built a hut out of bamboo sticks that we fixed between the trees, and pieces of plastic. We were determined to live in the wilderness and never go back. We stuck it out there for a whole night. By the morning, there was not much of our excitement left. We were frightened and cold. My brother had fallen asleep in a strange position. I went outside to sit in front of the hut and looked out over an open patch of land. There was a white mist above the ground. Suddenly, out of nowhere, a young fawn was standing right in front of me. It was panting, and steam was coming out of its nostrils. The fawn and I looked one another in the eye. I sat motionless, as though I had been turned into stone by astonishment. My body was glowing. Then the animal made a magnificent leap and disappeared between the trees. I crawled back inside the hut, woke up my brother and said that I wanted to go home. My brother nodded and put an arm around me. We walked home like this and found our mother in the yard, wringing her hands. And we got a thrashing from my father that evening." Mochizuki looks ahead dreamily. "I will never forget the way that fawn looked at me. So gentle, so gentle."

"A beautiful story, Mochizuki-san," says Zhiqiang Li.

"All of a sudden, we've seen quite a different side to you."

"How do you mean?" asks Mochizuki, prickly once again.

"Oh, never mind," says Zhiqiang Li. "The next one, please."

The eyes turn towards Zhiqiang Li.

"Oh, it's my turn. Well, when I was about five, I was taken by a rich aunt on a winter sports holiday in Japan. It was near the town of Nagano. First we went by plane, and then by train, and after that by bus. Finally we had to walk a long way with our rucksacks up to a hotel high in the mountains. It was the first time I'd ever seen snow. I remember seeing the mountain peaks, with collars of bare black trees. It was like a pen-and-ink drawing. Once we arrived at the hotel I was given a sledge to play with, in a dip in the ground in front of the hotel. I felt the snow with my bare hands, and even stuffed it in my mouth.

"I went to lie on my back on the sledge and looked up at the sky. It was crystal clear. And then, out of the blue sky – don't ask me how – it began to snow. Big fat snowflakes were falling on me. It was magical. I still think about it often. People say it's impossible for snow to fall out of a clear blue sky. But the memory is so vivid that I really can't believe I made it up later. I still get goose-pimples when I think about it." Zhiqiang Li rolls up her sleeve and looks at the skin on her arm. Mochizuki leans politely over her arm.

"They've already gone down," says Zhiqiang.

"I once almost drowned in the sea," says Lucia Valenti. "I was at the beach north of Palermo with a girlfriend. I'd gone too far out in the water, and suddenly I felt no ground under my feet. When I looked back at the beach, it was a long way away. The bath towels people were lying on seemed no larger than postage stamps. After that I must have passed out for a while, because out of nowhere I was looking at running women. There were thousands of them, and they had long wavy hair. Their hair flowed together, in a huge swaying motion. I was looking down at all this from above, as though I was floating. It was really lovely, looking at that hair. Then I threw up, and I found myself lying next to my friend at the bottom of a dinghy. Some fishermen had seen us and had sailed out to pick us up. One of the fishermen took me home. My mother was furious, and she hit me so hard that the fisherman had to get between us. My friend got into trouble too. The hair, that beautiful hair… I will never forget it."

"God, you know, I remember something," says Jack Fowell, "I was once hanging from a piece of elastic, jumping off a bridge in Sydney. You scream your lungs out; a friend told me about it. It cost a hundred dollars, but what an experience! It is indescribable. I did scream, but it wasn't even jumping that was the most liberating part – it was the falling. How can I put it? As if the whole world is transformed in front of your eyes. I've never dared to do it again, but it was fantastic. Fantastic!" Fowell repeats, looking exultantly round the group.

"I used to be very fat," says Bettina Welt. "When I was going through puberty, I piled on the kilos. I got to the age of twenty and I was fed up with being fat and feeling unattractive and awkward. I decided to change my diet and began training and doing breathing exercises. It was unbelievable how this made me start to slim down.

There was a whole series of dreamlike moments, one after another. The moment my collarbones became visible; the moment my clothes felt too big; the moment I could breathe so deeply that it seemed I could float upwards; the moment I put on a bikini and looked good in it, even in the fluorescent light of a changing room; the moment I discovered I could run around again....it was amazing how quickly it all happened."

"You'll have to tell me more about that sometime," says Silva.

"I'll do that," says Bettina Welt.

"I once saw a man in Paris," says Bertus Hogenelst, "who was mad. He was standing in dirty rags talking to himself on the square in front of the Palais de Justice. I watched him while I was sitting on a bench. He was standing perhaps fifty metres away. He stretched his arms out sideways, and dozens of sparrows came fluttering around his head and arms. He spoke to them. Very unusually for sparrows, the birds stayed around him. They beat their wings in the air, quickly, like bats. It was so strange. It must have lasted for, oh, a minute I think. I've never been able to explain it."

"When I was at nursery school, around Christmas time I was given a metal tray," says Mark Croo. "It was a 'girly' present, and I still don't understand why they decided to give me this particular tray. I cried with frustration. Other boys got Dinky toys or cranes, and I felt really ashamed. However, at the same time I was secretly pleased with it. The tray was bright red and there were animal pictures on it. Later I lay looking at it for hours from my bed. I found the pictures beautiful. To this day I can still remember the embarrassment, the shame and the delight at the beauty of the pictures on that bright red background, and how all these feelings jostled for supremacy in my mind."

"You haven't blushed once, Marc," says Robynne Green, teasingly.

Marc Croo blushes.

"I was once standing on top of a mountain in the Rocky Mountains," says Robynne. "I was sixteen. I was with a friend, and we had climbed the whole day to get to the top. We looked out over a cloudscape, and in the distance we could see mountain-tops sticking out. A huge ravine yawned at our feet. Then I felt a strong urge to jump, and I actually moved forward to do it. My friend only just managed to grab hold of me. After that we went down to a mountain hut, both very emotional. My friend simply wanted to know why I had suddenly wanted to jump. I couldn't answer that question, and even today I can't. It felt as if a totally overwhelming power had me in its grip."

"I once came back from the dead," says Gerardo Silva loudly, in the silence that follows Robynne's story. "Nine years ago, I had a stroke. Half my body was paralysed, and my eyes didn't work too well. I had to wear prism glasses. After I had been taken to the hospital by ambulance, I was put through a scanner and then in a sort of tent, connected up to tubes and lines. I don't know exactly what happened to me, but I couldn't communicate anything. I seemed to be imprisoned in my body. I really started to panic. Then I fell asleep, or maybe they put me under. I dreamed that I was weightless and was floating high in the air with my arms spread out. There was a long white cord coming out of my navel. This was moving in the wind, and connected me to the abdomen of a wetsuit that lay on the ground far below me. I swooped down towards the wetsuit. First I missed a couple of times and flew past it. Then I slid into it. It felt nasty, cold and clammy. When I came round, my body still felt rubbery. It took months for the weird feeling to disappear completely. But flying, that was magical."

With a nod, Silva indicates that he has finished his story. The group eats in silence for a while.

"It's strange," says Robynne Green, "almost all these stories have something to do with nature."

"Yes," says Bertus, "it's funny."

"I found it really interesting," says Silva, laughing.

Zhiqiang Li bangs on the tablecloth with the flat of her hand. "Yes, that was certainly a worthwhile exercise. You are all expected to be in this room at two o'clock this afternoon, for a review of the case. Many thanks."

The members of the team get to their feet, stumbling, talking and laughing, but even before everyone has reached the door to the corridor the relaxed, disorderly atmosphere has died away and tension has begun to engulf them again. Lucia Valenti looks pale, Mochizuki sways as he walks, Silva has his hand over his heart, Robynne Green has a slight twitch by her left eye, Bettina Welt's upper lip has come out in a sweat, Bertus Hogenelst and Marc Croo rush to the toilet.... They disperse and go to the corridors and lifts.

Zhiqiang Li is standing in the middle of the dining room with her hands at her sides, looking at the team. They have very few leads, she thinks. Only Yvonne Lacoste, Yukiko Inoue and Watanabe are contented, because they have clear aims: translating, typing reports, researching, drawing maps, ensuring that the information flow is organised. The others are working in a state of great uncertainty; they still do not know what they are looking for. Neither do they know that an entire new team has been selected and put on stand-by in case they do not succeed,

Bettina Welt transmutes the humiliations of her first few days into a feverish energy. She has covered the walls of her hotel room with her photographs even more densely than Bertus Hogenelst did with his. Her whole room – the bed, the desk, the floor, the chairs – is strewn with files on which she has written headings in felt pen, and when necessary with lipstick, in thick, crooked handwriting. The bathroom door stands slightly open. Articles of clothing, towels and a rogue pair of mismatched shoes are protruding from it. Bettina lies on the floor, doing abdominal exercises, and looks at the photos.

She has been to look at the archives that have piled up in Yukiko and Yvonne's office, in search of all of the visual material related to the case. This has led her to a few photos which had not been included in the general collection within the reports distributed to the international team. She has taken back to her room the files in which these photos were found and spent the whole morning going through them. One of the photos is of the victim Hendrik Mechanicus, supplied by his Japanese host family. Mochizuki had discovered that it had been taken in the Harajuku area.

Mechanicus stands almost casually in the middle of the street with his hands at his sides, leaning slightly to one side and giving a forced smile for the camera. It was not known who had taken the photo.

Next to it hangs the photo of the victim Marcus Bopp, which Mochizuki had obtained from Frau Fischer. Bopp stands there on the beach, tanned, his demeanour as posed as that of Hendrik Mechanicus. It was not known who had taken the photo. According to the reports, the location was Kamakura. There are also three photos that Bopp had had taken with Frau Fischer. The pair are pulling silly faces at the camera. There is a series of the victim Irina Skoynich, taken in 1994 by her friend Morio Abe, in Irina's studio. These are eight artistic colour photos on high-gloss paper, in differing oblong formats: portraits of Irina posing in her colourful shawl in front of her paintings. These have the effect of framing her pastel-tinted face against wild expressionist backgrounds; her face is like a separate object, either half-recumbent, upright or tilted sideways in the soft folds of the fabric of the shawl. Her eyes and mouth are relaxed. Abe created this series when things were clearly not going well between them. Typical pictures taken by a lover, thinks Bettina, and gets up from the floor to look the photos more closely.

There is a series of snapshots of the victim Jacob Parker at a Christmas party for children attending his Harvard Academy for International Communication. The photos were taken in the afternoon of Christmas Day, 1996. 'Children's English Class' is chalked on a blackboard. Parker is wearing a stripey suit and a Freddy Kruger serial killer mask. The children are wearing Disney masks. In the hall in the background is a plastic Christmas tree with tiny lights. The photos are bizarre, showing the large masked man towering, tall and ungainly, above the slight Japanese children. In one photo the children are singing, while

Parker keeps time with something that looks like a rubber cudgel with an orange light on the end. Bettina Welt shudders. Nice little school, she thinks. Sense of humour, this Parker. She whistles a tune between her teeth. Irina was almost always wearing the shawl, she thinks. Let's see if we can find out anything about the shawl.

She rummages impatiently between the files on the floor, and then on the desk. "Skoynich, Skoynich," she mutters to herself. She pulls a file out from under a pile of papers on the bed and flicks through the contents. Victim's clothing... trousers, blouse, jacket...shawl. Details of the shawl: 200cm by 100cm, silk. Colour: orange, yellow, brown. Brand: Kenzo. Probably bought...? Characteristics: smells of Estée Lauder/White Linen perfume. Perfume bought by Abc at the Mitsukoshi department store in Ikebukuro. The victim had had two identical shawls of this type. She always wore one of them.

Hmm, thinks Bettina, we've got something here. She lobs the file containing the papers back next to the other one on the floor. "Scheisse!" The file slides a little way along the carpet and comes to a stop with a jolt against a pile of other files. The uppermost ones slide sideways off that pile, open side down, so that the contents spill out against the skirting board. "Typical," says Bettina, and pushes gently against the files with the end of her shoe. She bends over and tries to push the contents back into the file. They are too slippery, and the whole heap collapses. Sighing, Bettina sits on her haunches next to it and sweeps the loose papers untidily together. She throws the heap onto the bed among the files that are already spread out there, and impatiently begins to sort everything out. Gradually her movements become slower and more thoughtful. She looks at notes in one file, and then another; she looks at diagrams and drawings. "Hey, here's another one," she says loudly to herself, and excitedly pulls a photo from one of the files about Ian Wackwitz. Then, more quietly, "I hadn't seen this one." Wackwitz sits, clearly posing, next to a small table on a large terrace in front of the café. With one arm he leans on the little table; his other hand is raised to head height, making a V-sign. Wackwitz is smiling enthusiastically, his lips clenched, as though he is saying 'cheese' for the shot. On the reverse of the photo there is a sticker bearing the text, 'Developer: unknown. Location: Roppongi, café Red Hat'.

Japan makes the best quality prints, thinks Bettina, while she fishes a roll of adhesive tape out of a bag. She fiddles around for quite a while with her short nails, cursing, to find the very end of the little roll of celluloid; then she bites off four pieces of adhesive tape with her incisors, spits a piece of tape in the direction of the wastepaper basket and sticks the photo onto the beige wallpaper made of plasticised linen. The adhesive tape comes unstuck several times. Bettina pushes it down hard. This causes messy wrinkles in the tape, but it stays down. Bettina sits on the bed and contemplates the pictures. She concentrates hard on the enlarged passport photos and the photos of the victims after they were found. She is tired of looking at them. But underneath, just above the edge of the desk, is an interesting set. To the left of the picturesque Irina series are the photos of Hendrik Mechanicus and Marcus Bopp; then the Christmas horror series of Parker and the silly-face series with Frau Fischer; and finally, the photo of Ian Wackwitz. The photos of Mechanicus, Bopp and Wackwitz are in different formats, but display the same amateurish quality. Bettina reaches for the telephone under the bed and dials the number of the administration team.

"Yukiko! Are there really no negatives of the photos of Mechanicus and Wackwitz?" she asks. While she is waiting, she lights a cigarette from a crumpled packet and tries to look around the room for an ashtray, held back by the short telephone cable. Defeated, she sits down again and knocks the ash into the hollow of her hand.

"No? Okay, well, that was to be expected. We have to find out where the photos were developed. Ah. Too bad! No, it doesn't matter. 'Bye, talk to you soon." She stands up, takes an ashtray from the night stand, empties her grimy hand over it and walks over to the wall, her lit cigarette in one hand and the ashtray in the other. She looks at the photos from very close up. Certainly taken by a Japanese, she thinks. Or at least, by an Asian. Europeans and Americans don't take posed photos; they always try for a certain naturalness. Asians, on the other hand, are renowned for their formal photos. How can I find out who developed them? The people who supplied them to the police, the host family of Mechanicus and Frau Fischer, don't know. Wackwitz's were found in his apartment. Just a moment…. She stubs out her cigarette, puts the ashtray on a chair and takes the photos off the wall, then looks at them carefully through her powerful magnifying glass. Then she puts them into an empty file and walks out of her room, taking the file with her.

If we found that the photos had been taken by the same

person, she thinks, that would at least be an interesting discovery. She hastens excitedly along the corridor.

"No, what am I saying? It would be a breakthrough in the investigation," she intones quietly in German, in time with her rapid footsteps.

In the corridor, she is accosted by Lucia Valenti.

"I have to tell you," says Valenti, "there are Fish Murder games in the shops. There's a PlayStation version that you can hook up to a TV monitor. I'm going to give a demonstration in a moment, in the small meeting room."

Conspiratorially, they hurry along the deep carpet of the corridor. They pass Fowell, who is walking in the same direction. He wolf-whistles at them.

"Prat," says Lucia Valenti.

"Creep," says Bettina.

"Knuckle-dragger," says Lucia.

"In his dreams," says Bettina. Laughing, they go into the conference room.

Valenti sits cross-legged in front of a television on the floor, adroitly manipulating a kidney-shaped plastic box with pistachio-green buttons. The members of the team trickle into the hall and stand behind her. On the screen, a yanagi-ba rotates against a black universe full of stars and planets. There is a soundtrack of swishing sounds. A computer-generated muscular hand with pronounced veins appears at the bottom of the screen. The hand ends up grasping the knife, against a background of loud electronic crackling sounds; then a zoom-out brings into frame a blond-haired figure with a prominent nose. His hairy, bare, wide-angle legs disappear into a pair of cowboy boots; attached to one of these is a leather sheath, into which he dexterously slides the knife. He wears frayed, cut-off jeans. As Lucia Valenti manipulates the buttons, swaying her upper body left and right, the killer wanders menacingly onto the screen into a three-dimensional labyrinth of streets. He is whistling Beethoven's Seventh Symphony. His puffy renaissance shirt is bright green and shiny, and the sheath on his boot emits silver flashes of light. Richly coloured pink text floats over the image from the corners of the screen:

Help Police in Tokyo
Kill Kill
殺
Have a nice time catching kill
Take care not get kill
死

"Fantastic English again!" Lucia Valenti calls out above the noise.

At once nimble and angular, the Aryan slices with the knife at the text on the screen. It disappears in gold flashes of lightning with a loud *ker-plonk*. Meanwhile, the narrow streets of the labyrinth are being populated by long-nosed round-eyed bimbos dressed in floaty skirts, and by angular, fashionably dressed men. Their hair and clothing twirl in digital streams of light. Policemen dressed in blue are crouching all over the set, behind wooden shutters. At the top of the screen the players are presented with an arsenal of weapons. Lucia sends one crouching figure to obtain a bazooka, another to get a ninja star. Soon the screen is a chaos of flashing messages,explosions,whizzing bullets, and sizzling fires. Lucia extinguishes things, catches things, swings swords and clears up bodies. The idea is to outflank the killer before he strikes. Lucia Valenti grunts, her shoulders hunched as though she is driving an imaginary car. Now and then she utters a cry.

"God almighty," says Fowell, as Mochizuki brings the scene to a premature end with a swipe at the electrical switch.

"The developers of the game have assumed that the perpetrator is a foreigner," says Lucia Valenti. "I would like to know why."

"In that case we will pay a visit to the developers, Valenti-san," says Mochizuki. "You and I will go there."

Lucia Valenti nods. They leave the room together. "The bastard looked as if he liked that idea," says Fowell, and looks around, laughing.

"*Stop it now, Mister Fowell,*" says Bertus Hogenelst. Robynne Green looks at him, surprised at the sharpness of his tone. Bettina Welt keeps pace with Mochizuki and gives him the file with the photos. Mochizuki, who is carrying nothing into which to put the file, hands it over to Lucia Valenti, who has a bag.

"Don't forget to drop them off at the lab," says Bettina Welt to Lucia.

With all his strength, Mochizuki uses his stomach to push Lucia Valenti into the jangling, overfull train to Shimokitazawa.

He himself receives a helpful knee in the back from the uniformed station master. There is still room for a young man dressed in brand-new punk gear. The doors hiss shut, trapping his long orange spiky hair. The youngster waits stoically until his hair is freed at the next stop. No one pays any attention. Some travellers sleep as they strap-hang, propped up by their fellow passengers; others concentrate on reading their small books undisturbed. The normal roar of the train is overlain by the metallic resonance of badly connected Walkman headphones. Lucia tries with all her might to suppress a burst of laughter she feels bubbling up within her. Mochizuki gives her a look of surprise.

"'Hormone'," she says. "Why is the company called 'Hormone'?" Mochizuki shrugs his shoulders and resumes his bored gaze over the heads of the crowd pressed together in the train carriage. Stumbling, they leave the train at Shimokitazawa. At the bottom of the station staircase, Mochizuki imperturbably studies the map of the area, while Lucia Valenti attempts to quell her increasingly hysterical laughter. Helplessly, she walks behind Mochizuki through a maze of little streets with concrete garden fences. Her heels scrape firmly over the crumbling tarmac. Now and then a quiet, resolute walker goes past. A child practises high jumps back and forth over a piece of elastic strung crosswise over the road. Lucia and Mochizuki have to stoop to get under it. The air is like warm honey.

"This area is like the one in the video game," says Lucia, containing herself. Mochizuki nods politely and distantly.

"Here it is," he says, when they have reached a small building composed of blocks of concrete, with a blue door. "Hormone."

Lucia sneezes.

"Bless you."

Lucia nods. Mochizuki presses a copper doorbell. The door is opened by a young man with an even smile, dressed in an Armani suit. He bows to both visitors. Once they are sitting opposite him, he is positioned so that the business logo on the wall encircles his head like a halo. HORMONE: FOR BEAUTIFUL AND ENJOYABLE LIFE. Lucia Valenti concentrates on the raised points of the lapels on the man's purple suit. He has introduced himself as Saito. A silent secretary wearing rustling nylons brings tea. Lucia blows gratefully onto the steaming green liquid. She holds the base of the cup between both hands, as if seeking to warm them.

"*You like Japanese tea?*" Saito laughs, baring his impressive row of implants. Lucia nods.

"You can speak in Japanese," she says. The hot tea has calmed her down a little.

"In the Fish Murders video game, you portrayed the murderer as a blonde *gaijin*," says Mochizuki gravely. "Did you have a reason for doing that?"

Saito nods with some solemnity. "Every detail of the game was considered carefully. Have you seen how the streets in the game, just like those in Tokyo, form a labyrinth around the empty centres where the rulers used to live? Those empty areas in the centre used to be protected by snipers. They used bamboo throwing stars, weighted with lead and filled with a deadly poison! That is a historical component of the game: we educate the young players without making it obvious. For the profile of the perpetrator, as a starting point we used a Western model deriving from sociology. This is an incremental model. It assumes that human striving always develops according to the same stages. The first is the need for food, then for shelter. Once these have been fulfilled there are the longings for sexuality and love, and finally, and this is the most complicated stage, the desires for respect, power and recognition."

"Maslow's theory. The hierarchy of needs," says Lucy.

"Quite right, Valenti-san," grin the implants. "And in sociology, there is also a theory about fame versus sacrifice."

"Wilson?"

"Right again, Valenti-san!"

"I am a sociologist."

"Then you will also know that in the West there is a culture of individual fame, but in East Asia there is a culture of the collective in which the individual is suppressed. We would rather be small Buddhas than stars. A serial killer operates partly out of the drive towards individual notoriety. So it must be a Westerner!" The teeth smile triumphantly.

"Hmm. A naive and tendentious argument," says Lucia.

Mochizuki looks at her sideways, shocked.

"Is there also a reason why you chose to make the killer a man?"

"Certainly," nods Saito. "Our team tried to think of everything when we created the 'Fish Murders' game. Having a man as the murderer appeals to the public that we want to reach. There is a lot of talk among intellectuals at the moment about a book called *Countess Dracula*, by Tony Thorne. It's about the female killer Erzsébet Báthory. We didn't want to be part of that. To differentiate ourselves clearly from it, we chose to portray the killer as a man."

"Don't you think that encourages stereotyping?"

Saito laughs. "We are a business, not an educational establishment. Our purpose is to make a profit. But where we can, we add an educational touch to our material as well."

"In that case, maybe you should have another look at the English," says Lucy.

"How is that?" asks Mochizuki.

"It's full of mistakes."

"*Jinglish*," laughs Saito.

"What did you say?"

"*Japanese English*. That's what Japanese like."

Mochizuki nods approvingly. "Then at least we can understand it," he says.

Outside in the sweltering heat, the child is still jumping back and forth over the elastic.

"I will tell Bettina that I have seen a child," says Lucy.

"Why?" asks Mochizuki, surprised.

"She said she was longing to see a child. In and around the hotel you never see any children, she says."

"Oh," says Mochizuki vaguely.

Lucy claps her hand to her mouth in shock and stands stock-still.

"Mochizuki-san!"

"What!?"

"I have left my bag with Bettina's file of photos on the

rack in the train."

"*Maaaaah! Shinjirarenai!*" says Mochizuki. Sweat breaks out over his whole face. He starts to walk briskly ahead of Lucia, as though she no longer exists. Silently, he takes one train and then another; nimbly, he passes through the swarming crowds on the platforms, Lucia trailing along behind him as if on an invisible lead. They stand wordlessly in the carriages, pressed against one another, staring at the ochres and umbers of the city flashing by, while Mochizuki dabs at his face with a brand-new folded handkerchief. At a counter in a cool concrete concourse he identifies himself gruffly, and they are both immediately permitted to pass through to the racks marked 'Articles Found Today'. Rows of laptops stand on metal boards. Along the wall hang thousands of umbrellas; then nine dresses, tidily ranged on coat-hangers; and next to these, suspended on a nail, is something that looks like a mediaeval icon.

Lucia screams. In a glass box that is green with algae, there is a small crocodile gasping for breath. Mochizuki tugs her towards the bags, which are arranged by colour and size.

"Search!" he says.

Lucia removes a black bag, the first in an endless row, from a wooden rack.

At the hotel, information is beginning to come through from the telephone hotlines. The manager of a shop dealing in gadgets thinks he has found a tiny photo of the victim Larry Maxwell in his shop. He believes he recognises Maxwell from the passport photos published in the newspapers. Fowell is dispatched to follow this up, and asks Watanabe to accompany him in case an interpreter is needed. It is half-past eleven, and they take the train to Kichijoji. They sit next to one another, awkward and weary. Fowell has circles under his eyes. Watanabe looks straight ahead. Every few minutes his eyes dart towards Fowell's surly profile. The train carriage is full of schoolchildren in uniform, the boys strictly separated from the girls. The girls lean casually from vertical chromium poles. Suddenly, a remarkable performance begins. The girls go and sit on the floor among their school bags, then take off first their sneakers and then their tight white socks. A few girls sitting on the seats follow their example, still deep in conversation, as if this were the most normal thing in the world. The boys look on, bored. Fowell smells thirty pairs of girls' feet. Long thick white socks emerge from the school bags. Embarrassed, Fowell watches the scene. Watanabe sits next to him, saying nothing, staring at his shoes.

"What in God's name are they doing?" whispers Fowell.

"Oh, that's the latest fashion," Watanabe says solemnly. "Loose socks. They are not allowed to wear them to school. They are now coming back from school and exchanging their school uniform socks for loose socks. This often happens in the trains in the mornings. Then they take off the loose socks and put on their clean ones. The railway companies have already announced that measures will be taken. Soon it will not be permitted, just like PHS's in the train."

"PHS's?" asks Fowell, his gaze fixed on the girls.

"Personal Handy Systems," answers Watanabe. "Mobile telephones; very small, brightly coloured ones. Every self-respecting teenager has one. But they interfere with the communication channels of the railways. And the socks, they smell." With a movement of his head, he indicates a group of girls sitting on the floor. They pull their socks up their calves, then fold them over so that the socks fall in baggy pleats down to their shoes. They attach the upper edges of the socks to the skin of their legs, just below the knee, using adhesive stickers. The children apply the stickers in the way that women apply lipstick; very quickly, and, for a brief moment, quite wrapped up in themselves.

"Unbelievable," says Fowell.

Watanabe offers no reply, but observes the entire scene impassively.

Looking back once more, Fowell gets off the train and follows Watanabe, who is hurrying ahead. "What do those characters mean?" Fowell points, still looking behind him, to the board above the exit of the station. "They look like a bear sitting down, and then a square." Watanabe turns round. "Exit," he says laughing, without changing pace. They walk under an archway decorated with plastic flowers, then into a roofed pedestrian arcade. "Sun Road," explains Watanabe. They are drowned in the ear-splitting noise of competing advertising jingles coming from enormous speakers set above dozens of small shops.

"Here it is," says Watanabe, and strides rapidly into a small, candy-coloured shop. Fowell manoeuvres himself between two booths concealed by pink rubber curtains, bending down to pass under the low storefront.

"Are you from the police?" asks a small, thin man with

a friendly face. Watanabe nods briefly. And then begins the bowing and hesitant emitting of utterances. The two men appear to move apart and then to be drawn together, like magnets. They exchange name cards, and Watanabe introduces Fowell. The shopkeeper is not accustomed to shaking hands. His thin hand feels limp, and he keeps Fowell at a distance. As Fowell releases his hand, the man's arm falls next to his body, as if the action has been completely unexpected. Then Watanabe and the shopkeeper lean over a small object on a glass counter. Watanabe beckons to Fowell. The shopkeeper gives them a magnifying glass. Fowell peers for a long time at a picture even smaller than a postage stamp.

"Yes, that is Maxwell," he says eventually. "What kind of photo is this?" He tries to prise it off the counter, but it is stuck.

"It is a Print Club photo," says Watanabe.

Fowell looks at him interrogatively.

"Come with me." Watanabe leads him to the booths at the entrance to the shop. He disappears behind one of the pink rubber curtains. Fowell bends his head and follows him into the booth. Watanabe stands on a raised section and manipulates a number of blue buttons and a flaming red joystick. Pictures appear on the digital screen in front of him. "Would you like to have a photo taken with me, Fowell-san? Shall we have our photo taken with that panda there?" Watanabe is looking at the screen. Fowell doesn't answer, but examines the screen. "That is the background to the photo with Maxwell in it," he says, pointing at a picture of Manhattan by night. At that moment the panda lights up, very large and clear. There are four bright flashes.

"That's it," says Watanabe, pushing Fowell outside the booth. "Now, wait a moment." He stands with his arms folded, his eyes on a slit on the outside wall of the booth. After a while a piece of paper slides out, the size of a postcard. On it are twenty-four pictures of Watanabe and Fowell with the panda. Fowell has his mouth half-open and is pointing; Watanabe is standing with his eyes tightly shut. "Not a good shot," says Watanabe, "let's take another one."

"No, no, leave it," says Fowell. "I get the idea; a sort of passport photo machine for children."

"Exactly," says Watanabe. "Print Club."

"Ridiculous name," says Fowell, as they go back into the shop. Farrell bends over the small photo on the counter once again with the magnifying glass. "There's someone else there," he says. "You see, Watanabe, there, in the shadow, just in the divide between the pink curtains. Could you ask the man again where exactly he found the photo?"

The man takes them outside and points to a wooden board plastered with hundreds of Print Club photos. "A lot of people leave one behind here," he says. "There are so many people coming past here every day. Print Club is a craze. Schoolgirls exchange the photos. They have Print Club books they stick them into. There was a little girl rummaging around in the waste basket here. She took out a Print Club book, peeled off a photo and stuck it onto the board. I went over to her to ask her where her mother was; I mean, she was only about four. I asked whether she wanted to give me the little picture, so that I could throw it back into the wastebasket. The child began to scream that she wanted to keep the picture because there was a gaijin, a foreigner, on it. I just let her keep it and had a closer look at the photo she had stuck onto the board. I hadn't noticed there was a gaijin on it. Then I made the connection with the photos of the murdered gaijin that were in the newspapers. Is that him?"

Fowell does not answer. "So these photos are little stickers?" he asks.

Watanabe nods, and demonstrates by peeling one from the card in his hand and sticking it on to the board.

"*Kilroy was here*," says Fowell.

Watanabe looks at him in incomprehension.

"That means that here, in this endless desert, we have left behind a little token of our identity," says Fowell, and goes back into the shop. He pries the small sticker with the picture of Maxwell off the glass countertop and tucks it into his wallet.

"Oh, Kilroy," says Watanabe, catching on, "from the Second World War."

"Precisely," says Fowell and punches Watanabe amicably on the chest. Startled, Watanabe flinches.

"What exactly is this gentleman selling here?" asks Fowell, pointing at the plastic egg-shaped objects displayed under the glass top.

"Tamagotchi," says Watanabe.

"Tama- what?"

"Tamagotchi. You don't have them in Australia yet?"

"Not that I know," says Fowell, "but then I'm not a schoolgirl."

"This gentleman deals in items that are the latest

136

crazes," says Watanabe. "Look over here," and he points to a rack on the wall. "Loose socks."

"Jesus," says Fowell, "and the PlayStation with the Fish Murders. But the eggs, what are those?"

"A Tamagotchi is an electronic chicken," Watanabe answers solemnly. "It was designed to teach children how to care for animals."

"Pardon?"

"I'll show you," says Watanabe, and asks the man for one of the eggs. He is handed a light blue one, which he gives to Fowell. On the flat front of the egg is a small digital screen. "You have to switch it on," says Watanabe, and takes the egg from Fowell's hand. Using a pen, he presses a recessed button at the back. Then he shows Fowell the screen. It shows a pulsing egg. "'Tamago' means 'egg'," says Watanabe, "and 'gotchi' means 'dragon'. Soon, Tamagotchi will come out of the egg and ask for food, entertainment, nappy changing and medical care. You can provide these with these three buttons." He points to the pale yellow butttons on the flat section of the egg.

"When Tamagotchi wants to go to sleep, you have to switch off the electronic light, and when he defecates, you have to clean up the electronic poo. If you've taken good care of him, he will grow up, change shape and live a long time. If you neglect him, he will die. You can monitor his health, age, weight and degree of contentment. I think the record for longevity stands at twenty-seven days at the moment. When Tamagotchi dies, you can bury him in a graveyard on the Internet. There are also Tamagotchi doctors and other Tamagotchi experts."

"Fantastic," says Fowell. "I'll take one. Would you like

one too, Watanabe-san?"

Watanabe chuckles. "No, my daughter already has some. They've only just come back onto the market again. They were sold out completely for a couple of months."

"What do they cost, Watanabe?"

Fowell buys one. "What an educational day," he says as they walk back to the station side-by-side. "The children in the train, they would all have a Tamagotchi?"

"Yes," says Watanabe, "and loose socks, and Print Club photo cards; the girls, at least. The boys have other things again. I don't know so much about those. I only have a daughter."

"What a world," says Fowell.

Watanabe nods abstractedly. Still walking, Fowell taps Watanabe gently on the shoulder a couple of times and performs a couple of sclerotic skipping movements. Watanabe freezes at his touch and walks stiffly onward.

"We have got something!" says Fowell. "We have found something!"

Watanabe nods politely.

In the first review of the cases, during the afternoon of the fourth day of the investigation, Mochizuki, Lucia Valenti, Bertus Hogenelst and Jack Fowell report on their investigations concerning the victims Marcus Bopp, Marco Polo, Hendrik Mechanicus and Larry Maxwell.

The other members of the team have not yet made enough progress to have anything to report. Robynne Green and Marc Croo are still particularly busy analysing the files on the victims Jacob Parker and Hughes de Keuninck.

To everyone's relief, Mochizuki is in a good mood and does not harass Watanabe. The result is that Watanabe can quietly get on with his simultaneous translation.

Mochizuki begins. "After the visit to Frau Fischer, a female friend of Marcus Bopp's, I went with Watanabe and Welt-san to the three bars that were visited by Marcus Bopp on the first of March in the company of Frau Fischer. At first, Welt-san suggested investigating on her own, but, partly because of the unpleasant character of the area, I thought it better for Watanabe and myself to go along. I know the area well because I have made enquiries there in the past, about the drug trade. The bars we visited were thick with smoke. But this fact probably has nothing to do with drugs; none of our victims used drugs, and all the bars were vetted by the Japanese team before you arrived here. At that time we did pick up twenty users, but nothing suggested a connection with this affair.

"The three bars we visited mostly attracted the same kind of clientele: the kind of people who first visit the SixtyNine, which is a reggae bar, then go on to Tonoyama, which is a club that requires you to become a member, and finally Zazai. Zazai is an unpainted concrete basement where there is room to dance, unlike SixtyNine and Tonoyama. We were only able to get there very late. At midnight, there was almost no one there. Around three o'clock in the morning, it was teeming. By the time clients enter Zazai, they have already drunk so much that they need a while for the drink to wear off. In addition, they have to buy expensive vouchers to exchange for what they consume. Ninety percent of the clientele of the three bars are foreigners. All these establishments are managed by Japanese people.

"At the SixtyNine, after asking around a little we met Raul, the young man Frau Fischer had seen talking to Marcus on the evening she went out with him. Despite the fact that he had only met Marcus Bopp in the three bars, Raul appeared to know him reasonably well. He remembered the evening of the first of March and recalled that Marcus had had a breakfast appointment with a male friend. Marcus left Zazai at around three-thirty. The 'breakfast friend', about whom he had not revealed anything more to Raul, is one of our suspects. Raul's alibi was watertight. He had picked up a young Japanese man in Zazai that night and taken him home. Raul's apartment is above a pachinko parlour, a gambling joint which is open all night. The boss of the pachinko parlour saw both young men going upstairs while he was standing in front of his door taking the air. Later that morning, the members of the pachinko parlour's cleaning team saw both men coming downstairs and walking out into the street, and a little later, strolling back with plastic shopping bags from Seven-Eleven. A visit to the closest Seven-Eleven supermarket was enough to confirm this account of events. After the SixtyNine, where we interviewed the staff and the clients without finding out anything worth mentioning, we went with Raul to Tonoyama, a small bar only as large as a six-tatami room, which is full if there are ten people sitting in it.

"All the people there had encountered Marcus Bopp. He stood out because he was a little older than most of the customers and came across as a bit more conservative. He wore a three-piece suit and probably went directly from work to the bar. In Tonoyama you have to order a whole bottle of spirits, which is then stored for you until the next time. The bottles are kept behind the bar, with a little plate around the neck showing the name of the customer and the date of purchase. There was a bottle of vodka in Marcus's name, dated the eleventh of January 1997; so, about two months before his death. The bottle was half-full. According to the bartender, Marcus drank moderately and often alone. Sometimes he talked with whoever happened to come and sit next to him. There were thirty-one people in Tonoyama at the time of our fifteen-minute visit. People were standing like sardines in a tin, packed next to one another. An American woman there had known Marcus reasonably well. He had once confided to her that he found it very difficult to build up a circle of friends in Tokyo. Other than that, our interviews with the staff and clients revealed no more information. Then Mr. Raul was kind enough to accompany us to Zazai – by that time it was already nearly three o'clock. There we met the Japanese man who was identified as having been with Raul on the morning that Marcus was murdered.

"We have a glimpse of a possible perpetrator, ladies and gentlemen. A breakfast appointment. It was a 'male friend', ladies and gentlemen, so a man. It is unlikely that this friend should be sought among the clients of the bars: the appointment was made elsewhere, not in one of the bars. I will now hand the floor to Valenti-san so she can talk about the investigation into the murder of Marco Polo."

"At first I didn't make any progress at all in my investigations into the Marco Polo affair," says Lucia Valenti, "and after two days and long evenings of fruitless combing through files, with Mochizuki-san's permission I decided to make use of my colleague Toni Albuixech in Perugia, in Italy. Perugia was the last place that Marco Polo officially lived, and I thought that a more in-depth look there might reveal more information. Toni Albuixech was one of the Italian candidates for our team. We had agreed that I could bring him in if necessary. He is a stand-by for our entire investigation. Among other things he combed through all the language institutes in Perugia for me, and in doing so he came across five Japanese girls who had known Marco Polo.

"Marco Polo appears to have been a slum landlord and the owner of a launderette, and was certainly a very ardent lover of Japanese girls. Four of the five girls had had a relationship with him. Two of them worked as his managers; one at the launderette, and the other managed a dozen apartments for him. They were each under the impression that marriage with Polo was as good as in the bag. None of the girls was worried when Polo had no contact with them for months, and none of them knows any of his family. A visit to the town hall revealed nothing. Polo's official address turned out to be that of a Japanese student: the Via Martelli. Before then he was registered at the address of his parents in Rome. A telephone call to the registrar's office in Rome revealed that neither of his parents is still alive.

"Polo had the correct licences for his launderette in Perugia, and had no criminal record in Italy. The apartments were rented out in the black economy. In Japan, his residence permit had expired. He regularly spent time in a Zen monastery in Japan. The girls in Perugia could not say where the monastery was, but they thought the sect was relatively unknown and unusual.

""Polo appears to have led a turbulent life in Italy, and to have set himself on a spiritual path in Japan. That is not especially strange; there are certainly other Westerners who use Japan for the 'purification of the soul'. Japan and Zen.... You probably know the combination well.

"For details such as the names of the girls, their addresses here, their addresses in Italy and the names of the schools where they were studying, I would refer you to the reports.

"According to Albuixech, it was striking that the girls looked so similar and that they did not read any newspapers or watch television. Their spoken Italian and English is poor. Polo spoke good Japanese. None of the girls had heard of the Fish Murders until then. One of them said that this was because the television news was too difficult to follow, and that even if a Japanese newspaper is available in the city it is at least a couple of days old, so they don't buy any newspapers.

"Over the past two days, Mochizuki-san's Japanese colleagues have interviewed the families and friends of the five Japanese girls, a task not to be underestimated and one that may involve more than a hundred people. One thing is striking in all the witness statements: the girls were actually very secretive about their relationship with

Marco Polo. Even the two girls who thought they were going to marry him did not make either their families or their friends aware of this. I have thought at great length what the significance of this might be. I think that in the eyes of the girls, Marco Polo was not 'proper' enough to be introduced to parents or friends. There must have been something wrong with Marco Polo…"

"May I interrupt you here?" Mochizuki asks, through Watanabe.

"Could I point out to you that there is a very obvious reason for Japanese women to keep quiet about their relationship with Marco Polo? Our culture is the most homogeneous in the world. Such relationships do happen if we are internationally orientated, but most parents would dread seeing their daughter with a foreigner. We are not against foreigners, but we do find that there are too many problems involved with the arrival of foreigners within our culture, within our families. And I think you could say that as a general rule, we prefer the certain to the uncertain."

"Can you really talk in that way about 'we', Mochizuki-san?" asks Lucia. "How can you be so sure that over a hundred and twenty million of your compatriots think the same way about this as yourself? I know that it is always said about Japan that the population is homogeneous and behaves in the same way, but is that really true in daily life? I can hardly believe it is."

"If you have really immersed yourself in my country then you really should know that what I have just said is true. We Japanese have no choice. We don't grow up like wild plants, like you in the West. We are perhaps born that way, though I personally doubt even that, but we are immediately pruned like the hedges in the garden of the famous Versailles. Every twig that grows crooked is firmly cut away immediately. We must be prepared for the society in which we end up, where overgrowth is not tolerated. That society is the same for everyone; so in that sense, it can be maintained that we are all the same, and therefore that I certainly can speak for my fellow citizens."

"But Mochizuki-san, isn't that actually true of us as well? That we Italians also end up in the same society? That a society may in any case be diverse? That you have to have different kinds of people in order to make up a society?"

"To a certain extent," answers Mochizuki with a straight face. "But over the course of my career I have seen and heard a good deal, and on that basis I think I can say that we Japanese differ from one another less than you Westerners do."

"I don't believe that at all," says Lucy. "But even if you are right, that doesn't contradict my theory. What do the victims have in common with one another? We have already learned a lot about the structure of the perpetrator's character, but what links the victims? Aren't we perhaps fixating too much on the fact that they were all foreigners? Of course we must not ignore that aspect, but it might have been mentioned too often and it has not got us anywhere so far. It seems to me that Marco Polo was not only an untrustworthy figure, as a slum landlord and womaniser; equally, I see him as a split personality. In Italy, he was duplicitous; in Japan, he visited Zen monasteries. We are looking for one person in a city of fourteen million.

We don't have a single piece of information about this person, except that he is most probably a man. There are eight victims. One of them, Marco Polo, gives the impression of having been divided. I am wondering: are there elements in the other victims that point to the same kind of split personality?"

"I suggest that we postpone this discussion," answers Mochizuki. "Silva-san and Hogenelst-san still have to present their reports. The Zen monastery where Polo stayed in Japan has not yet been found. We've only researched the best-known ones in and around Kyoto. The more obscure sects will be looked at in the next few days. Hogenelst-san, over to you."

"I have spoken to the father of the victim Hendrik Mechanicus, to the Japanese host family, to a friend of Hendrik's, and to the staff of the Japan-Netherlands House, where he worked," says Bertus. "The Japanese host family with whom Hendrik was lodging has also been interviewed several times by Mochizuki-san's Japanese team. I went there, but did not learn much more. The conversation with the victim's father was painful. The mother faxed me a series of letters which the victim had sent to his parents from Japan. From these letters we learn the following:

1. Hendrik had only one good friend in Tokyo, Tim Smith, about whom I will tell you more later.

2. Hendrik went into psychotherapy a little before his death.

3. He hoped to return to the Netherlands with a Japanese bride.

4. He attempted to do some serious writing.

5. He regularly visited the mountain village of Daigo.

"I have had a conversation with Tim Smith, an American and a classmate of Hendrik at the" – Bertus looks at his notes – "*The Japan-America Conversation School for the Japanese and English Languages and International Communication.* Quite a mouthful, isn't it? Hendrik and Tim went together a couple of times a month to the mountains west of Tokyo, mostly to the areas of Takao and Jimbo. They left Tokyo early and took the train to Hachioji, then the bus to the village of Daigo, the final stop. From there they used to walk the whole day, or on one occasion, two days. They had sleeping accommodation with a dance group in the village of Daigo. So far, so good. I already knew these facts from the letters. But what the letters did not say was that an awful lot was talked about during these expeditions.

"Tim Smith told me that Hendrik often didn't feel well. Hendrik himself called it a 'loss of identity'. He often had what he called 'a strange feeling' in his head and suffered from feelings of anxiety for reasons he could not pin down. He said that the adrenaline sometimes coursed wildly through his veins for no reason. Tim said that he himself had felt powerless and was unsure what he should advise Hendrik to do.

"When I asked whether Hendrik behaved differently at school or among other people, he answered in the negative. He told me that Hendrik had once said he was surprised that no-one noticed when he had an anxiety attack. When that happened he had trouble breathing, he came out in a sweat and he could hear his heart beating.

That happened regularly during his Japanese-language classes and at work, or when he went to lunch with his boss Adinda Buisman.

"Tim Smith had a theory about Hendrik's emotional state. Hendrik tried to write a book about his youth. He did this in English. Tim Smith thought he was the only person who knew about the book, because Hendrik had expressly and repeatedly requested confidentiality. However, Hendrik wrote about it in detail to his parents. Once a week, Hendrik and Tim went to a tea house together to go through the manuscript. At these weekly sessions, Tim helped Hendrik improve the English text, and Hendrik paid Tim private English teacher's rates. Tim thought that writing the book took Hendrik into an odd mental space. He described how excited Hendrik was during the conversations about the text. Tim had a copy of the manuscript, which bore the title *Broken Rituals*, and entrusted it to me. I've read it. It is a rather nicely written tale of a youth spent in the Netherlands. The principal themes are nostalgia for bygone eras that Hendrik did not himself experience, the celebration of primitive cultures, and community spirit; hence the title. It is clear that Hendrik himself is the protagonist, even though the manuscript is written in the third person. It is striking how Hendrik the protagonist meets his end: a Kafka-esque mental illness overwhelms him in a strange city. One of the passages concerns the fear of going out naked by accident. When on the street or in a train, the protagonist continually checks whether he is wearing any clothes. According to Tim, Hendrik really was afraid that he might do this. Despite his fears, Hendrik was often charmingly funny in Japanese, the language that he had just begun to master. Once when he ordered a snack with his tea, while they were working on the manuscript, it was served with a decoration of little green plastic leaves. Tim called the waitress over, dexterously fished the leaves off the plate with his chopsticks and in rapid Japanese, said – Bertus checks his notes – '*Nihon no tabemono wa zenbun oishii dakedo, kore wa mada taberarenai*'; this means 'I find Japanese food delicious, but this here, I can't get used to it'. To his great satisfaction, the waitress went away giggling audibly.

"Tim had advised him to seek professional help for his problems, but did not know whether Hendrik had actually done so. We know from the letters to his parents that this did happen.

"Hendrik and Tim often talked about the consequences of culture shock, because Tim too had sometimes felt very nervous. However, he had put this down to living in a strange city full of millions of people.

"So I do not think Lucia Valenti's theory is unreasonable at all. The mental health of our victims is indeed worthy of more consideration."

"I completely agree," says Jack Fowell, and leans towards Lucia Valenti. She tilts sideways on her chair, leaning as far away from him as possible. Silva shoots a dirty look at Fowell, who begins his story. "I've been looking at Larry Maxwell's diary. My research is not included in the latest report, because I was occupied with it until late yesterday evening. The ladies of the administration team can hardly have slept a wink last night, because I already have a printout of the report here."

Yukiko passes out the photocopies of the report.

"in this report I have arranged the passages in the diary by subject. They are very abstract and chaotic," begins Fowell. "I have arrived at three main themes, which I have called 'The Angel', 'The Whip' and 'The Friend, I'. 'The Angel' refers to a figure or picture that is sometimes an image, sometimes a statue. I quote:

The statue of the Angel must be transformed into the Whip. The Whip must be compact and must be understandable only to a few. James Joyce must play a role in this. The portrait of Joyce forms the map of Tokyo.'

"Another quote:

'Sometimes I sit on the smooth bronze of the shoulder of the Angel, in the crease between her wing and her neck. The cold of the bronze presses through the fabric of my trousers. My buttocks and genitals are at one with her, and above this the sky moves.'

"You get an idea of how difficult it was to make any sense of all this. There are a lot of references to 'the Whip'. What or who 'the Whip' " is, I do not know, but 'the Whip' must, I quote again:

'be compact, be understandable only by few, like a poem, and include all my friends. The Whip must roar and let fly around him, must connect and punish, and especially must be love.' "

"Could 'The Whip' be the title of a film?" asks Lucia, after this has been translated with difficulty and followed by a long silence. "Bearing in mind that Larry Maxwell was a video artist?"

Jack Fowell rises straight from his chair, and in doing so upsets his coffee cup. Looking at the brown stain soaking through the white linen of the tablecloth, he says, "God almighty. Of course Lucia, that's it."

Lucia pulls a face.

"That's all well and good, but it doesn't make the story any less weird," says Mochizuki.

"You're right again about that," says Jack Fowell, and starts to sit down again. "What shall I do about the stain?"

"Nothing," says Mochizuki. "Carry on with your report."

"'The Friend I' could also be the title of a film, I realise now. It is as though 'I' is someone, fictional or real, with whom Maxwell discusses everything. I quote:

2nd February, 1997. 'I' is not surprised and agrees with me that the Whip must roar. 'I' is generally in agreement with the Whip.

4 February, 1997. Long conversation with 'I'. I myself had the idea that there was someone else. 'I' denied it. He sometimes breaks off an exchange of ideas before I have finished with him.

8 February, 1997. I have told 'I' that I don't trust him; that I don't trust anybody. We spoke about The Great Mistrust.

10 February, 1997. They are there with a lot of people and they have the most impossible names. They are Americans (I trust them the most) and Europeans, and they speak in tongues. One Asian as well. Them I dislike.

15 February, 1997. 'I' says he wants to see me. We talked about American women's hair; one of the reasons why they couldn't get me to the USA, even if I were paid for it: the hair of American women. Brrrrr….

"Those are the quotations from 'The Friend 'I'' up to now. These passages are dated until shortly before Maxwell's death. There are two to five days between the 'conversations'. The last 'conversation' is dated the seventeenth of July 1997, and the story goes as follows.

Saw 'I'. The conversations are better when I do not see him. His jaw and mouth disgust me, and also his thin hair. These things should not disturb me. But in the end, 'I' just functions as a mirror.

"As I said, this 'I' could be a fictional friend," says Jack Fowell. "But let us just assume that he is real. In that case, who is he? Maxwell sees him sometimes, and then does not. If 'I' is real, then he is a suspect and we have to track him down. From Maxwell's diary entries there is nothing to lead us to him; there are no locations or telephone numbers mentioned, and in Maxwell's address book there is no one who has not already been interviewed, even under the 'I' section. We know that 'I' is surrounded by Americans, Europeans and Asians. That sounds like a large international company. Larry can hear them speak. He says that they 'speak in tongues'. And 'I' has thin hair.

"From this reading, Larry Maxwell was a troubled man, and he had a mysterious friend. Is a pattern beginning to form here? And then the key question: could the letter 'I' be the first person pronoun? Is 'I' Maxwell himself?"

As Fowell delivers his account, more and more of the group rearrange their limbs; long breaths are drawn; tea and coffee are poured out and drunk without thinking; erratic doodles appear on the edges of notepads. Watanabe is hoarse from translating; every few seconds he takes a swig of water, as if he is powered by machinery.

"My story about Irina Skoynich is still on the agenda," says Gerardo Silva. "I have the feeling that we are getting somewhere." There are nods and sighs and throat-clearings in preparation for another round. Yukiko and Yvonne serve tea with crushed ice from glass jugs.

"Mind if I smoke?" asks Bertus.

Gerardo Silva starts to speak as soon as the smokers have returned to the group in the conference room. "My visit to Irina's friend Mario Abe delivered an interesting observation that I have already talked about with Bertus, but would now like to share with you all. Abe told me that he speaks with Westerners differently – that is to say, more openly and personally – than with Japanese. He said that he has, to quote, 'a membrane in his head'. He switches, as it were, between one mental world and the other. I will begin with the conjecture that this explains to a great degree why the investigation was stagnating – excuse me, Mochizuki-san – before the creation of the international team. It would appear that our methods of making enquiries are different from those of the Japanese police. Let us hope that that this is to our advantage.

"With regard to the observations of Jack Fowell, Bertus Hogenelst and Lucia Valenti concerning the state of mind of the victims, I can add that Irina Skoynich went to an American psychiatrist because of depression. In Irina's address book I found a good female friend of hers in Poland. I have spoken on the phone with this friend, Katharina Labovitch, who lives in the city of Poznan. She has faxed me the letters she received from Irina between January 1995 and May 1996. I have arranged for you to have copies of the English translations of all these letters, but I would like to read out one from the beginning of 1995, because it suggests that in the past years of her stay here Irina was lonely, which makes all the greater the possibility of the existence of a mysterious contact."

Silva reads out:

Dear Katharina,

I am sending you something I've written, to calm my perpetually restless spirit. The painting is going well, but I need other, more intellectual outlets for expressing my recurrent confusion, exasperation, homesickness.... Here it is.

The best place in the world to research the phenomenon of culture shock is undoubtedly Japan. This is because the Japanese think they are unique, born of the gods, and consequently everything different is kept at a distance. On an island, this attitude is easy to maintain and lasts a long time. Everything from abroad (Mickey Mouse T-shirts, Coca-Cola and hamburgers, spaghetti Bolognese, white shirts, Mozart, Andy Warhol, Viennese hunting hats, and currently also ethnic products such as Mexican ponchos, Afghan carpets rugs

154

and African fertility statues), is available in this crazy city. Western advances (democracy, individualism, free relations, rights to a private life, feminism…) are unrecognisably changed in shape or negated and feared.

Any foreigner in Japan is the 'other'. There are only two kinds of people: Japanese and Aliens. You notice this at Narita International Airport, where the crowds pouring into the country are split up into these two categories, and after that it's never straightened out again. Aliens must keep their Alien Registration Cards on them and allow their fingerprints to be taken, and for the rest of your life in Japan you have to answer questions like: What do you think of Japan? What do you think of Japanese people? Do you like Japanese food, Japanese culture? Can you eat with chopsticks? Do you speak Japanese?

The Alien must put to one side all his values and norms and start again, learn to walk again, whether he is Chinese or Polish. Even Japan's closest neighbours, the Koreans, the Chinese and the Russians, don't have any kind of foothold.

Culture shock is symptomatic of a disease that can have consequences just as significant as other mental illnesses, and sometimes people develop a genuine split personality. I too have fallen prey to this. Being ill can assume terrible forms. The illness seems to consist of four phases: a honeymoon phase, marked by excitement and fascination; a crisis phase – the Deep Trough – characterised by rejection of the new culture and homesickness; a recovery phase; and an adjustment phase.

In the honeymoon phase, you arrive and feel you're on holiday. Everything is different, everything is new, everything is incomprehensible and therefore interesting. The length of time you stay within this phase depends on your character. Some people never emerge from it, never learn to read, speak, write or understand Japanese, and perhaps are the best off for it.

The more curious type of Alien quickly immerses himself in the language and the culture and understands these more and more; and then he comes slowly to the realisation that he had misjudged everything and in fact understands nothing. This surprises him at first; he has never before encountered such a phenomenon. We are now about halfway towards the crisis phase: the Deep Trough.

Once he is accustomed to the idea that he cannot operate within his old norms and values, it begins to dawn on the deeply shocked Alien what lies ahead. He must adjust himself, and this means that he must change himself, because that is less work than changing 127 million Japanese; and nothing is as tiring, boring and humiliating as changing yourself. We have now arrived in the Deep Trough.

In the short, energy-sapping period just before the Deep Trough, the Alien generally goes so far as to try to change the Japanese. During this Don Quixote period, unimagined feelings of loyalty to one's own country emerge, and there is an intense homesickness. This period is followed by the Deep Trough, which consists of a very virulent combination of hatred of the self and hatred of Japan. Leaving is usually impossible: one has invested too much in order to give it all up now. One has to 'make it all right again'.

Typically, the Alien gets out of the Deep Trough through a combination of studying the self and studying Japan. But just as with the honeymoon phase, there are people who get stuck within it. They are the worst off, because they are kept afloat only by cynicism and sarcasm. The people who remain stuck are in the minority; a larger number of Aliens are thrown back and forth between manic excitement, anger, absurd hatred, tolerance; they go up to heaven and back down to hell again....

It can be years before the upswings become less high, the troughs less deep. This continuous rising and falling causes a communication problem between foreigners who are already very isolated, because A, in the Honeymoon phase, and B, in the Deep Trough, feel in two totally different worlds, so overall have quite different perspectives.

I will give you examples of two Aliens I know. Let me begin with Antoinette (English), who is stuck in the Honeymoon phase. Antoinette is unnaturally cheerful and of a very positive disposition. She smiles continually. She has spent at least seven years in Japan but speaks no more than a few words of Japanese. She has a great many Japanese friends and is mainly interested in subjects like acupuncture, shiatsu, Zen, reiki, macrobiotics and aikido. She thinks that Japan is densely populated with practitioners of these disciplines. The reality is that only a very small minority takes any interest in such things. Because Antoinette always moves in these minority circles, she thinks they represent Japan. For their part, these rather atypical Japanese are attracted to Antoinette, with her blonde hair, her freckled arms, her open, spontaneous manner, her ditziness. Antoinette thinks the Japanese are an extremely spiritual people.

One example of a permanent denizen of the Deep Trough is Bruce from Australia. Bruce, too, speaks not a word of Japanese after ten years in Japan. He is a fashion designer, slightly addicted to cocaine (which is subject to heavy penalties), and has several times tried to break into the Tokyo fashion world. In doing so he came into contact with the ruthless world of business and went bust several times. Everywhere, Bruce sees businessmen, suffocating in their ties, who suck up to rise on the ladder while kicking down the people below. Bruce thinks all Japanese are unscrupulous bloodsuckers.

Most foreigners lurch back and forth in the grey area between Antoinette's heaven and Bruce's hell.

I myself have been in Antoinette's kingdom and Bruce's catacombs. When I arrived in Japan it seemed like heaven, and stayed that way for a long time. The weather was always good, I was healthy and cheerful, I could stay up all night without becoming tired, earned plenty of money and spent it right away, went around with crooks and layabouts and took pleasure in everything and everyone. Because for example the clothes, getting your hair cut and people's behaviour are all so different from what you are used to, at the beginning it is very difficult to assess people and situations. I remember that I sometimes used to worry vaguely about the fact that I felt so good; there was something unnatural, a little isolating, about this happiness. There was no good reason for it. I could eat what I wanted without becoming fat, drink alcohol without becoming drunk or hung over. My memory worked too well. I remembered names, faces and telephone numbers that were of no importance at all. Useful things, such as the Japanese language, slightly eluded me. It was at the same time terrifying and wonderful.

The nadir came about four years after the zenith. I had been going to school for two years to learn the language, saw a Sumie teacher every week, and I had Morio. Everything seemed in order and I had learned to behave appropriately again. I had struggled hard to reach this point, and the result was that I now seemed to consist of two different people: the European Irina and the Alien. These two halves had different opinions and were continually at odds with one another.

In that same year, almost all my good friends left. It is uncanny how you lose friends in Tokyo; nobody stays, everybody is passing through. When four of my five friends left inside two months, my two separate identities began a war. I lost six kilogrammes in three weeks. A wearying dislike of everything Japanese overwhelmed me. I had worked so hard to belong, and I felt alone. I dyed my hair black in order to stand out less and forestall the eternal stares. (It is now red again.)

Around that time, I had an interesting dream. I dreamt that the Japanese had little ovens at home in which they incinerated themselves millimetre by millimetre, so that by the time they died, most of their *bodies had already been cremated. They found that very efficient. If you should doubt the fact that I was in hell, then you'd better believe it.*

My emergence from this particular hell was initiated by self-analysis. I found a Western psychiatrist (he was American) and spent six months in recognising, accepting and uniting my two identities. If I look back on it now, it seems remarkable how much effort that cost. Now, three years later, I glide effortlessly from one identity into another. It is eight years since I came to Japan. Now that I don't try so hard to fit in, perhaps I fit in more than ever. I still feel I have mountains to climb, but the peaks have flattened and the valleys are smoother. The stark young mountain range is being eroded and is changing slowly into a gently sloping landscape. But it doesn't make me feel happier; rather, I feel melancholy.

Darling Katharina, keep writing to me. I shall keep you posted.

Many hugs and kisses,

Irina

PS: I am enclosing an invitation to my exhibition. It's in a small gallery. It's really expensive to hire the space for a week, but I did so anyway. After all, I have to keep busy.

"So that's that," says Silva, tired from reading. "Thanks to this letter, I have been able to form a much better picture of who Irina really was. From the letter it is clear that she was lonely and felt depressed. She likens the phenomenon of culture shock to an illness. We can say that something like this was true of Larry Maxwell and Hendrik Mechanicus, and perhaps also of Marcus Bopp, although his case is less clear to me."

Mochizuki looks around the table surprised. "I never knew that it was so difficult for foreigners here," he says.

Watanabe translates this and says shyly, "Neither did I." Both men give a slight, apologetic bow.

"I suggest that we leave it there for this evening," says Mochizuki quietly. "I wish you all a good night's rest."

Silva walks directly up to Lucia Valenti and puts his arm through hers. Speaking rapidly in Spanish, they disappear towards the bar.

Third of September

My research into the photos was delayed because Lucia had left the photos behind in the train and had to spend the whole afternoon in the railway's Lost and Found Department. This meant that Mochizuki returned to the hotel on his own. He was furious. Watanabe had to leap into the breach again. Lucia only came back during dinner, though she was successfully waving the envelope with the photos. Now the lab won't get them until tomorrow. Lucia described her bizarre expedition along the racks of the Lost and Found Department. Following that, there was a conversation over dinner about how lost and found objects are dealt with in Japan. Everyone who has been here before has an example of how extraordinarily honest the people of Tokyo are. Once, Croo was changing over the lens on his camera. He put an extremely expensive telephoto lens down onto the pavement for a moment, next to a busy crossing in the middle of Tokyo. A quarter of an hour later, he realised that he had forgotten to put it back into his camera bag. After ten minutes' hurried retracing of his steps – so, twenty-five minutes later – he was back at the scene of the disaster. The lens was still standing there, but neatly set to one side, so that pedestrians would not step on it.

Yvonne Lacoste had once left her bicycle somewhere in the middle of Shinjuku without locking it, and had forgotten to pick it up before she went to France to celebrate Christmas and New Year. She had accepted that the bicycle would have gone by the time she got back, and had not even returned to where she had left it. Weeks later, when she happened to be passing, the bicycle was still there. From the statistics on the number of people who pass through Shinjuku station every day, she calculated that more than sixteen million people must have walked past the bicycle in the meantime. Bertus and I were the most surprised when we heard that. We are both from Amsterdam, where they even steal the bungee straps from your bicycle.

After the meal I went straight back to my room and studied the photos of the victims once more. The way the bodies are arranged suggests that the perpetrator is a woman. You hardly ever see a man laying anything out in that way. The photos of the crime scenes remind me of magazines about interiors and kitchens; everything is positioned so snugly.

Li's game was good value again. Li is a real psychologist. She looks into your eyes too long and too intensely. However, she is kind, and it is a pleasure to observe her carefully groomed appearance. I wonder how many of those red outfits she has.

During the reviews, we asked ourselves: what if the murderer keeps flying in and out? Lives in Indonesia and commits the murders in Japan, or something like that? Mochizuki assured us that the borders are very closely monitored, but so what? Li told us that criminals usually remain near the scene of their last crime. Croo said that he had never heard of travelling serial killers, but Silva immediately came up with a couple of examples in America. But, and this is important, in these cases the murders were invariably also committed in different states. There were no cases where a murderer had kept going away and coming back.

Once again, it was really worth watching Watanabe eat. When he peels a mandarin, using an extremely sharp knife he carves perfect diamonds in the skin four times, for crying out loud! Then he takes the edge of the peel and strips it away from the flesh of the fruit as if he is opening a miniature box of gold dust, with such concentration. He drapes the small sections of peel around the edge of his plate, like the cars on a caterpillar ride at a fun fair. Then the skinning begins. The skins are deposited in a heap in the middle of the plate. All through this process there is the constant dab, dab, dab of a tissue against his lips.

Within the team, relationships are beginning to take shape. Fowell wants to pursue Lucia Valenti but doesn't dare go after her, and half-heartedly lets his hangdog eyes fall on me. He wears a revolting brown suit that needs to go to the dry cleaners.

Lucia and Silva seem to get on really well. They speak Spanish together, they gesture while they are doing so, thay hang around in the bar the longest. Robynne Green sits looking at Bertus Hogenelst and becomes alert and witty when he comes in. Bertus is kind to everyone, a team worker; everyone likes him.

I cannot work Croo out. That blotchy face, the weird checked clothes, the blushing. Yvonne and Yukiko are similar types, easy to work with; at least, if I come along with yet another vital thing to be done.

I have begun to work through the very earliest files. The photos that Lucia lost later in the day came from these. I have had them enlarged fifty times and hope they will reveal something.

Fowell went out with Watanabe. I saw them leave the hotel together. A fine pair, the tall lopsided Australian and the small, poised, tidy Japanese.

Lucia Valenti went with Mochizuki to visit a business called Hormone. So this afternoon I was well rid of Mochizuki.

The evening was given over to comparing the findings of Fowell, Silva and Hogenelst. We can now say with certainty that Maxwell was lonely, like Skoynich and Mechanicus.

I feel wrecked, but I cannot sleep.

The *Japan Times* informs us that Osaka wants to bid for the Olympic Games in 2008.

On Channel Two I saw a fantastic documentary about special education for acutely shy people. In Tokyo alone, there are millions. They are mostly boys, and some of them have enlarged cervical vertebrae from looking downwards. They get special gymnastics lessons to exercise their neck and shoulder muscles. Others go through the day with a dark scarlet complexion. Compared with this, Croo is clearly an amateur as a blusher. The blushers are taught how to apply a special make-up over their whole face. There is a light green anti-blush foundation, and this must be applied under a skin-coloured layer. There are also role-play games that use actors to bring the shy pupils out of themselves.

CHAPTER 5

"Good morning, everybody. Shortly we will be going through our reviews again," says Zhiqiang Li, opening the breakfast meeting. "The temperature?"

The members of the group demurely describe their moods.

"Thank you," says Zhiqiang Li. "Where were you when Elvis Presley died? Robynne, will you begin?"

"I was in Salt Lake City. We heard about it early in the morning. The young people wanted to have a church service. The adults were against it. They thought Elvis was the embodiment of evil," says Robynne Green, hurriedly.

"You seem rather bored of talking about this," says Li .

"Yes," says Robynne. "Look, I'm not interested in playing this game every day."

"Well, we are in fact playing it today," says Li, autocratically. "Gerardo?"

"I was standing in a queue in front of the best baker's in Mexico City, reading the newspaper. It was front-page news. Some people in the queue were weeping," says Silva. He laughs. "Elvis Presley never really did anything for me."

"That day, I was being interviewed by a group of students from Todai. It was a time of great social change," says Mochizuki. "The students wanted to talk about the role of the police in modern society. The last question from the panel was, 'if you had been able to choose to be someone else, who would it have been?' I answered, 'Elvis Presley'. I received loud applause."

The team also applauds, faintly.

"I heard it on the radio at home," says Li . "I cried."

"Sure, that's a really inspiring story," says Robynne Green.

"Yes, well, I can see that today's going to be no picnic," Li says tartly.

"I heard it at school from my teacher," says Lucia Valenti. "Then all the pupils were asked what they wanted to do, The whole class sang '*It's Now or Never*'. I found it very moving."

"Elvis Presley is not dead," says Fowell, briskly.

There is laughter within the group.

"I can't remember," says Croo. "I only remember the period afterwards. A lot of new albums came out. I bought them all. I still like Elvis."

"I wish to God I didn't have to know any more about it," says Bertus. "I've no interest in Elvis Presley. I think he is grossly overrated. Rubbish."

Fowell looks disapprovingly at Bertus. "The King is alive," he says.

"You are tired," says Li.

"We can decide that for ourselves," says Fowell. "I suggest we finish with the game. We have too much to think about."

"All right," says Li. "Are the others agreed?"

There are nods. Li looks ill-tempered. "Is everyone keeping a diary?" she asks. "We must have some way of practising mental hygiene."

"Why don't we do exercises in the mornings?" says Mochizuki. "We do that at the office, and I miss doing it when I have to be here early."

"Forget it," says Fowell loudly.

Mochizuki looks around the table quizzically. People shake their heads; some laughing, others vehemently. Mochizuki shrugs. "Let us start by going through the profiles of the perpetrators," he says, and looks at Watanabe, who is about to sit down and get ready to translate. "I will offer the table first to Croo-san, who will explain why he thinks there is a strong chance that the perpetrator is a foreigner. Of course, Croo-san has studied crime in Japan extensively over the past few months."

"Yes," says Croo, "I would first like to tell you about crime in Japan in general, after which I shall look at a few particular characteristics. The crime figures in Japan are strikingly low. The simplest explanation for this, which is that the average Japanese person is honest and well-mannered, is usually overlooked. People prefer to attribute it to the presence or absence of a 'different brain structure', in books of dubious scientific content. *The development of the left side of the brain in the Japanese* is an example of this kind of frequently cited book.

"The use of narcotics is a serious crime in Japan. It does happen, but is subject to stringent penalties. A great deal of alcohol is consumed; this does not fall under the anti-drug laws, and there is a surprisingly large number of drunks in the streets and in the trains. Nevertheless, Tokyo is astonishingly safe, anywhere and at any time. You can confidently leave your shoes and umbrella, or even your expensive garden tools, out on the street next to your door. A housewife can leave her wash in an unstaffed and unguarded launderette, or abandon her shopping in a bicycle basket if she has to pop into one more shop. Front doors are often unlocked; there is very little breaking and entering. The shoplifting statistics are the lowest in the world.

"In the suburbs of Tokyo there are unstaffed vegetable stalls provisioned by farmers, women who come into the city by train with huge boxes on their backs. The people who live in the area take the vegetables from the stalls and leave the money for payment in a cardboard box. In the evening, the owners of the stalls come back to pick up the unsold vegetables and the money. They can be certain that nothing will be unaccounted for. I once spent a couple of days observing the course of events at one of these stalls from the window of a house opposite.

"If you lose something, you can usually get it back from the *koban*, that is, the local police box, or the local municipal office. A wallet that I myself lost, containing a hundred and twenty thousand yen in notes, was handed in at the koban by the finder, a boy of seventeen.

"Fighting on the streets and in bars is almost unknown, so anyone can walk the streets in safety, even at night.

"The low crime figures in Japan have to do partly with the efficiency and quality of the legal system, partly with the character of the community. I would first like to say something about the legal system. Its role in society is greater than in most countries. For the Japanese, crime simply doesn't pay. The chances of being apprehended are much higher than elsewhere in the world. And there is much less negotiation possible between lawyers and judges than in other countries. Because of this, the penalties laid down are adhered to more often than elsewhere, and they are stricter. Policing is very efficient, partly because of the large number of officers and the attitude they bring to their job, partly through the widespread use of undercover information.

"Japanese companies exert strong psychological pressure. There is fierce competition because of the enormous population density, particularly in the big cities, and there is also strong social control, with the citizens being obliged to conform. Japanese who are convicted of a crime, or who are suspected of committing one, whether it is shoplifting or murder, feel a deep sense of shame. This extends over the family and friends of the accused. The family feels responsible for the crime, and family members often commit suicide after the verdict. Shame is a very large component of this culture.

"That said, crime rates have risen in Japan in the last hundred years, especially with respect to acts of violence that appear to lack any motive. The Japanese call these violent excesses *torima*; 'passing devils'. There is usually some kind of loss behind them; for example, failing a university entrance examination. Here again, shame is the key word.

"In addition to loss of face, 'indirectness' also plays a role. Assertiveness, physical or verbal, is not appreciated in any situation and is seen as extremely impolite. Japanese people speak very indirectly and politely with one another; this is something to which the Japanese language is extremely well suited. In language and deed they work towards harmony and avoidance of conflict. They bring up their children from birth to be like this. Assertiveness is not tolerated at all, by parents or at school, and there are strict penalties for a child who acts in this way.

"At a job interview, an interviewee begins by listing his weak points and the reasons for thinking why, all in all, he is not suited to the position for which he is applying.

"The homogeneity of the population also plays a role. Only a very small percentage of the population is not Japanese, and it is very unusual for a foreigner to become a naturalised citizen. This creates a special connection among Japanese people. Some go so far as to maintain that there is a kind of telepathic communication between them. They see themselves as being members of a large family, and most of all they are trained in group living. As I have already mentioned, because of this there is a high degree of social control.

"This social control certainly has advantages, such as the high degree of security for those who follow the rules. In most cases, employees can assume that they will work their whole life at the same organisation for a reasonable salary. They rise, slowly but surely. Promotion has to do mostly with length of service. Employers offer the whole family many opportunities for recreation. Some companies have their own swimming pools, golf courses and sports fields.

"Life in the cities is lived very fast, but the group structure provides a lot of help and support at an individual level. Each group, whether a company or a neighbourhood, has its own facilities to satisfy the needs of its members: a masseur, a flower arrangement group, a tea ceremony club, reading clubs... Currently, there are also a large number of so-called 'laughing clubs'. At these you have to laugh on demand, even if your life is nothing to laugh about. A laughing lesson begins with the utterance of the words 'hah, hah, hah', and ends with a heartfelt group bellow, I have been told."

"Ha, ha, hah," laughs Robynne Green. "Is that true, Mochizuki-san?"

Mochizuki nods solemnly.

"Insofar as crime does take place," continues Croo, "it is committed by members of organised gangs, which spend their time fighting to resolve internal disputes, dealing in narcotics and guns, organising prostitution, swindling, especially in real estate, and engaging in extortion. These yakuza do not get involved with normal members of the public. They distinguish themselves openly with colourful tattoos over their whole bodies and amputated little fingers.

"In sharp contrast to the peacefulness of everyday life is the fact that pornography is available on every street corner in the form of photographs and manga magazines. It is consumed in enormous quantities by young and old. Even in the train you see men unashamedly looking at pornography. Many newspapers have a sex page. Images of trussed up, bleeding women are nothing out of the ordinary. No one appears to be bothered about this. It's often claimed in the media nowadays that the unashamed indulging of gruesome fantasies is precisely why Japanese society is so peaceful.

"Now and again a discussion arises about whether pornography and sex manga should be prohibited. This was the case during the Miyazawa affair, which I researched. I have already told you a little about that. He was the serial killer who murdered pre-school children. Miyazawa was arrested by Mochizuki and his team, and within one week he confessed to five murders. When the police went through his room in search of evidence, hundreds of videotapes were found, along with pornographic magazines and manga. These contained gory horror material and Lolita-like stories. The reports on Miyazawa's interrogation leave no doubt that he was a sex murderer.

"After the media reports had brought the subject into the public eye, a debate developed, with psychologists, journalists, TV personalities, newspaper readers and TV viewers taking part. They basically fell into two camps, with opinions that were diametrically opposite.

"Group One maintained that it was impossible for to protect children from pornography and manga because these are available everywhere, even in vending machines and from litter bins in the street. Dealing in it should be prohibited.

"Group Two said that serial killers have always existed, even before the trade in pornography and manga, and will always exist, even if these are banned. By banning pornography you would undermine press freedom and create a black market, which would mean that crime increased, rather than decreasing.

"Group One answered that criminality is reduced not by tolerating crime, but by punishing it.

"Group Two's response was that pornography is fantasy. As long as perverse and violent feelings can be experienced through fantasy, perverse and violent actions are circumvented.

"In the Miyazawa case, this last argument was clearly false.

"It really doesn't look as though a law is going to be passed in Japan against the sale of pornography and manga. This country will therefore continue for some time to be an unusual combination, populated by modest, honest individuals who take pleasure in looking at books of rape scenes when they are on the trains. Now and then it will throw up a terrible criminal like Miyazawa; but hopefully, it will still manage to retain those unstaffed vegetable stores in the suburbs.

"My view is that there is a very strong likelihood that the perpetrator in this case is a foreigner. I offer you the following in support of this idea: notwithstanding their extensive enquiries over the past six months, the Japanese police have not succeeded in tracking down the perpetrator. In the Miyazawa case, they quickly knew where they should search. They were in a position to place the events in a socio-cultural context, and were able to form a picture of the personality of the criminal, of his background and of his motivations, from the places where he was able to operate.

"In conclusion, I would like to return to the established facts of our investigation. On the clothing of two victims, a couple of blonde hairs were found which originated with one and the same person. There is a strong likelihood that these are the hairs of the perpetrator. Japanese people do not have blonde hair. We are therefore almost certainly looking for a foreigner. But another possibility is that at some point these victims came into contact with the same person, who left hairs on their clothing. In that case we are on the wrong track, and the perpetrator could well be Japanese. But at this stage there is no evidence that points towards their having such a blonde-haired friend in common.

"I will sum up once again. One: the Japanese police are completely in the dark because they cannot assess the social background of the perpetrator, so the perpetrator is most likely a foreigner. Two: blonde hairs have been found, so the perpetrator is probably blond."

"I think I've read," says Bertus, "that the number of crimes involving perversion is quite high. I saw in the *Japan Times* that in Yokohama a man was picked up who sold schoolgirls' used underwear in vending machines. The unwashed panties had a photograph of the owner attached. When I read that kind of thing, I do think: oh, that is strange."

"That may well be so," Croo replies, "but you should remember that pornography is tolerated because of the argument that it is an outlet that averts real crimes. For example, in Japan there's a lot of gambling. Just look at the many pachinko parlours and opportunities for people to play mah-jong for a lot of money. Some people think that these small morsels assuage a larger hunger: they steer people away from committing major crimes."

"Well," says Bertus crossly, "the drug policy does not particularly display the tolerant attitude that you describe."

"That is a separate issue that is not up for discussion here," says Mochizuki. "Our drug policy is strict, and I am proud of that."

No one backs Bertus up. He sits there looking a little guarded.

"I would now like to open the floor to Zhiqiang Li," says Silva in a loud voice. "We are making progress with the profile of the perpetrator."

"Yes," says Zhiqiang Li. "I will now focus on the criminal himself. There are reports about this investigation in the newspapers every day. That means that the murderer very likely knows he is the subject of an intense manhunt. It could affect his behaviour. It is possible that he is keeping a very close eye on the progress of the enquiry. He may even be in contact with the police; phoning in tips, getting to know how things stand with the investigation. In the meantime, he is looking round for the next victim. He comes across a particular haircut, a well-known perfume, a particular kind of skin... and then he ends up in the Shadow Phase again. He will play his game very openly, because he wants to lure the police towards him.

"He despises himself for what he does and who he is. He yearns for punishment; the prospect of lifelong incarceration, the electric chair or a lethal injection exercises a gravitational pull on him. The possibility of being caught sometimes provokes such a murderer to commit more crimes. We must try to stop that happening. Once you have caught him, in all likelihood he will confess to his crimes and beg to be punished strictly."

The members of the team sit together in silence. "Back to business," says Mark Croo abruptly. "I have a train to catch. Enjoy your work, everyone."Croo has almost three quarters of an hour to wait at Shinjuku Station before the Narita Express departs. He decides to take a walk through the enormous complex.

He drifts with the crowd through tiled passageways bathed in fluorescent light, going up and down staircases and escalators, via lifts and along moving walkways, to the lowest level, four floors underground. Immediately he finds himself among huge crowds. There is something rather pleasant, almost something erotic, about the swaying mass of people smelling slightly of soap. He also discerns the smell of hot iron. He sticks his head above the carpet of stiff black hair. Yves Saint Laurent, Isetan, CiCi, Issey Miyake, Pleats, Keio Department Store, LoveLove...in the blink of an eye, he reads the horizontal, recognisable text between the vertical columns of vivid characters written with a brush. Glossy advertising posters are framed by a damp, yellow-tiled wall covered in city dirt. Croo allows himself to be drawn along, floor after floor, up and down, as he had often done during his lonely months in Tokyo; past kiosks, shops, merchants noisily advertising their wares, steaming noodle tents, sleeping vagrants. He smells hot curry. He sees a poster of a dirty man in rags riding his groin on the magnified face of a blue-eyed, creamy-white photographic model. He has made her red lips dirty and damp. It looks as though she has eaten liquorice. On the ground floor, Croo gives a hundred-yen coin to a woman sitting on the ground. Her feet and legs are wound round with grey bandages. She calls out after him: 'American.' The roar of trains and air extractors and the high-pitched squeak of broken fluorescent lights mingle with her mad laughter.

The south side of the ground floor opens onto a broad,

leaden-grey square overarched by dirty concrete. Standing motionless amid the milling mass of people is a Buddhist monk. As if driven by a machine, he rhythmically strikes a copper stick against the bell in his left hand. The noise rings out clearly above the reverberating rumbles and thuds on the square. Croo stands watching in fascination, then looks at his watch and gives a start. He runs as best he can, stumbling, pushing and zigzagging in a long upward slalom, while he takes his train ticket out of his wallet. He puts the end of the yellow ticket into his mouth while he closes his wallet and leaps into the train, just between the hissing doors that are already closing, landing right next to the conductor. He removes the little card from his mouth. With horror, the man in the tight uniform takes it between his white-gloved fingers and clips it. Bowing, he hands back the defiled object.

Croo blushes.

Just past the towers of Disneyland in Chiba is QueBook, the shop owned by the late Hughes de Keuninck. It is a small dusty space with a glass window on the ground floor of a grey apartment building. Along the walls on wooden planks, old books are piled to the ceiling. There are handwritten signs dividing them by subject. Coloured posters on the walls depict Patrick Süskind's *Perfume* and Thorne's *Countess Dracula*, about Erzsébet Báthory.

That's Silva's female serial killer again, thinks Croo.

A cleaning team clad in bright blue overalls, with metal bottles on their backs and masks over their noses and mouths, is busy spraying the books with a liquid smelling of cinnamon. The men bow slightly to Croo as he walks past. Croo sniffs the tingling aroma and sneezes.

"Excuse me. There's nothing better than the smell of old books, but that aroma is a thing of the past here. The hot weather has brought on a plague of bugs. As if we haven't had enough to put up with. Good afternoon. My name is Lambert. I was Hughes de Keuninck's best friend." The stout, blond man with childlike ruddy cheeks and deep-set, slightly slanted eyes shakes Croo's hand.

"My condolences on the tragic loss of your friend, Mr. Lambert. I'm sorry that you have to be troubled by the police again."

"I telephoned the police myself," says Lambert. "I only hope the murderer can be caught."

"The case is in full flow, I can assure you of that," says Croo. "There are sometimes more than a hundred people a day working on it. I heard from the Chief Inspector that you have found a list?"

"Yes," says Lambert, "I have inherited Hughes' possessions. I'm storing some of his papers at home. There was a list of names among them whose significance I did not understand until yesterday. If you will come with me to the back of the shop, I will show you something. I knew that my friend Hughes had a fascination with horror and thrillers, but I didn't know he had got mixed up with stuff like this; it must have brought in some much-needed cash. Have a look here."

Lambert leads Croo to a metal trap-door, descends a wooden staircase and gestures around the dusty, low-ceilinged concrete space, where untidy piles of magazines and video tapes are stacked against the wall. "All pornography, Mr. Croo. I discovered the cellar yesterday, when it had to be fumigated because of the insects. I telephoned the police immediately. The shop had been reopened, but they came here right away to seal it up again and open up the cellar. They took over the bug-spraying from the company that I had originally contracted to do it."

"Yes, I heard about that," says Croo.

On the wall, categories are spelled out in black paint. Soft, Hard, Romantic, Violent, SM... Mark Croo takes a book from one of the piles, leafs through it and blushes deeply. He turns away from Lambert, and with his back to him, says, "why do you think this may be important for our enquiries? Pornography, and not just the milder sort, is still tolerated in this country. Just as long as no pubic hair is visible." His blush has diffused; he turns on his heels, the closed book loose in his hands, and gestures at Lambert nonchalantly.

"There is also pornography originating from America and Europe that is actually illegal. There are even Japanese films, made by amateurs, which are especially violent. These films are apparently rented to a select public. The list I found appears to be the members' list of this club. You may well have read that people who are addicted to pornography..." he says this with a voice choked with tears, "that those sorts of people may be the kind who take the risk of committing crimes. A couple of years ago, there was the Miyazawa affair here. That guy had his whole room full of it. There's a lot of pretty weird material here, Mr. Croo." He swallows rapidly, twice in succession. "I looked through a number of them yesterday evening. I'd never have imagined Hughes was into this kind of stuff. I sat here watching the tapes till very late. There were women being injured, with knives, and I thought: the murderer, he is also crazy about knives… in the end, I wanted you to have the list. I could have handed it over to a policeman here, but I thought, if you could see it with your own eyes… You probably have so much material available to you. I wanted to play you a little segment of a film." His tears are now real.

Mark Croo walks up to him and puts the book back onto the pile. Then he reassuringly pats Lambert on the back a couple of times and nods. "Go ahead and play it," he says.

Lambert blows his nose, then switches on the video recorder on a stool in the corner. Mark Croo sits on the ground, his arms round his knees. Lambert comes and sits next to him with a remote control. He fast-forwards and rewinds the tape a little. The speeded-up pictures form a mishmash of leather, white flesh, blood and steel.

"You see?," says Lambert, and allows the tape to play at normal speed. They sit together, silent and embarrassed. Mark Croo turns pale. "Er, thank you," he says, "I get the idea. Could you just give me the list of members as well?"

Lambert hands over a sheet of paper in a transparent plastic folder. Croo reads through the list.

Yoshiaki Abe
Hiroshi Bota
Dave Daalen
Min Doi
Rai Enamlanhal

Henri Faber
Mike Feininger
Saboro Gata
Satoru Hiroi
Kenichi Ichigawa
Hans Keslinger
Kunikaze Komamoto
Jake Limelight
Kenji Morita
Takeo Morita
Yoshi Nohara
Koki Nohara
Hank Onodera
Adam Randell
Oguri Satou
Jiro Tsunoi
Jonathan Wanadoo
Jeromy Wanderfogel

Next to the names are handwritten combinations of numbers and letters.

"All men," says Croo. "No addresses?"

Lambert shakes his head.

"The clean-up team will go through everything here with a fine-toothed comb," says Croo. "If there are addresses, they will certainly be found. Thank you very much, Mr. Lambert, for your cooperation. It is very possible that this will help us make some progress." He waves the bundle of paper in front of Lambert's face. "I will start work on this right away and will have the tapes and magazines sent to my hotel today. I understand that this has been a great shock for you. I'm sorry." Both men lower their heads and walk silently up the wooden staircase in single file, leaving the stuffy cellar below them. They squint in the grey light coming through the dirty windows of the shop. Lambert holds the door open for Croo.

"I wish I could help you in your enquiries, Mr. Croo. I feel so powerless."

"Regrettably, Mr. Lambert," says Croo, "I will have to examine the material on my own. To go through a whole cellar of pornography, you must be an accredited police officer."

"Yes," says Lambert and smiles weakly. "Much success with it."

Croo walks rapidly back onto the street. Lambert watches the long thin legs in the checked trousers walk away until, with an almost comically sharp movement, they turn the corner.

It is eight o'clock in the evening. Marc Croo sits cross-legged on his bed and looks around his hotel room. For the first time, he is not surrounded by heaps of files from the Japanese police, translated into English by Yukiko and Yvonne. Stacked high on his desk and the office chair are the magazines from the QueBook cellar; against the wall opposite him is a pile of video tapes. Croo counts them, his head inclining slightly as he does so.

"Two hundred and four," he says out loud. I can't stop

being around porn, he thinks. If it's not at the university, it's in a police investigation. Sighing, he swings round and lets his lower legs hang from the bed, like a swimmer getting used to cold water before launching himself into the pool.

"Well, let's get on with it." Croo pushes down with his arms, swings his checked-trousered legs horizontally to the front so that he hangs between his thin arms like a basket. He rocks back and forth in this position for a moment, then pushes himself forward in an elegant arc and lands on the thick carpet in his stockinged feet. He has a hole in his right sock. One of his toes is sticking out. He slots in the first video tape, swings the stand round on its wheels so that he can see the television screen from the bed and takes the remote control with him to the bed. He lies there, almost motionless and with his eyes closed, holding the remote control in his hand, arms folded behind his head, his bare elbows poking out, red and pointy. Then he springs to his feet energetically, switches the recorder on, takes a pen and a notebook from the night table next to the bed and sits ready to make notes while he reads the untidy rolling credits of the film.

By midnight, Croo has, against his better nature, already achieved three embarrassed climaxes while watching the videos. It is a long time since he has come so quickly and so strongly. His face is flushed.

At three-thirty he falls asleep with his trousers still open, the remote control in one hand and his pen in the other. His head rests on an improvised cushion of magazines that form a colourful collage of bound, injured, spread-legged flesh and items of underwear in lace, rubber and leather.

Fourth of September

I would really like to have a long sleep. But again, that is quite impossible. The clear lozenge-shaped sleeping tablets that I got from Li sit temptingly in front of me. But I don't dare take them, as I'm afraid I'll be woozy from sleep tomorrow. Croo talked about criminality in Japan today. He knows a lot about it and told us interesting facts about Japan to demonstrate that the killer could be a non-Japanese. I was not completely convinced by his argument, but I found the presentation very illuminating. We went through the perpetrator's profile with Li again. That was also useful and was something we needed. In the afternoon I had gone to the laboratory with Mochizuki. The photos were not yet ready; there had been problems with the enlargement.

Mochizuki has begun to be a bit nicer to me, and I'm beginning to find him a more sympathetic person. What's odd about the man is that he doesn't let on whether he is having a tough time. He is always in the same volatile mood, eats impatiently and irritatedly, slurps and sweats.... he charges blindly towards his goal, like a tank. That makes him annoying and awe-inspiring at the same time. If something offends him, he is stoical.

Eating together is problematic; the mixing of intimacy and tension. I'm trying to force myself not to pay much heed to his compulsiveness. The harder I try, the more difficult it is not to stare at him.

Over dinner I talked with Li and told her I felt so ambivalent about Mochizuki. She looked at me with those wide-open doll's eyes of hers and suggested that maybe I had 'an authority problem.' She referred to it as if it was some kind of disease. I just answered that in Amsterdam people cannot survive without having this kind of 'problem'. Unfortunately she didn't quite understand what I meant.

The investigation is now focussing on Croo's activities. A cellar full of illegal pornography has been found under QueBook. Croo has had the videos delivered to his room. I wonder exactly what he's up to at the moment.

It is crazy to see how, despite the enormous pressure, people still find ways of getting together, making jokes, arguing. I saw Silva walking down the corridor with his arm around Lucia. I think Lucia was crying.

While waiting for the photos I spent the afternoon sitting reading old and new reports. I've compared them with one another and I think we are now making progress more quickly. It is frustrating that we as foreigners are kept in a silo. There is no contact with the old Japanese team, which is now on standby for whatever chores come up. Mochizuki likes to organise everything in such a way that the gap cannot be bridged. When we had to go along to his office this afternoon, he left me standing waiting outside the door!

It is illuminating when all results of the investigation of the last days are brought together during the reviews. Patterns start to emerge. The victims were lonely and sought someone they could trust.

I am less anxious and tense, although the case is really

eating me up, like a rat gnawing at a ball of grain. That's also true of the others; everyone looks really tired, except for the girls from the office.

I saw on Channel Two that Prime Minister Hashimoto had donated two hundred billion yen in development aid to Minister Li Peng of China. Pictures of people in Shanghai taking a dump on the street and Chinese crawling all over one another. English-language schools on the street, under a few trees. It was as though using these images the Japanese wanted to show that they are also Asians, but much more sophisticated.

Bertus called out, just after the meal, 'Who would like a sandwich with chocolate shavings?' He'd managed to get hold of some whole-grain bread from somewhere. Where the chocolate shavings came from is a puzzle. Sent by his wife, maybe? They turned out to be the main event. Those of us who are from the Netherlands and Belgium were particularly excited about the bread and chocolate shavings, even though the food at the hotel is excellent.

Croo called the chocolate shavings 'n*gg*rtoes'. Six long days in Japan now, and the connection with home has to be made with the aid of 'n*gg*rtoes'. Calling home is difficult because of the echo and the fact that we are not allowed to talk about the case.

CHAPTER 6

At six o'clock in the morning Marc Croo is sitting on his bed, following his routine of comparing the advertising pages in pornographic magazines with the notes he has scribbled in his notepad. At eight o'clock he appears at breakfast, looking impatient. I hope to God we're not playing a game today, he thinks; that would just distract me. He does not rise to Robynne Green's banter. He eats quickly and automatically, then hastens back to his room. At ten o'clock he telephones the Kenji Casting Bureau, using the number he has found in a pornographic magazine, and makes an appointment. He can be there at twelve.

He introduces himself as Marc Mortier.

"You make pornographic films?" he says to Kenneth Curbain, who is still sleepy.

"Yes," answers Curbain. He is a handsome, rather ponderous man. Half-Japanese, half-Western, Croo reckons.

"I'm working on a book. I'd like to see how you work. Is that possible?"

"That would be difficult, Mr. Mortier, unless you can go along with what I need. A little problem has come up this afternoon. Someone has dropped out. You can take on the role if you want."

"What kind of role?" Croo asks.

"It's no big deal," says Curbain, "everything's staged. We have an American woman who wants to get her clothes off, everything revolves around her. You would just have a minor role. You would have to pour some candle wax over her, we would chain you up, and you would be wearing clothes. You will have to twist back and forth on a chair while you are sitting on it tied up. Your face will not be in the frame, but your hands and buttocks will. Those especially. We need a shadowy male character who takes care of some stage business. Can you go along with that?"

"The candle wax," says Croo, "is that painful?"

Curbain takes a candle from a stand on a cabinet in the office. "Just roll your sleeve up a moment," he says. He lights the candle and casually twirls it round in his hands. As the wax begins to drip, he moves the candle back and forth above Croo's arm. The drops fall. Croo feels a slight shock, but no pain.

"And what about the more sensitive parts? The stomach, for instance?"

"Pull your shirt up a bit," says Curbain laconically. Croo complies and leans horizontally against the back of his chair. Curbain lavishly drips wax onto him.

"No, it's not painful," says Croo.

"It's just like a bed of nails, anyone can lie on one. People don't know that," says Curbain. "Can you do it? You'll get sixty thousand yen, the girl gets five hundred thousand. I'm telling you this to show you we're straight with people. If you want to watch what goes on – whatever your reasons – you will have to participate. You don't imagine I can just let you come in and stand around and see how it's all done?"

"Couldn't I be one of the film crew today?" Croo suggests.

"No, I've got my usual crew. Besides, do you know anything about cameras?"

"No," says Croo.

"Good," says Curbain, "then that's sorted. You can take part, and on top of that, you've got lucky. Sixty thousand, cash in hand at the end of the day, on the black. Take it or leave it."

"Fine," says Croo. "I'll do it."

"In that case, let me invite you to lunch."

"So you're a writer?" says Curbain, once they are sitting in a restaurant.

"Yes," says Croo, "and in my book there is a scene in which a pornographic film is being made, but I have no idea how it all actually happens."

"Been in Japan long?" enquires Curbain.

"A year," answers Croo.

"Is your book set in Japan, or outside?"

"In Japan."

"Okay. Because you have to understand that in Japan the porn industry is quite respectable. No sleazy back rooms or underpaid minions. We rent a clean apartment, we have a professional film crew and we pay the models well. I do it to earn money for my artistic videos. You've probably heard of Araki, the photographer? He came through the porn industry. An interesting guy with an international reputation. Our stylist is an artist from Australia who has to put food on the table, and our makeup artist-cum-wardrobe manager is a failed fashion designer, also from

Australia. So I'm happy to lend a hand to a writer. What kind of book is it?"

"A detective novel," says Croo.

Curbain nods understandingly. "You can tag along with me," he says, "then you can get to know the two Australians, Cleopatra and Bruce, beforehand. We begin filming at three o'clock this afternoon. We hope to be finished around ten this evening."

Bruce, thinks Croo, where have I heard that name before?

"Hi, I'm Cleopatra," says a small, delicate woman. Her golden chains and necklaces jangle as she comes towards him and shakes his hand; she looks like a pharaoh in full regalia. "And this is Bruce."

A bald, lanky, tortoise-like man in a vivid orange jacket shakes Croo's hand heartily. "Hi, welcome," he says. He wears copper earrings that resemble flattened champagne glasses; they are so long that they brush his shoulders. With a flourish he takes off his plastic jacket. It falls onto a chair with a crackling sound. He says to Cleopatra, "Frida was so annoying again last night!" Amiably, he turns to Croo. "Frida is my cat." He continues, including Croo in the conversation by turning alternately from him to Cleopatra. "I was having a nice sleep when Frida suddenly jumps in through the hole above the air conditioner, you know where I mean. I'd put a brick against the rubber flap in the opening. The brick falls onto my glass table. The whole table ended up in splinters, in the middle of the night. I'm on my futon, I sit straight up from the shock, and I say to myself, so, she is home." He continues to look from Cleopatra to Croo, then laughs uninhibitedly, with long, whooping out-breaths. Cleopatra also laughs, matching his rhythm; this draws Croo into the laughter as well.

"So, shall we get things ready?" chortles Bruce.

"Yes, that's fine," says Croo, tittering.

"Get your clothes off," says Bruce casually.

"I'll go ahead into the studio," says Cleopatra, and disappears through the door.

Croo undresses, embarrassed

"That hair will have to come off," says Bruce.

"What?" says Croo, shocked.

"No pubic hair in Japan, don't you know that?" says Bruce blithely. He has already started shaving Croo; the latter, pale with fear, looks at the head bending over his pubic area.

"Relax, man! Don't worry about it. Just think of me as your friend."

The dry razor scrapes along Croo's pubic hair. To Croo's surprise, the superfluous hair comes off quickly. Bruce plies Croo's organ from left to right as if he is handling the leaves of a sick house plant; it is still sore from Croo's masturbation the night before.

"You're a little bit tense," says Bruce brightly. "That's it, just push forward a little.…"

Bruce hands over an immaculate white towelling robe. Still complaining about Frida the cat, he amiably gives Croo a gentle push towards the studio door.

In the studio, Cleopatra is standing on a ladder. She is hanging up an empty picture frame, inside which various frightening-looking objects are dangling from a nylon cord. She totters on her platform soles.

"What are those?" asks Croo, somewhat self-consciously.

"Items I made myself," answers Cleopatra, stretching out to attach the frame to a hook in the ceiling. "I've already exhibited them a couple of times, but I've not sold any, of course. A lot of people who came to the exhibitions thought they were 'devilish'. The gallery owner strewed salt by the door to ward off evil spirits. Now I only use them here, then I get paid in advance." She turns around to Croo and laughs. "Oh, you do look cute," she says.

Embarrassed, Croo looks at his thin, bare, hairy legs poking out of the short bathrobe.

"Sorry," says Cleopatra. She grasps the material of her long black skirt and pulls it up to knee height, then descends the ladder. "Have you met your co-star yet?"

"No," says Croo, cautiously.

"Don't worry about it, she's really nice. She's called Jessie. She needs the money."

Croo nods.

"Here she is," says Cleopatra. A fleshy woman comes into the studio in an identical bathrobe. Cleopatra goes over and embraces her. "How are you, darling?"

"Fine, fine," says the woman, smiling broadly. "And you are Mr. Mortier?"

Croo offers his hand.

"Nice to meet you," says the woman affably. "Is it your first time?"

Croo nods.

"Don't worry," she says. "Everything will go fine. Piece of cake."

Then the camera crew comes in and everything happens very quickly. Curbain gives instructions which Croo follows blindly. He wonders where the American woman has got to. Suddenly she is above him with her mouth. "Just suck," says Curbain sternly. Surely not, thinks Croo, while he lies on a table top, half-covered by Cleopatra's gold-brown shawl, which still carries the scent of her. Nothing happens. But then he hears slurping sounds at the level of his groin, and looks down. He sees only a blonde Abba wig moving up and down. She is sucking her own fingers, thinks Croo. A little later, she crawls up towards him. She kisses his cold neck.

Croo allows himself to be chained up, and in this state sways his upper body back and forth on the chair; he gets into a leather suit that is too small; he stares out of the window when Curbain asks him to; he drips candle wax over Jessie's writhing, blindfolded body. The camera shots take a long time. He cooperates mechanically. His buttocks are filmed from behind while his flaccid organ bangs against Jessie's genitals, which are smeared with Vaseline. They feel sticky and clammy.

"Slot shot," calls Curbain, after yet another change of costume, "Watersports scene. Could you just ask Bruce for a bucket?" he asks Croo, who is exhausted.

Croo trudges to the dressing room. "Do you have a small bucket?" he asks Cleopatra.

"A watersports scene?" she asks. "Fine, then we're almost finished."

Croo delivers the small plastic bucket she gives him to Curbain in the studio. Curbain takes it and calls over to Jessie, who is lying on a table with her legs spread. "Okay, you can do it now."

"I can't go," says Jessie quietly. "I just have to go out

onto the balcony. If I get cold, then I'll feel like going." A cameraman holds the door of the balcony open for her. "Could you leave, Mr. Mortier? It inhibits me if you're watching."

"Yes, of course," says Croo quickly, and goes back to the dressing room.

"All done," says Cleopatra, laughing. "Tired?"

Croo nods and goes to sit in a deep armchair in a corner of the sparsely furnished entrance. There, he falls asleep. He is woken by the noise of the camera crew passing through. "How long was I asleep?" he asks Jessie, nervously. She is fully clothed and holds a thick envelope that someone has given her.

"Oh, I'd say about an hour," says Jessie. "Do you want to come and have a drink with us?"

Croo nods. "What's the time?"

"A quarter to twelve."

"I've never slept so well," says Croo. Curbain gives him an envelope.

"O-tsukaresamadeshita," says Curbain loudly.

"O-tsukaresamadeshita," repeat the staff.

"… shita," says Croo automatically in unison, and bows.

"Where shall we go?" says Curbain. "To Andy's? You know Andy?" he asks Croo.

Croo shakes his head.

"Andy is an Englishman who has a yakitoriya under the railways in Yurakucho," says Curbain. "This guy's been in Tokyo a year and he doesn't know Andy's. Shame, shame," he says, to no-one in particular. "Have the lights in the studio been switched off?"

The members of the group go into the dressing room

and sit on their knees in a circle. Curbain motions to Croo. "Go and sit next to Jessie."

The members of the group bow their foreheads to the floor. Like a judo group, thinks Croo. Why would they do that?, he wants to ask Curbain; but Curbain, bowing, has just begun to take his leave of the Japanese camera crew.

"Have you ever heard of Jeromy Wanderfogel?" Croo asks one of the members of the film crew who has stayed with them, once the group has been provided with beer, saké and snacks. The man looks at him uncomprehendingly.

"Wanderuvoguru," he says and beckons at Bruce.

"Maybe you've heard of Jeromy Wanderfogel?" asks Croo.

"That weirdo?" says Bruce soberly. "I won't work with him. You have to enjoy what you do. I do this for the money, but also for the fun."

"Where can I find him, this Wanderfogel?" asks Croo.

"No idea," says Bruce and shrugs indifferently. "Have a drink, man, don't be so serious."

"So who is Wanderfogel, then?" Croo asks Curbain later.

"No idea," Curbain answers. "I'm not in the violent porn business. He is a pervert, everyone knows that. How do you know his name?"

"From a porn magazine and the credits of a film," says Croo.

"Where can I find him?"

"Just ask in QueBook," says Curbain.

"I've already been there," says Croo.

"Then drop it, man," says Curbain impatiently. "What do you need the guy for?"

"I want to watch a really violent film being made, for my book."

"You don't mean that," says Curbain, dismissively.

"I do, really," says Croo. His heart thumps against his throat, which is dry from tension.

"Bruce knew someone who worked with him," says Curbain, "but the poor woman is dead. Murdered. You still interested in Wanderfogel?"

"You mean that Wanderfogel murdered her?" asks Croo.

"If we knew that, we'd certainly go to the police. Someone I knew was also murdered, you know. A video mate of mine. You must have heard of the Fish Murders? You do read the newspapers? All casting bureaus, including ours, were checked out by the police. They didn't find anything at ours that was illegal, not even a strand of pubic hair. If any parts of the genitals come into the frame we cover them over neatly with a little blob, or pixelate them. You'd laugh your head off. In close-ups the whole frame is simply pixelated out. You just hear the moans in the background. My films are sold to love hotels. I can only imagine where Wanderfogel's films end up. I know they were rented out under the counter at QueBook. I heard that from poor old Larry, the guy I knew, the one who was murdered."

"Wasn't the owner of QueBook also murdered?" asks Croo.

"Holy shit, is that so?" asks Curbain, genuinely shocked. "Did you hear that Bruce, Cleopatra, Jessie? Marc Mortier here says the boss of QueBook has been murdered as well."

"Did you know him?" asks Croo, as neutrally as possible.

"No, not personally, but every foreigner knows QueBook, don't they? But when was he murdered? You've been to QueBook?"

"I don't know," says Croo. "There was obviously someone different in the shop."

"Did you know him well, then?"

"No, no, not personally, but I knew QueBook."

"Jesus, Jesus, Jesus," says Curbain. "The person Bruce knew, what was she called again, Bruce?"

"Irina," says Bruce.

"And Larry and the owner of QueBook. Good God, Mortier, what's going on here?" He yells this out. People stare at him.

"I don't know," says Croo.

"Soon they'll have a go at you or me, Cleopatra," says Bruce, with an expression of horror on his face. "That what's going to happen. Murdered in this incredible city. You wouldn't want that to happen to your fucking drunk great-grandfather in Perth, but it will happen to me, you'll see."

"You have to get away from here, Bruce," says Cleopatra, quietly.

"I want to meet Wanderfogel," says Croo.

"You're sick," says Bruce.

"I'll be careful. I want to get something really special for my book."

"You can make it up, Mortier, you don't have to go looking for a crook to find that stuff out."

"Yes I do," says Croo.

"You're nuts," says Curbain. "I'm not going to get involved with this."

"I really want to have it," says Croo after a silence.

"You know what? I'll ask around a bit and see what I can do," says Cleopatra. "I know quite a few people in this business. Maybe there's someone who once worked for Wanderfogel. I'll give you a call if I find out anything, okay?"

"Idiot," says Curbain. "Look – we meet Marc Mortier, and straight away we hear about three stiffs. You know what I'm going to do tomorrow? I'm going to the police."

The table is quiet.

"Jesus," says Bruce. And then, after another silence: "Christ, Curbain is going to the police. Unto such a point have we come. Curbain is going to the police. We are at an historic turning point in an era, ladies and gentlemen, Curbain is onto it. Curbain is going to the police." His laughs and whoops last a long time.

Curbain nods. "And I will, too," he says.

"What are you going to say?" asks Croo.

"That I met you and immediately learned about three stiffs. As far as I'm concerned that's a bit too creepy, Mr. Marc Mortimer. Then they can have a look at how the pieces fit together. There is a whole international team working on the case at the moment, so it should be dead easy. It's got something to do with Wanderfogel, I'm telling you. You'll go to the police if you know something?"

"But what do you know?" asks Croo.

"I've no idea, man. I only know I've suddenly heard about three murders, and I don't like that one bit."

"Where is the international team?" asks Croo.

"I've no idea, but that's easy enough to find out. I swear I'll call them tomorrow."

With red-rimmed eyes, Croo sits on his hotel bed. It is seven-thirty in the morning. He has sent a report to Mochizuki and now he can sleep for a couple of hours. He carelessly sweeps the magazines and the cardboard cases of videotapes from his bed; then, for the third time in forty-eight hours, he falls into a deep, refreshing sleep.

"I am a slut and a whore and addicted to sex," Robynne Green says to Zhiqiang Li, vehemently.

Zhiqiang Li's consulting room is comfortably furnished with a white leather three-seat sofa, two matching armchairs, a glass coffee table and a white, deep-pile carpet. Zhiqiang Li sits attentively, even a little reverently, bending forward in one of the armchairs, her elbows supported on her shining nylon stockings just below the edge of her red dress, her chin in her hand, listening to Robynne.

Robynne is draped over the other armchair, apparently exhausted, gesticulating with her arms and hands, her long legs stretched out.

"You said that last time as well," says Zhiqiang Li. "What do you think about sluts and whores? Are they bad? Inferior? Despicable?"

"No," says Robynne. "I have nothing against sluts and whores, but I don't want to be one of them myself. I despise myself."

"You don't despise other sluts and whores?"

"No."

"Shall we first look at what you understand by sluts and

whores?" says Zhiqiang Li.

"Sluts are women who will go to bed with anybody."

"And you do that, so you are a slut," observes Zhiqiang Li. "And whores? As far as I know, whores are women who trade love for payment. You do that as well?"

"No. By whores, I mean the same as sluts. People who are unfaithful."

"Good, so we can retract half of your accusation: you are a slut, but not a whore."

"Okay, so let's move on," says Robynne Green, with a furtive laugh. Then, with a rigid gaze, she looks out of the wide window that overlooks the quivering, steaming city. Not a single sound from outside is audible within. The air conditioner hums, and in the distance the lift bell pings at regular intervals. Zhiqiang Li is silent.

"It ruins my days. It wrecks my concentration. I think of him the whole day, so I can't do my work properly. I really want to go to bed with him, and I will do, but he doesn't want to. That makes me absurdly angry," says Robynne. "And it's certainly not the first time this has happened to me. I've been in love with other men since I got married. For a long time I didn't have any problem with that, but now, now of all times, it's driving me mad. My anger, the stupidity of my own behaviour, I can't stand them. It would be too idiotic if I managed to seduce him. I mean, a colleague for heavens' sake. And on top of that, during an investigation as important as this one. Disgusting!"

"It seems to me important that you distinguish between the emotion and the behaviour," says Zhiqiang Li. "Do you blame yourself for finding him sexy, or do you blame yourself for having tried to seduce him?"

"For having tried to?" says Robynne. "I'm still trying to do it. When I leave this room soon I'll be at it already, you'll see, then it'll just be a matter of everything falling into place; Robynne puts on her best clothes, then the ogling can begin. He is not blind to it, I can tell you. I can see how he looks at me, but he has a wife, and he's faithful to her. He is a real sweetie, and I want to have him."

"I'm asking you, is it the emotion that disgusts you, or the behaviour?" repeats Zhiqiang Li.

"Both. If I didn't feel the emotion, then I wouldn't manifest the behaviour."

"You can't do much about the feeling; that just happens to you."

"Damn' right."

"But the behaviour is something you can control. Can't you allow yourself the feeling and discard the behaviour?"

"Oh yes, at least in theory, but I know I'm too weak to do it."

"Too weak?"

"Yes."

"Don't you mean 'too incorrigible'?"

Robynne laughs. "Yes, that is what I mean. Nice one, Zhiqiang."

"A moment ago, you said you were addicted to sex. What exactly do you mean by that?"

Robynne's face clouds over. "I mean that sex gives me a kick, and sometimes I do everything I can to get that kick, even against the intentions of my better self."

"That sounds as if you got it from a book," says Zhiqiang Li.

"That's right," says Robynne surprised. "Not long

202

before I came to Japan, I read a book about women and sex addiction."

"Listen, in this case I would steer clear of the word 'addiction'. Everyone feels desire, and can get pretty obsessive about it. That is not only true for you. I would like to talk about the distinction between feelings and behaviour."

"I wouldn't," says Robynne. "I would just like to talk about feelings."

"Why?"

"Because it makes me all mixed up and makes my life impossible, especially now, in this situation. I despise myself. I spend the whole day sitting staring at photos of mutilated, murdered people, I hear the most repellent details about serial murders, and meanwhile I sit fantasising about having sex with him. Nice, eh?"

"In my experience, sexual feelings often become more intense when death comes along."

"Really? How is that?"

"For example, it is a well-known fact that many men get an erection just before they die."

"Yes, I've heard that somewhere."

"Even the coffin-bearers at a funeral often experience erotic feelings. And what do you think of nuns gazing at the bloodstained body of Jesus? There is sometimes a connection between bodily violence and erotica."

"Yes, but isn't that sick?"

"Do you find it sick?"

"Yes. So you don't?"

Zhiqiang Li reflects for a moment. "It depends. I am very much in favour of what you might call 'freedom of emotion'. Thoughts are free, Robynne. We cannot blame ourselves, or other people, for having certain emotions, because they are foisted upon us, as it were. We are ambushed by them, from outside, from inside – who can say? They might simply be chemical reactions; no one knows exactly. However you look at it, an emotion is not something we can just decide not to feel. In that respect, we are powerless. But it's quite different when it comes to translating emotions into behaviour. That is something over which we do have power. Behaviour can undoubtedly be twisted, or illegal, or immoral, or unscrupulous – in short, damaging to others."

"Hmm," says Robynne.

Zhiqiang Li is silent.

"There's quite a lot to think about there, Zhiqiang."

"A form of behaviour can also be harmful to you yourself," continues Zhiqiang Li. "That's not good, either. Imagine that you did manage to seduce him. Who would be hurt by that – you, him or both of you?"

"Him, because he has a wife. And me too, because I would be ashamed, about his wife."

"And what about you? You're married as well."

"Yes, but I've been going to bed with other men for years. For me, that's normal."

"Does this have anything to do with the fact that your parents are Mormons?"

Robynne gives a loud laugh. "My parents had to know sometime."

"Is that why you do it?"

"Oh, who knows?"

"How can you be so sure that he doesn't want to go to

bed with you because of his wife? Has he told you that?"

"No."

"Maybe he just doesn't find you attractive."

"Yes, maybe it's that." Robynne's mouth contorts, and tears roll down her cheeks.

Zhiqiang Li adeptly reaches down to the cardboard box on the floor next to her and passes Robynne a tissue. "And the anger," she continues, while Robynne continues to cry, "tell me a bit about that. Who are you so angry about?"

"Him. The fact that he has the nerve to turn me down."

"You poor thing," says Zhiqiang Li.

Robynne Green is laughing and crying. "It's always like this with me. When I'm angry, I start crying. What should I do, Zhiqiang?"

"I don't know. What do you want to do?"

"I want this obsession to go away, so that I can concentrate on my work."

"For the time being, it is not going to go away. You can be sure of that."

Robynne stops crying and nods. "Yes, you're probably right."

"What are you going to do?"

Robynne sighs, passively opens her hand, which had been balled up into a fist, and lets the damp tissue fall onto the carpet. "I've no idea. I'm so fed up with myself."

"Hmm," says Zhiqiang.

"What should I do, Zhiqiang?"

"To begin with, I would try not to get angry at yourself because of desire, an emotion. Just watch how it goes, think about it, and we'll talk about this a bit more in a couple of days. You can't solve everything in a single session."

"You're right," says Robynne. "Thank you."

"You're welcome."

Bertus Hogenelst runs spryly up the steps from the seventeenth floor of the hotel to the eighteenth, where he wants to check the latest hotline calls at the call centre. At the top of the stairs he has to stop for a moment to catch his breath. His heavy breaths echo against the tiled walls. The sunlight shines through the dusty windows, pale and slanting. It is six o'clock in the morning, and Bertus wants to do some work before breakfast, because he fears there won't be a conference at the table and that instead they will all have to play one of the games dreamed up by Zhiqiang Li.

He takes a packet of cigarettes and a lighter from the pocket of his corduroy trousers and looks at the Mild Seven Lights cover. He has finished his supply of Caballeros that he brought from home. He reluctantly shakes a filtered cigarette from the unfamiliar packet.

He half-screws up his still swollen eyes, looking into the sunlight, while he lights his cigarette. He pulls a face. Just carry on smoking, he thinks. His eyelids already feel less heavy. He feels the nicotine hit his brain, and he is immediately able to think clearly. He thinks about the lists of telephone numbers he examined in his room the evening before. There was not a single instance of phone numbers corresponding in the lists of outgoing calls from the victims. That means that the victims had no friends, acquaintances, doctors, dentists or other contacts in common. Neither did the victims know one another. It is the sixth day of the investigation, and up to now no-one has had a single hour of free time. Bertus thinks briefly about Robynne and their agreement to visit the galleries in Ginza. With a groan, he stubs out his dog-end in a sand-filled ashtray hanging on the wall and goes to the administration room. The door is open a crack. There is no one there yet. He walks in and looks around the well-ordered room. The desks are made of grey steel, even more old-fashioned than the ones he and his staff work at in Amsterdam. The computers are enormous, yellow, musty leviathans. The records are housed in wooden chests standing on their sides. There are neatly arranged cardboard folders in primary colours. Hotel furniture is piled up in an alcove. From a room a little further in, a low voice is audible. Bertus walks towards it and opens a door. On the other side of a partition, a member of the hotline staff is wearing a headset and talking to people phoning in with information. The conversation takes place in a language that Bertus cannot identify; possibly Korean. Behind the telephonist is an old-fashioned cosy corner with a low round table, where the latest reports about the hotlines are available to look at. Bertus has never been in this room before.

The hotline reports are usually distributed around midday. He goes to sit on one of the chairs in the cosy corner. The woollen fabric of the upholstery pricks uncomfortably through his trousers into his thighs.

He looks through a couple of stacks of files, and finally leans over a yellow file bearing the words 'Most Recent'. His thighs are now itching unbearably; half-standing, he reads through the reports. They contain a surprising number of confessions from people who claim to have committed the murders. Bertus counts three in the past twelve hours, five from the twelve hours previously. Strangely enough, all these confessions were from Japanese men. Then his eye falls on a report that reads:

Woman with coloured shawl reported in telephone cell BC983 in Iitabashi by a resident of an apartment opposite the telephone box, in the spring of 1997. The woman with the shawl often made calls from the telephone box, sometimes even daily. At the beginning her calls lasted a long time, perhaps an hour. Later, the conversations were more frequent but shorter; about a quarter of an hour per call. The caller said she had recognised the colour of the shawl from a photograph in the newspaper.

Bertus removes the report from the file and takes it to the administration department. The copier has not yet been switched on, and he has some difficulty getting the ultra-modern device up and running. "I think we have to call this one the tip-off of the week," he says softly, while he walks round the copier to find the right opening into which to insert the document. "Telephone box PC983 in Iitabashi. I'm off to find Mochizuki."

He thinks he remembers Mochizuki wanting to work through the night at the hotel. Mochizuki will probably be resting now, in one of the rooms allocated to external team members. On the off-chance, Bertus knocks.

Mochizuki opens the door slightly, then opens it further to allow Bertus to enter. In his light blue pyjamas and bright green slippers, his defences are down. He listens to Bertus sleepily; but as soon as he hears the number of the telephone box, he reaches for his telephone. The Japanese that he barks down the receiver is strange to Bertus's ears. None of the sounds is the slightest bit familiar.

"I have telephoned NTT," Mochizuki says in his throaty English, once he has replaced the receiver in the cradle. "It will be checked. By five o'clock this afternoon we will have a printout of all the numbers called from that telephone box in the year to June 1997."

"Will you contact Silva about this?" asks Bertus.

"Yes," says Mochizuki. "I'll see you back in the dining room."

While the NTT staff are retrieving the information about telephone box PC983 in Iitabashi, Mochizuki and Watanabe are on the packed platform of the Ginza line at Akasaka-Mitsuke station.

People are waiting patiently, in long orderly lines, for the rush-hour trains. The arrival of each orange Ginza Line train is proclaimed by the sharp ring of a bell. With the arrival of each train, the queue becomes a little shorter. As the final passengers try to maintain their equilibrium against the railings of the sliding metal doors, railway employees, armed with white canvas cloths, politely but firmly push them further into the carriages. Then the doors hiss shut and the mass of people inside is compressed further. Here and there, parts of skirts, jackets and handbags are caught in the doors. The doors slide open again and the railway employees, cloths held out with both hands, cram the projecting articles back into the carriages.

As the train starts moving Mochizuki curses softly, gesturing impotently at Watanabe, who is still standing on the platform. In the packed carriage he thrusts his whole body forwards, slides open the window and calls out, "Aoyama-Itchome, I'll be waiting by exit B4!" Watanabe nods and raises his arms in frustration. Assisted by his fellow passengers, Mochizuki manoeuvres himself out of his diagonal position, then pulls a small book from his case and begins to read it intently, holding it ten centimeters from his face. In this way, he shuts himself off from the world around him.

"I'm very sorry, I couldn't stay with you," a flushed Watanabe gasps to Mochizuki, who is waiting by exit B4.

"I've been waiting here a quarter of an hour," says Mochizuki crossly.

Watanabe bows silently.

"Just have a look at the map there and find out where the Goethe Institute is," instructs Mochizuki.

Watanabe studies the neighbourhood map on the board in front of the station exit. "Far side, third right, second left, fourth right," he says, and sets out ahead of Mochizuki. The latter follows, grumbling and dabbing at his forehead with his handkerchief.

In the hall at the Goethe Institute, a strange chaos reigns. There is a heap of earth on the marble floor, with spades stuck into it. Using red strips of material, Japanese boys and girls, adolescents in loose clothing, are busy connecting a mobile, an artefact of thick bamboo poles hanging from the ceiling, with the branches of a tree outside the building. The red ribbons are already wedged between the glass doors, which open and close automatically.

"What's going on here?" Mochizuki snaps at Watanabe.

"If you'll wait here for a moment, I'll go and find out," says Watanabe. With his hands in his pockets, Mochizuki stands gloating as he watches the boys fail to subdue the mobile turning and swirling on its nylon cords. A boy on a ladder is hit on the head by a bamboo pole and winces from the pain; a girl sitting outside on a swaying branch of a tree gives a sharp cry. Every time someone comes near the glass doors they noiselessly slide open and shut, giving yet another impetus to the movements of the mobile inside the building and the tree outside.

"Ask whether the doors can be fixed so they don't move," shouts the boy on the ladder. A girl runs over to a line of closed doors in a side corridor. Watanabe reappears in the company of a tall man dressed in sober grey.

"Mochizuki-san, my apologies for the noise. We have a performance here this evening. I am Uwe Solle, head of the Cultural Department. Would you like to come along to my office? Mrs. Welt is waiting for you there."

Mochizuki bows, beckons to Watanabe and follows the man through several corridors to a comfortable, light room containing pine furniture and a large number of plants. Bettina Welt is present. Name cards are exchanged. Uwe Solle speaks excellent Japanese.

"You make notes," Mochizuki snaps at Watanabe.

Watanabe takes a small cassette recorder from his bag and looks enquiringly at Mochizuki.

"Give it to Mrs. Welt."

Bettina takes the device from Watanabe without betraying a trace of pique. "Do you have any objection to our recording the conversation?" she asks Solle. The latter shakes his head.

"Goethe Institute, Herr Solle, fifth of September 1997, nine o'clock in the morning," she says softly into the microphone.

"You knew Ian Wackwitz?" Mochizuki asks Solle.

"Yes. I did not know he was dead until I saw his photograph in the newspaper. I knew him only superficially, but I do know the places he mostly frequented. We organise various kinds of cultural performance here. Wackwitz was a member of a Japanese-German group of performers under the directorship of a Japanese man, based in Hachioji. You can't really call what they do either dance or theatre; they mingle into a sort of combined theatre. The members themselves refer to what they do as performances, but these are not really what we in Europe understand by performance. It is a mixture of Japanese and European theatre, modern and traditional; they call it to Buto. They are coming to perform here in the hall this evening. We have an excellent theatre, but in general they avoid conventional theatrical venues. They are not very well-known, but I find them extremely interesting and want to give them an opportunity. They attract a very young audience. I take it you would like to speak to their director?"

"Very much," says Mochizuki, "but first tell me what you know about Wackwitz."

"I don't know much about him myself," says Solle. "He used to hang around here, built props and scenery, and sometimes took part in performances. He handled the procurement of materials for the performances. He set a budget, we went through it together, I paid him what he thought he would need. After the performance, when the entrance money had come in, we totted up the accounts. Usually I got money back, because he was very frugal and sensible about what he bought. I arranged any payments for guest artists with the leader of the group."

"Who is the leader, and where can I find him?"

"Kazuo Yamaguchi. He is coming here late this afternoon. If you want, I can call him and try to set up a meeting with you."

"If you would be so kind."

Solle telephones, speaking good Japanese. He puts his hand over the receiver and looks enquiringly at Mochizuki. "This evening, after the performance?"

"Couldn't it be earlier?"

"Late afternoon then, maybe about half-past three?"

Mochizuki shrugs his shoulders. "Couldn't it be earlier than that?"

"Yamaguchi-san is still in Hachioji. It will take at least two hours for him to get here, door-to-door." Mochizuki raises his hands, takes a step towards Solle, grasps the receiver and speaks loudly to Yamaguchi. Then he angrily bangs the receiver down onto the cradle. "He hung up."

"Would you like to see the performance?"

Mochizuki shakes his head.

"You can use this room for the interview," says Solle. Mochizuki nods, and gestures to Bettina that she can switch off the recorder.

"The places you end up going to on a case like this," he

213

says, when they are back on the street, under a high tree on which a group of girls is perched. "I'll be interested to see whether this gives us something to work on."

"Let us hope it does," says Watanabe softly.

"I do not have much time, Mochizuki-san," says the huge, bald Yamaguchi almost menacingly, a couple of hours later. "I have to lead the general rehearsal."

"Fine, then we'll keep it brief. How did you know Mr. Wackwitz?"

"I didn't know him well. He was the handyman for my group when we performed. He often used to stay in the group's house in Daigo. Apart from that, I don't know anything. May I go?"

Mochizuki stands up. He is dwarfed by the muscular giant standing impatiently in front of him. "May we go and have a look at the house?"

"That is not a request, it's an order," says Yamaguchi. "Here is the address and a description of how to get there." He writes and draws on a crumpled piece of paper which he takes from his trouser pocket, like a celebrity giving out an autograph. "At the shop by the last stop on the bus route, ask for Saburo. He has a Land Rover and can take you there. You'll have to pay him. The door of the house is open." He bows and walks out of the room.

Angrily, Mochizuki follows him down the corridor. "Yamaguchi-san, it is not for you to decide when this interview is over."

Yamaguchi stops abruptly. "No?"

"You could just as well have given me your information by phone. Instead you kept me waiting for several hours."

Yamaguchi puts his square, grubby hands on Mochizuki's

shoulders and gives him a push. Mochizuki's back slams against the wall of the narrow corridor. Bettina Welt emerges from Solle's office, closely followed by Watanabe. Bettina runs after Yamaguchi.

"Let him go," shouts Mochizuki, gesturing with his head in the direction of the strutting Yamaguchi.

"Let him go," shouts Watanabe in English.

Bettina turns round and walks back to the Mochizuki, who is gasping.

"Lowlife artist! Charlatan! I'll get him," he says. "We will go, right now. Watanabe-san, you go back to the hotel. Welt-san and I will work on this together."

Bettina looks at him, astonished.

Fifth of September

It is ten past one in the morning. This afternoon I was sent to the Goethe Institute by Mochizuki. He was going to be waiting for me there, with Watanabe. They were late! I spent an extremely uncomfortable half-hour with Uwe Solle, head of the Cultural Department at the Institute, because I didn't really know what I'd been sent there for. So I was really furious with Mochizuki.

Today I could have given Watanabe a crack on his big symmetrical head, the way he allows himself to be enslaved.

Talking of hitting, Mochizuki was grabbed right in the short and curlies by the leader of the dance group, Yamaguchi. Mochizuki, who's no shrimp himself, was not even in the same league as the huge bald shiny guy, and was thrown against the wall. It was the first time I'd seen him lose his cool. But he recovered immediately and asked me to accompany him to Daigo, a village in the mountains. After a journey by train and taxi, we got a lift from a guy called Saburo. Mochizuki fished Saburo out of a little shop right by the bus stop. He smelled of booze, but took us safely to the house of the dancing group, where we interviewed about ten young Japanese members and two Germans. They told us that Wackwitz had often stayed at the house. And Mechanicus had been there once, with someone called Tim Smith, during their walks together. So Mechanicus and Wackwitz might have known one another! I still have to write a report about this and take it to the administration department.

Marc Croo has been expelled! No-one knows when or how he left. Mochizuki did not want to open up about it at all, but this much is clear: in the context of this investigation, our staid Mr. Croo has taken part in a pornographic film and accepted money for doing so. It would be laughable if it hadn't turned out to be so serious. Bertus Hogenelst was very shaken by it all. He had known Croo from a previous case and was clearly very attached to him. He kept telling anyone who would listen how stupid Croo's behaviour had been, after all the press reports about pornography in Belgium last time, but he also thought Croo should not have been thrown out so quickly, just like that. Mochizuki said he had authority to expel Croo according to the rules established at the conference in Honolulu. Taking part in the film was one thing, he said, but accepting money for it was unforgivable. What was Croo supposed to have done? Said he would do it for nothing?

Mochizuki is dead scared of the press, of course. That seems to me the deeper reason for why Croo was expelled so quickly. Mochizuki is contemplating a raid on the Kenji Casting Bureau to seize all their visual material. If the press gets wind of Croo's escapade, all hell will break loose for Mochizuki. That's the way I see it.

So, exit Marc Croo. Nothing definite is known about any replacement. God forbid that we have to play Li's game again!

This evening I went for a walk towards Shinjuku. After eight o'clock it was still very warm, and already pitch-dark. I tried again to go through neighbourhoods keeping parallel to the main road, but I couldn't do it; the sidestreets spiral and simply come to dead ends. Not once was there a square at the end. With all their old-world tranquillity, these neighbourhoods are in huge contrast to the huge smoky highways. There are children living there, girls in colourful yukata who sit playing with sparklers, boys messing around with insect cages. The screech of the cicadas is deafening. There are still small supermarkets open until very late. People in plastic slippers make their way to the sento with towels and soap boxes in their hands. There are cooking and bathing noises, crying babies, the buzz of televisions, the smell of soft soap; the domestic and familiar and the strangely exotic at the same time. And there are red fire buckets in front of the houses.

The purpose of the expedition was to buy paper clips, thumbtacks and fridge magnets for my room. In a gigantic stationery shop by the station I spent more than an hour choosing between thousands of kinds of thumbtacks. Then I picked the paperclips and magnets at random, dazed by the range on offer. I am writing this with a new soft rubber pen. I also bought seven erasers on impulse.

Soon I'll do some more channel surfing. I'll see how the preparations for Diana's memorial day are going. Princess Diana was hugely popular in Japan. Now, after her death, hair salons have emerged which specialise in Diana hairstyles. You see them on the street and in the trains; Asian versions of Lady Di.

The Austrian empress Elisabeth Amalie Eugenie Habsburg-Wittlesbach von Bayern, otherwise known as Sisi, is also doing well. On television I also saw a delicatessen which only deals in Sisi merchandise: biscuit tins, chocolate Sisis in coloured silver paper like Easter bunnies, Sisi tarts, Sisi ice cream.

I mustn't forget to look into the matter of the sect leader who is suspected of murdering a lawyer and his wife in Yokohama. Sects are a good business in Japan. Some of them have tens of thousands of members and own skyscrapers in the middle of Tokyo. I do sometimes ask myself whether the case we are investigating could have something to do with a sect.

My photos still haven't arrived!

CHAPTER 7

Robynne Green has boarded the Romance Car from Shinjuku station to Odawara. The driver of this almost silent train sits high in a canopy atop the locomotive; the bullet-shaped nose below it is made entirely of glass. Mochizuki has advised Robynne to reserve one of the seats with numbers one to ten. She sits on Seat 4 in the transparent nose while the train whisks its way as fast as an arrow through the mountainous landscape. When she alights at Odawara station, the air is surprisingly clear and fresh. Grateful for having been able to leave the mad, hectic city behind her for a while, she inhales deeply several times. The station and the low houses with cobalt-blue roofs that lie against the rocky mountain slopes have a friendly, provincial simplicity. At the kiosk on the platform, she buys a balsa-wood lunchbox of cold rice and fish and a tin of chilled oolong tea, then takes them to a bench and sits down. The rice is nicely sticky; the fish is fresh, cold and refreshing. Robynne dips into the orange-white food with the chopsticks provided with the lunchbox. She hears a mechanical female voice announce the arrival of a train; the announcement contains regular pauses.

She smiles at the various announcements and requests provided for passengers who are arriving and departing: "please stay behind the yellow line until the train has come to a complete stop; remember the step, and the opening between the train and the platform; do not forget to remove your luggage, jacket and umbrella from the racks; we wish you a nice day and a pleasant journey; thank you for using the Odakyu Line's Romance Car, and we hope that you will use the Romance Car again in the future."

Robynne deposits the empty balsa-wood box and tea can into a rubbish bin and stretches herself in the mountain air. Finally, she thinks: fieldwork in the open air. Long lines of gleaming taxis stand in front of the station. She approaches one at the head of a line.

The chauffeur crosses his arms in front of his face.

"Good luck, you prat," says Robynne loudly, and walks towards the second row of taxis. She bends down towards the window. The driver looks at her, at once curious and apprehensive.

"*Havarudo Interunasuyonaru Komyunikeishion Akademi Kaiwa Kakuin wo shiteimasuka?*" she asks.

"*No, no, no English*," says the man.

"*Demo watashi wa nihongo ga dekimasu yo.*"

"*No, no, no English*," the man repeats frantically.

"But right now, at this moment, I'm speaking Japanese to you," says Robynne.

The driver shakes his head.

Robynne bangs angrily against his door and looks around her, lost. A third taxi driver has got out. He walks up to her.

"May I help you?" he asks, in English.

"Certainly. Do you know where the Harvard Academy for International Communication is?"

"That school is closed," says the driver. "An unfortunate incident occurred."

"Yes, I know that," says Robynne, "but I'd still like to go there."

"Are you sure?" asks the driver, looking concerned. "Do you know what happened there? There are angry spirits hanging around there."

"I would still like to go there," repeats Robynne. "Can you take me there?"

"If I have to. We, the people who live in Odawara, stay clear of it. You know what happened to the director?"

Robynne nods briefly.

"Are you from the police?" he looks at her curiously.

"Can you take me there or not?" says Robynne , sharply this time.

"Yes, *lady*, if that's what you want, but I warned you. My apologies."

"Thank you."

The journey takes a little less than ten minutes; they drive inland, through a landscape that immediately becomes steeper. The sea shimmers behind them. The driver asks Robynne all about herself: where she comes from (America), what she thinks of Japan (nice), what she thinks about Japanese people (pleasant), whether she can eat with chopsticks (yes), whether she likes raw fish (really good!) and whether she likes natto (no).

"Aha, there's not a single foreigner that likes it, that stinking soya bean paste of ours," he laughs, "it could be called the Japanese people's version of cheese, don't you think? But then we Japanese don't like the smelly cheese from the West. What do Americans think about that? Do they like French cheese?"

"Some do, some don't," Robynne answers patiently.

"Hmmmm," says the man, reflectively but cheerfully. "Do you really not speak any Japanese?"

"Yes, but I can't get anywhere with it in Japan," says Robynne acerbically.

"Must be poor pronunciation. Say something in Japanese."

"No," says Robynne, and emits a sigh as the car comes to a halt in front of a low concrete building.

"The school," says the driver. "You should throw some salt over your shoulder when you come back outside. You shouldn't risk bringing bad luck onto yourself."

Robynne nods.

"Do you have any salt?"

"Yes," she lies. "Can I call you for the return journey? Do you have a meishi?" She rattles this off in her best Japanese.

"Ahhhh. Very good, very good," says the man approvingly, and with a twinkle in his eye he gives her his card.

Robynne walks over the pavement to the door of the school building. The door is opened by an unusually small man in a brown striped three-piece suit. "Please come in, Mrs. Green. My name is Joshua Popenoe." He offers Robynne his hand. He gives her a name card; she gives him hers. They study one another's cards politely for a few seconds. "Nice to meet you," they both say simultaneously. Popenoe smiles broadly. "Everyone calls me JoshPop," he says.

"That name suits you." Robynne laughs back at the small, jocular American. "Where do you come from, JoshPop?"

"Boston, "says Popenoe.

"You were Mr. Parker's assistant? My condolences on the loss of your employer, JoshPop," says Robynne, more formal now, once they are each sitting on one side of the steel desk.

Popenoe lowers his head. "Thank you."

"I would very much appreciate it if you could tell me everything you know about your employer."

"I understand. Well, let's cut the crap. Jacob Parker was not a nice man, Mrs. Green. Ours was strictly a business relationship. To tell the truth I was already looking for another job, without his knowledge. I know nothing about his private life."

"In what way was Jacob Parker not a nice man?"

"He was ruthless and dishonest in business, he treated his staff badly, and he cheated his clients. He lied. Have a look at these photos." Popenoe indicates a bulletin board. "Those are the portraits of all the teachers, male and female, who have worked here. They are all holding diplomas from Harvard, do you see? And here you can see photos of the Harvard campus. Parker told his clients that all his staff came from Harvard, but he had the diplomas printed himself. Our staff did not come from Harvard. Oh no, they were all backpackers who needed a job. They could have one here if they were prepared to appear in one of those photographs. Some of them were not native speakers of English.

"For the Polaroids of the campus, Parker once visited Harvard. He just went round and took photographs. He also forced me to lie and cheat. One time, one of his female teachers didn't turn up, so he telephoned another one who lives around here who was on a free day. He shouted at her that she'd failed to come in, and she had to come over immediately. The woman stayed calm and said she couldn't because she had her hair dye in. Parker usually drew up the rosters for the students himself, on small scraps of paper. He had the teacher sign them at the bottom and made a copy for himself. After the phone conversation with the teacher, he began to make a new roster right in front of my eyes. He forged her signature and copied the new roster, which showed that she had been scheduled to work that day. The next day, when she came to his office with her roster to show that she had actually been scheduled to have a free day that day, Parker accused her of having forged it. She resigned immediately, and she refused to leave until Parker had paid her off, right down to the last yen. She just sat there, where you're sitting now, until he angrily threw an envelope with the money into her lap. The crazy thing was, he actually believed that she was the one who had been in the wrong, not he. He was furious."

"Do you still remember the name of the teacher?"

"Yes, she was a German lady, Leonora Schmitt."

"Do you know where she lives?"

"She used to live here in Odawara, right near the station, but I don't know whether she still does. I can point the house out to you."

"Could you go there with me soon, in my taxi? Have any documents come to light since the police took everything away from here?"

"No, not that I know," answers Popenoe. He gets up energetically. "Shall I call a taxi?"

"Oh no, please don't," says Robynne. "I'll do that myself in a moment. I have a card from a taxi driver that I can stand, at least just about. Please continue."

"There is not much to tell," says Popenoe. "Parker was a shit who used to cut corners. He always stank of drink and spent hours on the telephone."

"On the telephone? Who was he telephoning?"

"I've no idea. Girlfriends, most likely. He regularly used to shut himself up in his office with the telephone."

"Where was his office? Is it still intact?"

"More or less. Come this way."

On Parker's dreary, brown imitation-wood desk is an outsize pink telephone with a dial.

"Gosh," says Robynne , "that's an old one. You don't often see those nowadays. Isn't that an old payphone?"

"Yes," says Popenoe. "The students could call from here. Parker made money on everything."

"What's the number of this phone?"

"Oh, I don't know that. It wasn't used for incoming calls, only for calling out."

"I must have that number," says Robynne agitatedly. "Do you have a couple of ten-yen coins for me, JoshPop?"

Popenoe feels in his trouser pocket.

"Thank you."

Popenoe bows, rather obsequiously for an American.

Impatiently, Robynne dials Mochizuki's number, hangs up and dials it again. "Damn." She swipes irritably against the orange curtains. A musty smell comes off the material as it sways back and forth. Come on, Mochizuki, answer me, she thinks. "Could you please leave me alone for a moment?" she says authoritatively to Popenoe. He hastily leaves the room. Robynne tries Mochizuki's number again. She bangs the receiver onto the cradle impatiently and looks around the room. There is a metal filing cabinet against the wall. She opens one of the doors. The shelves are empty and dusty. On the floor of the cabinet is a cardboard box. She pulls it right out of the cabinet. It is full of socks rolled up into balls. She untucks a couple of pairs. They are short, loose-knit girls' socks in pastel colours. Holding a handful of socks, she walks to the corridor and calls out, "JoshPop, quick!"

Popenoe hastens in obligingly.

"In the cupboard in Parker's room, there is a box with socks in it."

Popenoe nods. "Parker wanted the children in the children's room to take off their shoes. Then he gave them extra socks."

"Only the girls? These are all girls' socks."

"No, the boys too, but they were embarrassed about the bright colours. Parker had already promised that he would make a boys' box, but nothing came of it."

"Did he go to buy the socks himself?" asks Robynne. "Didn't he ask you to do that? You being his assistant?"

"Yes, er, no, he went to buy the socks himself," says Popenoe, bemused. "Is that strange?"

"Maybe that's what I should ask you. Is it strange?"

Popenoe thinks quickly. "Yes, it is strange, a boss who goes out to buy socks like that himself."

"Do you see?"

"What do you mean?"

"It is strange, that's all I mean."

Popenoe nods.

"May I call the taxi now?" asks Robynne.

"Of course."

Robynne goes back into Parker's office, throws the socks back into the box and walks to the front door holding the box in her arms.

"You want to take them with you?" He takes the box from her.

The taxi driver opens the lid of the boot and gets out. Popenoe puts the box into the luggage compartment.

"To the teacher's house," Robynne says to Popenoe, who slides in onto the back seat next to her and immediately starts talking to the driver. Robynne tries to ignore the two men's chatter.

At Leonora Schmitt's house, Popenoe gets out of the taxi and indicates that Robynne should stay where she is. After he has rung the doorbell, Robynne sees him deep in conversation with someone who has opened the door slightly. Once, the door almost closes. Popenoe pushes it back open and points at the taxi. A thin, rather stooped woman with bright red hennaed hair darts a hostile glance at Robynne.

Robynne gets out and walks quickly towards her. "Police. My name is Green," she says, and offers the woman her hand.

"I want nothing to do with this business," the woman says, anxiously.

"You have to, Mrs. Schmitt. May I come in?"

"Well, no, I'd rather you didn't. Do you have a search warrant?"

"Make my day, Mrs. Schmitt. I can obtain a search warrant, or I can require you to come to the police station

228

with me. It will be quicker and easier for both of us if you cooperate."

Leonora Schmitt opens the door in silence.

"This is about Parker," says Robynne.

"Yes, I'm sure it is," says Leonora Schmitt.

"I heard from JoshPop what Parker did to you."

"Yes, he was standing there watching," says Leonora Schmitt, and looks fiercely at Popenoe.

"Sorry," he says.

"So I don't have very good memories of that man, Mrs. Green. He was a horrible obnoxious person, a brute. From the first day I worked for him, I hated him. He prowled around and looked through the windows in the doors of the classrooms while I was giving lessons; he stuck his nose into everything, how I was dressed, how I was made up. Nothing was right in his eyes. He even made me pose with a diploma from Harvard, for a Polaroid photo which was posted up at the school."

"Yes, I heard that story from JoshPop."

"He was also paranoid about students having private lessons. He was afraid that I secretly made arrangements with his students. He was right about that. Four of my students asked if I could give them private lessons, then left the school. They used to come to my home without him knowing. They still come here every week. Would you like some tea, Mrs. Green?"

"Thank you, I would."

"I'll be getting back," says Popenoe.

Robynne nods. "JoshPop, I will be contacting you again. Thank you for your help and information."

"Not at all, any time. This is my private card, so you

can reach me at home as well," says Popenoe, and walks quickly out of the room.

"Has he gone?" asks Leonora Schmitt when she returns, bearing a tray with tea and cups.

Robynne nods.

"The coward," says Leonora Schmitt and puts the tray onto a low table.

"Parker was not just unpleasant," she says, while she stands over the tea tray, "He was also pathetic. He ingratiated himself to get up the ladder and kicked down the people below him. You could see through him right away. People made fun of him. He noticed that, so he quickly did everything possible to curry favour with his employees and clients. One afternoon he laid on a Christmas party for the children at the school. First he put socks by the door for all the children to put on, and then he danced with the kids. They were wearing Disney masks. And Parker was wearing a Freddy Krueger mask, of the serial killer, for heavens' sake. He kept playing the same stupid song, 'Rudolph, The Red-Nosed Reindeer', and spent the whole afternoon trying to get the children whipped up into a frenzy. They got caught up in the excitement of it all. I found it scary. Parker was going around like a lunatic, beating time with a police truncheon, or something like that. It amazes me that he himself was the victim of a serial killer. I think he could just as well have been the murderer. At the beginning, I even helped him with his institute! The first phone line he applied for is still in my name. At that time he didn't even have a resident's permit, and because I had a student visa at that time, I was able to apply for a phone line from NTT. I went to the NTT office with him, I bought the line in my name, and I paid for it. I never got my money back. I still have the papers."

"May I see them?" asks Robynne, breathlessly.

"Yes, you can even keep them if you can arrange for me to have the money reimbursed. A line still costs sixty thousand yen." She goes to look for the forms in a side room then gives them to Robynne.

"Thank you. Could I also ask you to give me the addresses and telephone numbers of the four private students?"

Leonora Schmitt looks at her. "That will present me with some problems, Mrs. Green."

"No, Mrs. Schmitt, it won't present you with any problems, because Parker is dead."

Back from Odawara just in time for the afternoon review, Robynne has reported to her colleagues on her expedition to the Harvard Academy for International Communication and is now telling them about her visit to Mrs. Schmitt.

"Leonora Schmitt was still in possession of the application papers for the first telephone line that Parker requested. The telephone number does not appear on the list of calls compiled by the Japanese police because this number was registered not in Parker's name, but in the name of Mrs. Schmitt. All the other telephones in the building were in Parker's name. I called Mochizuki-san about this at around half-past eleven from Odawara station, and by the time I arrived at the hotel Schmitt's students had already been interviewed – yes, Mochizuki-san's team is lightning-fast. One of them apparently lives right by the school. She told us that Jacob Parker used to sit in his office very late into the evening. She could see him clearly from her house. He used to sit behind the lighted window, with a bottle in front of him, and make phone calls."

A tense silence has fallen over the conference room.

Robynne continues. "With the help of NTT, Mochizuki-san has just come up with the numbers dialled from the payphone in Parker's office in the months before Parker's death. One number appears very frequently. It is the number of the Help! Foundation, a help and information line for foreigners in Tokyo."

"Well," says Bertus Hogenelst, "as we say in the Netherlands, this adds a few sods to the dyke. But why does that number not appear in Parker's address book?"

"Because the number is 03-03-03-03-03-03, which anyone can remember."

"Then it could be that other victims also had that number in their heads," observes Bertus.

"Indeed."

"Very good, Green-san," says Mochizuki. "Do you have any idea what the connection is with the box of socks?" He stoops, then puts onto the table the cardboard box containing the rolled-up socks that Robynne had found in Parker's cupboard.

"No, but I'm following that up, Mochizuki-san."

Mochizuki nods.

"I am sure you are, Green-san. I would now like to tell you more about Croo-san's adventures," he says, his face impassive. "I am going to show you one of the videotapes from Hughes de Keuninck's cellar. The recording was made in Japan. It is not what you would call pleasant material. Croo-san has viewed dozens of these tapes. Please prepare yourselves." Mochizuki switches on the video recorder. A close-up of a pale breast comes into frame. The nipple stiffens under a stream of smoking candle wax. The scene is accompanied by sickly muzak.

"Oh God!" says Lucia Valenti. The music swells, then the camera moves back a little. Now there are two breasts in the frame, and also the glittering point of a long, sharp knife. The point pierces the soft white flesh right by the nipple; then the movements speed up, and with a quick slash of the blade the nipple is sliced off. The frame fills up with blood. Lucy utters a cry and abruptly moves her chair backwards, then sits with her head between her knees and moans.

Mochizuki switches off the machine. "Oh," he says.

Silva goes over and ministers to Lucia, rubbing her back.

"Sorry," she says, "I cannot stand the sight of blood." Yukiko brings her a glass of water.

"We have seen enough," says Mochizuki. "The rest of the film is best left to the imagination. You probably remember the case in England concerning two young boys who murdered a toddler. Croo-san studied this case. Croo-san studies everything that combines the media and crime. Every now and then there are discussions in the media about the influence of violent visual material on society. We suspect, for example, that the English boys were strongly influenced by the film *Child's Play*, in which violent acts are committed by a doll. It is interesting that in addition to the videotapes, Croo-san was in possession of a list of the members of the video club. It contains all the names, but not the addresses. However, my team has been able to follow up on all the members, with one exception. Some have no alibi for the evening on which Hughes de Keuninck was murdered. I will read out the names of these people – all of them.

Min Doi: Professor at the University for Economics in Tokyo, Japanese.

Jiro Tsunoi: Photographer, Japanese.

Johnathan Whittaker: Psychiatrist, American.

Kunikaze Komamoto: businessman, Japanese.

And finally, there is the unknown person: a certain Jeromy Wanderfogel.

"We have started investigating the movements of these first four individuals. We know nothing about Jeromy Wanderfogel, who also appears on the list. The name Wanderfogel also appeared in the credits of the film of which you have just seen a fragment, and in a number of others. As you have been able to read in Croo-san's reports, he approached the Kenji Casting Bureau. He found the telephone number of this bureau in a pornographic magazine that he was researching and was signed up by a certain Mr. Curbain, a maker of soft-porn films."

There is suppressed laughter. Mochizuki clears his throat and continues. "In this way, Croo-san hoped to establish contact with the pornographic actors in Wanderfogel's films. He did not succeed, but Curbain seems to have been a friend of the victim Larry Maxwell, and Curbain's assistant Bruce was superficially acquainted with the victim Irina Skoynich. It is this Bruce who is mentioned in

Irina's letter to Katharina in Poznan. Bruce believes that Irina Skoynich had worked with Wanderfogel.

"When Curbain heard from Croo-san that Hughes de Keuninck of QueBook had also been murdered, he was very shocked. He said that he would go to the police the following day. He did not do so, so the police have started looking for him. The two Australians, Bruce and Cleopatra, and the American, Jessie, have also been questioned in the meantime. As a result, Croo-san could not build on the relationship of trust he had established on the day the film was made. They still didn't know who Croo-san really was, but they would certainly have been wary about helping him get hold of Wanderfogel's number. Given that we questioned Curbain only one day after Croo-san had asked about Wanderfogel, in Croo's eyes Curbain would have suspected that Croo-san had reported him to the police. Croo-san was very angry about this.

"The reason he was expelled was not just that he played a role in a pornographic film and accepted money for it. His anger at my decision to go and interview Curbain himself also played a part. He was going his own way too much. Because of that he could not think clearly any more, and he was making mistakes. We cannot have that kind of behaviour in a team that is so carefully monitored. If the press gets wind of this...."

Bertus Hogenelst coughs noisily. Robynne Green lays a soothing hand on his shoulder.

"So what should he have done, Mochizuki-san?" asks Bettina. "Should he have said he would do it for nothing?"

"He gave me the money," says Mochizuki. "What should I have done with it? Put it into my bag?"

"Send it to a good cause," suggests Bertus.

"The press. We cannot have that," continues Mochizuki. "None of this alters the fact that at the moment, Wanderfogel is our chief suspect, and we don't have any leads on him. In the last twenty, years no one under the name of Jeromy Wanderfogel has entered Japan. His name and films are known in the pornographic world. But apparently those are not the circles he moves in."

"Jeromy Wanderfogel. Too bad the name doesn't begin with an 'I'," sighs Gerardo Silva.

"Many murderers operate under different names. It could well be that he did as well," says Zhiqiang Li. "It even seems likely."

"Yes," says Mochizuki, "We haven't been able to get any more information from Cleopatra, Bruce, Jesse and Curbain than we already have. Irina Skoynich and Larry Maxwell were depressed. Here too there was a superficial relationship. Bruce knew Irina from a bar, and Curbain knew Maxwell from a café that was popular with people involved in films."

"All psychiatrists and psychologists in Tokyo, both Japanese and of other nationalities, have been questioned for a second time – this time, in connection with the victims Irina Skoynich, Hendrick Mechanicus, Larry Maxwell and Hughes de Keuninck. These people all spoke with their psychiatrists at some point, about a telephone helpline. "Welt-san will now report on what followed our visit to the Goethe Institute."

"The bus to the village of Daigo had already left when we arrived at Hachioji station," begins Bettina. "Daigo is very remote, so this meant that the last bus to the village had gone. So we took a taxi for a journey that lasted more than an hour. At the village shop we asked Saburo to take us further up into the mountains in his Land Rover. When the road was not much more than a track, he set us down by a black-painted farmhouse with a thatched roof. There were about ten young Japanese and two Germans staying there, and they told us that Wackwitz had often stayed at the house. Mechanicus had also been there with Tim Smith, during their walks in the area.

"Both Wackwitz and Mechanicus did chores in exchange for their lodging. There are thirty sets of bedding in the house. Cooking takes place over a large fire in a pit in the yard. The setup is a kind of communal society where people come and go. They can receive Yamaguchi's training for free, while on his side he can choose the amateurs for his performances. It is considered a great honour to be allowed to take part in a performance. The amateurs are exploited and treated with disdain by the core group. At the house, Yamaguchi himself has the status of a guru. The dancers receive no money; they have to pay to stay there.

"The Daigo house is being trawled for clues today by one of Mochizuki-san's teams. People who live in the area are also being questioned. I shall be evaluating the results with the help of Watanabe-san later this evening.

"Members of Yamaguchi's core group described Wackwitz as a subservient, diligent young man with a moderate degree of talent," continues Mochizuki. "Yamaguchi-san would have preferred him not to participate in the performances, but Wackwitz kept badgering him until he was admitted to the select group of performers. This was condoned because he had done chores for the group.

"Now comes the clincher. He often telephoned for hours from the pay phone at the dance studio. Here again we are dealing with someone who makes long calls. This afternoon we compared the list of outbound conversations from the three telephones: from Jacob Parker's, which was in the name of Schmitt; from the telephone box near Irina Skoynich's studio; and from the telephone at the dance group. There is one number common to all of them: 03-03-03-03-03-03, the number of the Help! Foundation."

Intense conversations break out between the members of the group.

"We komen dichterbij," Bertus says to Robynne.

"What did you say?"

"We komen dichterbij."

"You're speaking your own language, you idiot, you're speaking Dutch."

"Oh," says Bertus, dumbfounded. "Sorry. I said, 'We're getting closer'."

"Yes," says Robynne.

"it's ludicrous," Fowell says to Bertus, "that the Japanese police were unaware there is a helpline for foreigners."

"And that we didn't come across it," says Bertus.

"We've got it!" says Bettina and drums her knuckles hard on the table.

"The tasks will be shared out anew," shouts Mochizuki above the noise. "We shall have to work right through in the days ahead. There will be no opportunity for free time. Be quiet, please, everyone," he calls out authoritatively. "Just for clarity: there are now three suspects. The breakfast friend, the person known as 'I', and Wanderfogel. Three men."

Sixth of September

Late this evening I went to watch one of the performances by Yamaguchi's group. They have their own little theatre in a cellar in Nakano Fujimitsu. It's called Plan Z. The performance (in Japanese, pronounced '*paafoomansu*') was introduced by a maundering journalist who specialises in commenting on buto performances. He was reasonably clear at the start when he talked about the founders of this form of dance, the '*ankoku butoh*', the dance of darkness. After Japan's defeat in wartime and the atom bombs on Nagasaki and Hiroshima, he said, the only kind of dance that could arise was a contorted, grotesque kind that addressed itself to the earth. I can only reproduce the names of the founders because after the performance I brought back a grimy piece of printed paper – Hijikata and Ono. The first is dead, the other is in his eighties and very sprightly – he's still dancing! The journalist's talk became more woolly as he departed from the facts, and it ended up in a hopeless tangle of imagery, for which he received resounding applause from the audience, who must have numbered about sixty. For all its weirdness, the performance was fascinating: a tangle of white-powdered nudity, ripped kimonos, gaping toothless mouths, rolling eyes, contorting torsos, clawing hands, twisting feet, knees bobbing about.... All this was given an electronic accompaniment by a serious young man behind a sound mixer. It should be said that buto has a certain beauty if it is performed by Japanese people, but as soon as Westerners take part it turns into people pulling funny faces.

Yamaguchi accepted the applause for the choreography, which according to the journalist was completely improvised by the dancers, and invited the public to go and have a drink with the dancers in a room next to the theatre. I went along and sat at a large wooden table, but the journalist began to witter on so much that I couldn't stand it any more, and took the train back to the hotel. On the way, a drunken salaryman accidentally puked over me.

Although we're not allowed to talk about the case with family members, I said to Matthijs on the phone today that films and books about the hunt for serial killers are not much good because they are not true to life. The hunt for a serial killer has more in common with an office job than with a Wild West film. It involves an awful lot of reading, discussing and evaluating, we eat regularly, there is a lot of overtime, the rooms in which we work are stifling and people exercise a pretty rancid sense of humour.

But the case is beginning to become more interesting. Let me line up the issues, so that when I am old, wise and grey, I can look through them again and think back to these times. Our world has collapsed into a desire to find the perpetrator; it has become everyone's obsession.

The victim Wackwitz has led us to the remote isolated house used by Yamaguchi's performance group in Daigo, a village in the mountains. The victim Hendrik Mechanicus also visited that house, with his friend Tim Smith, during their walks.

Phone calls were made to from this house to the 6 × 03 number of the Help! Foundation.

On the list of members of an illegal pornographic video club, Croo saw the name Wanderfogel. This name has also appeared in the credits of several pornographic films. Croo took part in a porno film; Wanderfogel was named by Croo in conversations with the film crew. Some of them knew Wanderfogel by name; he appears to be a producer of violent pornography.

There may have been some kind of relationship between Wanderfogel and the victim Irina. She might have worked for him.

Bruce helped produce the porno film. In Irina's letter to her friend Katharina (Poznan, Poland)0 someone called Bruce was mentioned.

No-one called Jeremy Wanderfogel has entered Japan in the last twenty years.

Bertus is following up a tip that came in from the helpline: a woman with a coloured shawl was spotted in a telephone box, near Irina's studio. The 6 × 03 number of the Help! Foundation was called from this phone box.

Robynne Green researched the Parker affair. She has found an old telephone that was not in Parker's name but in the name of Schmitt, a former employee. The 6 × 03 number of Help! was often called from that phone.

Marcus Bopp had a secret 'breakfast friend', and there was an equally secret conversation partner, called 'I', mentioned in Larry Maxwell's diaries.

This conversation partner is a man, probably with blonde hair; he wears leather; he has a weak chin; he works somewhere where many languages are spoken (speaks 'in tongues'); he is likable and inconspicuous; he possibly makes or has made home-made pornographic films; he was friendly with the victims; and he met them for breakfast somewhere in the city.

The Help! Foundation is being approached this evening.

The atmosphere in the team has become more gloomy since Croo's expulsion. I agree with Bertus that expulsion was too drastic a move; Croo might well have brought us closer to the truth. We're not allowed to have any contact with him now.

Today is the eighth day of the case.

On TV there's a lot about 'Aki Basho', the spring wrestling competition. The programme looked at the diet of sumo wrestlers. They were shovelling down impossible quantities of noodles and rice with vegetables. Even the way their hair is made into a 'topknot' was gone into in detail.

I watched a couple of bouts. Akebono is my favourite. He has a beautiful smooth skin and an elegant, almost feminine style. He pitched Kyokushuzan out of the ring with a graceful throw. He had more trouble with Takanohaha.

Right now, at this moment, I'm taking a sleeping pill for the first time, with a large glass of tap water that smells of chlorine. I can feel my heart beating about this because I'm a bit scared. It is as if I am relinquishing control. I really don't like that.

CHAPTER 8

At half-past six the following morning, on the seventh day of the investigation, the members of the team are sitting in an emergency meeting. The mood is one of deep dismay. They have recently learned from an exhausted Mochizuki that a ninth murder has been committed.

The body of 'Father' Arturo Adel, a 39-year-old Filipino missionary, was discovered by two security staff working at a shopping centre in Shibuya-ku. The remains were found on waste ground at the foot of the hill on which the shopping centre had recently been constructed. The nature of the injuries, and the way in which the body was arranged, laid out on a dish-like array of stones, left no doubt that Adel had been the serial killer's latest victim

There is a tense silence in the conference room. People rub their eyes and necks and massage their temples.

"Shit, shit, shit," says Robynne Green.

Coffee is drunk silently. Breakfast has been ordered and served early, but is all but untouched. Mochizuki takes the floor.

"This crime must have been committed around two o'clock this morning. I have assigned nineteen police officers to make initial enquiries about the victim. As soon as the identities of the people who should be questioned have become clear, I will dispatch one of you to the scene.

"Our pathologist has already examined the scene of the

crime and the remains. There were large pools of blood at the scene, and these appear to contain the HIV virus. There is no evidence of the HIV virus in the blood from the human remains. This means that there is blood from two people at the scene of the crime. The area is now being searched, for drag marks among other things. I am afraid that there might have been two victims last night, and one of them has been moved elsewhere."

"That is not a trademark of the murderer we are looking for," says Bertus Hogenelst sharply. "Why didn't you wake us up, Mochizuki-san? Why did you hand over the most sensitive part of the investigation to the Japanese team? Is that in conformity with the agreement?"

"I thought you really needed your sleep," answers Mochizuki, his countenance impassive.

"I beg your pardon?" says Fowell. "Since when have you been not just our chief inspector, but also our Mother Goose?"

"Mother Goose?" repeats Mochizuki.

"Their mother," translates Watanabe, with another helpless gesture of his hands. "Their carer."

"The timing of this murder doesn't match the previous ones," says Robynne .

"God forbid, could a copycat have emerged here?" says Li loudly.

"Copycat?" Mochizuki lets the word roll around his tongue in an exploratory manner. Then, shaken, he asks, "You mean, someone who is imitating the murderer?"

"It often happens," says Li.

"That really would be a disaster," says Fowell.

"We must not let ourselves be led astray by speculation,"

says Mochizuki. "In fact, we cannot work on this latest case today. Until all necessary information has come in and been processed, we will have to stick with the order of the day."

Bertus sighs, vexed. "I'll complain to the conference coordinator about him, the pig-headed idiot," he whispers in Robynne's ear.

"First things first," she whispers back, and gestures that Bertus should now pay attention.

"Late yesterday evening the director of the Help! Foundation was called out of bed, and we made appointments for initial interviews and enquiries at the Foundation," says Mochizuki. "There are two hundred and fifty-two volunteers working at the Foundation. We can go there after two o'clock this afternoon when all the permanent staff have been assembled. I would therefore now like to divide up the tasks again. In the light of these sudden new developments, I must regrettably cancel the free time of Lacoste-san today, and of Inoue-san tomorrow." Yvonne and Yukiko nod.

"The Director of Help! is an American lady called Molly Tender. She will not tell the staff in advance what we are coming to enquire about. Molly Tender has explained to me how the Foundation is structured and assured me that we are free to look around anywhere. However, she did point out that the Foundation is obliged to keep the names of its clients confidential. At the administration department of Help! there is a permanent staff of five women, including Molly Tender. It is housed in an annexe of the Lutheran Church in Iidabashi. I would like to send Green-san there this afternoon."

Robynne Green nods. "As you wish," she says.

"Then there is a small department where a team of four counsellors, mainly pastoral counsellors, receive clients. Their clients are referred by the administration department. The counsellors all work part-time, on an on-call basis. They are all willing to be available this afternoon. The department is located in Shibuya, in an annex to the Baptist Church. I would like to send Valenti-san there." Lucia nods silently.

"There is also a Volunteer Training Department. Training is compulsory for all volunteers before they staff the phones. There is a training session in the undercroft of the Baptist Church this evening. Could Silva-san go there?"

"Fine," says Silva.

"And finally, there is a small office for telephone counselling. This is the one with the six-times-zero-three number that was phoned by the victims. The office is on the third floor of the Lutheran Church, also in Iidabashi. Could Hogenelst-san go there this afternoon, after midday? One of Mrs. Molly Tender's staff will be available, as well as two of the volunteers who staff the telephone lines."

Bertus looks up from his notes slightly grumpily, and nods.

"You can obtain the information you will need today, such as the addresses and locations, the names of the Help! Foundation staff and so on, from Ms. Lacoste and Ms. Inoue at their office, after nine o'clock.

"I would like to ask Welt-san and Fowell-san to act as my watchers here today, so that I can deal with the Arturo Adel affair in my office with my Japanese staff."

Bettina Welt and Jack Fowell nod in agreement, take up their notes and go to sit next to one another at the table. Fowell brings his face close to Bettina's and says something. Bettina says something in reply, while she attempts to avoid Fowell's breath by leaning backwards.

Bertus comes and stands behind them. "I can't let Mochizuki do that," he says. "I'll make sure of that."

Bettina turns towards him amicably. "The investigation is proceeding. Don't try to prod the Japanese into changing, Bertus. It's not a good time to do that."

"Whether he's Japanese or not, it's a disgrace what this man gets up to, and if I try to say anything about it, I draw a blank. He's just an idiot!" Bertus's face is red with anger.

Once Mochizuki has disappeared back to his headquarters, Bettina takes the opportunity to go back to the house used by the group of performers in Daigo, on her own and unannounced. It is also a way of avoiding having to spend a day at the hotel with Fowell. The midday heat bears down on the platforms at Hachioji station. In the beige bus that takes her to Daigo it is so humid that the windows steam up heavily and cannot be wiped clear.

Just in time, Bettina recognises the area in the forest where a tree has fallen down. It marks the location where she has to press on the button with the pink light that requests the bus to stop.

The shady traffic circle is pleasantly cool. The rushing streams far in the distance sound surreally familiar to Bettina, as if she is coming home.

At Saburo's stuffy little shop she stands still for a moment. Should she ask Saburo to drive her up to the house? She steps into the darkness of the shop. Inside it is quiet; it smells the way that cardboard wrappers of ice cream taste when they are licked. She calls out several times, first shyly, then gradually more loudly. Nothing stirs. It is quiet at the back of the shop as well. Bettina walks carefully towards the back room, between old-fashioned freezer chests and low shelves bearing groceries. Cautiously, she slides open the wooden door. On the tatami, in the dark room at the back containing only a few cardboard boxes, Saburo lies in a deep sleep. He reeks of alcohol that he has recently consumed. Whisky, thinks Bettina. She shrugs her shoulders, slips outside and walks to the mountain path that leads to Daigo.

The rushing of swiftly flowing streams becomes louder. Bettina stands and shifts back and forth to listen to it. Or is it the sound of the wind in the treetops? Walking in the cool air does her good after all the excitement, in a hotel that was too cold, in Tokyo, where it was too hot. She feels a surge of excitement in her stomach.

Daigo is further than she thought. Her feet are aching by the time she recognises the point where the road becomes an unsurfaced track. Cautiously she follows the track up to the house and immediately sees a pair of sliding doors open to the external wooden veranda. She calls out "*Gomenkudasai*," then mounts the three steps to the veranda.

A thin woman emerges and looks at her short-sightedly from behind a pair of dirty spectacles.

"Is Mr. Yamaguchi available?" asks Bettina. The

woman shakes her head and stands there defensively, almost blankly, her arms hanging limp.

"Are you here alone?"

The woman nods. "Who are you?"

"I am a member of the international police team investigating the Fish Murders," says Bettina. "I have been here once before, with Mochizuki-san. Does that name mean anything to you?"

The woman shakes her head.

"And who are you?"

"Momo Ashikawa," says the woman, and bows. "I am Yamaguchi-san's assistant and principal female dancer."

"May I ask you a few questions?"

Momo Ashikawa nods stiffly and walks abruptly inside. Bettina wants to follow her, but Momo has already returned outside with two flat, square cushions. She carefully places them adjacent to one another on the wooden veranda and indicates that Bettina should sit down. Bettina gives her a sharp sideways glance.

Momo answers her questions in a monotone. She looks directly ahead, staring through her spectacles at the motionless bamboo thicket from which comes a deafening cacophony of cicadas.

"I'm mainly interested in the foreigners who sometimes come to stay here," says Bettina. "How many foreigners come here to stay, usually?"

"Oh, that depends," says Momo. "Sometimes there are a lot, at other times very few. There are some who have been coming a long time."

"How long has this house been owned by the group?"

"About ten years. Why?"

"Can you remember which foreigners have stayed here in, say, the last year and a half?"

"Oh yes," says Momo, and thinks for a while. "Ianu-san, of course, but he is dead, you know that."

"Yes," says Bettina. "When did you hear that?"

"A couple of days ago, from Yamaguchi-san. We were very shocked. Then we realised we had not seen him for quite a long time."

"Didn't you miss him? He used to do jobs for you and your group."

"Yes, but we were really better off without him. We found he didn't fit in."

"Why not?"

"Because he gave the impression of being unstable. To function in our group, you have to have a strong character and listen carefully to Yamaguchi-san. We found Ianu-san too selfish and fragile. Our group must progress, must develop, even go overseas. To do that, you have to be strong."

"Why did Wackwitz give the impression of being unstable?"

"He was very solitary, and in the evenings he used to make phone calls too often and for too long. That is not the way we do things here. For example, we have little contact with our families."

"And who else was there?"

"Oh, a man from the Netherlands."

"Hendrick Mechanicus?"

"Er, no, yes, Hendrikku- san did come, but also Jannu-san."

"Jan?"

"Yes."

"Jan who?"

"I don't know, I don't know any of their surnames. The foreigners here were only known by their first names."

"And Hendrick?"

"Yes, sometimes he came along with a tall American. They used to sleep here so they could continue walking the next day."

"Tim?"

"Timmu-san! Yes, that was his name."

"Any more?"

Momo furrows her brow and enumerates them: "Jannu-san, Hendrikku-san, Jeromi-san, Timmu-san, Ianu-san …"

"Jan, Hendrick, Jeromy, Tim and Ian? Who is Jeromy, does he still come sometimes?" asks Bettina, as neutrally as she can. She feels her cheeks glowing. Momo nods. She appears not to notice Bettina's excitement.

"He helps us sometimes with the video equipment. He is good at filming and repairing cameras. He films the training for us here sometimes when we work outside."

"What does he look like? What's his surname?"

"I've no idea what his surname is. He is tall and thin. He wears a scarf around his head. In the evenings, sometimes he dresses up. I think he is a leather freak. He puts on a motorcycle suit and he goes to the city, I think. Later he comes back with the clothes."

"Whose clothes are they?"

"They are a part of our costume collection. But we haven't used them for years. Now we use kimonos, or we dance naked. We used to wear a lot of uniforms and things like that. It's an old police uniform, I think."

"Is the uniform here?"

"No idea. I think Jeromy-san thinks of it as his property. He's been using it for a year or two. We're not really bothered."

"May I see if I can find it?"

"It would be better if I did that," says Momo. "Do you want to come with me?" She stands up, and Bettina follows her into the gloomy house. A six-tatami-mat room behind a sliding door is full of colourful costumes. Many of them are torn, and the heap gives off a strong smell of mothballs.

Bettina watches Momo kick the pile of clothes around. "There is no leather here, you can feel there isn't," she says, then kneels down and begins to fold up some of the pieces of clothing. Bettina sits next to her and helps her fold and tidy. They do this in silence for about twenty minutes.

"No," Bettina says, "it isn't here." Momo stands up and beckons to Bettina. They walk over the wooden floor of the verandah; Bettina in her socks, Momo on her strong brown bare feet. She springs down adroitly from the walkway and stretches a hand out to Bettina. In her stockinged feet, Bettina jumps onto the dead spruce branches on the ground. Just as Momo has done, she bends down to look below the frame of the house. Underneath the house, right in the centre, is a dark, shapeless bundle.

"Just as I thought," says Momo. "He's hidden it. He must have been embarrassed."

Bettina nods. "How often does he come here to pick it up?"

"No idea, I'm not always here. But he always phones before he comes here."

"Could you phone me if he phones?" asks Bettina, with a catch in her breath.

Momo nods thoughtfully.

Bettina gives her a card. "I'm going to swear you to secrecy. You must not tell anybody what has occurred between us."

"Not even Yamaguchi-san?" asks Momo, her eyes round with astonishment behind her spectacles.

"Not even Yamaguchi-san," Bettina confirms.

At two o'clock the same afternoon, Robynne Green introduces herself to Molly Tender, the director of the Help! Foundation. Molly Tender is a large woman in her late forties. She wears a huge girlish summer skirt with a bow at the back. Her feet are stuck into white orthopaedic sandals and are crooked from arthritis. Breathing heavily, she goes ahead of Robynne into a small office. Her blue eyes are bright in her broad, open face, and her voice is surprisingly clear, warm and strong as she says to Robynne, "Please sit down, Mrs. Green. What can I get you? Coffee?"

"Yes please, Mrs. Tender, and a glass of water if you wouldn't mind."

"A Cola Light, perhaps? I drink twelve every day, maybe more. An addiction, you could call it. Go ahead, have one." She bends down from her chair and reaches under her desk to a cardboard box with cans in it.

"No, thank you, I'd prefer water."

"I understand that you have come here in connection with those sickening murders," says Molly Tender. "But I won't ask you how your enquiries have brought you to our humble organisation. I am at your disposal. Maybe it's best if I explain how we work here."

"I'd very much like to hear that, Mrs. Tender."

An Asian woman comes in and puts a tray onto the desk.

"Thank you, March," says Molly and looks at the woman fondly. "Would you mind very much if I took my shoes off, Mrs. Green? They make my feet ache."

"Please feel free."

Molly Tender pulls off her white sandals. As she massages her knobbly toes, she starts to speak. "Help! was started in 1973. It was set up by a few missionary wives who regularly had to deal with displaced people in the foreign community. They were the ones who had to offer a floor to people who were stranded or homeless, because nowhere else offered help. They were the ones who took people into their homes when Japanese hospitals, the Salvation Army and other organisations could not offer any more help. And it was they who got to hear the stories of isolation, culture shock, depression and loneliness, at their kitchen tables, particularly at night and at Christmas or New Year. At that time there were only about ten missionary families in Tokyo. Not nearly enough to cope with all that suffering. The women decided to organise themselves and open a telephone helpline. They staffed the telephone in shifts. At the beginning, they operated from rooms at their homes.

"During the 1970s, a result of economic growth, many

more foreigners came to Tokyo; principally Europeans and Americans. In the 1980s people also came from other parts of Asia: Thailand, the Philippines, Korea, Indonesia. At the beginning of the 1990s, when the economic recession really began, they were augmented by a lot of people from the Middle East. They arrived in their thousands, from Pakistan, Iraq, Iran, to work in the construction industry, to collect the rubbish, to sweep the streets... Many came on tourist visas and worked illegally.

"A separate category was made up of hostesses and prostitutes. They came mostly from Thailand and the Philippines. These girls had a huge need for help. To cope with the steady stream of people with these needs, the missionary wives began training other women to work on the telephones. Our training emerged from this, and over time its quality has become high. The course is run twice a year.

"It is still mainly women who apply to take this training; they are the wives of managers and industrialists who have themselves come to feel a sense of isolation because of their husbands being transferred to Tokyo. They are women who have been accustomed to having a certain standing within the community.

"Because they were having to deal with so many different belief systems, they decided that they would no longer enforce the Christian character of the counselling, and instead adopted a non-sectarian approach. Out of all this, Help! was established. We now have two hundred and fifty volunteers, and the lines are open twenty-four hours a day. Our volunteers work at least one shift per month. We provide counselling in crisis situations, and for personal, legal and financial problems. We are part of a network of lawyers, hospitals and other aid organisations.

"We have a good reputation in the community, including the business community. We are still not subsidised by any public body, but we receive money from churches, from the business community and from organisations and individuals to keep the wheels turning. And we hold a yearly fundraising campaign, the 'Friends of Help!'."

"At the moment we receive about forty thousand calls per year – that is, about a hundred a day. The problems range from the very simple – people who have lost their way in the metro system – to the very serious – attempted suicide, crime... We get telephone calls from perpetrators and victims, from elderly people and children, from business people and vagrants... And of course we do our best to provide a listening ear, and if people can afford it, we offer face-to-face counselling. We help the poorest people free of charge.

"We have four counsellors available on an on-call basis. Not nearly enough, but it's a start. We are constantly grappling with financial problems. I have young women working for me who are married to Japanese men. They work too many hours for a low salary. March Ogino from the Philippines, who brought us our coffee, is the accountant. Then there is Emma Doi, a Dutchwoman, who is my personal secretary; Stephany Dan, an American, who is the coordinator of volunteers; and Henrietta Kuwahara, also from the Netherlands. She does the fundraising and organises the admission of clients. They speak Japanese and they know what it means to live as a foreigner in this society. We are a close-knit quintet, and I would ask you to tread as carefully as you can when you present them with that dreadful case of yours. They are my children, as it were, and I owe them a lot."

"I would like to question them. I promise to be as brief as I can and to take up as little of their time as possible."

"Fine," says Molly Tender. "Can I do anything more for you?"

"Later in the day perhaps. Thank you very much, Mrs. Tender, for telling me all about the Foundation. If you have no objection I would now like to have a word with your ladies."

Molly Tender accompanies Robynne to the small office where the women are concentrating on their work. The furniture is worn and the computers are old-fashioned.

"Girls," says Molly Tender fondly, "this is Robynne Green."

The women of Help! look tired, but they have the same bright eyes as Molly Tender. They break off from their work and invite Robynne to come and sit at a table in a side room. It is shabby and bare, but clean and tidy. An orange enamelled medallion with a praying figure of Mary on an oak board is hanging on the wall.

"I have to ask you some questions. We have a lead that has brought us to your organisation. I would like to ask for your cooperation."

The women around the table look at her solemnly.

"Please don't look so serious. First, please tell me what you all do," says Robynne.

"It's really nothing special," begins March, with an off-hand laugh. "We do our bit to keep the place going. We are months behind with the administration and finances, but you just get used to that. We do what we can."

"I myself don't really understand what brought me to do this kind of job," says Henrietta Kuwahara. "The days are long and it's poorly paid, but I have never felt so useful before. There's a real need for what we do. I'm a loyal member of the congregation at the Tokyo Union Church, but I have to wonder whether the churches are doing enough for the homeless, the lonely... I don't think they are. Our volunteers are so well trained, so competent, so motivated... It's still women who have to take on the burden of providing assistance. Terrible, isn't it?"

"Right on the button, Henrietta," says March, the small Filipina. "I manage the finances, along with Molly," she says to Robynne. "As I said, it is a bit of a mess. But the phone bills are always paid on time, so that we can stay open. And our creditors are not troublesome, and they are discreet, thanks to our good name in the foreign community. If it leaks out that a police investigation is going on inside this organisation I am afraid that it will all be over as far as the goodwill is concerned."

"I am Molly's secretary. I organise her appointments and write her letters. I am a punctual person. If Molly didn't have me..." Emma says.

"That's true," says Molly from the central office space, where she is shuffling papers around. "I'm a scatterbrain, emotional and impulsive."

"And you?" Robynne asks Henrietta.

"I approach charities and businesses. I organise an annual fundraising campaign and cultural events such as concerts and exhibitions. In addition, for four hours a day I organise the referral of clients to our team of psychiatrists and psychologists. So I work partly for Molly and partly for the clinical department, which has a different director."

"How does the referral process work, exactly?" asks Robynne.

"I have phone contact with the people who have been advised by the helpline to go into therapy. They call me and I write a report on their problems. On the basis of this report I steer them towards one of the counsellors who specialises in their type of problem."

"So you are in close contact with the clients and you know what their problems are," says Robynne.

"Yes, but you should understand that that information is confidential and cannot be released without a reason, even to the police. All our volunteers work under aliases. The foreign community is relatively small, and our service has to remain anonymous at the telephone counselling stage."

"I understand," says Robynne Green.

"I should explain who I am and what I do," says Stephany. "I am the coordinator of the volunteers. I'm in charge of our training programmes, I draw up the monthly work roster and I coordinate the contacts with repeat callers."

"What are repeat callers?"

"People who call us regularly, for example a couple of times a day, sometimes over a period of years. We have developed special guidelines for them. In contrast to normal callers, they are subject to a time limit, for example, otherwise they would simply clog up the lines. They are often people who have made depression a lifestyle; our 'professional victims'. They mostly refuse to go into therapy and keep calling us with their immediate problems."

"I find your organisation impressive," says Robynne.

"I hope that will continue to be the case," says Henrietta pointedly. "An investigation like yours, it's certainly not the kind of thing we need, I'm sure you understand that."

"Yes, I do understand that," says Robynne.

Lucia Valenti is in a room in the annex to the Baptist Church in Shibuya, waiting for the four professional counsellors from Help!. Bored, she looks around her at the small room furnished with old chairs and tables. There is a blotchy, light green carpet. Lucia drags her heels over it, making marks, and picks at a stray piece of rattan on the armrest of her chair. She lets it snap rhythmically against the curved bamboo: snapsnapsnap. The noise echoes, bleak and bare, round the gloomy little room. Pale light falls through a window of reinforced glass onto the yellowing patterned wallpaper. A faulty fluorescent light bulb flickers irritatingly. The air conditioner roars. The room is cold and damp and smells of old mattresses. Lucia shivers.

The four counsellors arrive at the same time; two men and two women. One of the men introduces himself as Ron Sullivan, director of the clinical department. He introduces the other three: Bob Thomson, counsellor and pastor; Ginny Cohen, specialising in drugs and alcohol; and Grace DeVries, specialising in relationship therapy. A little later, Henrietta Kuwahara, who has been just been interviewed by Robynne Green, comes in panting.

"May I inspect the reports?" asks Robynne.

"Well, that depends which reports you mean," says Ron Sullivan, "but if you're referring to the information about our clients, then I'll have to say no for today and discuss it tomorrow with a lawyer."

"What I want to know is whether, among the Help! volunteers or your clients, there is someone who answers to the following description:

– is male;

– has thin, mousy hair;

– wears leather;

– has a weak mouth and chin;

– speaks English with a South American or North European accent;

– has a fascination with knives;

– has a normal life socially, and in the community;

– his name may begin with an 'I', or he may be known as Jeremy Wanderfogel."

"No," says Ron Sullivan. "Look, Mrs. Valenti, you must understand that we can't open the files on our clients just like that. I have no reason to think any of my clients has the Fish Murders on his conscience. I am ready to repeat that statement under oath. As far as the volunteers are concerned, I haven't known them all very long. You would do better to ask Molly Tender about that."

"In that case, I know enough for the time being," says Lucia. "If I were you I'd make another appointment this afternoon, Mr. Sullivan, with a lawyer, because I'm afraid we will have to look at those files."

"I'll do that," says Ron Sullivan.

The counsellors look at one another for a moment; then Grace DeVries starts to speak. She is a large, swarthy woman with long, loose hair. Her voice is strong and she articulates precisely and clearly.

"Henrietta has an initial conversation by telephone. The client is referred to her by a volunteer on the helpline. She finds out the nature of the problem and puts the client into a particular category according to what it is. On the basis of this classification she discusses with Ron Sullivan who is the best person to deal with the client. After that, the relevant counsellor is informed. If he approves therapy, then an appointment is made for a course of sessions."

"Is a client ever turned away?" asks Lucia.

"As a general rule, no. But there is sometimes a waiting list."

"However ill they are, our clients are seldom referred to psychiatric hospitals because then they are in a Japanese organisation and can end up becoming even more isolated. We attempt to keep our clients independent as long as possible. As long as a person is in a fit state to carry on living as a foreigner in this city, things are not as bad as he might think.

"Henrietta, Ginny, Bob Thompson and I are psychologists and are under the supervision of Ron Sullivan, who is a psychiatrist. We cannot prescribe medicines, not even Ron, because we studied at American universities. So Ron works with a Japanese psychiatrist who writes the prescriptions and signs them off.

"The clients have to come to us, we don't do home visits. That applies also to our therapeutic strategy. Though there is a crisis team. If somebody becomes ill on the street, for example from taking drugs, the crisis team swings into action. The team works very closely with the police and a hospital. We are prepared for any possible situation."

The same afternoon, Mochizuki receives the report informing him of the name of the Zen monastery at which Marco Polo sometimes used to stay. It is in the mountains of Minakami and is affiliated with the Rinzai sect.

On their arrival, Watanabe sets Mochizuki down at the monastery gate and remains sitting in the car.

Mochizuki has never been inside a monastery. He looks around uncertainly. He is admitted by a prior in a black robe. Cautiously, he steps into another world. The prior leads him over the wooden floor of the dojo. A tremendous din echoes from inside the monastery building: stamping, shouting, the sharp clang of a bell.

"The work ritual," explains the prior. At the outside gateway a man is lying on the ground. To Mochizuki's shock, the prior hits the man with a long stick. The man goes for a short walk and then returns and lies down, motionless, with his forehead pressed against the wooden floor.

"That is against the law. You are not allowed to hit someone with a stick," Mochizuki says to the prior.

"This man is an entirely willing participant in this ritual," the prior answers dryly.

"Ritual? You hit him really hard."

"Mochizuki-san, do you think a ritual is a thing of the body, or of the mind?"

"Of the mind," says Mochizuki.

The prior shakes his head. "Of the body," he says. "A ritual must be felt."

They walk further, along long passages, at the end of which the prior opens the door of a washroom. In a stone room shaven-headed monks are standing in silence, carefully washing rice. They look like statues formed of stone just as much as the washroom itself, silent and untouchable. Mochizuki wants to go inside to talk to them, but the prior forestalls him and says he must wait.

Outside there is a dull clang and the sound of clear copper bells.

"The *zazen* has begun," says the prior.

For forty minutes they watch from a distance as thirty monks, clad in black kimonos and white under-kimonos, sit on long platforms in rows, silent and motionless, with their backs to the middle of the room. Their hands are folded so that the four fingers of each hand rest against the others, the tips of the thumbs against one other. Mochizuki tries to imitate them with his own large, square hands. A monk carrying a piece of wood walks up and down the row of seated monks, striking the shoulders of any who allow themselves to be distracted.

After the meditation, a service begins in another room. Mochizuki listens intently to the unfamiliar, penetrating tones of the chants.

Then it is mealtime. A wooden fish hangs on the ceiling of the dining room. This is struck with a clapper while rice gruel is scooped from wooden buckets into black bowls. Bowls of vegetables and miso soup are set down onto low tables. Mochizuki sips cautiously at the thin gruel, while a tumult breaks out again in the kitchen. The monks fill pails with water, then clean the floors and walls at a furious pace, stamping their feet hard as they do so. The prior tells him that the chores are changed every four months: cooking, cleaning, shaving heads, working on the land, clearing snow…

Mochizuki accosts a small group. The prior allows him to do so unhindered.

"Is life difficult here?"

"The first months are the hardest. A lot become sick then," answers a man with a sunny expression on his face.

"Does anyone ever die?" asks Mochizuki.

"That happened once," says another man, laughing.

"And why are you yourself here?"

"*So ne*," replies the monk, and scratches his chin reflectively.

"Does it have to do with enlightenment?"

"Enlightenment? What do you mean?"

"Er, *satori*, spiritual liberation."

"*So, ne.*"

Mochizuki turns to the prior who is still standing just behind him and asks, "Why in heaven's name did you hit that man?"

"To give him a chance to stretch his legs a little."

"What's he doing lying there?"

"He is begging to be taken on as a monk."

"Did Marco Polo have to do that as well?"

"Yes, of course."

"How long has that man been lying there?"

"Three days."

"When will he be allowed to go inside?"

266

"*So, ne.*"

"Was Marco Polo a good pupil?"

"*So, ne,* no, not really. He did not have enough discipline. Monastery life made him unhappy, but he himself did not know that yet."

"is there a telephone here?"

"No, but there is a telephone box on the road outside."

"Are the monks allowed to go outside in the evenings?"

The prior thinks for a moment. "That is not the intention, but it is not prohibited."

"Did Marco Polo ever go out in the evenings?"

"I wouldn't know. That is not something we check on."

After this conversation, during which the monks gathered curiously round Mochizuki, they divide up into groups, disciplined once again. The prior explains that some are going to clear leaves, others to work on the land. Mochizuki and the prior follow one group into the monastery building, where an old monk in a yellow kimono is sitting on a wooden chair. The other monks ask him questions in a respectful tone. To these he gives bizarre answers which he shouts out loudly, even though the monks are standing very close to him.

Mochizuki stands perplexed, listening.

"What was the shape of your face before you were born? What is the sound made by a copper bell without a clapper? How many millimetres does the crown of the head wear away per year? If a snail on the back of a running cat emerges from its shell in the same direction that the cat is moving while the cat is running on the roof of a train against the direction that the train is moving, does the snail move forwards?"

The prior says that a team that does chores is to start work again shortly, and after that there will be more sitting meditation.

Mochizuki feels he has seen enough, and takes his leave. In the car he breathlessly gives a report to Watanabe, who has been sitting waiting for him all this time.

They drive down the road towards the telephone box. Mochizuki gets out and dictates the number to Watanabe. The two men then drive back to Tokyo in silence; Mochizuki deep in thought, Watanabe respecting the silence.

Later in the evening they report back to the international team. Even by this time Mochizuki's surprise has not yet completely worn off, and this comes through in his voice.

"I requested NTT to investigate whether the same number had often been called from the phone box down the road. That was quickly worked out, because the phone box was seldom used. Except for one period of time, the phone conversations all took place in the evenings, and the first ones were long – they lasted an hour, or even longer. After that they were more frequent, but shorter; ten or twelve minutes. The calls were made to Help!

"The prior said that Marco Polo was unhappy at the monastery, but that he didn't know it himself. Ladies and gentlemen, don't you think that's an interesting statement from that man?"

"Mochizuki-san, how is it that life in a Zen monastery is so surprising to you?" asks Bertus in puzzlement.

"I was barely aware of the existence of monasteries like this," says Mochizuki. "Sometimes it seems as if foreigners know more about our traditional culture than we do ourselves. It is always the foreigners who talk about Noh and Kabuki theatre, about Taiko drums, about Zen Buddhism. I've never come into contact with these things myself. Part of Marco Polo's life unfolded in the strange world of that Zen monastery.

"I need time to think about this," he says. "I wish you all a restful night. I can be reached at my room here in the hotel. As the investigation is speeding up, I will be staying at the hotel from now on."

Seventh of September

The unthinkable has happened: a new murder has been committed. The victim is 'Father' Arturo Adel. There is a lot of confusion because two kinds of human blood have been found at the scene of the crime. So not only Father Adel's. Were there two victims, and has one of them been placed somewhere else? Is this in fact 'our' killer's doing? The murder took place a couple of hours earlier than the other murders. Has a copycat murderer started work? Or is the murderer panicking because he is being hunted, and might he be getting careless?

It's beginning to get really frustrating. The more things happen, the less I can tell Matthijs. Because of that our phone conversations have become a bit unreal.

On the off-chance I went to the dance group's house in Daigo. We knew that Wackwitz and Mechanicus had been there, but the fact that it was also one of Wanderfogel's stamping grounds is new. Could Croo's porno film have had some sense in it? If so, then it is particularly bad that Croo was thrown out.

I didn't take the clothing under the house. Mochizuki was all praise and deep bows. The unbelievable has happened: Mochizuki is taking me seriously.

Green and Valenti followed a trail to the Help! Foundation today. My photographs are still giving the lab problems. It doesn't help to get angry.

I am terribly sleepy from the sleeping pills that Li gave me, but it may also be because we were all rounded up so early. A lot of people in the team are suffering from insomnia, according to Li.

An hour ago I heard noises in Lucia's room next door. Valenti has been very quiet up to now, but now Silva is clearly visiting her. It sounds as though they have got very cosy. Valenti told Silva loudly that in Japanese, 'to come' (as in to climax) is 'to go'. A Japanese man says 'I go' when he's coming. Gales of laughter from both of them.

I found Mochizuki particularly moving today when he was telling us about the Zen monastery. He had no idea that that kind of institution still existed within his own culture. Isn't that crazy. In the West, Zen is all over the place.

I went to the big stationer's in Shinjuku today and am writing this with yet another new pen. This time it's a 'My Kitty'. I now have twelve new pens.

The Far East network informs us that:

– A condolence book for Mother Teresa has been opened at the Indian embassy;

– An American supermarket has been opened in Osaka;

– There are pregnancy courses for foreigners in Tokyo.

The trial of Asahara, the sect leader, is taking some strange turns. Asahara used the word "phowa" in connection with the murder of the lawyer and his wife, but also in connection with other murders. This appears to be a religious term from Sanskrit that means the 'transforming of souls to higher spheres'. Although it is obvious to one and all that he is guilty, Asahara has good lawyers, and they are trying to offload the responsibility onto one of his followers.

CHAPTER 9

The Baptist church is an ugly building, probably dating from the 1960s. The towers, which barely project above the roof of the nave, are covered in triangular beige tiles. The wide cracks in the walls, the results of earthquakes, have been messily patched up with cement. Quirkily shaped flat pieces of pink natural stone have been pressed onto the concrete of the staircases that lead up to the various entrances. On one of the staircases, in front of the main entrance, there is a small group of people standing around smoking.

"Pardon me, would you happen to know where the Help! training is taking place?" Silva asks, of no one in particular.

"In the basement," says a middle-aged woman adorned with jewellery. "Are you a new trainee?"

"No," says Silva, and quickly walks further up the staircase, away from her Poison perfume, through the big glass front door.

After a look around, during which he comes across a huge kitchen with cupboards bearing labels, he finds a staircase carpeted in moss green, leading downstairs. He walks past a row of humming beverage vending machines towards the muffled sound of voices in a large room, then pushes the door open and enters a harshly lit classroom where people are sitting in groups on plastic folding chairs, talking softly. He stands for a moment on the beige lino-leum tiles, looking lost, gazing around, and then approaches a woman sorting out papers on a grand piano in the corner of the room.

She looks up. "Mr. Silva? I am Stephany Dan. I coordinate the training for the volunteers." They shake hands. Stephany Dan, a stout, pale woman with flaming red hair, looks at him amicably. Silva sees Native American origins. From her large nose, two deep grooves run down to the corners of her wide mouth. She looks like me, thinks Silva, with a slight shock.

"What exactly can I do for you?" she asks Silva. "I have already been interviewed, by your colleague Mrs. Green yesterday."

"First of all, I would like to know how you work here. Would you have any objection if I spent a morning observing the training?"

"I would have to run that past the group. Our volunteers and trainees value their anonymity, you understand."

"What happens if a client rings in and gets a counsellor on the line whose voice he recognises, or vice-versa, a counsellor recognises a client's voice?" asks Silva.

"Then the counsellor says, 'I believe we may know one another. Would you like another counsellor?' Usually, the answer is yes."

"I see."

"In a moment I will explain your presence to the group, and if no one has any objection you can observe us," says Stephany. "This morning we are discussing AIDS. Please take a seat. We start in five minutes."

She introduces Silva as a minister from Mexico who is

interested in the work of the Foundation. No-one in the group objects to his being there. He has placed his folding chair slightly outside the circle of trainees, adjacent to the grand piano in the corner. He takes a small notebook out of his trouser pocket.

After Stephany has given an introductory talk and distributed piles of paper, she hands the floor to a slim, bald man. He is introduced to the group as Frank Laing. Frank immediately begins speaking rapidly.

"The foreign male community in Tokyo has created a new myth. A persistent rumour is doing the rounds: Japanese condoms are too small for Western men. In order to convince you once and for all that this is untrue, I would now like you to feel under your chairs."

Their faces expressing disbelief, the trainees grope around under the seats of their chairs. With some difficulty, they each pull out an envelope. Frank Laing has also taken one out from under his chair, and is busy extracting the contents. A few women in the circle giggle and a fat man laughs in long, high peals. Frank Laing has taken off his shoes and socks and asks his audience to do the same. In front of the haphazardly cleaned blackboard, he sits on a steel desk. With slow concentration, he rolls a light-green condom onto the bare toes of his left foot. He pulls it up as far as his instep, then over his heel, and rolls it up his leg until it extends to just below his hairy knee. Then he looks around the room triumphantly.

"So it's nonsense!"

Amid a growing mood of hilarity, pink, black, flesh-coloured, striped and polka-dotted condoms are rolled over bare feet, nylon stockings, socks and trouser legs.

274

Onto his right leg, which is wound around with a thick bandage, Frank Laing rolls a condom decorated with an American flag.

"With this experiment we have proved that it is not true that Japanese condoms are too small for Western men. The condom is at the moment the only method – I repeat, *the only method* – of protection against AIDS. Do not be confused by reports in the media. There have been reports of AIDS cures since 1990, but we are now about seven years down the road and that cure has not yet arrived. Do not be misled by the reports about new cocktails of medications. These cocktails extend and improve life for AIDS patients, but they have serious side-effects and we know nothing about their effects in the long term.

"Thirty percent of our incoming calls are about AIDS and the problems connected with it. In this training session and the following three, you will be brought thoroughly up to date with the medical, social and psychological aspects of this illness. This first session is easy, so you can get used to the subject, which on the whole is not comical or a matter for levity. Is there anyone in this room who has friends or family members who have died from AIDS?"

Fourteen hands go up.

"Is there anyone in this hall who has lost friends to AIDS?"

Seven hands go up.

"Is there anyone in this hall who has family members who are suffering from AIDS, or who are seropositive?"

Two fingers go up.

"Is there anyone in this hall who has AIDS, or who is seropositive?"

No one reacts.

"AIDS is coming ever-closer," says Frank Laing. "You will get many frightened people on the phone. People who have had unsafe sex or whose condom has split, people who have questions. They will talk about their sexual organs, and those of their partner. They will use all kinds of names for the sexual organs, in various languages, because not all of our callers have English as their mother tongue. Among you here today, there are also various nationalities represented. I would like you to sit in groups of five and list all the names, both inoffensive and vulgar, that you can come up with for:

One: the female sex organs,

Two: the male sex organ,

Three: the sexual act."

The trainees remain seated. Low-pitched laugher emanates from some of them.

"Don't delay," says Frank Laing. "You must get over your embarrassment."

The trainers spread themselves out over the hall and lean over the notepaper in their laps.

"You have half an hour," Frank Laing calls out. "After that I will write them all on the board, so you will never forget them."

From each gently murmuring group, laughter is occasionally audible. Frank sits watching passively from behind his desk. Silva walks up to him.

"How many of these people here have been connected with Help! for some time?"

"Er... those would be Stephany and me, and Griepsimee Essayan, the dark woman in that little group behind at the back of the hall. She is a trainer. And Walt Pebbles, the balding man over on the left, and Peter Tate, the man with the long hair." Frank points them out.

"I would like to have a word with you and those people before long."

"I will tell them," says Frank, "but after the trainers' meeting, please. We have one after each session of the course."

"That's fine," says Silva. "What time will you be finished, and where should I wait?"

"Oh, you can go and sit upstairs in the kitchen," says Frank. "You should see us come out around eleven."

"I don't really feel like being present for an hour while people think up synonyms for the names of the sexual organs and the sex act," says Silva, in a reserved tone. "I'll go and sit in the kitchen beforehand."

"That's fine," says Frank laughing. "Do you know a good synonym for 'female sex organ'?"

"Hairburger," says Silva, and escapes over the shiny linoleum and through the doorway, leaving Frank choking with laughter.

"I won't waste your time and energy with small talk," says Silva, when the trainers are sitting with him around the large table in the kitchen.

"Our enquiries into the person who committed the Fish Murders have brought us to your organisation. I have brought each of you a file with information about the murders. Please read it carefully and review your thoughts over the past year. In the next few days, please think about all the people with whom you have been in contact via this organisation." Silva counts them off on

277

his fingers: "Counsellors, volunteers and professionals. Clients. Trainees. Staff members. Management members. Benefactors…"

"There has been another victim. His identity is as yet unknown. The HIV virus was detected in the blood of this victim. Your organisation receives many telephone calls in connection with HIV and AIDS. Please make very thorough notes of these conversations. Call us immediately if you encounter anything that could have something to do with the murders, even if it seems insignificant. Better to make one telephone call too many than one telephone call too few. In the files, I have also provided a summary profile of the likely perpetrator."

"We don't have much to go on as far as a profile is concerned," says Frank Laing. "We are a telephone helpline. We never see our clients."

"Did I say that the perpetrator was a client?" asks Silva.

"What kind of signs should we be looking out for? I don't really understand," says one of the trainers.

"Anything, anything at all. You must think for yourselves, not in collusion with colleagues, about whether there has been something, in the past year…" Silva counts off on his fingers again: "that has attracted your attention, that you don't understand, that you have a strange feeling about, that scared you, that brought about an inexplicable unpleasant physical reaction…."

"What then? What should we do then?" asks Frank.

"Call me immediately," says Silva. "My card is in the file."

"We'll do that," says Frank, and he looks around the table. The trainers nod gravely.

Frank half-rises from his chair, awkwardly and partly supporting himself on his hands. "Thanks again for that word," he says, grinning.

"Not at all. I'm counting on you."

"One more thing," says Silva, as he turns next to the door, "do you have a diagram of the structure of this organisation, on paper?"

"No," says Frank Laing, "but I can draw one for you. I've been working here for eleven years. If you can let the trainers go home now, I can draw one on the board."

"Fine."

Silva walks behind Frank into the training room. Now that it is empty, their voices ring out. As he explains, Frank Laing draws on the dirty blackboard with a squeaky chalk. When he stretches above his head to draw a rectangle for 'management', Silva sees that he still has the condoms and the bandage on his legs.

Bertus Hogenelst is pushed out of the yellow Chuo-line train onto the platform of Iidabashi station. His foot almost gets stuck in the space between the train and the platform. He stubs his ankle painfully.

Limping and groaning softly, he allows himself to be swept forward by the crowd towards the exit. There are groups of middle-school girls in the crowd. From their blonde ponytails and uniforms of Scottish plaid, it is evident that there is a French school in this area. Brash and loud, the children do not give the rest of the crowd a glance.

Bertus allows his train ticket to be sucked in by a metal slit at the exit to the station, then squeezes himself through the narrow swing doors covered in artificial leather. Once away from the crowd, he rubs his ankle with a pained face.

Then he takes out of his pocket the map that Yvonne and Yukiko have drawn for him and studies it, frowning. A policeman comes out of the *koban* right next to the station exit.

"Can I help you?"

Bertus nods. "Do you speak English?"

The policeman shakes his head self-consciously. "Can I help you only."

"Church," says Bertus.

"Church," repeats the policeman, reflecting.

Bertus shows him the map that Yukiko has drawn.

"Ah, *kyokai. Yes, yes, yes.*" He points clearly using his hands and his fingers: up the hill, third street on the left. "*Kentukki Furaido Chikken,*" he says.

Bertus thinks for a moment. "Ah! Kentucky Fried Chicken."

"Straight on, second street on the right." The policeman draws a horizontal line in the palm of his hand with his index finger and indicates the middle of the line: there! He points in front of himself and with both hands he draws in the air the shape of a church.

"*Domo arigato gozaimashita,*" says Bertus. This is the first time that he has used this phrase in a real situation. He has kept practising it in his hotel room. Sweating, he makes his way up the hill. His shirt shows large spots of sweat that make him embarrassed, and he suddenly has an unbearable itch in his crotch.

The Lutheran Church is a lumpish, white-plastered building. The corridors are firmly carpeted in red, and they smell of beeswax and bleach. There is no-one to be seen.

Bertus scratches himself at length, lurking and gazing around. Then he ascends a wide wooden staircase and fetches up on the third floor, in a maze of small corridors leading onto small offices. In one of these, a balding Japanese man sits behind three towering piles of paper, staring straight ahead.

"Help!?" asks Bertus. The man makes a vague gesture to the left and then stares ahead absent-mindedly once again. A small, fat woman in a skirt that is much too tight comes up to Bertus.

"Help!? asks Bertus again. She takes him cordially by the hand and leads him through the labyrinth. Bertus cannot walk beside her because the corridor is too narrow. He limps awkwardly behind her. With her free hand, she points at his foot.

"*Itai?*" she asks.

Bertus nods, hoping that this is the right response.

She indicates a door. "Help!"

"Thank you," says Bertus, and gives her small hand a friendly squeeze.

"*Atsui?*" she asks, and points unabashed at the patches of sweat on his shirt. "*Bye,*" she says then, and waves girlishly.

"*Bye,*" says Bertus and waves back using the same small movements. Then he knocks on the door she has indicated. A shock of flaming red hair appears. Stephany Dan immediately puts a finger to her lips.

"Mr. Hogenelst?" she whispers, and gestures that he

can come in. The walls of the small room are hung with blackboards and pieces of paper bearing internal memos, frayed letters, cut-out cartoon strips and photos. Two telephone counsellors sit side by side, separated from one another by a sound-proof screen and speaking solicitously into the microphones on their headsets.

In a corner of the room there is a fridge with coffee stains on it, humming loudly. Stephany Dan takes two folding chairs from the corner and points to the door. Bertus takes the chairs from her and puts them next to one another on the narrow corridor under a noisy electric fan.

"At least we can talk quietly here," says Stephany. They sit down on the chairs. Their red hair flutters up and down in the rhythm of the fan, hers bright and fiery, his dull and thin.

"Move up a little bit, redhead, out of the wind," says Stephany, laughing.

"What's going on in that room?" asks Bertus.

"First I'll explain everything to you, then you can go and have a quick look, quietly. The counsellors think you are the director of the SOS line in the Netherlands, you see. You're visiting so you can learn from us. They will just carry on working quietly. They have headsets, as you saw, and there are no trainees coming along this afternoon."

"Trainees?"

"Yes, they come and listen in, and later they take on shifts themselves. Then the experienced counsellor listens in. After three listening shifts and three work shifts the trainees can work the lines independently, as long as the experienced counsellor is happy for them to do that."

"How long does a shift last?"

"The day shifts last four hours, the night ones six."

"You said that the counsellors listen in. Could I do that later?"

Stephany thinks for a moment. "Yes, I don't see why not," she says eventually, "but you would have to sign a confidentiality agreement."

"Are there reports on the incoming calls?"

"Yes, brief notes on special forms. They are put into drawers, and then arranged according to the nature of the problem. An hour before their shifts begin, the counsellors have to be there to read through the forms for the month before, so that they can get a good grasp of the nature of the particular problems, and the clients don't have to start again from the beginning. The form has the name, sex, age and the nationality of the client, at least if the client provides them. We don't ask for them. We can often guess the nationality and the age. We usually give clients nicknames. We do that especially for the ones we refer to as repeat callers, to make it easier for us. Of course the clients have no idea of their nicknames. Our counsellors work under aliases, so they are not immediately identifiable as counsellors in the outside world. There are lists of the nicknames in the office drawers."

"Do you also help Japanese people?"

"Yes, as long as they speak English. We have a small group of Japanese clients, some of them repeat callers, and a number of Japanese counsellors. They are mostly people who have lived overseas for a long time."

"Do you also have clients' addresses or telephone numbers?"

"No, we never call clients back."

"Could I listen in now?"

"Sure," says Stephany. "I'll just get hold of a confidentiality agreement form."

Bertus takes his chair and goes into the little room. He sits next to one of the counsellors. The counsellor gestures at a second telephone. Bertus takes the receiver off the hook. The counsellor presses a button.

"Then I stuck my hand into the aquarium," Bertus hears a quavering woman's voice say.

"Hmm," says the counsellor.

"And then I suddenly noticed that the fish was bleeding. And there was also a bit of poo coming out of it. Can fish have AIDS as well? I was so worried last night!"

"You mean you're worried you might have caught AIDS from a fish?" asks the counsellor.

"Yes. Is that possible?"

"No, madam, I can put your mind at rest. That's absolutely out of the question."

"Are you quite sure?"

"Yes, I'm quite sure of that."

"Are you quite sure you're sure?"

"Yes, I'm quite sure I'm sure, madam."

"Oh, wonderful. That's a load off my mind. Thank you very, very much."

"Not at all, madam."

"Bye."

"Good-bye, madam."

The telephone rings again immediately.

"Help!, good afternoon, can I help you?"

"Yes," says a woman's voice, "I would like to make parasols. You know, from paper, the Japanese ones."

"Yes?"

"And now I'm wondering where you can buy the ribs, you know, the little sticks under the paper. I've got the big one already. Made of bamboo. It was easy to find."

"One moment please." Without turning a hair, the counsellor rapidly thumbs through a thick red book.

"I will give you a couple of addresses." Bertus gives the counsellor an incredulous look. The counsellor laughs.

"Not at all. Goodbye, madam."

The telephone rings again as soon as the connection has been broken.

"Haaaaaai, this is Yuki" says a girl's voice, slurred.

"Hi Yuki, how are you?" asks the counsellor. *This is a repeat caller,* he writes on a notepad, for Bertus's benefit.

"Oh, not so good. Who are you?"

"I am James," says the counsellor.

"Can I speak with Iman?"

"No, he's not here at the moment. Don't you want to talk to me? You have ten minutes, you know that don't you?"

"Yes, yes," the girl says quickly.

"Have you been drinking, Yuki?"

"No, I've had some pills."

"What kind of pills?"

"Sleeping pills."

"Have you taken many of them?"

"No, well, maybe ten."

"Ten? That's too many, Yuki. How long ago did you take them?"

"About fifteen minutes ago."

"I'd like you to try to bring them up, Yuki. Just take the

telephone with you to the toilet."

"Nooooo," whines Yuki.

"Come on Yuki, we've done this before. Ten is too many. You just need to make some lukewarm salt water in the kitchen. Are you at home? Okay, could you go and prepare some salt water?"

"Yeeeees," moans Yuki.

Noises are audible through the receiver. *She has a mobile phone*, the counsellor writes on the notepad for Bertus. *Just like all Japanese girls*, he adds a moment later.

"I'm going over to the toilet now, James."

"Yes, Yuki, you do that. Have a good drink of salt water, then put your finger down your throat."

There is a sound of gagging and vomiting, then of a toilet being flushed.

"That's good. That was quick. Has it all gone, do you think?"

"Yeeeees."

"Do you feel better now?"

"Yeeeees. I am so frightened, James."

"Yes, Yuki, I know you're frightened. And can you tell me what you're frightened of?"

"No."

"Yuki, we've asked you that many times. Why don't you just come in and see one of our psychologists?"

"They're all swindlers," says Yuki angrily.

"They're really very good people. I think you need some therapy."

"Oh, you all say that. You're all in it together. My time is up. Bye, James."

"Goodbye, Yuki." The counsellor gives a big sigh and

takes off his headset. "So that was Yuki," he says. "And that's what always happens. It drives me nuts."

"How long has she been calling?" asks Bertus.

"About ten years," says the counsellor, and sighs again. "My colleague there looks as though she has a heavy call going on. Go and have a listen." He points to his neighbour. Bertus takes his chair and takes the receiver off the hook. He hears a low sobbing sound. The counsellor is silent. The sobbing continues uninterrupted. Bertus cannot hear whether it is coming from a man or a woman.

Then comes a voice. "She wears a necklace with a metal point."

"Yes?"

"Last night she came home… "

There is sniffling and gurgling that goes on for a long time.

"Just take it easy," says the counsellor "I have all the time in the world."

"She stabbed me with the point," says the voice. "She flew at me, yanked the necklace from her neck and went on the rampage like a madwoman. I'm still injured."

"Your wife abused you with an iron pin?"

"Yes, last night." The man cries out, in a high voice.

"Where are you now? Are you safe?"

"I'm at home."

"And where is your wife?"

"I don't know."

"Have you been to see a doctor?"

"No."

"Are your injuries serious?"

"I don't think they're so bad that I need to go to a

doctor. It is more the shock. She was rampaging around like a madwoman...."

Bertus gently puts the receiver on the hook and sighs. Why do people volunteer to spend four hours listening to this kind of story? What is it that makes me come over to a faraway country to look for a serial killer? He opens the drawer under the desk. The counsellor helpfully moves his chair back slightly. There is a well-thumbed, plasticised list of names in the drawer. Bertus's eyes move down towards the 'I's:

Nickname	Real name	Languages
Ida	Emma Rabinowitz	English, Russian
Idi	Hideo Nøre	English, Finnish, Eskimo languages
Igmar	Boris Norg	English, Danish, Swedish, Portuguese, Japanese
Iman	Frank Laing	English, Spanish, Portuguese, Japanese, German, French
Inder	Radi Komas	English, Japanese, Spanish, French, Norwegian, Hindi
Ingeborg	Kaatje Visser	English, Dutch
Irdin	Shikil Mohammed	English, Punjabi

Nickname	Real name	Languages
Irma	Griepsimee Essayan	English, Armenian, Japanese, Greek
Isaac	David Mayflower	English, Hebrew
Ivan	Vladimir Seki	English, Russian, Polish

Bertus goes into the corridor and photocopies the list. Then he sits at an empty desk in a corner of the counselling room and looks around. Stephany comes in and gives him a cup of coffee poured from a grubby thermos flask, along with some little bags of sugar and milk powder and a plastic stirrer, then leaves the room again. Bertus drinks reflectively, bites on the cardboard rim of his cup and looks at the blackboard hanging on the opposite wall. It also shows a list of names. Bertus's hand makes an involuntary movement. He splutters on his coffee, drops the cup, holds the warm fabric of his trousers away from his thighs, for all the good it might do, and stares wide-eyed at the blackboard. Then he runs out of the room and along the corridor. He looks wildly around him, then calls out: "Stephanyyyyyy!"

Doors open everywhere, and people stare at him.

"Stephany! cries Bertus again, hoarsely. Stephany comes running. Her large bosom sways up and down.

"Please be quiet," she hisses angrily.

Bertus puts his heavy arm around Stephany's robust

waist and drags her into the counselling room. She looks at him, shocked.

"There," he points. The counsellors listen imperturbably, concentrating on their clients.

"There!"

"What?" asks Stephany "and please be quiet."

"There, there. It says Marc O'Polo there," whispers Bertus. "Why is 'Marc O'Polo' written up there?"

Stephany takes his arm and pulls him along the corridor. "That's the list of repeat callers," she says. "Those names are not real. They're the names we've given them. I've just explained that to you."

Bertus swallows. "Please excuse me." He turns and goes back into the counselling room. Stephany follows him. Bertus stands in front of the blackboard and reads carefully.

"I have a list of the repeat callers on paper," whispers Stephany. She rummages around in one of the drawers of the desk. "Come out to the corridor with me."

Bertus takes his chair again and puts it under the fan again and takes the list out of Stephany's hands. Stephany sits next to him and puts her hand on his arm.

"So what's all this about, Mr. Hogenelst?" Their hair is being ruffled rhythmically. Neither pays any attention. Bertus leans over the list and reads through it quickly.

"Faids?" He asks.

"Fear of AIDS," says Stephany. Bertus carries on reading.

Repeat caller	Nationality	Minutes	Problem category
Angel	Australia	15	Psychological
Bean Paste	Japan	None	Heavy breather
Beethoven	Germany	15	Loneliness
Boris Yeltsin	Russia	15	Drink
Cardboard	Sweden	10	AIDS
Cowboy	England	10	Psychological
Desert Storm	USA	10	?
Elvis	USA	10	?
Flipper	?	15	Loneliness
Goethe	Germany		Loneliness
Hercule	Belgium	15	Pornography
Imelda	Phillipines	15	Depression
John lennon	USA	15	Psychological
Lassie	?	10	Sex
Liz Taylor	USA	10	Suicide
Madam Mao	China	15	FAIDS
Manolito	?	15	Loneliness
Marc O'Polo	Italy	10	Psychological
Maria	USA	10	Religion
Nakasone	Japan	5	Psychological
Napoleon	?	10	Psychological
Picasso	Switserland	10	Sex
Piggy-back	Poland	20	Loneliness

Repeat caller	Nationality	Minutes	Problem category
Raicoat	USA	10	?
Rembrandt	Netherlands	20	Loneliness
Sadam	?	5	Power/weapons
Samovar	Russia	25	Homesickness
Skippy	Australia	5	Homesickness?
Socks	USA	5	Sex
Tokyo Runner	USA	5	Sex
Tomboy	Finland	15	FAIDS
Underwear	?	none	Heavy breather
Weather Forcaster	?	10	FAIDS
Yuki	Japan	10	Anxiety

Bertus groans.

"So this is it at last," he says, and looks at Stephany. "This is it!"

"Would you like to see the descriptions of these people?" asks Stephany. She puts her hand on Bertus's arm again.

They go into the counselling room while Bertus looks abstractedly at the coffee stains on his trousers. "May I make a phone call?" he asks, when Stephany comes back with a pile of coloured files.

Stephany nods and takes him calmly by the shoulder. "There." She points at a telephone hanging on the wall at the end of the corridor.

"There will be a few people coming here," says Bertus, when he is back sitting on the chair next to her. "Is there a conference room we can use?"

"I'll arrange one," says Stephany, and puts the pile of coloured files onto Bertus's lap.

"Ah, says Bertus softly, and opens the first file.

Robynne Green lies on the hotel bed in her *nemaki*, hands folded behind her damp head, and reflects on her visit to Molly Tender and her staff. She has taken her report about this visit to Yukiko and Yvonne. She had gone downstairs using the staircase again. Her thoughts wander. On the floor above, just behind the door to the stairwell, she had smelled Bertus Hogenelst. In the ashtray screwed to the wall she had observed a half-smoked filter cigarette; she had fished the stub out of the sand using two fingers and looked at the brand. Mild Seven Light. The brand which Bertus had gone around with since he had finished his Caballeros. She had pinched the filter between her lips for a moment and then pressed her whole body against the wall at the spot next to the ashtray, where he had stood smoking a cigarette and must also have leaned against the wall. Shocked by her own behaviour and glad that no one had caught her in the act, she had gone back to her room to take a shower and rest for a couple of hours.

In the room next to hers, Lucia sits behind her desk once again, writing her report about the Help! Foundation.

Mochizuki is at his head office in the Kasumigaseki district, occupied with the Arturo Adel affair. Drag tracks have been found at the scene of the crime, probably from the heel of a foot.

In the small conference room at the hotel, Bettina Welt, Jack Fowell and Silva are leaning over the huge enlargements that Bettina has had made of all the photos of Bopp, Mechanicus and Wackwitz in which reflections of the photographer are visible.

In Mechanicus's eyes, in Wackwitz's beer glass and in Bopp's sunglasses, which hang a little awry on a chain around his neck, there is a reflection of the same person taking the picture each time: an inconstant, distorted, shadowy form.

In Mechanicus's eyeball, he is tall and thin; in the ridges of Wackwitz's beer glass, he is short and fat; and in Bopp's Ray-Bans, he is stretched out diagonally. In the photo with the Ray-Bans, thin, lank hair is visible; medium-brown, blowing in the wind. The sun is reflected off the silver buttons of a black leather jacket, worn open over a white T-shirt.

Next to Bettina's photos lies a copy of the print shop photograph of Maxwell, blown up to A3 size. In the background there is a quarter-sheet showing a black-clad form which seems to be moving back suddenly behind the pink curtains.

"The figure in this photo, meaning the perpetrator, realised that he had accidentally been caught for eternity in the company of one of his future victims, and tried to get rid of the card from the print shop," says Fowell.

"You might think he would have torn up the card right away," Silva remarks. Fowell gives Silva the card of the picture showing himself and Watanabe with the panda.

"Just try it," he says. "The paper is so stiff that if he'd tried to tear it up he would have drawn Wackwitz's attention to what he was doing."

"You're right," says Silva, tugging hard at the card with both hands. He takes a magnifying glass from the table and peers at the image. "He seems to be wearing a cap, look." He gives Bettina the magnifying glass.

"It's hard to say," she says. "You can't see it clearly enough. It could even be a shawl. We now have images of the perpetrator, but he's still just as vague as he was before. It's enough to drive you mad."

She bites her lip reflectively. "I would swear these photos were taken by an Asian. This vague figure, who must be our murderer. Or certainly someone who's lived in Japan for a long time and has adopted the habits of people here. He asked his victims to say 'cheese' when he took their photos."

The trio continue to examine the collection of material lying on the table.

"These are the photos of the deboned meat and poultry," says Fowell. "I've divided the pieces of meat into three groups: those where the butchering went well, those where it went reasonably well, and those where there was an error. If the knife is not used quickly and skillfully then there are rough edges, in the meat and the poultry. Even in the case of the most successful parts you can see rough bits here and there.

"Now have a good look at the shots of the injuries of the victims. They are perfect – even better than my best-executed cuts. The perpetrator must be in a profession, or once have been in a profession, that has to do with cutting; a butcher, a fisherman, a surgeon, I don't know. On De Keuninck's video as well, it struck me that the cuts were very skillfully executed. The nipple could have been sewn back on after that shot, I reckon."

Bettina Welt turns pale.

Something begins to beep in Fowell's jacket pocket. "Shit," he says grinning. "Tamagotchi's calling. Let me just see what he wants now." He brings the egg with its small screen up close to his face.

"I'll just turn this light off," he says. "Tamagotchi wants to go to sleep". He dexterously presses the little buttons under the screen a couple of times. "So, where were we?"

"The pornographic video," says Bettina.

"Which pornographic film? The one Croo starred in? When are we going to see that?" asks Fowell, maliciously.

"The video that caused Lucia Valenti so much distress," replies Bettina Welt coldly. "We know that one of the members on the list at Hughes De Keuninck's pornography club was also connected with the making of that video film we saw. Jeromy Wanderfogel. He undoubtedly operates under a false name, because in the last twenty years no-one of that name has travelled into or out of Japan. The videotape was made three years ago. If we assume that Wanderfogel is the perpetrator, then Croo's theory about a slow process of development, from an observer being perverted to his becoming a murderer, makes sense. Wanderfogel can also be connected to Irina

Skoynich, via Bruce. On top of that, Wanderfogel has been to the house in Daigo, where he probably met Wackwitz and Mechanicus."

The trio are now looking at Bertus Hogenelst's material: the passport photographs of the victims. "Bertus has noticed that they have an expression in common, around the mouth," says Silva. "A certain frailty, an expression of sulkiness and perhaps dissatisfaction. You can even see it in De Keuninck, even though he is laughing."

"Yes," says Bettina, "now that you mention it."

"But now we have a dilemma," says Silva. "We know almost certain that the perpetrator is to be found among the ranks of the Help! Foundation. In Fowell's reports about Maxwell's diary there is the following sentence. *'They are there with a lot of people and they have the most impossible names. They speak in tongues.'* Up to now we have been thinking in terms of a large international company, but at the Help! Foundation there are all kinds of nationalities. The victims all made their initial contact with the perpetrator by telephone. So he can't have seen their faces. Therefore, he didn't select them on the basis of their appearance."

"This is unbelievable," says Fowell, rubbing his hands together. "It's only a question of days now, maybe even hours. Mark my words."

"I hope you're right," says Bettina Welt.

The door is pushed open and Mochizuki comes in, breathing heavily. He puts two round glass canisters on the table.

"These are the hairs that were found by the remains of Irina Skoynich and Maxwell," he says. "Blonde hairs. I've just brought them from the laboratory."

Jack Fowell, Bettina Welt and Silva line up to peer at the glass canisters with the magnifying glass.

"Scary," says Bettina, "I feel as if I'm close to the murderer when I look at these." Jack Fowell tries to put a hand on her shoulder. Bettina turns away quickly to avoid the gesture. Then the telephone rings.

Mochizuki, Watanabe, Jack Fowell, Gerardo Silva and Bettina Welt have joined Stephany Dan and Bertus Hogenelst at a peeling table in the clammy undercroft of the Lutheran church. There is a bar against one wall. It smells of stale beer and cigarette ends.

"And in a church, too," says Jack Fowell pushing away a full ashtray.

"This is where the international youth club holds its meetings," says Stephany.

"We have him, we have him!" says Bertus, hoarsely. He has almost lost his voice.

Mochizuki says something authoritatively in Japanese. "Show me the files," translates Watanabe, almost as gruffly. "Please," he adds, more gently.

Mochizuki looks him irritatedly. "Please yes please," he says forcefully.

"Look, this is the list of repeat callers," says Bertus raspily. "There are all the nationalities of our victims here: one Swiss, Germans, Americans, a Polish woman, a Dutch woman, a Belgian, a Filipino, Australians, an Italian: Marc O'Polo."

"Holy shit," says Jack Fowell.

"You can say that again, Jack," says Bertus softly.

"How is it that Marco Polo is simply called Marc O'Polo and the rest of them have nicknames?" asks Mochizuki.

"We thought it was an alias. I mean, who is called Marco Polo nowadays? It's not a name you could take seriously," says Stephany.

"God almighty," says Jack Fowell. "We thought that too, at the beginning of the investigation, didn't we Bertus? We thought it wasn't a real name."

Bertus nods. "A number of these people have been dead for a long time, Stephany. Why didn't you notice that they don't call any more?"

Stephany puts both her plump hands in front of her mouth, which is wide open from shock.

"Oh," she says, "how terrible." She lets her hands fall. She looks at her palms in her lap, as though she is praying.

"We are behind with the archiving of the monthly reviews. Months behind. Financial problems, it's chaotic. You mean all these people are dead?" She looks up from her hands and lets them slowly fall to her hips. "I've had all of them on the line at least once," she says, dazed.

"Read out loud what is in the files," says Mochizuki.

Bertus pushes the file towards Jack Fowell. "You read them out, man, my voice is almost gone."

"Let me read them," says Stephany, now quiet, "then you might be able to concentrate better."

"Thank you, Dan-san," says Mochizuki. "Watanabe-san, make a recording!"

"Shall we begin with Marc O'Polo?" asks Stephany. There are nods of agreement.

Stephany reads out:

Man
Italian
Age: 30 – 40
Problem category: psychological, loneliness, delusions, guilt, etc.
Marc is an intelligent man who resides in Japan at intervals.

Sometimes he stays with girlfriends, in which case he uses their telephones to call us; at other times he calls from a phone box. He sometimes spends time in a Zen monastery. There are undoubtedly many women in Mark's life; he speaks about them alternately with dismissiveness and fondness. These women are always Japanese.

Marc's problem is not entirely clear. He is lonely, embittered about 'the Japanese', suffers from culture shock and apparently combines several lives: he is probably well-educated, does 'business' in Italy, leeches off girlfriends, talks about fidelity, marriage and having children, feels guilty about certain (pregnant?) girlfriends, is interested in spiritual matters.

Despite his problems, Marc appears to get along fairly well in Tokyo: he eats, sleeps and bathes.

Instructions for the counsellor:

Don't give Marc much more than ten minutes to 'let off steam'. Try to make it clear to him that his problems are too wide-ranging to discuss on the phone. Emphasise the need for a visit to a psychiatrist or psychologist. Give him clear information about this, even if you have done so before.

"Maria," continues Stephany.

"No," says Mochizuki loudly, "we'll look for the victims first. The Australian?"

"Angel" says Stephany. She reads out:

Man
Australian
Age: 30 – 35
Problem category: mental
Angel is well-spoken, intelligent and mixed-up. He often speaks about angels, hence his name. He makes films, and he appears to confuse himself with the characters that he invents for his films.
Angel is probably very ill (schizophrenic?) and in urgent need of professional help and medication.
Several themes that keep coming up in his conversation are: a whip, James Joyce, American women's hair.
Guidelines for the counsellor:
Try to connect with Angel and give him the number of the referral line. Do not buy into his fantasies. Tell him he has a quarter of an hour, and tell him when that time is up. Tell him that you have the impression he is ill and in need of help.

"That's him," says Fowell, "our Maxwell!"

"Read out the notes about Goethe," says Mochizuki, looking up from his notes.

Man
German
Age: 30 – 35
Problem category: loneliness (?)
Goethe is called Goethe because of his romantic idealism. He has come to Japan because he hopes to find a 'purer world' here. Sometimes he can go on for weeks believing that this is actually the case.

He then comes out with fantastic, overheated stories about the beauty and the serene character of, for example, Japanese women. Once this mania has passed, he becomes depressed about 'the world in general'.

Goethe is doing his best to find a social network. He works at the Goethe Institute, among other places; he has something to do with the theatre there. He says that he has 'never been accepted or understood'.

He regularly visits friendship clubs for foreigners and Japanese, without ever finding a real friend there, male or female.

Instructions for the counsellor:

It is not certain whether Goethe's problems are susceptible to therapy. A course of five to ten sessions would probably be beneficial, because he calls so often. Tell him this.

Because it is not entirely clear why he calls, his time has been reduced to ten minutes. He may well call once in each session. If he calls less often, he can stay longer on the line. (See the notes from the meeting about repeat callers in the repeat callers' drawer for the latest decisions on this.)

"Bingo! And now Hercule," says Mochizuki. Stephany looks down the list.

Man
Belgian
Age: 30 to 35
Problem category: pornography
Hercule is called Hercule (after Hercule Poirot) because he comes from Belgium and likes detective stories.
He is addicted to watching pornographic films, to which he

masturbates. Sometimes he watches six films an evening, he says, and
afterwards he's very ashamed. Moreover, the films that arouse him are
becoming more and more violent.
   He probably also deals in films.

Instructions for the counsellor:
   Let him know that you are not sitting in judgment on him regarding
his problem. Do not go into details about the pornography.

"Oh," says Bertus, shocked.
"Now the man from the Philippines," says Mochizuki.
Stephany looks at him for a moment and reads on.

Imelda
Man
Filipino
Age: ?
Problem category: depression, anxiety
Talks a lot about the 'greed of people in this world'. Gives
examples, among others Imelda Marcos, the wife of the ex-President
of the Philippines, who owned more than a thousand pairs of shoes.
The visible prosperity of Tokyo also causes him a lot of anxiety. He
himself lives very simply, he says, and tries to eat as little as possible.
   He gives the impression of being exhausted.
   He could be a clergyman; he knows a lot about counselling.

Instructions for the counsellor:
Give him a quarter of an hour to twenty minutes. Tell him about
our referral line and about the Filipino Catholic Church, where they
have a good care team.

"Oh, that's Father Adel," says Bertus.

"Yes, of course," says Mochizuki in English. "Now, the Swiss."

Stefany glances down the list:

Picasso
Man
Swiss
Age: 35–45
Problem category: sex
Picasso is so called because he almost always starts a conversation with a story about art. Then he claims that his problems would be solved if only he could paint.

If he is asked about the nature of his problems, he becomes vague and speaks in general terms. They appear to have something to do with his sexuality. He often talks about 'the sensitivity and artistry of homosexuals'. He also asked once if the counsellor thought that everyone was bisexual.

He has something to do with security.

Instructions for the counsellor:
Give Picasso ten minutes per session. Try to bring him to the point of clearly defining his problems, about which he is probably embarrassed.

Let him know that you will not condemn him if he expresses homosexual or bisexual feelings. Tell him about the possibility of therapy. Do not get involved with personal questions. He often asks about your own sexual proclivities. Tell him that is not the point under discussion."

"Marcus Bopp," says everyone in unison.

"Now Rembrandt," says Mochizuki.

Man

Netherlands (?)

Age: 25 to 30

Problem category: loneliness

We have given him the name Rembrandt because he presumably comes from the Netherlands.

Rembrandt's problems are unclear, but they are certainly of a kind that compels him to call us almost every evening. He appears to have got his act together: he studies (Japanese), and has a job.

Instructions for the counsellor:

Give Rembrandt twenty minutes. He likes to talk about his experiences with Japanese people. He likes Japanese women. Make it clear to him that he could talk for an hour if only he didn't call so often. Try to get him to talk about his loneliness and about his own situation. He tends to lapse into generalities.

"That is Mechanicus," says Bertus.

"Yes," says Mochizuki. "And now it will be revealed why Parker had a box in his cupboard with socks in it."

"Socks"," says Stephany.

Man
United States
Age: 35 – 45
Problem category: sex (?)
When Socks gets a man on the line, he wants to talk. If he gets a woman on the line, he wants to talk dirty. He always tells the same story: his pornographic fantasies about naked girls just wearing socks. He is really ashamed about this obsession and says he wants to stop talking dirty. He also says he exposes himself to young girls.

Socks is the director of an English-language school. No-one is aware of his proclivities.

Instructions for the counsellor:
Do not condemn him. Emphasise the possibilities for help. Be very clear: do not go into the details of his fantasies.

"Piggy-back," requests Mochizuki quickly.

"Piggy-back," reads Stephany.

Woman
Polish
Age: 30 – 35
Problem category: loneliness, cultural adjustment issues
She is so named because of her strong inclination to befriend the counsellors. Has almost no friends, speaks the languages she does speak badly. Paints and draws, sometimes exhibits. Sometimes calls

when drunk (drinks a lot, even when alone) and when she does, is flattering and beguiling to the counsellor, whether it's a man or a woman.

Instructions for the counsellor:
Tell her she is calling too often. This is an indication that things are not going well for her. Try to convince her that she must change her situation, because no one else can do it for her. Do not get involved in invitations to exhibitions or evenings out in bars…"

"Poor Irina," says Silva.

Stephany is silent. The tape recorder grinds rhythmically in the centre of the large table. The five police officers look straight ahead, rub their faces, shut their eyes in disbelief.

"We have him," says Bettina Welt.

Stephany shuts the coloured files and slowly pushes the pile into the middle of the cool brown formica table. Watanabe stands up and switches off the tape recorder. Mochizuki stretches, then pulls up his trousers. Bertus Hogenelst clears his throat. He has tears in his eyes.

Jack Fowell bangs his fist on the table, and then strikes the flat of his hand against his right cheek. Stephany Dan weeps soundlessly. Bettina Welt stands up to comfort her.

"We're almost there," she says. "We almost have him."

"Those were our victims," says Mochizuki sharply. "There is still an unknown victim, with AIDS. How many people on this list have AIDS, Dan-san?"

Stephany counts them.

"Four say they have AIDS: Cardboard, Tomboy and Weather Forecaster. Only in the case of Cardboard do we know for certain that it is not faids. He sent us his test results."

"Where do these people live?"

"We don't know."

"Then we now have to look at the potential victims. Mrs. Dan, would you read out from the rest of the list?"

"*Madam Mao,*" begins Stephany, with a quavering voice.

Woman

China

Age: 25 – 30

Problem category: faids

Madam Mao says she has AIDS, in contravention of the fact that she does not have sexual relations and has not done so. She thinks she has caught AIDS from a dog, a cat, a rat, and so on. In particular she is dead scared of monkeys, because somewhere she has got hold of the idea that AIDS was transferred from monkeys to people. Madam Mao is a very child-like young woman, and despite the fact that we have already told her everything that we know about AIDS several times, this fear still dominates her life. She is exhibiting symptoms.

She gets tested regularly and is negative.

Instructions for the counsellor:

Emphasise that correct information is important. Tell her not to believe what she reads in gossip-mongering and sensationalist magazines. Direct her to pharmacies and hospitals that provide information in Chinese (see list).

"From now on, just the most important information, if you wouldn't mind," says Mochizuki. "You can leave out the Japanese people. And also the ones who don't suffer from depression."

Stephany sums up:

Repeat caller	Nationality	Age	Problem category
Beethoven	Germany	?	Loneliness
Cowboy	England	40-45	Psychological
Flipper	?	30-35	Loneliness
Liz Taylor	USA	40-45	Suicide
Madam Mao	China	?	FAIDS
Napoleon	?	?	Psychological
Yuki			

"Yuki, she is Japanese ," says Mochizuki quickly.

"I have heard her speaking," says Bertus.

Mochizuki nods briefly. He thinks quickly. "There is no more time to be lost. One of these people is in danger. We don't know where they live, we cannot have them followed. We will continue this conference at the hotel. If you will all go straight outside, I will call the taxis. Dan-san, are you in a condition to come along with us?"

Stephany Dan nods.

"Just to be clear about everything once more," says Mochizuki, once they are back at the hotel, "their Socks is our Jacob Parker; their Picasso is our Marcus Bopp; their Goethe is our Ian Wackwitz; their Piggy-back is our Irina

Skoynich; their Rembrandt is our Hendrik Mechanicus; their Hercule is our Hughes De Keuninck; their Imelda is our Father Arturo Adel; their Angel is our Larry Maxwell; and finally, their Marc O'Polo is our Marco Polo."

"Now, we must be careful. Among the repeat callers we have mentioned are potential victims of our perpetrator, who is very probably a telephone counsellor, most likely male, whose alias begins with 'I'. The repeat callers do sometimes get other telephone counsellors on the line, but if our perpetrator encounters a repeat caller then he entices him in, in one way or another. We have seven suspects:

Name	Alias	From
Radi Komas	Inder	India
Hideo Nøre	Idi	Finland
Boris Norg	Igmar	Denmark
Shikil Mohammed	Irdin	Pakistan
Vladimir Seki	Ivan	Russia
Frank Laing	Iman	Venezuela
David Mayflower	Isaac	Israel

"Hideo Nøre, Boris Norg, Vladimir Seki and David Mayflower are blond. Frank Laing is bald." Mochizuki pauses and asks Stephany, "How long has Laing been bald?" Stephany starts, then thinks for a moment and says, "a couple of weeks."

"Was he blond before that?" asks Mochizuki.

"Grey."

"We will include him," says Mochizuki quickly. "If we assume that the perpetrator was not wearing a wig while committing the murders, that brings the number of suspects to five. None of them has ever been seen in Help! wearing a black leather jacket, or other leather clothing. Neither has any of them been seen completely dressed in black. From the photos we can't see whether the perpetrator is fat or thin, tall or short. And we don't know where the repeat callers live, so we can't protect them."

The sun shines pitilessly on the large windows, but inside the conference room it is too cold. The women wear thin shawls; the men wear jackets. The air conditioner hums; blocks of ice tinkle in the glass when someone takes a drink of water. The starched tablecloth is a brilliant white. Beneath it is a thick undercloth which retains deep circular marks from the bottoms of glasses, cups and saucers. The members of the team lean back on their brown artificial leather chairs; now and then some of them pore over the table to look at their papers again. They look tired.

"The question is, how we move ahead from here," says Mochizuki.

"I don't think we should arrest anyone or question

anyone at this stage," says Bertus hoarsely.

Some people nod; others shake their heads.

"We should listen in on their conversations with clients," says Robynne.

"Exactly, Green-san," says Mochizuki, through Watanabe.

"Nice one Robynne," says Robynne, sighing.

Zhiqiang Li gives a short, clear laugh. Watanabe looks at her reproachfully.

"Could you set that up with Mrs. Molly Tender?" Mochizuki asks Robynne.

She nods and stands up. "Is everyone agreed on this course of action?" she asks, looking around the group and leaning on the table with her long hands.

She hears seven yesses.

Robynne walks out of the room. The smokers disappear to the corridor. Zhiqiang Li, Yvonne Lacoste and Yukiko Inoue sit next to one another and talk animatedly. Fowell goes and stands next to them. They ignore him.

Robynne comes inside, followed by the smokers. She goes up to Yvonne Lacoste, who breaks off from her conversation and looks among her papers, then passes round blue forms.

"These are the confidentiality agreements from Help!," she says. "Could you all just sign one?"

"The rosters of the seven counsellors are as follows," says Robynne, when she has everyone's attention again. "Inder: Tuesday next week, from six in the evening to midnight. Iman: Monday next week, from midnight to six in the morning. Irdin: tomorrow, from ten in the morning to two in the afternoon. Isaac: tomorrow morning from six to ten. Idi: the day after tomorrow, from ten in the morning to two in the afternoon. Igmar: Tuesday in two weeks' time, from six in the evening to midnight. Ivan: the day after tomorrow, from midnight to six in the morning. Could you assign the jobs, Mr. Mochizuki?"

"Yes," says Mochizuki, who has been sitting and writing. "Inder: Valenti-san. Iman: Green-san. Isaac: Silva-san. Igmar: Welt-san. Ivan: Fowell-san." He stands up and walks out of the room.

"Good, so now we know," says Bettina.

Mochizuki turns by the door and looks at her expressionlessly. Then he goes out of the door and disappears into the corridor.

"Stupid bastard," says Bettina softly. Watanabe looks at her, shocked. Zhiqiang Li laughs.

"Who's going to do Irdin and Idi?" says Bettina.

"Conference suspended until tomorrow morning," says Silva. "I will not be there. I have to go and listen to Isaac. Hopefully he will try to sweet-talk Napoleon into meeting him at a breakfast café."

"Mochizuki wants to catch the perpetrator in the act, and I wish him luck," says Robynne Green. "That way there is the least chance that a skilful lawyer would get him off."

Eighth of September

I have to go to bed because I'm tired of racking my brains. The stress is terrible. I think tonight all members of the team will lie dicing and mixing and kneading, just like a row of bread machines. We are now very close to the denouement. We all worked until after twelve this evening.

I'm aching everywhere and I feel spaced-out, as if I had drunk too much. We are getting ever-closer to the perpetrator but he is still shadowy, doesn't have any real form. That is spooky. My head is full of useless images: Croo's stove, Irina's shawl, Robynne's flirtatious features, droves of people on zebra crossings, shiny pebbles on the staircases of the metro ... What a mess!

To make matters worse, we've just had a pretty strong earthquake. The telephone fell off the desk. It gave me a huge shock; my nerves are so keyed up.

At the end of the afternoon I went for a little walk. I bought some pretty Atom-Boy notebooks and a few more Animal Backstyle things. In the same street there is a shop that sells stuff for children: little boxes, mugs, bento boxes, T-shirts, and what-not, all pink, with a silly cat on top: My Kitty.

The only thing on TV is programmes about Lady Di.

On the Far East Network on the radio, some men are talking about the need for name cards in the form of stickers available from vending machines. They're called Nana Club. Nana Club has been developed by the same business that launched Print Club. I saw an interview with the founder of the company, a man dripping with sentimentality.

Deeply moved by his own beneficence, he told us that Print Club and Nana Club are both highly esteemed by his employees. I didn't have the impression that the employees in question had become financially better off as a result; rather that it was a matter of obligation.

Whoops. Another series of earth tremors. It really seems as if the earth is sharing in our excitement.

CHAPTER 10

The following morning, the breakfast conference is inaugurated by Mochizuki. "At the moment, Silva-san is in an office one floor below the Help! telephone counselling room. My permanent staff installed listening equipment there last night. The Help! lines will be tapped twenty-four hours a day. Here in this hotel, two rooms have been equipped with recording and reception equipment, so we will also be able to listen to the counselling sessions taking place on the Help! lines.

"I will divide you into two groups. Each group will be responsible for one phone line. We will follow the same shifts as Help!. In the mornings, these are from six to ten; then from ten to two; then from two until six in the afternoon; from six to twelve midnight; and from midnight to six in the morning."

"In the next few days, Valenti-san and Hogenelst-san will listen in on Line 1, in room 12 on this floor; Silva-san and Green-san will take Line 2, in room 14, also on this floor. Each of you will work a shift of four or six hours. During the times that our suspects are working their shifts at Help!, someone will be available in the office in the Lutheran church below the Help! telephone counselling room. Lacoste-san and Inoue-san will each be in a listening room here at the hotel, and will process any information you obtain.

"What we are trying to do is get the perpetrator to set up his meeting and follow it through. If possible we would like to catch him in the act, in the company of his victim and in possession of his weapon. I will provide you with firearms. Go to the shooting range at my department and you will be issued with weapons. I will assist you with the permits to go there today. From this afternoon, unmarked police cars with drivers in plain clothes will be standing by at the entrance to this hotel twenty-four hours a day. If you are stressed, do not hesitate to consult Li-san."

Mochizuki looks at his watch. "It is ten to six. If everything is going according to plan, Silva-san should be at his post. I would request that you go to rooms 12 and 14 and switch on the equipment, and then we can all listen in to Isaac's shift at Help!."

A few hours later, Bettina Welt and Mochizuki are hiking up the meandering mountain path to the village of Daigo. Relieved that they have been able to leave the heat of the city, they set an energetic pace. Each is wearing small rucksack. The air is heavy with the scent of conifers and damp earth.

The air is full of sounds; the rustle of the wind in the pines and spruces; the chirping of the cicadas; the splashing of fast-flowing streams and small waterfalls. Mochizuki speaks to Bettina in rapid, leisurely Japanese. He appears to have forgotten that she is a foreigner.

"It's a good idea to tuck your trousers into your socks," he says. "There are hornets here that can give you a nasty bite, especially on your legs." He leads by example, stuffing his khaki trousers into his dark green socks. He puts his

317

rucksack on the ground, then reaches into it and takes out a light blue handkerchief which he drapes loosely around his neck.

They walk on. Black butterflies as large as bats flutter back and forth in front of their faces.

"We are early," says Mochizuki. "It won't be dark for some time. Isn't it about seventy-five minutes' walk to the house?"

"Yes," answers Bettina.

"So we have some time for a rest on the way," says Mochizuki. "A little bit further up there should be a shrine, according to the map. It's half-way along our route, which is convenient. Shall we stop there soon and have something to eat there?"

"Where can we get food?" asks Bettina.

Mochizuki knocks triumphantly on his rucksack with both hands. "My wife has prepared a nice bento box for both of us."

"How kind of you. Thank you."

Mochizuki gives a relaxed, affable smile. In silence they walk further up the steeply rising path. To their left is the damp escarpment of the mountain into which the path has been cut; to the right, there is a ravine. Here and there they come across a pile of freshly sawn wood giving off a sharp, sweet fragrance. After they have walked for forty-five minutes, a bright red wooden gate looms up on the left. Behind it is a path hacked out of the rock.

"Here is the shrine," says Mochizuki. He passes in front of Bettina and goes through the gate. A little further on there is a smaller red gate. Behind this, in the long shadows of the trees, they see a dark wooden building.

There are old stumps of thick deciduous trees sticking out of the earth. An open area is strewn with heavy yellow sand that has been raked over. Mochizuki puts his rucksack onto one of the tree stumps and walks over to the main gate of the shrine. He goes over and faces the shrine, then bows, claps his hands three times, puts his hands together in front of his face and prays for a moment.

He bows once more, then walks back to his rucksack. Bettina has gone to sit on one of the tree stumps. Mochizuki undoes his rucksack and pulls out a flat wooden box with a linen strap. He unties the strap and divides the box into two layers. In the centre of each box, rolled in a serviette, is a pair of chopsticks.

"Please take this," says Mochizuki, and he hands one of the boxes to Bettina. She inhales the delicious aroma that rises from the box.

"Thank you," she says, surprised, and feels ashamed because she has maligned Mochizuki so often in the past. "It's done so beautifully, and it smells delicious," she says, a little shyly.

Mochizuki bestows her a genial smile. "Yes," he says, "My wife is a very good cook."

They eat in silence for a while. Then Mochizuki says, "I am curious to know whether you are right, Welt-san."

"I oh hi ho ah etlanan er hub be," says Bettina fervently, with her mouth full. "Sorry," she says, and chews quickly. "I don't see what other explanation there could be," she says again, once she has finished masticating. "Leather clothes, and hair as well, and maybe a knife, Mochizuki-san. Lying underneath that house over there, not inside. And just think: what better place could there be to hide yourself away than that house? You've been there. There are all kinds of people coming and going. It is dirty. There are clothes and hair and fingerprints all over the place. You can sleep on one of the futons. As long as you lend a hand and bring along food and drink, no one asks any questions. Every evening after the performances, people get drunk, eat, talk, quarrel, sometimes fight. Nobody keeps track of who stays, or for how long. It's a perfect place for someone who wants to shut themselves away. It reminds me of squats in Germany and the Netherlands. Some members of the Baader-Meinhof group holed up in squats in the 1970s, and it was a heck of a long time before the police even got onto their trail."

Mochizuki nods, munching.

Bettina takes a thin nylon pair of trousers out of her rucksack and goes over to one side of the shrine. "Do you think it's going to get much cooler soon?" she asks from behind a bush. Attached to the branches of the bush are strips of paper tied in bows.

"Yes," says Mochizuki. "You should put on a sweater as well."

"Shall we hang a wish up here?" asks Bettina, when she reappears from behind the bush, wearing the black trousers.

Mochizuki nods, delighted. "I have some paper here." He tears two sheets of paper from a notebook, quickly writes a few characters onto the uppermost sheet, puts it behind the second sheet and hands the paper and pen to Bettina.

Bettina thinks for a moment, with a dispassionate expression. With some effort, she writes a few words.

She returns the pen to Mochizuki, along with the paper bearing his wish. Together they walk to the bush next to the shrine. They fold their wishes into narrow strips, like paper fans, and secure these among the others that encircle one of the branches. Mochizuki once again makes the gestures of prayer, putting his hands together, raising them slightly and letting them fall again, then puts the lunchboxes into his rucksack.

"Shall we go?"

Bettina looks at him mischievously. "Should we read the other prayer requests? He might have written one."

Mochizuki looks at her sharply. "No! Not if it is not necessary. If we don't find anything today, we can always come again. This place is for the villagers. I would prefer not to disturb anything within it."

"You're right," says Bettina. "I was wondering whether there might be any prayer requests from Tim Smith, Wackwitz or Mechanicus hanging there."

"Those would have vanished long ago, in the wind and rain," says Mochizuki. "It is appropriate that our wishes are offered to the gods by means of the weather."

The exterior wooden shutters of the house have been slid in front of the doors of the verandah. They appear to be tightly closed.

"There's no one here," says Mochizuki. "Good!" He steps up onto the veranda and moves one of the shutters slightly to one side. Then he stands still and raises a finger in warning. Bettina freezes in position, with one leg on the veranda. There are moaning sounds from inside the house.

Mochizuki slides the black wooden shutter fully open.

It gives a thud. Directly behind it is a sliding paper door, which Mochizuki slides open as well. They peer into a dimly-lit tatami room. At the back is another paper door.

The moaning has ceased. Suddenly the inside door is opened, and two people scramble out from under a blanket. Mochizuki signals to Bettina that there is no need for concern.

"Good evening to you both," says the young Japanese man. He walks through the tatami room towards Mochizuki in his socks, while he zips up his trousers. Behind him a stocky blonde woman stands up. She wraps the blanket round herself.

"Do you live here?" asks Mochizuki.

"No," says the young man. "We should go now; we're out walking."

"You don't have to leave on our account," says Mochizuki. "Is there anyone else here?"

The young man shakes his head. "They're all in Tokyo," he says. "Doing a performance. It'll be late when they get back. Three or four in the morning, I should think."

Mochizuki nods. Bettina is surprised how naturally he plays his role, as if he and she were also intending to engage in intimacy. She smiles, moves to stand next to Mochizuki and gives him an arm. He presses against it for a moment.

"Come on Kiki, let's go," says the man. The woman nods. The boy goes back into the room and slides the door tightly closed.

Judging from the noises inside, they quickly pack up their possessions. The woman comes outside first, now dressed in a thick nylon jacket. "It's getting cold this evening," she says to Bettina. Bettina gives her a friendly nod and goes to sit on the edge of the verandah.

"Would you like a piece of watermelon?" asks the young man, bringing a pair of bags from the room and putting them on the veranda.

"Thank you very much," says Mochizuki. The woman takes two large pieces of watermelon wrapped in cellophane from one of the bags, removes the wrapping and cuts the pieces in half. She gives Bettina and Mochizuki a piece each and goes to sit on the verandah next to Bettina. Mochizuki and the young man sit together a little further along. They all eat in silence and spit the seeds into the gathering dusk.

"It's getting dark quickly," says Mochizuki. "Not so good for walking."

"Our car is down there," says the young man. "And we know the path well, don't we, Kiek?"

Kiki nods.

After a few more silent minutes of seed-spitting, Kiek collects the slices of melon peel and puts them into a plastic bag, then puts this into her rucksack. "You have to keep this house clean," she says. Bettina nods. Kiki and the young man raise their hands in farewell and set off down the path from the house.

As soon as the couple have rounded a few corners on the path down to the valley and disappeared from view, Mochizuki and Bettina begin their preparations. Together, they scrape out a shallow trench behind the house. Darkness creeps rapidly towards them from the bamboo wood.

"We should have a look under the house first, before

we have to use our torches," says Bettina. Mochizuki nods and breaks off from what he is doing.

"I will stay here. Could you please squeeze under the house? You're much smaller than I am."

Bettina nods and works herself into the crawl space below the house, between the joists under the verandah. It smells of warm sand. Beneath the house, right in the centre, there is a parcel.

"It's still here," she calls out softly to Mochizuki.

"Don't disturb it," he calls back warily.

"It's leather. I can smell it."

"Okay. Come back out now."

When Bettina looks as if she is becoming trapped between the joists, he reaches over to her and boyishly offers a helping hand.

"God, it's got really cold suddenly," says Bettina.

Mochizuki takes two aluminium sheets out of his rucksack and lays along the trench. "Then we will use these."

"Looks pretty good," says Bettina, examining the trench with a critical eye. "I'll bring the blankets from indoors to put over them, would that be okay?"

"Make sure you take your shoes off if you go inside."

Bettina comes shuffling back to the trench with her heels squashed down on the back of her shoes. She spreads the blankets out over the aluminium sheets. "There we are. We can get under the blankets."

Standing next to the trench, Mochizuki puts on the black nylon jacket and gives Bettina a woollen hat. Bettina puts two pairs of night vision binoculars at the top end of the trench. They both feel for their weapons and tug at the straps of their holsters.

"*Josh*," says Mochizuki, "then let's get started."

Bettina slides under the blankets next to him. They both lie on their stomachs.

As the time passes, they take turns to get up quietly from the trench and stretch their stiff legs, or relieve themselves behind a bush. After they have each made several excursions, they hear footsteps on the path.

Mochizuki nudges Bettina with his elbow. "That Momo of yours was right. Here he comes. She worked that out well."

"Yessss," whispers Bettina, and slowly moves her hand towards the binoculars.

The thin figure of a man is vaguely discernible in the light of the stars. He has a shawl wrapped round his head. He walks casually to the side of the house and goes to sit on the veranda. He takes a wrapped piece of watermelon from a plastic bag, peels off the cellophane, then eats and spits. Mochizuki end Bettina peer intently through their binoculars. The man coughs. It is an eerie sound, and very close. Mochizuki moves his hand toward his firearm. The man takes another bite and spits out the seeds again. He is wearing a striped T-shirt with long sleeves and a sleeveless denim jacket. He shivers in the cold mountain air. Then he throws the watermelon peel into the bushes, and with an eel-like movement, disappears between the joists under the veranda.

"*Josh*," says Mochizuki, right by Bettina's ear. She nods and slowly brings out her gun. She leans on her elbows and aims it at the place where the man has disappeared. Mochizuki continues to watch through his binoculars.

They both lie motionless.

"He is creeping to the front of the house," says Mochizuki in Bettina's ear. "He's taking the parcel with him."

After a few minutes they see the figure slip into the house from the side, carrying the parcel in his arms. They lie alongside one another, stiff with tension.

The dark shape glides soundlessly and almost invisibly through the same aperture, back onto the veranda outside. Then the man goes down to the mountain path, shoulders hunched up against the cold, and sets off at a brisk pace.

Mochizuki stands up slowly and stiffly and looks over to where the path descends to the valley. "We'll wait a little longer, then call," he says, and gives Bettina a mobile phone. "We'll wait here another hour, until he is almost in the valley. Then we'll start walking and Watanabe will drive up. It is five past eleven. If we're lucky, the dance group will not yet be on their way back and we won't meet them."

By the light of her torch, Bettina calls Watanabe, who is sitting in the car down in the valley. Watanabe waits for the man in black to go past the car, then drives uphill. Halfway to Daigo village, he stops on the quiet mountain road to let Mochizuki and Bettina get in. They stretch their stiff muscles gratefully.

"Are the trackers at their places?" Mochizuki asks Watanabe.

He nods. "Four along the road. And there are two taxis in the valley with police officers behind the wheel."

"The station at Hachioji is covered too?"

Watanabe nods. "Twelve men."

"Very good," says Mochizuki tautly. "Nothing can go wrong."

The first tracker calls the telephone in the car.

"The suspect went past two minutes ago. I'm going to follow him now."

The tracker is clad in a tight elastic camouflage suit. He has been trained as a sniper by Mochizuki's unit and has undergone a refresher course in the past few weeks. He has emerged from the training well-fed and well-equipped. He was selected by Mochizuki for his stoical disposition and perseverance. Twelve other men of his calibre have been kept in reserve. His face and hands have been smeared with dark brown camouflage paint.

His eyes are covered with plexiglass goggles, attached to his head with a broad band of elastic, to conceal the gleam of his eyes in the dark. His trouser legs disappear into black cotton boots with soles specially developed by a famous sports shoe manufacturer for his line of work – a combination of polyurethane and sealed Alpha gel. The big toe is separate, so that the foot resembles a kind of devil's paw. The boots are fastened by a long row of metal pull tabs on the calf. These *chikatabi* are specially designed for stealth, and for climbing trees and poles.

Like an eel, the tracker slides through the forest.

The man being followed hesitates for a moment as he sees the two taxis on the road in the valley. The tracker stands motionless in the forest behind him. With his hand shading his eyes, the quarry first looks inside one dark taxi, then inside the other. The tracker knows that both taxi drivers are pretending to be asleep. The quarry knocks on the window of the second taxi. Nothing happens. He knocks harder, this time with an object; a ring or a key. A light goes on. With difficulty, the driver eases himself up from his recumbent position.

"Taxi?" asks the man in black.

"I was asleep," the taxi driver says gruffly.

"Could you take me to the station, please?" the man asks politely, in perfect Japanese.

The taxi driver shrugs.

"Otherwise I'm in for a long walk. It's already too late to hitch-hike, there'll be no one coming along this way now. And there are no more buses."

The rear door swings open and the man gets in. The driver starts the engine and drives away slowly. In the forest, the tracker takes a mobile telephone from his breast pocket and passes on the details of the taxi the man has taken. Then he gets into the other taxi, next to the driver, who has just sat up, and begins to undo the metal hooks of his chikatabi.

"They're going to the main entrance, on the city side," the driver says. "Did you mention that?"

The tracker nods. "It's crawling with people there."

On a platform at Hachioji station, where the yellow Chuo line train for Shinjuku is running late into the night, two drunken businessman are asleep on a bench. One of them has his mouth wide open. The train is already at the platform, and the man in black gets on. He puts his cloth bag onto his lap and looks around. The train is half full. Most of the passengers are asleep; some are sitting and reading.

A conductor shakes the drunken salarymen on the platform. One of them vomits as he tries to stand up. Once he has done this, he takes off the tube attached to his cheek with a sticking plaster and puts it in his bag, next to the rubber pump with the imitation vomit. The two men stagger into the train and sit opposite the man in black. He gives them a friendly smile, then takes a book out of his cloth bag and opens it. Mochizuki's colleague with the vomit in his bag observes that the book is Silva's *Cold Blue Fire*.

On a platform at Shinjuku station, where the yellow Chuo line train comes to a halt an hour and a half later, the tracking process becomes as complex as choreography. Mochizuki has put a huge number of trackers into place. Despite the late hour, thousands of people are still up and about in the station complex. Three hundred work for Mochizuki. They are dressed as salarymen, hostesses and students, like many other people hurrying to get the last train home. They are divided into three groups waiting on the three staircases for the man in black, some upstairs, some downstairs.

Once the man has disembarked and taken one of the staircases up from the platform, two-thirds of Mochizuki's tracking team can go home. The group on the platform can also ease off as soon as the man is on the staircase and walking into the concourse. The man in black has forty-four men and women walking in front of him, behind him and beside him. The six trackers in front fall away as he changes course. When he goes left, the trackers to his left peel off. They number twelve in total, and have been instructed to walk straight ahead. It is as though the man in black is at the centre of a school of fish, with groups veering off independently, first one way and then another. Twenty-six trackers remain. Unnoticed, they accompany the man in black into the Kabuki-cho area. The man goes through a door. Two trackers follow him into a large eatery called Sin, open day and night. It is abuzz.

The two remaining trackers are Hiroshi Onitsuka and Kyoko Sakai, two of Mochizuki's promising young assistants. They are wearing normal, nondescript student clothes: jeans and corduroy, bulky white ASICS sneakers covered in squiggly lines. They each order a Sin Highball. The man in black has ordered a fresh orange juice. He is reading *Cold Blue Fire*. Nothing changes for a while. At around one o'clock, Kyoko Sakai takes her acid-green mobile telephone to the ladies' toilet to call Mochizuki.

In a bar on the same street, Robynne Green, Lucia Valenti and Jack Fowell are standing sipping drinks. Gerardo Silva and Bertus Hogenelst are close by, in anonymous cars with drivers. Watanabe is at the hotel, in the room with listening equipment, behind a table with a bank of telephones. As Kyoko Sakai returns to her table for the third time, from another visit to the toilet where she has called through to say that the situation is still unchanged, a small Asian woman comes into the restaurant.

She stands, looks around uncertainly and then goes over to the table where the man in black is sitting. He turns and kisses her exuberantly on both cheeks. Then they have a substantial breakfast, Japanese-style, with soup, fish and seaweed. The woman talks almost without a break. She looks serious, and sometimes rubs her eyes as though she is crying. She shows the man something on her arm. He leans over her arm for a moment, nods sympathetically and makes an occasional remark. He keeps adding food to the woman's plate from the dishes on the table. After forty-three minutes, the two stand up. The man pays at the cashier by the door. Before they go out of the door he puts his arm over her shoulder.

Kyoko Sakai and Hiroshi Onitsuka start following them. The first has a small device in her hand that enables Watanabe to follow the precise route they are taking.

"They're walking in the direction of Sendagaya go-chome," Watanabe informs Mochizuki by telephone, "they are now on Meiji-dori, up by the Shinjuku Park hotel. They are crossing the street and going left, past the lumber yard and the bento kiosk, towards the back of the park. They're walking parallel with the park fence."

"They're going to the place where Wackwitz was murdered," Bettina says to Mochizuki.

He nods. "He is becoming careless," he says. "Call Green-san. Keep her on the line. I'm drawing a red line on this map here, look. Tell Green precisely where she, Valenti and Fowell must go. They can set off now. Watanabe-san, call the others in the cars. We are going to start encircling them as quickly as possible. Welt-san, once you have made the call please join the team. There is a grey Toyota ready for you downstairs."

"They are going onto the service road," says Watanabe. "They are now walking right along the perimeter of the park. The road there is unsurfaced, and there are wooden houses there. Most of them are empty. It's going to be dangerous for Sakai-san."

Watanabe and Bettina talk intensely on the phone. Via the device held by Kyoko Sakai, Mochizuki sends a message that she and Hiroshi Onitsuka should cease tracking. They slow their pace, turn round in a flowing movement and head back.

Bettina joins Robynne Green and gives her a detailed description of the route. In turn, Robynne describes it to Fowell. Lucia Valenti watches over his shoulder as he writes, and then she quickly settles the bill. Go past the Shinjuku Park Hotel, cross over Shinjuku-dori, pass between the lumber yard and the bento kiosk, go left towards the perimeter of the park, and then right along the unsurfaced road .

"Come on, let's go."

They walk along the route two by two, keeping a sizable space between the pairs. There is almost no one out on the street any more; in the side streets it is dark, and silent now that the chirping of the crickets has stopped.

They reach the overgrown gardens of a row of empty wooden houses. Members of the Japanese team are standing there waiting for them. From this moment on, each member of the western team is given cover by a member of the Japanese team. They all step over a barbed-wire fence and draw their weapons.

When each has a weapon to hand, the pairs break up. The members of the international team steal towards the fence on the far side of Shinjuku Park, their Japanese covers following.

Bettina Welt and her Japanese shadow are the first to see the quagmire, the place where Wackwitz was murdered. Bettina lowers her weapon and gestures to those behind her to do the same. On the path there is no-one to be seen. The members of the group retreat quickly to the overgrown gardens, then step back over the barbed wire onto the surfaced road that runs behind them.

"They must be here somewhere," whispers Bettina. "They couldn't have gone back, could they?" Her voice is uncertain, almost pleading.

"Jesus Christ," whispers Fowell, "we've blown it."

"No need to give up hope right away," Lucia Valenti whispers back. "That path along the edge of the park is a dead end. They can't have gone back. There are only three possibilities..." – she counts them off on her fingers – "the path, the houses or the gardens. We must split up, everyone for themselves, into the gardens and houses. There is no alternative. Whoever finds them nabs them immediately at gunpoint and calls the others."

The others nod. They step back over the barbed wire, into the gardens and creep noiselessly, both arms outstretched, their weapons pointed first in one direction and then another. Fowell only just manages to suppress a panicky cry when he steps on a dead cat, and sees that his Japanese colleague behind him is startled by it as well. The feeble light from the street lamps falls onto the gardens.

The vegetation is dense. The bamboo is especially noisy when anyone brushes against it. Fowell thinks he can see a light flickering behind the frosted glass sliding doors of one of the dilapidated houses. He fumbles at the door with one hand. The door slides open almost soundlessly on its wax-coated wooden runner. Inside, a human being or an animal on a bed of newspapers turns away. Fowell smells printer's ink and feels a vein on his forehead throbbing fiercely. Behind him he hears a sharp intake of breath from his shadow. He puts his torch onto its lowest setting and directs the beam. A wizened brown face looks at him, dazzled. Fowell smells alcohol and a recently extinguished cigar. He puts his fingers to his lips. The woman with the squirrel-like face smiles, nods and lets her head fall back onto a colourful bundle of clothes. Just before he switches off his torch, Fowell sees that she has arranged them on newspaper. He creeps back into the garden.

A couple of houses further along, Bettina Welt has slid into a utility room with an earth floor and walks down a narrow corridor with a wooden floor. Although the house is unoccupied, everything from the previous residents is still in place; two pairs of bright green plastic slippers by the door, neatly placed next to each other, a faded red washbasin on a hook on the wall, an aluminium kettle on a butane gas burner. The gas bottle is placed tidily beside it. Its rubber hose is perished and lies, like the skin of a snake, on the floor between the burner and the bottle.

There is a thick layer of dust everywhere. The house is lit faintly by the street lamps behind it and a lamp in the park at the front. In the dust on the wooden floor of the corridor, fresh footprints are visible. Bettina lets fall her outstretched arm holding the weapon. Leaning forward millimetre by millimetre, she peers into the room at the end of the corridor. Her Japanese shadow leans with her, keeping pace and with his weapon at the ready.

Bettina sees the man with the small Asian woman, presumably Madame Mao, the Chinese from the Help! List of repeat callers. They are sitting next to one another on a pair of small boxes that form part of a circle. The man has his back to the hallway. He takes a knife from his bag and shows it to the Chinese woman. She does not appear to be the least bit frightened. She leans over towards him. He puts his arm on her shoulder.

Bettina takes a couple of steps backwards and yells out as hard as she can: "Five, five, five, they're in house number five!"

As she hurtles forward and shouts "You are under arrest!" the knife is only about twelve centimetres from the woman's larynx. Bettina's Japanese shadow has moved to the far side of the couple. He shouts something in Japanese.

"Freeze, freeze, I want you to freeze!" shouts Bettina, keeping her gun aimed at the pair in the room. She continues to repeat these words in a crisp monotone; like a mantra.

When Fowell and Valenti make their appearance, this is how the four people are positioned: in a kind of frozen *tableau vivant* depicting the moment just before a tenth murder. A little later, Bertus Hogenelst, Robynne Green, Gerardo Silva and their shadows arrive at the scene.

CHAPTER 11

Robynne and Bertus are pressed against one another, standing in the jam-packed train on the Ginza line.

"Let's agree not to talk about Frank Laing today."

"Okay," says Bertus, huskily.

"Instead of that, let's play some games. Do you like games, Bertus?"

"No, apart from Monopoly I hate all games."

"Even if it's one I made up? I'm simply crazy about games."

"What a strange woman you are, Robynne Green."

"Then let's begin with the story-telling game. I'll tell you a story and then you tell me one."

"Go ahead."

"Good. Do you know why everyone has somebody else's hair?"

"What?"

"No one has their own hair. I hate my own hair. Don't you hate yours?"

"Never really thought about it," rasps Bertus.

"Well I have. I'm convinced that my neighbour has my hair. Her hair is of course thick, long and red."

"And so that's the kind of hair you would like to have," says Bertus.

"*Would like* to have? It's mine! I recognise it! I pine for it! I have a right to it! This is how it all went. A long, long time ago, even before we were born, we were in Heaven. Heaven was a gymnasium, and the gym teacher was God. We could spend the whole day playing street football. You were defending a pile of wooden blocks. The last one in was the winner. The winner had to give a signal. On that signal, everyone in the hall ran into the centre, threw his hair onto a huge heap and ran back to the wall. Those were the rules of the game. On the next signal, which came from the losing side in the game – you have to pay close attention here – everyone ran back to the heap and tried to get his own hair back. I was never paying attention when that happened. That was how I lost my hair to my neighbour. Terrible eh?

"Just look around for a moment, Bertus. Disgusting, don't you think? All those Lacoste polo shirts. And all the handbags! I've already counted five polo shirts with little crocodiles on the bench seat there." Robynne points.

"Don't point," whispers Bertus, and blushes.

"It is high time there was an invasion of crocodile snatchers," says Robynne, "and then people who wear Lacoste would not be allowed entry to the Club."

"Which club?"

"The Club of Nice People."

"The Club of Nice People," repeats Bertus wearily. "Am I allowed to be a member?"

"We'll have to establish the rules first."

"Oh, Robynne."

"Which would you rather be, Bertus, a bear or a snake?"

"No idea."

"Come on, a bear or a snake?"

"A bear."

"Why?"

"I don't know."

"Oh, you are stuffy. But you do owe me a story."

"Jesus, Robynne, I don't know any stories, and certainly not any as crazy as yours. Besides, I've almost lost my voice."

"You could make one up. If you just made the effort."

"No, Robynne, I've not going to do that. I'm not interested in doing it, but you tell as many as you want."

Robynne stares ahead, a little aggrieved, and then turns around to Bertus again. "I would really like to have a proper adventure with you. Should we run away together?"

Bertus changes colour and then looks at her quietly. "I'm afraid that's out of the question, and you know it, Robynne."

"Do I hear a little regret in your voice?"

"No," says Bertus, reluctantly.

"Pity."

"It's out of the question."

"Does that mean that you would like to really?"

"No. That is not what it means."

"Now I've lost track. Is it something that you'd really like to do, or not?"

"I don't want to."

"Yes, but would you like to?"

"No."

"Why not?"

"Because I'm too old to do things like that. And because I love my wife. Are we nearly there?"

"Yes," says Robynne. "First, we're going to have coffee at Mozart."

"Mozart?"

"A well-known coffee shop in Shibuya."

"Sounds good. I could do with a cup of coffee."

"I could do with a cup of coffee," says Robynne mockingly. "You sound like an old man when you speak like that."

"I've told you that myself."

"Not bad," says Bertus, as they stand in the middle of the small Café Mozart, looking for a table. "I hope my legs can fit under one of these little tables."

"Let's go and sit there, by the window," says Robynne. Forced to do so whether or not they want to, they walk to the rhythm of Mozart's music, past portraits of Mozart, past little statues of Mozart...

"It's a pity the waiters aren't wearing Mozart wigs," says Robynne.

"I hate hearing music everywhere. You start moving to the beat involuntarily," says Bertus, "against your will, as it were."

"Ah, Bertus knows the 'against her will' game!"

"Oh Christ, be quiet, please!"

"Just call me Robynne. No, listen, I have to tell you, the 'against her will' game is really fun. I played it with a girlfriend for months. We used to come up with titles for romantic novels. They always had to finish with 'against her will'." Robynne recites slowly and rhythmically. 'She felt magnetically attracted to figure skaters, against her will. She turned into a Frenchwoman, against her will. He became a Zen priest, against her will. He slammed her against the wall like a lizard, against her will'. Your turn now, Bertus."

Bertus thinks for a moment.

"She danced the tango with Jesus, against her will."

"That's the idea," says Robynne, "you're beginning to learn."

"He wore a Rolex, against his will," says Bertus.

"Not quite so good. What shall we order?"

"A Wiener Mozart Special," says Bertus, studying the menu, "against my will."

"Wouldn't you also like to get to know me better, against your will?" asks Robynne. "Oh Bertus," she says, permitting herself to continue seriously this time, "I'm so crazy about you. I feel so comfortable with you."

"I think of you every night as well. Against my will."

"Really?" asks Robynne. Bertus has the impression that her eyes are moist.

"Well," says Bertus, "yes it's true, but we're not going to do anything about it. Okay?"

He reaches over the table and strokes Robynne's left cheek. The gesture carries a mixture of fatherliness and sadness.

Robynne looks right into his eyes and says, "Okay, we're not going to do anything about it."

"There's one more thing I would like to know," says Bertus. "You're married as well. What about that?"

Robynne's face clouds over. "My marriage is my anchor. Other than that, I do what I want."

"And that works well?"

"No, it doesn't work well, but it doesn't work so badly, either."

Silently, they drink their coffee out of flowery cups which have been brought on silver trays.

They are strolling through one of the main areas of Tokyo. Robynne points at the ink brush manufacturer. There are paint-brushes the size of brooms. Entire horse's tails are fitted like beards into copper ferrules attached to mahogany handles.

At the knife maker's they stand close to one another, feeling the blades with their thumbs.

"What workmanship," says Bertus.

"What workmanship," Robynne repeats. They laugh, as though they have been co-conspirators in playing a trick on someone.

"I'd like to go to the Gallery Lunami now," says Robynne, "in honour of you. They are showing the work of Hans van Olmen, a Dutch painter. Do you know him? He lives in Amsterdam. He must be about your age."

"No, there are so many painters living in Amsterdam that I really think there should be a moratorium on the profession for a while."

"I find him interesting. He's been doing well in Tokyo in the last few years." She precedes Bertus through a glass door as they enter an enormous apartment building. They take a lift and then a service staircase, pass through a complicated network of grey corridors, and go past a huge bicycle shed and a small empty theatre hall. Then Robynne opens a grey metal door and they find themselves in a small gallery.

"How do people know how to get here?" asks Bertus. "How did you know the way?"

"I know the gallery circuit like the back of my hand. This is an annex to a larger gallery. There are hundreds of places like this, hidden away in large buildings."

"That's nice," says Bertus. He walks past van Olmen's placid, minimalist canvases.

"I can see why the Japanese like his work. It's so unpretentious, so aesthetic."

"Yes," says Bertus reflectively, "and not decorative either. That's strange. And it's also very Dutch."

"How's that?" asks Robynne. She stands close next to him and looks at his face.

"The work has a certain blandness that you don't often encounter elsewhere. I like it very much. Though there are other Dutch painters who work in this restrained kind of way. There is no Baroque in it at all."

"It's a rather niche taste," says Robynne, "the style is a matter of absence rather than presence."

"Yes," says Bertus, surprised, "and one that is really not Dutch at all."

"No, Japanese, rather."

"When I'm back in Amsterdam I will buy one of his paintings, as a souvenir of this day with you."

Robynne looks at him astonished. "Do you mean that?"

"Want to bet? I'll send you a photo of me and the artist."

The next galleries on Robynne's programme are also hidden away among labyrinths of corridors and staircases. Standing very close to one another, they look at contemporary Korean sculpture, Japanese paintings and a video installation by a Thai artist.

"Very interesting, Robynne," says Bertus. "I really like it. May I buy you dinner somewhere near here, and if so, do you know anywhere good?"

"I'd like to, but let's go to another neighbourhood. Ginza is expensive. There is a good *shabu-shabu* restaurant in Akasaka-Mitsuke, one stop from our hotel. Then after we've eaten we'll be right near home. It's called Shabu Gen."

"What is shabu-shabu again?"

"Ah, you'll find out. We'll take a taxi." Robynne steps onto the road and puts her arm up. A taxi stops immediately.

"When they're driving, taxi drivers can't see so quickly that it's a gaijin who is standing by the road," says Robynne, grinning.

At Shabu Gen they are led to two high stools at a smooth wooden circular bar. Behind these, six chefs in immaculately clean aprons are shouting frenetically. Their glistening, razor-sharp knives descend incredibly fast onto thick wooden chopping boards. White marbled meat is being thinly sliced. Using enormous ladles, chefs with broad smiles are filling copper bowls with clear, aromatic stock. Plates are rapidly being filled, with a range of thinly sliced meat, baskets of mushrooms, chrysanthemum leaves, tofu and raw noodles. Steaming green tea is being poured into huge mugs, which are then slid over smooth wooden counter to the customers.

"First you dip your meat into the stock," says Robynne, "then the vegetables, the tofu and the mushrooms, and finally the noodles. These there are sauces for the meat; a spicy miso sauce and a mild sesame sauce. When you add the noodles, the stock is nicely flavoured by the food that you have dipped into it. You get a soup bowl and drink the soup as a dessert. What would you like to drink with it? I recommend beer."

"Beer, then. Oh, isn't it nice here, Robynne. And that

343

was a nice afternoon. Thank you very much."

"it's a pleasure. Did you keep a diary during the investigation?"

"No."

"Neither did I. Zhiqiang Li insisted on it, though."

"We shouldn't talk about work."

"That's true. Shall we play another game?"

"No, we've had enough of games."

"Pity."

"Idiotic music everywhere" says Bertus, as they are walking out of the restaurant together. "Just listen to it! *'You Are The Sunshine Of My Life,'*" he sings in a squeaky, high pitched voice, and emphatically times his stride to the beat. "*'You Are The Apple Of My Eyeyeyeye.'* You're walking along a shopping street next to a woman who's a complete stranger, and before you know it you're keeping pace with her, and your shopping bag is swaying to the beat of some love song or other. It's horrible."

"What are you talking about?"

"Never mind," says Bertus. His voice has almost completely gone. His footsteps, usually so heavy, have become as light as a feather.

In the basement at the police headquarters in Kasumigaseki, a warden opens a thick iron door and lets Silva pass through.

Frank Laing stands up from a concrete bed, walks up to Silva with the posture of a maitre d'hotel, and shakes his hand heartily. His eyes are shining and he laughs affably.

"Hairburger," he says. "I couldn't stop laughing about that for the rest of the day."

"Yes," says Silva, surprised at the sympathy he feels for Laing. He would like to have been able to put a friendly arm around the thin shoulders. Instead, he sits on the closed lid of a low toilet. Frank Laing goes back to sit on the bed. There is no furniture in the cell.

"Why, Laing?" Silva says harshly.

Laing abruptly turns his face away from Silva, towards the closed cell door. He manoeuvres his body into an oddly extreme defensive posture and says, "That is not so simple." His voice sounds different from before, with a higher pitch.

Silva involuntarily moves his hand to the inside pocket of his jacket, where a tape recorder is running soundlessly. Outside the cell door, Bertus Hogenelst is sitting on a wooden chair, with a bright orange earpiece in his left ear.

"What have you got there in your pocket, Inspector? A revolver? You don't need to be afraid of me, you know that, don't you? How could I do you any harm?"

Silva ignores him. "What is not so simple, Frank?"

"Don't call me Frank. I prefer to be called 'Iman'."

"Or shall I call you Jeromy Wanderfogel, Laing?"

"No, there is no Wanderfogel now."

"Where did you leave your last victim, Iman?"

"Have you ever heard of butoh, Inspector?"

Silva sees that Laing is still wearing a white bandage around his leg. "Butoh?"

"*Ankoku butoh*, does that mean anything to you?"

Silva shakes his head.

"The dance. The Japanese dance by which the dead

345

were brought back to life after the bomb, Inspector. The esoteric dance, the dance that imagines life after the atom bomb. The weighty dance focussed on the Earth, the contorted dance that wants to show the inside of the body instead of the outside."

"Ankoku butoh," says Silva, "isn't that the style that Yamaguchi practices with his group?"

Frank Laing straightens himself slowly from his complicated posture. He drops down a little, bending his thin knees, rolls his eyes up so far that only the whites are visible, opens his mouth wide and stretches out his tongue until it touches the point of his chin. High above his head, his thin hands flap like bats. Holding this posture and wobbling on the outside edges of his feet, he walks towards Silva very slowly. His stomach forms a hollow; his back is contorted like that of vicious cat. Silva takes a couple of steps backwards.

Laing drops out of character immediately, and sits down again.

"I asked where you left the last victim," says Silva.

"There are three great masters of Butoh," says Laing. Silva is silent.

"Hijikata is dead. Ohno is in his eighties and still dancing. And beautifully, Inspector, really beautifully! With those wrinkled old legs under a tattered lace skirt. And then of course there is Yamaguchi. He regards Hijikata as his father. Hijikata went to prison once, did you know that?"

Silva shakes his head.

"He danced naked with an enormous golden penis fitted onto him. You couldn't do that after the war."

"Why are you telling me this, Laing?"

"Iman," Laing corrects him.

"Iman," says Silva compliantly.

"The beauty of death," says Laing, "that's what all these people are concerned with. That fact is quite fascinating, Inspector. At the end of his life, Hijikata spoke almost exclusively with his dead sister. He hadn't had his hair cut since her death. It trailed on the ground when he had it down. He used to put it up in a knot with two big cooking chopsticks."

"What does that have to do with you?"

Frank Laing stands up again and stretches up on his toes, high and trembling. He lets his head hang back a long way. In this posture he tiptoes backwards up to Silva. His bald head looks particularly weird. Silva realises that he has never before seen a face on a head in this way. The mouth looks as though it is situated in the forehead. It opens, and a high-pitched voice says, "the inside of the body is very beautiful."

Laing straightens his head, comes back down from his tottering position so that he is back on his feet as normal, then stands looking at Silva, eye to eye. He allows his hands to hang down loosely from his raised forearms, as if water is dripping from them, then marches on the spot, bringing his knees up high.

"That's the way they walked in Hiroshima, just after the bomb," he says, continuing the strange movement. "The skin was dripping from their hands. It had melted."

Silva has to concede that that was precisely what it looked like.

"It must have seemed to them as if the world had ended. That is what Yamaguchi's dancers portray: the insane moment of the Last Judgement. And they do it beautifully, with twisted body parts, their energy directed towards the earth."

"*The Night of the Living Dead*," Silva says sarcastically. "But I still don't understand what this has to do with you."

"The Last Judgement, Inspector. Justice, that fascinates me."

"What does that have to do with the people who died?"

"Everything." Laing looks directly into Silva's eyes. Then he says, "there is no concealed victim."

"But next to the body of Father Adel, there was blood from two different people, Laing. Blood with the HIV virus, and blood without."

"The infected blood is mine, inspector. I have AIDS." Silva is silent.

"I cut my leg when I was dealing with Father Adel. That's never happened to me before."

"And the drag tracks?"

"Those would have been from my leg trailing behind. I didn't feel anything. Death makes you ecstatic."

"You are good with knives. Where did you learn that?"

"My father was a butcher." Laing goes and sits down as though he is about to have a fireside chat. He draws up his knees and puts his arms round them. Silva is silent. His heart thumps.

"Look, Inspector," Laing says quietly, "I belong to a triple minority group: I am a foreigner, I am a homosexual and I have AIDS. I've never complained about it and I've always tried to get involved with my fellow human beings, for example as one of the most active volunteers with the Help! Foundation. Whenever my health permits

I give lectures to other AIDS patients, in English, French, German, Spanish, Portuguese or Japanese. I do not spare myself. I am as poor as a church mouse and I live in a rabbit-hutch of an apartment that I have to disinfect with bleach every day."

"And now and then you refresh yourself by murdering a client, Laing?"

"If you want me to carry on talking, you will have to address me as 'Iman', says Laing.

"Iman," Silva says loudly.

"On the Help! counselling line, I used to receive telephone calls from perfectly healthy, heterosexual young white people who suffered no discrimination. People who told me how miserable they felt. They called every day. Repeat callers! People who had nothing wrong with them. Who thought they could get AIDS from a badly washed cup, while they had the latest leather-bound edition of the *Encyclopaedia Britannica* on their bookshelves. Stupidity, Inspector, deserves to be punished. And arrogance, Inspector, also deserves to be punished. You see a lot of arrogance here. It's typical of Tokyo. They are very full of their own importance, Inspector. That's because the foreigners are treated specially by the Japanese. Oh, how interesting they are."

"You executed them?"

"Yes. I enacted the Last Judgement. After all, what God can do, I can do too."

"And why the arrangement of the dead bodies? Why did they have to be served up like fish sliced open on a plate?"

"It was theatre, Inspector. And in a theatre you need

décor."

"So you see yourself as an artist?"

"Yes. I have been a film-maker."

"Jeromy Wanderfogel, hard pornography," says Silva.

"The portrayer of Armageddon. The ultimate butoh dancer. I turned the human body inside out."

"How did you end up in Japan, Iman?"

"I am the son of a butcher," Laing says pleasantly. "When I was ten, I was the best carver in the whole family. Later I became an assistant to the pathologist at the mortuary of a hospital in Rio. I laid out bodies and maintained the temperature of the freezers. Best possible job for a homo who'd been prosecuted."

"Were you prosecuted in Rio?"

"Yes, for intimacy with a minor. I was arrested and raped by a policeman in a cell. Since then I've always been on the run. Here in Japan I was able to begin a new life. I have done some very good work here within the foreign community, as a hypnotherapist as well."

"Come on, you're a hypnotherapist as well?!"

"I obtained my diploma here."

"A fine combination, Iman. Cutter-up of corpses and hypnotherapist."

"A very good combination," Laing agrees cheerfully. "The collective unconscious and death. Death is very interesting, Inspector. Really, there is nothing frightening about it."

"You can explain all that in detail to your psychiatrist later. How are you feeling now, Iman?"

"I have AIDS, Inspector, and if you have that you never feel very good, but I am not sick in the head, as you describe in *Cold Blue Fire*."

He quotes the words from memory. "Elastic ego boundaries. Limbic psychotic trigger reaction. Archaic, automatic behaviour patterns; changes in the frontal lobe…" Silva realises with a shock that Laing has read his book in depth.

"No, Inspector," Laing continues, "You underestimate me. I am not merely a machine powered by primitive fuel who lets fly at everything around him. I am an artist who has been purified by his illness and has risen above all laws. I can see what is wrong, and with extraordinary clarity. My Third Eye has been opened. That is something that occurs only in those who have meditated for a long time and undergone great physical suffering."

"And where is this Third Eye?" asks Silva.

"In the middle of the forehead, Inspector, you know that. It is there in your head as well, but in you it is closed."

Silva suppresses the urge to feel the location with his hand. "No feelings of guilt?" he asks casually.

Laing intones, as rhythmically as a drumbeat: "I do what I do because I want to do it; I do what I do because I have to do it; I do what I do because it must be done; I do what I do because somebody has to do it and I feel that I have been chosen to do it. When I stand before his throne soon, the Father of us all, whatever he may look like, will pass judgement on me. I trust that he will admit me to his kingdom of eternal joy."

"I shall pray for you."

Laing lets his knees slide out of the grip of his arms and turns slowly towards Silva. He places his feet together on the floor, puts his hands in his lap and bows his head elegantly, with a slight tilt, like a ballet dancer taking a short rest.

"I appreciate that, Inspector," he says with a beaming smile.

"An Employee in the Service of the Cosmos," says Silva gravely.

"Very well expressed, Inspector," says Laing, with another beaming smile. "You are a sensitive person."

11th of September

I am now addressing the old woman who I will be when I read this again.

"No, at that supreme moment I did not write in my diary. That is a pity and it is unforgivable, because it is mainly for you, old woman, that I am keeping this diary.

Yes, we know who he is and why he did it. Frank Laing, unhinged by the dance of darkness, Armageddon…"

I am now addressing the child who I once was and who would be proud of me.

"Yes, I arrested him. Do you know how I felt when everything was over? I felt nothing at all. I was just vaguely glad that I would now be able to go home soon."

I have slept, twice actually, during the day. At Mochizuki's expense I spent two and a half hours on the phone in broad daylight, and I was finally allowed to talk about the case with Matthijs.

We fly to Helsinki tomorrow. From there, everyone will go their own way.

For you, old woman, I will once again set everything

down chronologically, in order.

On the night of the ninth to the tenth of September I never even saw my bed, because on the ninth I had a telephone call from Momo Ishikawa, the principal female dancer of Yamaguchi. From what I've heard, she once had all her teeth taken out so that her head would be as good as possible for creating the dance of darkness. She conjectured that Jeremy Wanderfogel would be coming along to get the motorcycle suit. He had telephoned her to ask whether the group would be at home that evening. On the basis of this very small tip-off, I went to the house with Mochizuki. We had set up a huge trap for Frank Laing, involving hundreds of people. A human machine went into operation. In the early morning of the tenth of September, I arrested Frank Laing. It will make me famous, said Mochizuki. It will certainly make Frank Laing famous.

Mochizuki had planned a fun evening in a nightclub. We had to go there with him yesterday after dinner. The club was in a basement and was called Pussy Cat. It was endearing to know that Mochizuki spends his free time there, whether or not in the company of Watanabe. Mahogany panels, wall-to-wall carpeting, shepherd scenes, red plush... In the corner a grand piano, and behind it a pianist with alopecia.

The establishment was operated by a Mama-san who was called Midori because she always goes around dressed in green. She was short-sighted and wore a large pair of spectacles under a page-bob that was too young for her. Also, she was almost deaf – from an accident with an airgun when she was young, Mochizuki said. Because of that her head kept moving from one side to another. The resemblance to an owl was quite striking.

Despite all that she sang Spanish songs, into a microphone which had too much echo. 'Granada', at Mochizuki's request. They were real hostesses, who teased our men and completely ignored our women. Fowell sat with a certain Yoko on his lap. She sang too, a sort of jazz. The worst thing was that we kept being invited to sing by the piano. It was a sort of live karaoke. Books of song lyrics were given out.

Fowell sang 'Let It Be' badly with Yoko. Mochizuki sang the love duet 'Ginza no Koi no Monogatari' with Mama-san. He was pretty drunk by that time, but still sang it well enough. It was almost touching. The refrain (with dead seriousness): 'lonely in Tokyo, lonely in Ginza, this is the story of romance in Ginza'. At the end Watanabe cheered and clapped like an idiot. His ears were bright red, he was drunker than Mochizuki. The two sat together, slapping one another on the back as if they were equals.

I believe I saw Mochizuki hand over more than two hundred thousand yen to the Mama-san afterwards. We were waved goodbye, with a lot of fuss, by Mama Midori and her whole stable.

They were certainly discreet. They must have guessed who we were, but they didn't give anything away. For the five hundred metres back to the hotel we took taxis, at Mochizuki's insistence.

Today I visited the scene of the arrest and had another good look round. Wackwitz met his end in those weird surroundings. A little piece of Tokyo that by chance had escaped the attention of developers. In a year's time there will be a skyscraper standing there. Only ten minutes' walk away there is an enormous Tokyu Hands.

I bought presents there, for Matthijs and myself. A saw with teeth on both sides, socks with all the toes separate, chikatabi, inkstones, stamp pads, green copper paperweights in animal shapes, hand-made paper, India ink in plastic litre bottles and ink brushes.

Sylvia and Lucia Valenti are going out to eat this afternoon. Bertus and Robynne have spent the whole day in the city. Mochizuki and Watanabe are at home with their wives. Fowell wants to have a good time in the bar this evening with me and the ladies of the administration team. I'm going to look in and see how it's going with the old goat.

Tomorrow all hell will break loose with the media circus and I will appear on Channel Two, NHK, I think.

Is my hair done right? What should I wear?

CHAPTER 12

Frank Laing is flown to Honolulu, in a specially chartered Japan Airlines Boeing, under heavy guard. There he will be brought before an international jury. Meanwhile, the team is being taken to Narita airport in a special coach.

Jack Fowell sits alone, grinning at the plastic egg in his hand. "Look, Tamagotchi is going to have a poo." He turns towards Bettina, who is on the seat behind him. She peers politely at the little screen. The egg emits a tiny beep. "Time to clean up the mess," says Fowell. In the corner of the screen there is a steaming digital pile of excrement. Fowell presses a button and laughs loudly in the direction of Bettina, who is kitted out with new designer clothing and a careful coiffure. She turns her face away, embarrassed because Fowell is once again making her complicit in his vulgarity.

Zhiqiang Li, dressed in red as always, is deep in a women's magazine with Yvonne Lacoste and Yukiko Inoue. They are all laughing.

Silva is sitting alone on the back seat. He has his eyes on Lucia, who has just started an earnest conversation with Bettina, sitting next to her with an arm around the high headrest of her seat.

Mochizuki and Watanabe are sitting silently together on the seats at the front, behind the driver. Robynne Green has sat down next to Bertus Hogenelst, who has now lost his voice completely.

"It was a pity you didn't want to go to bed with me, Bertus," says Robynne whispering, putting her head on his shoulder for a moment.

The defenceless Bertus pulls out a notebook and a pen from his bag and writes 'please just stop it, Robynne!'

Robynne takes the pen from his hands and writes in reply. "Let's run away together. This is the moment."

Bertus takes the pen from her. "Please stop it, Robynne Green!"

"Don't you like me?" writes Robynne.

"Yes I do."

"Well!"

"The games, Robynne, I am so tired of them. Introduction games and farewell games from Zhiqiang Li, the what-would-you-rather-be-a-snake-or-a-bear game, the against-her-will game, the who-can-be-allowed-into-the-Club-of-Nice-People game, the story-telling game… And now again, the let's-begin-a-new-life-together-far-away game! No, no, no, Robynne. I am a tired old man and I just want to look out of the window for a bit."

"Let's play one last game," says Robynne, grinning.

No, Bertus shakes his head.

Yes, nods Robynne.

No, Bertus shakes his head.

"Okay," says Robynne. "Then I will tell you a parting story. The story about how it could have been."

"Spare me!" writes Bertus, laughing.

"No," says Robynne and begins to speak rhythmically, almost in a whisper. "There would always have been wine in the house. They would have drunk it in the company of good friends. They wouldn't have become a slave to it, because they would have been invincible.

"They would still have pinched one another's bottoms in front of other people, even in old age. The power of their nightly passion would never have diminished. They would forever have tasted the sweetness of one another's lips. Everybody would have been envious of them. All that they witnessed would have been graced by a soft light. Everything they heard would have been full of significance. And everything they did would have been done without difficulty and would have succeeded.

"They would have worked hard and achieved even more. He, old and tired, would have had a pension and would have had nothing to do other than wait for her at home and get his tool out now and again.

"They would have played host to many people and many animals. Their hospitality would have been the talk of the little town where they had set themselves up, and also far beyond.

"They would always have planned to die together, but they would never have done anything definite about it. He would have become ill and she would have given up everything to take care of him – or, as he always used to keep saying, it would be the other way round.

"He would have died before her, quite contrary to his expectations, because he would always have believed in what was unlikely.

"His death would have left her howling with grief. She would have saved up the pills he would have prepared to mitigate her anguish. And then she would have taken them.

"Her family would have mixed her ashes with his, at her request, so they would be mingled together forever."

"Oh," writes Bertus. "You'll have to be careful. You're like Frank Laing. He had too many fantasies as well." Then he tears the sheet, written on both sides, out of his notebook, crumples it into a ball and puts it into his frayed leather case.

Robynne looks at him angrily.

Glossary

In Japanese, plurals are generally expressed only by cardinal numbers. Nouns do not usually have plural forms: the word 'futon', for example, does not become 'futons'.

For the purpose of legibility, in contrast with normal linguistic practice, vowels which in Japanese are lengthened with a 'u' or a line have not been marked with a macron.

Ankoku buto
Dance of darkness

Apato
Cheap apartment

Atsui
Hot, warm

Bento
Boxed takeaway food

-chan
Suffix after a girl's name

Chikatabi
Split-toed shoes made of cotton fabric

Demo watashi wa nihongo ga dekimasu yo

But I speak Japanese!

Dojo
Exercise room, ceremony room

Domo
A word expressing a wide range of meanings, ranging from 'thank you' to 'how are you'. Literally: 'much, many'

Domo arigato gozaimashita
Thank you very much

dori
Street

Fugu
Poisonous puffer-fish

Furoshiki
Carrying cloth

Futon
Sleeping mattress

Gaijin
Foreigner

Genkan
Space at the entrance where you take your shoes off

Gotchi
Dragon

Gomenkudasai
Is there anyone there?

Hajimemasyoka
Shall we begin?

**Harvarudo Internasuyonaru Komyunikeishion Aka-
demi Kaiwa Kakuin wo shiteimasuka?**
Do you know the Harvard Academy for international
Communication

Itai
Pain

Ja, gaikokujin no eigo, wakaranaiyo
I don't understand the English that foreigners speak

Josh
Reflective exclamation

Kaki
Persimmon

Kanji
Japanese characters

Karaoke
Backing music. Literally, 'empty orchestra'.

Katakana
Phonetic syllables used to write non-Japanese words

Keisatsu
Police

Koban
Small police box

-kun
Suffix after a boy's name

Konnichiwa
Good day

Kotatsu
Low table with a lamp underneath for heating

Kyokai
Church

Maaah
Exclamation conveying irritation

Manga
Comic book

Meishi
Name card

Midori
Green

Nan deshitaka
What is that? What did he say?

Narita Express
Train to Narita Airport

Natto
Fermented soya beans

Nemaki
Sleeping kimono

Nihon no tabemono wa zenbun oishii dakedo, kore wa mada taberarenai
I really like Japanese food, but I haven't got used to this yet

Ocha arimasu desyoka
Do they have green tea?

Ocha kudasai
Green tea, please

Ofuro
Japanese-style bath

Otsukaresamadeshita
Expression of appreciation used after working with other people

Pinpon
Bingo!

Ryokan
Japanese-style hotel

Saishokushigisha
Vegetarian

san
Suffix used after the name of another person

Sarariman
Office employee

Satori
Sudden burst of spiritual enlightenment

Semi
Cicadas

Sento
Public bathhouse

Shabu shabu
Japanese dish of thinly sliced meat

Shinjirarenai
That's unbelievable

Shiso
Fresh-smelling herb used as an accompaniment to raw fish

Shiatsu
Pressure-point massage

So, ne
Now you're asking...

Sumie
Japanese watercolour technique

Tamago
Egg

Tatami
Straw mats

Todai
University of Tokyo

Tofu
Bean curd

Tonyu
Soy milk

Torima
Mindless violence

Wapuro
Word processor

Yakitoriya

Bar, also serving food e.g. chicken on a stick

Yakuza
An organised crime syndicate, or member thereof

Yanagi-ba
A kind of fish knife

Yoroshiku onegaishimasu
I'm counting on your assistance

Yukata
Thin cotton summer kimono

Zabuton
Flat cushion for the floor

Zazen
Sitting meditation

ABOUT THE AUTHOR

Suzanne Visser (born 1957) lived and worked in Japan for eleven years. She has previously published (in Dutch) *De pracht van het dagelijks leven* ("The beauty of everyday life"), *Terra Nostra, De verdwijning* ("Vanishing"), and *Een Man met mooie benen* ("A Bloke with Beautiful Legs").

She has lived and worked in Central Australia since 2002 and now writes in English. She speaks five languages.

www.ingramcontent.com/pod-product-compliance
Lightning Source LLC
Chambersburg PA
CBHW070043120726
47909CB00002B/281